*Zac, Angelo and Tariq—exotic,
dangerous and passionate*

Billionaire Heirs

Three powerful, exciting romances from
three favourite Mills & Boon authors!

D1387444

Billionaire Heirs

TESSA RADLEY

First published in Great Britain 2011
by Mills & Boon, an imprint of Harlequin (UK) Limited,
Eton House, 18-24 Paradise Road, Richmond, Surrey TW9 1SR

BILLIONAIRE HEIRS © by Harlequin Enterprises II B.V./S.à.r.l 2011

The Kyriakos Virgin Bride, The Apollonides Mistress Scandal and *The Desert Bride of Al Zayed* were first published in Great Britain by Harlequin (UK) Limited in separate, single volumes.

The Kyriakos Virgin Bride © Tessa Radley 2007
The Apollonides Mistress Scandal © Tessa Radley 2007
The Desert Bride of Al Zayed © Tessa Radley 2007

ISBN: 978 0 263 88359 6

05-1211

Printed and bound in Spain
by Blackprint CPI, Barcelona

THE KYRIAKOS VIRGIN BRIDE

BY
TESSA RADLEY

Dear Reader,

In my teens a wide variety of books about Greece enthralled me. Romances set on islands owned by gorgeous Greek heroes. Gerald Durrell's laugh-out-loud funny autobiography, *My Family and Other Animals*, about growing up on the island of Corfu.

I devoured *The Odyssey* and, utterly fascinated, I went on to read tales of travelers who had followed in the wake of Odysseus. I loved Greek myths and legends—some of them were tragic, some were touching and almost all of them overflowed with passion and emotion. Among my favorites was Pandora's Box. So when I created my own Greek hero, Zac Kyriakos, and his heroine, Pandora Armstrong, I couldn't resist playing with this theme. What happens when you unwittingly start a process that you can't stop? Can you ever make it right again? And how can love ever survive such a setback?

I hope you enjoy reading *The Kyriakos Virgin Bride*. Please visit me at my website www.tessaradley.com to find out more about my new books. I always love hearing from readers!

Take care,

Tessa

Tessa Radley loves traveling, reading and watching the world around her. As a teen Tessa wanted to be an intrepid foreign correspondent. But after completing a bachelor of arts and marrying her sweetheart, she became fascinated with law and ended up studying further and becoming an attorney in a city practice.

A six-month break traveling through Australia with her family re-awoke the yen to write. And life as a writer suits her perfectly; traveling and reading count as research and as for analyzing the world…well, she can think *what if* all day long. When she's not reading, traveling or thinking about writing, she's spending time with her husband, her two sons—or her zany and wonderful friends. You can contact Tessa through her website, www.tessaradley.com.

For the hardworking hosties at eHarlequin.com—some of whom I've known since I first started writing. Rae, you held my hand when I needed it most. Jayne, you're a cyber lifesaver. And Dee, Lori, Dream and the rest of the team…you're all simply awesome!

To MJ and Karen, your guidance is always valued. Thank you, always!

Tony, Alex and Andrew—where would I be without you guys to keep me sane? And Karina Bliss, Abby Gaines and Sandra Hyatt, you're fabulous friends.

One

"I do."

Pandora Armstrong spoke the vow in a clear, steady voice, and a warm tide of radiance swept over her. She sneaked a look up at her groom. Zac Kyriakos stood like a rock beside her, feet apart, facing the archbishop. Serious. Intent. Utterly gorgeous.

He was staring straight ahead. His profile could've been culled from any of the statues or friezes in the Acropolis Museum he'd taken Pandora to explore three days ago. The arrogant nose that ran in a straight sweep from his forehead to the nose tip, the strong jaw, the broad and high-boned cheekbones all resembled the marble statues she'd seen. But it was on his full mouth that her gaze lingered. Jeez, his mouth…

Full and sensuous, it was a mouth made for pure sin.

Zac glanced down and caught her staring. His colder-than-glass green eyes blazed, possessive. And that sexy to-die-for mouth curved into a smile.

Desire shot through her. Pandora tore her gaze away and stared blindly at the bouquet of creamy white roses clasped in her free hand.

Dear God. How could she feel like this about a man? And not just any man. This was Zac Kyriakos, who made her feel feverish and shaky. What had he done to her?

Enthralled her?

She blinked, fighting the urge to wipe her eyes, in case she woke up and discovered she'd dreamed the whole thing. How could she, Pandora, Miss Goody Two-Shoes—except for that terrible summer three years ago—have fallen in love so quickly?

Dimly she heard the archbishop say, "You may kiss the bride."

The vows and the kiss were not part of the Greek Orthodox ceremony. Zac had requested the traditional vows for her sake.

She was married!

Married to the tall, dark and exceedingly handsome man whose right hand she clutched so tightly that her fingernails must be leaving crescent-shaped marks on his palm. Inside, her stomach cramped with nervous excitement. It wasn't every day that a woman married a man who until three months ago had been a stranger.

"Pandora?"

She lifted her head. Their eyes connected. Heat arced between them. Zac's eyes smouldered. Possessive. Hungry. But there was a question in those compelling eyes, too.

Pandora nodded, a small, almost imperceptible nod, granting him the permission he sought.

Zac's hand tightened on hers. The warm weight of his other palm rested on the curve of her hip covered by the embroidered wedding gown passed from Kyriakos bride to Kyriakos bride through centuries. A gentle tug turned her to face him. His head swept down. That devastating mouth brushed hers, warm and intimate.

And just like that Pandora forgot about the archbishop, forgot about the people packed into the pews. Forgot that this was Zac Kyriakos. Shipping tycoon. Billionaire.

The only reality was the sensual touch of his lips on hers. And the heat that shivered through her.

Too soon he set her away. Only then did she become aware of the flashing cameras and remember they stood in a church where nearly a thousand people watched. Instantly the trembling heat evaporated. Despite the blazing white August sun outside, she felt suddenly chilled.

"Goodness!" Pandora's eyes stretched wide as she stared at the noisy wall of paparazzi surrounding the bridal car as they turned into Zac's estate in Kifissia, the exclusive area north of Athens where the reception was being held.

"Overwhelming?" A flash of white teeth and a wicked grin lit up Zac's darkly tanned face. "A three-ring circus?"

"Yes." Pandora leaned back, trying to hide from the intrusive camera lenses. From the minute she'd stepped off the plane the paparazzi had been waiting to mob her. But Zac and his bodyguards had kept the hungry horde at a distance. Pandora supposed she should have anticipated the furious speculation the wedding between Zac Kyriakos and a reclusive heiress had roused. The great-grandson of a Russian princess and the legendary Orestes Kyriakos, Zac had inherited most of his fortune from his grandfather, Socrates, after Orestes had used his kidnapped bride's wealth to restore the state of the Kyriakos fortune to its pre-Great War glory. Both Orestes and Socrates had been legends in their own times, and Zac himself featured prominently on the covers of the world's finance magazines, as well as making the annual list of most eligible bachelors in the known universe for the last decade.

But naively Pandora hadn't given his fame a thought, hadn't expected to have her wedding treated like that of royalty.

"Smile. They think our wedding is romantic. A modern fairy tale," Zac whispered into her ear. "And you're the beautiful princess."

Feeling as though she were performing to the gallery, Pandora turned to the window and bared her teeth in a travesty of a smile. The cameramen went crazy. And then they were sweeping through the tall wrought-iron gates, along the private tree-lined avenue through parklike gardens.

"Pandora." Without warning, Zac's expression turned serious and he reached for her hand. "Remember what I told you when you arrived? Don't read the papers. Don't search for those photos in the newspapers tomorrow. The lies and half-truths that accompany them will only upset you. Concentrate on us, on our future together," he said, his voice unexpectedly fierce as his thumb caressed the soft skin on the inside of her wrist. "The speculation, the gossip and garbage the tabloids dredge up will destroy you."

"I know. I already promised you I won't read the papers." She sighed. "I only wish Dad had been here." Her father's absence was the only shadow that hung over an otherwise perfect day. But since a bad bout of pneumonia four winters ago had left his lungs permanently damaged, necessitating regular doses of oxygen, her father no longer risked airline travel. "I always thought he'd be there on my wedding day to give me away."

The realization was dawning that she'd left her father and her childhood home far behind. After today, she would spend the rest of her life with Zac. Loved. Adored. The pomp and people didn't matter. Nothing mattered. Nothing except Zac.

Zac's house—more like a mansion, with its tower and stone walls—appeared before them. This would be her home from now on, together with the town house he owned in London. Zac had also spoken about buying a retreat in New Zealand, near her father's station.

"Your father may not be here, but I am. I'll always be here for you." At the intensity in his voice she turned her head. His hard, hewn features were softened by the sun filtering through the bulletproof glass windows, his eyes curiously gentle. Her throat tightened. She cast around for words but couldn't find any that matched the moment.

"Are you ready to face the world, *yineka mou?*" he asked as the car slowed.

My wife.

Pandora shot him a dazzling smile, happiness overflowing within her. She smoothed down the swathes of silk of the antique full-skirted gown.

"I'm ready for anything."

Zac helped her from the car and they braved the informal

honour guard of smiling well-wishers that lined the path to the front door. Pandora couldn't wait to meet Zac's friends, the sister and cousins he'd talked about incessantly during his stay in New Zealand. She'd wanted to meet them earlier in the week when she'd arrived in Athens. Zac had smiled, his eyes crinkling in that irresistible way that she loved, and told her he wasn't ready to share her yet. He wanted to play the tourist, he'd explained, to show her around. There'd be time enough to meet his friends and kin and staff later…at the wedding. She'd acquiesced. Zac only had to smile at her and she turned to mush.

They'd met at High Ridge, her father's vast sheep station in the South Island. Zac had come to New Zealand to discuss the possibility of guests flying in for exclusive stays at a working sheep station in luxury accommodation while a Kyriakos cruise ship docked at Christchurch.

And it had been at High Ridge that the miracle had taken place—Zac had fallen in love with her. A whirlwind courtship followed. Three weeks. Packed with precious hours spent together. Then he'd stunned her with his proposal of marriage, the fabulous diamond ring, the promise to cherish her forever.

Recklessly, she'd said yes. And started to cry. He'd wiped the happy tears away, and his tenderness had made her love him even more.

Her father had been over the moon when they'd broken the news. He'd pumped Zac's hand up and down.

And then Zac had jetted off back to Europe, back to running the billion-dollar shipping company he'd inherited from his grandfather. And, although an ocean had separated them, they'd spoken on the phone every day. Morning for him. Night for her in New Zealand. During those long conversations, Pandora had come to know the man she'd fallen in love with. There'd been two more lightning-swift visits. And, finally last week she'd flown to Athens for five days of playing tourist in the city with Zac at her side. It had all culminated in the Big Day.

Today.

Now, as they moved forward into the massive arched entrance of Zac's home accepting congratulations, Pandora recognised some of the faces. She was kissed on the cheek by a famous Hollywood actress and her equally famous husband, a singer in a rock band. Several legendary businessmen wished her and Zac well, and she smiled at a star footballer and his fashion-icon wife.

Inside the huge house she glimpsed a European prince and his popular Australian wife, a socialite who'd sprung to fame from a television-reality show, and several stunning supermodels stood out from the crowd. Pandora's sense of inadequacy grew.

Her mouth dry with nerves, she allowed Zac to lead her to the dais where the wedding table was set with silver cutlery and exquisite antique crockery.

And still the congratulations didn't stop. People streamed past the table in a blur of faces. There was no time for intimacy as distant members of Zac's family, his colleagues and acquaintances smiled at her, until Pandora was sure that everyone in the room wanted a good look at her.

Did she measure up? Or had they expected more from the woman Zac married? The thought was daunting.

She searched the crowded tables. Evie and Helen, two of her school friends from St. Catherine's, were out there somewhere. For a decade the girls had been cloistered together in the strict boarding school in the backcountry. Except for vacations, Pandora had spent most of her life at St. Catherine's until leaving a few months before her eighteenth birthday three years ago. Since then, apart from a couple of vacations with friends' families, she'd helped her father at High Ridge.

Pandora felt terrible that she hadn't had a chance to greet her friends. She would search them out later, she told herself, looking at the sheer number of people with worried eyes. Even if they didn't see her, they'd forgive her. Understand that tonight her priority was her husband.

"Here comes Basil Makrides with his wife, Daphne," Zac murmured. "He's a business associate."

Pandora turned to smile at the couple. After the Makrideses moved off, there was a small lull.

"Where's your sister? I haven't met her yet." Pandora had hoped to meet his sister before the wedding ceremony. Had craved company while the skilled hairdresser styled her hair and a makeup artist tended to her face and the dressmaker who'd altered the wedding dress fussed in the wardrobe. It would've been nice to have Zac's sister there…or even the cousin or aunt he'd spoken about. To assure herself that they would like her.

That she would get on with them.

Zac's face darkened. "My sister didn't make the wedding. There was a problem."

Pandora took in his tightly drawn mouth. "Is she…ill?" She probed carefully.

"Nothing like that." Zac's tone was abrupt. "It need not concern you. She'll be coming later."

Pandora stiffened. Zac never treated her like some silly little butterfly whose opinions didn't matter. What was going on here? Was this about her…or was there something about his sister—

"I'm sorry. I was too terse." Zac's voice interrupted her thoughts. "My brother-in-law is the problem—he's not an easy man to be married to."

"Oh, dear." Pandora drew her own conclusions. "Your poor sister, married to a brute."

"He doesn't beat her. It's nothing like that."

"Oh?" This time her tone was loaded with curiosity.

But Zac shook his head. "I don't want to think about my brother-in-law. Especially not on my wedding day. He makes me angry."

"We don't want that." Pandora rested a hand on his arm. "You tell me about it when you're ready."

"You are the perfect wife," Zac breathed and brushed a row of kisses across the exposed crest of her shoulder, causing the man and woman approaching the table to tease him mercilessly. A camera flashed. Pandora jumped.

"Don't worry," Zac murmured close to her ear. "Everyone here tonight has been invited—and vetted. There are no members of the press, only family and friends. Oh, and one professional photographer with a spotless reputation for discretion, who will capture memories of the occasion for us to enjoy."

The press? Pandora's stomach balled at the thought. She hadn't even considered them, with their avid hunger for pictures of her and Zac together.

During the interminable dinner that followed, cameras continued to flash while Zac introduced her to wave upon wave of strangers. Celebrities, business acquaintances, distant cousins, hobbling great-uncles. She could see the curiosity in the women's eyes, sense the men's speculation.

Why had Zac Kyriakos, given all the choice in the world, married a little nobody from New Zealand? It was a question which Pandora asked herself repeatedly but couldn't answer. At last she pushed away the nagging feeling that there was something she was missing and let Zac hold her close while he continued to introduce her to their guests.

The first waltz was over.

Pandora stared at the flushed stranger with the sparkling silver eyes in the mirror. Looking away, she picked up a jug and poured herself a glass of chilled water and drank greedily. She'd slipped away to check that her makeup was still intact…to make sure it would withstand the army of cameras that flashed like streaks of lightning across the crowded dance floor, capturing endless images of her and Zac as they circulated the room.

Stroking mascara onto her lashes, Pandora admitted to herself that she found the whole situation overwhelming. How could she explain that despite the enormously rich trust fund that she would come into when she was twenty-five, she found the glamour of Zac's world—with its famous faces, the constant stares and the unrelenting glare of the cameras—unnerving?

With a sigh, she dropped the tube into her bag and zipped it shut. A last sip of water, then she made her way back to the noise and bright lights and glitz.

"Pandora, over here," Zac called to her. His height

made him easy to find and Pandora threaded her way through the crowd.

"This is my *theos* Costas—my uncle, my mother's brother." Zac introduced her to the man at his side.

Pandora smiled at the older man. Cheery blue eyes twinkled down at her as he took her hand in his.

"The pleasure is all mine." He lifted her fingers to his lips and brushed a gallant kiss across the tips.

"My uncle is a renowned ladies' man, so take care." Zac laughed, his fondness for the older man evident. "I don't know how Aunt Sophia puts up with it."

Zac's uncle shrugged. "She knows she's the one I love." The simple words tugged at Pandora's heart. "You have already met my son."

Pandora struggled to think who Costas's son might be.

"Dimitri."

"Oh, yes." Relief filtered through her. Zac's cousin. "He's the lawyer who drew up the prenuptial and the *koum*—" she stumbled over the unfamiliar word "—best man," she amended, "who held the crowns over our heads during the ceremony."

"*Koumbaro*," Zac corrected.

"Yes, *koumbaro*," she echoed the Greek word. Zac had explained that, as *koumbaro,* Dimitri would be godfather to their first child—one day. A wholly unfamiliar feminine quiver shot through her at the thought of a little boy with eyes like Zac. But first she wanted to spend a couple of years alone with her new husband.

"You learn our customs quickly." Costas looked satisfied. "It has been overwhelming? Meeting so many new people?"

She nodded, grateful for his understanding.

"You can call me *Theos*—uncle—like Zac does."

"Thank you, Theos. Zac speaks of you often." Pandora knew Zac's uncle had been a father figure to Zac during his teens. A lawyer by profession, Costas had taken an active role on the board of Kyriakos Shipping even though, as Zac's maternal uncle, he was not a Kyriakos himself. Only when Zac had gained control of the board had his uncle resigned to put all his energy back into his law firm, which he now ran with his daughter, Stacy, and his son, Dimitri. Dimitri ran the Athens office with his father, while Stacy worked in the London office, she recalled. Pandora remembered the respect and love with which Zac had spoken of his uncle during their long nightly transworld calls. "I'm so pleased to meet you," she said.

"We will talk more tomorrow," Theos Costas said. He clapped Zac on the shoulder. "Now, my boy, it is time to go dance with your bride."

"Hey, Zac, it's your turn to dance."

The call interrupted Pandora from asking what Costas meant by talking more tomorrow. She glanced around and saw two men approaching, grinning widely.

"Come, Zacharias."

Zac threw Pandora a rueful glance. "I was hoping to escape this."

"Not a chance." The taller of the men chuckled, his hawklike features alight with good humour.

Zac sighed dramatically. "Pandora, meet Tariq and Angelo—more of my cousins."

Pandora examined them with interest. Zac had spoken about both men with affection and admiration. When his grandfather, Socrates, had died, each of his three grandsons had inherited a sizeable part of his fortune. As the only son of the only son, Zac had inherited the biggest share. But Tariq and Angelo had been well provided for—as had Zac's sister.

Looking from one man to the other, Pandora could discern small similarities. Not only in the family resemblance in the cast of their features but also in the air of command each of the three radiated.

"Welcome to the family." It was Angelo who spoke. He had piercing eyes, the colour of the sea, and a crop of golden hair.

Pandora smiled. "Thank you."

Then Tariq took her by the shoulders and bestowed a kiss on each cheek. "Bring your husband and come and visit Zayad."

"Give us some time alone first," Zac growled. "We'll visit in a couple of months."

Tariq grinned. "Take your time. Now you better go dance."

Zac whisked her off into a large adjoining room where the ensemble was now playing Greek music and guests swayed in seemingly never-ending counterclockwise spirals. At their appearance a shout went up.

"Zac, here, join in."

Dimitri beckoned to them.

An opening appeared in the hands. Zac pulled Pandora forward. Then they were part of the swaying, shuffling mass. For the first few minutes it was as if she had two left feet, and she struggled to find the steps to the dance, frowning as she watched Zac's feet beside her. Right step, cross, right foot point to the back, forward, shuffle and a little hop.

Suddenly the rhythm came, fitting to the strum of the bouzouki on the bandstand. Euphoria swept over her.

She could do this.

As Zac moved, her body mirrored his steps. As his arms went back, hers did, too. As he widened the circle, she went with him and the line behind followed. It was heady stuff.

The music quickened. Zac's steps quickened. Her feet danced faster and her breath came more rapidly. All around her she could hear a few of the guests singing along in Greek.

She wished she understood the lyrics.

Zac's hand enfolded her right hand, while on the left she linked hands with Dimitri. The person on the other side of him moved forward. Pandora caught the woman's eye and they exchanged hectic smiles, then Pandora was concentrating on her feet again, taking care not to lose the rhythm.

The music changed, became softer, slower. She stumbled, Zac's arm came around her, steadying her, then his hand slid down her arm and took her hand again. Heat shot through her. The steps had changed. A frown pleated her forehead. She bit the tip of her tongue and concentrated furiously.

"Let the music take you," Zac murmured. "Relax. Your body must be fluid like the tide in the sea, not stiff like driftwood."

Pandora missed the next step.

His fingers shifted under hers. "Loosen your grip on my hand. You're trying too hard. Listen to the music, feel it ebb and flow through your body."

Pandora concentrated on the plaintive wail of the singer's voice.

"She's singing about her love who went away." His voice was low. "Each day she waits at the wharf for his boat to return, she is sure he will come back for her."

The music caught Pandora up. Loss and grief filled the singer's voice. Tears thickened the back of Pandora's throat.

"That's right. Now you have it." Zac sounded triumphant.

Pandora jerked back to reality.

She was following the steps. "How on earth did that happen?" she asked, amazed.

"Greek music comes from the heart. The dancing translates the music. Your body must feel the music." His gaze held hers. "It is easy. It's about what you feel. Don't make it difficult by thinking about technique, about complex things. Just feel the emotion. The joy of love, the pain of betrayal. The steps will follow."

A warm flush of accomplishment filled her. The music flowed through her, her feet shifted, her body sequayed forward as she followed Zac.

Again the music changed.

The line broke apart.

Zac tugged her hand. "We'll sit this one out." A waiter materialised with a tray of champagne flutes and tall glasses of ice water. "Would you like a drink? Champagne?"

She was hot and thirsty from the effort of the dancing. "Just water, please."

Zac handed her a glass. She sipped, the ice bumping against her top lip. Placing the empty glass on a passing tray, she said, "That was wonderful."

"Come, let's go somewhere cooler." He guided her, skirting the edge of the room. "You picked up the steps easily."

She laughed up at him. "Not easily. You'll have to teach me more—when we're alone." If that ever happened.

His mouth curved. "Perhaps on our honeymoon, hmm?" He led her through the open French doors. Outside, the night air was warm and stars studded the black velvet sky. Zac reached up and tore off the bow tie and undid the top button of his shirt.

Her heartbeat picked up. "So we're going to have a honeymoon? Some time together? Totally alone?"

"Oh, yes." He leaned against a pillar and, reaching out, pulled her toward him, his eyes darkening. "Totally alone. I think we deserve it."

"Where are we going?"

"I will surprise you. Suffice to say there will be sun, sea and only Georgios and Maria, the couple who look after the villa."

Excitement thrummed through her. "I can't wait. When do we go?"

"Tomorrow," Zac's voice turned husky. "I, too, can't wait."

Inside, the music had stopped.

There was an instant of simmering silence. She could feel Zac's gaze, intense, waiting.

Waiting for her to move. To do something. Say something. She did not know what he expected. So she did what *she* wanted. She rose on tiptoe, pressed her lips against his…and the fire caught. Zac moaned, his lips parting under hers.

His mouth was hot and hungry.

Distantly she could hear the next song starting. She blocked it all out. And concentrated on Zac. On that taunting, teasing mouth that she couldn't get enough of.

Then Zac was straightening. "This isn't the place for this. Anyone could see us. Come." He tugged her hand.

"Zac, we can't just leave," Pandora protested, casting a frantic glance back inside.

"Of course we can." He stopped. His gaze was hot, stripping away thought, leaving nothing but a raw awareness of his strength, his masculinity. Perspiration added a sexy sheen to those sculpted cheekbones and his mouth curved in a wickedly hungry smile. "Why should we stay one more minute when we both want to leave?"

"Because…" Pandora tried to summon her objections, to search desperately for a reason. But all she could think of was the way the silk shirt clung to his damp body. *His body.* Staring at the bare slice of skin at his throat, she swallowed, then said halfheartedly, "Because it's our wedding and we haven't cut the cake."

He shrugged. "The cake can wait. We can cut it at lunch tomorrow. Now come." Zac gave her hand an impatient tug.

"Lunch?" She stopped.

"For my family. To present my bride to them." He pulled her to him and linked his arms behind her back.

"Oh." She'd thought that once tonight was over she'd have Zac to herself. That from tomorrow they'd be alone. On their honeymoon, as he'd promised, without hordes of people and bodyguards. Obviously not. Enfolded in the circle of his arms, she still felt compelled to ask, "I thought we were going on honeymoon?"

"Afterward." He shot her a rakish smile, his face close to hers. "Be patient, wife. You haven't had a chance to meet my family—you told me that yourself. I've hogged you to myself for five whole days. But the whole clan are here—

it will be a while before they'll get together again. I thought we'd take the opportunity to let you get to know them a little outside the crush of the wedding."

"I see." Instantly, she felt contrary, confused. She wanted to be alone with Zac. But she also wanted to meet his family, his best friends. She wanted to have a chance to talk with Angelo and Tariq and get to know them better. She wanted to ask Dimitri and Stacy what Zac had been like as a little boy. And she wanted to meet his sister.

She wanted them to approve of her.

Zac was quite right. She should meet them. Tomorrow. Nerves started to churn in her stomach. "What if they don't like me?"

One hand came forward and tipped her chin up. "How can they not? You're perfect." His teeth glittered in the dim light, and she made out the glimmer of steel in his eyes. "Who would dare question my judgement?"

Her stomach churned some more. Jeez, she was far from perfect. Had Zac set her up on some sort of pedestal? She licked suddenly dry lips. What if his sister hated her? Zac would not tolerate anyone questioning his choice of bride.

Pandora bit her lip and told herself it would be okay. She was the chosen bride of Zac Kyriakos. His family would accept her or face the consequences. They would love her.

As Zac did.

They had to. She'd do her best to make it happen. And what she couldn't get right, Zac would sort out. She snuggled closer. Sometimes she forgot his power. Sometimes he was simply Zac, the man she adored.

"Stop worrying, everything will be okay." His head dipped and his lips met hers. Pandora's breasts brushed his chest and all her concerns vanished. All she could think of was Zac…his hungry mouth, the strength in the hard arms around her, holding her close, making every atom in her body vibrate with longing.

He tore his mouth away and drew a gasping breath of air. "Now can we leave?"

"Yes." She sighed.

Two

Zac strode to the drinks cabinet in the corner of the sitting room that formed part of the master suite and poured himself two fingers of the single malt scotch whisky he preferred. A couple of long, raking strides took him to the window. He stared blindly out, not seeing the city lights in the distance. All he could think about was the disturbing silence in his bedroom. His wife was on the other side of the door behind him. He wondered if she was ready for him.

His gut tightened.

He'd been waiting for this moment for three months. He'd been patient. A damned saint.

Throughout their courtship he hadn't dared stay in close proximity with his bride-to-be. He'd allowed himself only two fleeting visits, each flight on the Kyriakos Gulfstream jet taking twenty-five hours and necessitating a halfway stop in Los Angeles to refuel. The almost fifty hours he'd spent in the air had taken more time than he'd spent with his fiancée, but it had been worth it. To see her. To touch her.

Briefly.

Circumspectly.

And then he'd jetted off before he'd lost it. Before he pulled her into his arms, onto the wide bed in one of the luxurious wooden cabins he'd occupied at High Ridge Station and ravished her to the full extent of his need. His passion would have stunned her. It had shocked him.

Zeus, but she was temptation itself with her silky pale hair and wide-set silver eyes and her slight body with narrow wrists and ankles that made her look so delicate.

But now they were man and wife. All that separated them was a door. He swivelled and stared at the solid wooden door and swallowed.

He had to take it slowly, had to control the vast sea of desire that seethed inside him. The last thing he wanted was to terrify the wits out of his bride on her wedding night. Because Pandora was an innocent.

A virgin.

His virgin bride.

And now it was his wedding night.

Zac intended to savour every moment. Never in his thirty-one years had he made love to a virgin. His outdated sense of honour had always demanded that he choose women who knew the score as his lovers.

But his wife was a different matter.

He was horrified to discover he was nervous. His hands shook around the glass he held—and telling himself the nerves came from desire, not fear, didn't help. Zac stared into the amber liquid. He didn't drink as a rule. Had never been drunk in his life—nor even a little inebriated. He despised people who used their addictions as a crutch.

But tonight was different....

Tipping back his head, he downed the scotch and set the glass down. Plucking up his courage—Dutch courage, he thought mordantly—he made for the bedroom door.

Standing in the centre of Zac's rich burgundy-and-gold bedroom—her bedroom, too, now—and conscious of the immense bed behind her, Pandora watched as the heavy brass door handle twisted. Something squeezed tight deep inside her. The door opened and Zac stepped through.

He came to an abrupt standstill.

He'd showered, she saw at once, and changed his clothes. The close-fitting black pants and oversize white shirt were sexy as hell. She flushed as she realised he was watching her with as much interest as she assessed him. Instantly heat flickered in her belly and her breath caught in the back of her throat.

"You're still dressed." He sounded disappointed. "I thought I'd give you the chance to shower, to—"

"I need you to undo the buttons down the back," she rushed to speak. "I didn't think about arranging for anyone to be here to help me undo them." And no one had offered. Obviously the dressmaker who'd helped her get ready this morning had thought her bridegroom would relish the task. Just the thought made her flush. Quickly she continued, "I washed my face, but I need to get this gown off." She'd washed as well as she could, removed her makeup, brushed her teeth. Nothing more to do until the dress was gone.

"Of course! How stupid of me...I didn't think." He came nearer.

Excitement clamoured inside her. She tried not to shiver. But when he stood in front of her, the little tremors of anticipation started to race across her skin.

"Turn around," he whispered, dropping to his knees.

She needed no second bidding. The ancient silk rustled as she turned. She could hear Zac's steady breathing behind her, feel her heart start to pound as she waited....

A whisper of air caressed her ankles as he lifted the hem.

There was a small pull and she knew the lowest button was free. Little tug after little tug told her of Zac's successes as he worked his way up from the hem.

"*Zeus,* did the original seamstress have to use so many buttons? There must be at least two hundred—and they're tiny!"

"There are seventy-five buttons. The dressmaker doing the alterations counted them each time she took the dress off after a fitting. It takes forever to undo—even with a buttonhook."

"I dearly hope not." There was laughter in Zac's voice... and something else...something dark and sensual that caused her pulse to thrum through her head. "And I don't see a buttonhook."

She struggled to regain her composure. "If this were a fairy tale, you'd have waited one hundred years for this moment."

"I think I've been waiting my whole life," he muttered. Then he said, "If this were a fairy tale I wouldn't need a buttonhook. I'd have my magical trusted sword and I'd be able to slit a line down here—" His voice broke off and he traced a line from the small of her back, down over the curve of her bottom, and Pandora shuddered.

"Then I'd slide that dress off…." His voice trailed away, and she could hear that his breathing had speeded up.

"But you haven't got a magical sword, so you're going to have to do it—"

"The old-fashioned way. Slowly, taking my time, enjoying the experience," he murmured, and Pandora gasped as his hand slid up the inside of her calf, to her knee, where it stopped. "A couple more buttons and I'll be able to touch your thigh."

His fingers gave her bare skin a last caress, then slid away. Pandora sighed with disappointment.

"Don't worry, *yineka mou*, there will be lots of touching and stroking. We have the whole night ahead of us…and I'm going to take it very slowly. I promise."

"Then I think I might just die of pleasure tonight," she whispered, breathless from arousal.

"Aah, wife of mine, do not say such things. I am trying very hard to keep my cool. Don't melt it or it will all be over before we begin."

"I thought we'd already begun."

Zac groaned. "Wife, be silent! I need to undo these buttons as quickly as I can and you are distracting me." His breath caught and his hands stilled. "What the hell is this?"

"The garter. I wasn't sure if you followed the custom of throwing it…so I wore one anyway." Still kneeling behind her, his fingers moved again, soft against her thigh, running under the garter belt. "It's blue…for the rhyme. You know, *Something borrowed, something blue.* I thought the dress could pass as something borrowed." She was babbling now, but she didn't care. His touch was driving her crazy… and if she didn't babble, she might just grab that hand…

bring it around to her pebble-hard nipples for him to douse the aching.

But his fingers were retreating, and she could feel the garter sliding down her leg. He lifted her foot, hooked the garter off, then he spun her around, and rose to his full height.

She stopped breathing.

His face was taut, his eyes blazing, and he held the garter aloft like a trophy.

"Mine," he said hoarsely. "Every perfect bit of you is mine."

She didn't even have time to gasp before his lips landed on hers, hard and ravenous.

Stretching onto tiptoe, Pandora wrapped her arms around his neck, the impact of his chest against her rousing a wildness she'd never known, and she kissed him back as though she were starved, all the while pressing herself closer.

"Slowly, wife of mine, slowly," he panted, his big hands going to her hips, holding her off.

"I—"she punctuated it with a kiss "—can't—" another kiss "—wait."

"Ah, *Christos*."

His hands cupped her buttocks, lifting her, the priceless dress ruching up around the tops of her thighs, pulling her close until…until…she could feel his hardness through the fabric. With a rough mutter he hoisted her higher, and her feet dangled off the ground. Zac lurched forward.

"*Zac!* You'll drop me." Hurriedly, she hooked her legs around his hips, her feet tangling with the soft silk folds of the dress as she clung on for dear life.

She landed on the bed with Zac sprawled on top of her. Breathlessly she stared up into hot green eyes.

"I can't wait—not another minute." His body moved against hers, restless and insistent.

She could feel his heat, his hardness, could sense that he was hanging on to his control by a fine thread. "The dress—we'll ruin it."

"Forget the dress!"

"I can't. The dressmaker kept eulogising about it being a piece of living history. I'd feel so guilty—"

"Shh. Roll over, then. Let me get the damned thing off," he growled and shrugged off his shirt.

In a brief second Pandora took in his naked chest gleaming in the soft golden light of the bedside lamps, the curve of his chest muscles, the lean tapered strength of his hard stomach and groaned.

And promptly nearly died of embarrassment.

Balling her fists against her mouth so that no more humiliating sounds would escape, she rolled onto her stomach so that he wouldn't see her face, wouldn't see the desire, the wanting…and then cringed as the skirts of the irreplaceable dress caught around her legs. "Oh, no."

"I'll set you loose." There was laughter in his voice now.

"It's not about me—"

"It's about the damned dress, I know." A hint of very real masculine frustration mingled with the humour.

How could she explain that she'd hate to be responsible for tearing or damaging a priceless heirloom?

Then she forgot all about the dress. Zac's hands had slipped through the slit he'd already unbuttoned, were on her skin. Smoothing, caressing.

"Nghh," she moaned. "I thought you were supposed to be undoing the buttons."

"This is much more fun, *agapi mou.*"

She leaped at the brush of his lips behind her knees. "Zac!"

He trailed a row of kisses along her tender, sensitised skin. Stopped. She waited, her heart pounding, tensing for what might happen next.

She heard a rustle of silk, felt the sleek, slick wetness of his tongue on the back of her smooth thigh. She gasped, then buried her mouth in the bed coverlet, willing herself to be silent, not to moan like a wanton.

He was pulling at the fabric caught under her. She lifted her hips. He tugged again and muttered something succinct in Greek.

"I am going to have to undo these buttons. Every damned one...without a buttonhook." He muttered an expletive, then laughed. "This time I'll start at the top. It will be easier on my restraint."

Thank God.

Pandora raised her face from the coverlet and rested her chin on folded arms. The breath whooshed out of her as his thighs straddled her and his weight settled astride her.

"Am I too heavy?"

"No."

His fingers brushed her nape and she went rigid.

"First button." There was resignation in his voice now. "Seventy-five, you said? And I doubt I've undone even half. *Ai mi!* How long is this going to take?"

"Perhaps we can make small talk?"

"Small talk?" He gave a snort of disgust.

Pandora bit back a smile. "Like, about the weather."

"Yes, let's talk about the weather. It's so hot that I can barely breathe, and tonight I'm even hotter, despite the air conditioner in here. Shall I describe exactly how hot I am?" He didn't wait for an answer. "My skin is so hot that it's tight."

At his harshly bitten out words Pandora had a searing visual of his chest just before she'd turned over and hidden her face. The sheen on the bronzed skin, the curve of his nude chest muscles. Jeez, she'd wanted to touch him. His skin would have been sleek and warm to her touch....

"What else?" she gasped.

"I am throbbing with something—a hunger—that I have never felt in my life before. I'm thirty-one years old and I feel like a damned boy. A boy who wants to grab... and squeeze...and possess. Hell, I'm not hot—I'm on goddamn fire."

Pandora couldn't think of a single thing to say in response to Zac's raw outburst. But she could feel. She could feel the rub of Zac's fingers as he loosed the tiny buttons, could feel the winnow of air against her naked skin as he peeled back the gown. She could hear the faint hum of the air-conditioning and his harsh breathing in the sudden silence of the vast bedroom.

"Okay, that's the weather taken care of. Any more small talk you fancy making?"

She stared blindly ahead, her body burning with arousal at the fierce onslaught of his erotic, highly charged words.

"Damn! I've shocked you, haven't I? Shocked you with the reality of my desires for you. Sometimes I forget how young and—"

"Zac—"

"—how innocent you are. All those years in a girls' boarding school, then helping your father, working in his business… I should be shot." He'd stopped fiddling with the buttons. "I told myself I'd take it slow, told myself I'd—"

"*Zac.*"

This time he heard her and broke off.

Unable to see his face, she drew a deep breath. This was difficult, more difficult than she'd ever anticipated. "I wasn't always at school or with my father. I visited with friends—"

"Your father told me," he interrupted. "Vacations with school friends, carefully vetted—that's hardly experience."

"I'm not a total innocent."

"What are you saying?" There was a fine shake of tension in the thighs clamped around her hips. She baulked. It was too late for this discussion, a discussion that she'd thought totally irrelevant in today's day and age. They were married, for goodness' sake. What difference would it make?

She put it all out of her mind and said throatily, "That I want you."

He gave a growl. His hands were back on the dress, tugging, fevered with impatience. "Damn these buttons! Pandora, my wife, I want you, too—more than I can tell you."

"So show me, don't tell me."

"I thought you wanted small talk." He gave a soft, husky laugh. "Perhaps we can talk about flesh…" He lifted more fabric from her back. "Or skin." A finger slid into the indent of her spine, along the length of the shallow groove. "Shall I tell you how soft your skin is?"

An exquisite sensation rippled down…down…pooling in her abdomen, sliding lower. Pandora shuddered and flexed her toes, anything to slow the pleasure that threatened to consume her. "Talk's cheap," she gurgled, struggling for air.

"So you want action?" And then his lips were *there* placing openmouthed kisses in the hollow of her spine. And his tongue…

Jeez, his tongue! She bit the back of her hand, determined not to let the moans escape. The maddening caresses eased. And she breathed again. The dress gave some more, his hands were working quickly now. Frenzied.

"At last."

She felt the cool air on her exposed buttocks as he peeled the fabric away, heard his gasp.

"*What is this?* Is it meant to drive me out of my skull with desire?" His voice was hoarse, his Greek accent pronounced. "Because, I swear to you, it's succeeding."

As his fingers hooked under the tiny bits of white Lycra that made up the minuscule thong she wore, the tremors started again. Stronger this time. Tremors that he must feel. She pictured what he saw: a Y made up of three laces of Lycra. Then there was the narrow triangle of delicate white lace in front that he couldn't see.

She struggled to find her voice. "That's the something new."

"What?" He sounded shell-shocked.

"*Something old, something new.* Remember? The rhyme I told you about? I thought the dress could do double duty and pass as something old as well as something borrowed."

"*Forget the dress.*" He tugged it out from under her, dropping it on the floor. "I don't want to hear another word about that damned old piece of silk. It's taken up far too much of our time this evening already." He stroked a long sweep down her back and whispered, "Your skin is living silk. Pandora, wife, you are amazing."

She didn't—couldn't—answer. A blast of desire unlike anything she'd experienced in her life shook her. Then his hands were running over the naked globes of her bottom, a finger tracing the white thread of the thong that laced across the small of her back. And he was kissing the depression at the base of her back. That finger—oh, glory, that finger—traced the last bit of thong down between her legs. She bit down harder in case she started to scream.

The yearning ache between her legs caused her to shift restlessly…she wanted him to touch her *there*.

"Is this what you want, *agapi?*"

His hand was under the whisper of white lace now, at the heart of her, his fingertips exploring the wet crease, touching the tight bud.

A moan broke from her.

She wriggled, opening her legs wider. Another stroke. She went rigid as sensation shafted through her.

"More?" he asked. And touched again.

She fought the ache…the desire…all the while craving—

"More," she panted.

This time he barely touched her, just the lightest teasing brush of his fingertips, and a fierce heat swept that tiny bead of flesh. This time she screamed and came apart in his arms. Then she lay there breathless, spent, feeling as if a firestorm has swept over her and heard Zac's murmur full of dark delight in her ear.

"There's much, much more to come. And we have all night long."

Three

"It is done."

Pandora tilted her head at the sound of Zac's beloved voice and paused in midstep on the balcony outside his study. She'd woken to find Zac gone, only a delicate long-stemmed white rose and a note on the pillow beside her. His writing was strong and slanted and told her that something had come up to which he needed to attend and he'd see her at breakfast in the sunroom downstairs.

She'd risen, placed the rose in a glass of water and picked the discarded wedding dress off the carpet and hung it up carefully. A quick shower to freshen up, and she'd pulled the first thing that came to hand—a filmy sundress with splashes of colour that clung in all the right places—out of the large walk-in cupboard where her clothes had been hung. Leaving her long hair loose, she sprayed a dash of fragrance behind her ears and came to find Zac, still dazed and glowing from the incredible lovemaking of the night before.

Her groom was not in the sunroom, so she skipped through the open doors onto the balcony where they'd kissed last night, wondering what people—his family, his friends, his colleagues—had made of their sudden disappearance from the reception.

Oh, jeez. She shut her eyes. They hadn't even stuck around long enough to cut the cake. Soon she'd have to face the knowing stares of Zac's family at lunch. She shuddered at the discomfiting idea.

The sound of voices halted her embarrassing thoughts. From where she lurked on the balcony she could see two men through the French doors—Zac and another man with his back to her. It was the other man who'd spoken. As he turned and raised a fluted glass, she recognised Dimitri, Zac's cousin. His best man. His best friend. And also his lawyer.

Dimitri had prepared the complex prenuptial contracts and been present when she and Zac had signed them three days ago. Initially she'd pushed aside her instinctive objection that legalities weren't necessary between her and Zac. But she'd known that Zac was a hardheaded businessman, known her father would expect them. A law firm in London which her father used had vetted them for her and suggested only minor changes.

She hadn't needed a prenuptial contract to feel secure. Zac's love had done that.

Embarrassed, she hesitated outside, uncertain what to do next. The last thing in the world she wanted was to walk into that room and meet Dimitri's gaze. Not after she and

Zac had departed so hurriedly last night. She wavered. She longed to wish Zac a good morning, kiss him and let him see the love and joy that bubbled inside her.

Through the crack in the curtains Zac looked utterly gorgeous. She stole another look as he clinked his glass with his cousin.

"I thought I'd never find her, Dimitri," Pandora heard him say. "My wedding is definitely cause to celebrate."

"*Vre,* you have been lucky. And so beautiful, too, you lucky dog."

Pandora grinned. Men! Love was not enough, beauty was always important. But she was touched at the relief in Zac's voice as he'd said *I thought I'd never find her.* His relief in finding someone to love.

She felt the same about him.

Yesterday he'd told her he thought she was perfect. Well, she disagreed. *He* was perfect. She was the luckiest—

"It is done—finally. Now there is no going back." Something about the tone of Zac's voice interrupted her musings and stopped her from rushing headlong into the room. She paid close attention. "No one knows better than you that this prophecy has been the bane of my life."

"I know, cousin. But it's tradition. A tradition that haunts the Kyriakos heir."

She listened harder, intrigued. What prophecy? What tradition? *What on earth were they talking about?*

Dimitri was still speaking. He'd crossed the room, his back to the glass doors. Pandora strained her ears to hear what he was saying. "It's the twenty-first century—you would've thought that the family, the public, would be prepared to let it go."

"They can't." Zac gave a harsh sigh. "And neither can I. The risks are too high."

"You mean, the likelihood of Kyriakos Shipping's share prices dipping are too high, don't you?"

"That, too."

Pandora cocked her head. What was all this about haunting and share prices? For an instant she considered pushing the door open, striding in and demanding an explanation. But something held her back. Something that filled her stomach with cold dread.

For a moment she considered turning, walking away, pretending she'd never heard whatever this conversation concerned. It scared her. Made her stomach cramp and apprehension swarm around inside her head like a clutch of bewildered bees.

Yes, she should pretend. She could retreat, then stamp her way back down the corridor, make an entrance that they would hear. She could look Dimitri straight in the eye and pretend that she and Zac hadn't rushed off to consummate their wedding vows with indecent haste. She could pretend that she'd never heard a thing about the prophecy that haunted Zac. *And then what?*

She'd never find out….

How could she ask later? How could she just drop it into conversation? *Oh, by the way, Zac, tell me about the prophecy. You know—the one that you thought would never be fulfilled?*

She'd married a man whose deepest secrets she didn't know.

No.

She wanted—needed—to hear more. Even if it was

not all good. After all, Zac loved her. She had nothing
to fear. He'd married her very publicly. Made the love
he felt for her clear to the world. The apprehension
started to recede.

She was being silly letting the men's lowered voices
build a terror of conspiracy within her.

When the footsteps came closer, Pandora shrank away
from the door, panicking for an instant at what she would
do if they found her standing out here, eavesdropping. Then
she forced herself to get a grip. For goodness' sake, there
was nothing ominous about what they were discussing.

If only this stupid, ridiculous chill in the pit of her
stomach would go—

"To find a virgin, a beautiful virgin…my God, cousin,
the odds were against you. But I envy you this morning."

A virgin? What did Dimitri mean *a virgin? They were
talking about her.*

Then it hit her between the eyes. Jeez, she'd been so
blind. This was the reason Zac had married her. Not because he loved her. Because he needed a virgin bride.

"That's my wife you're talking about, Dimitri. Be careful." The warning growl in Zac's tone did nothing to as-
suage the bile burning at the back of Pandora's throat.

She'd heard enough. No way could she walk in there
and confront Zac and his cousin. Not about something as
intimate as her virginity.

She ducked her head and wheeled around, walking
faster and faster until she broke into a run.

The third door Pandora rattled was unlocked and opened
into a bedroom. Pandora rushed in, pulled the door shut be-

hind her and locked it before leaning her aching forehead against the hard door.

What was she to do?

"Can I help?"

The sweet voice came from behind her. Pandora straightened and spun around. The too-thin brunette in an ice-blue dress watching her with a questioning smile was a total stranger. Then the smile faltered and lines of concern etched into the other woman's forehead.

"Is everything all right?"

Pandora nodded jerkily. She wasn't ready to reveal what she'd learned to anyone, especially not a stranger. "I'm fine. Really."

Really, I'm not.

My world has just crashed down around my ears.

But she couldn't say that—she had a facade to maintain. A position as Zac Kyriakos's virgin bride. "I'm sorry…I've intruded," she said instead, and grimaced.

The brunette flapped a hand. "Don't worry about it. I'm Katerina—but most people call me Katy."

Katerina…*Katy.*

Pandora stared into familiar green eyes, warmer for sure but still the same hue. "You're Zac's sister."

"Yes. And you're Zac's wife." The bright smile was back. "You're beautiful. My brother has fabulous taste. And I know he's never going to forgive me for missing the wedding—" Katy's smile wavered "—but I hope you will. I've been dying to meet you. I only arrived in Athens this morning."

"Of course I'll forgive you." Pandora noticed the faint dimple beside the woman's mouth—just like Zac's. "And I'm sure Zac will, too."

"Maybe." The dimple deepened. "You're lucky, Pandora. I tell you, he's the best brother in the entire world. I hope we'll be friends."

Pandora instantly liked this warm woman. "Of course we'll be friends."

"Great!" Katy extracted a tube of lipstick from a small sequined bag, popped off the lid and ran it over her lips. "That's better." She eyed her reflection in the mirror. "My husband never understands why us women always want to look perfect all the time." She threw Pandora a wicked, laughing look. "He insists on kissing it all off."

"Is he here?" Pandora glanced around but saw nothing to evidence masculine occupation. Zac had said that Katy's husband was a difficult man to be married to. Had he not wanted Katy to attend Zac's wedding? Greek families were so close that would certainly add tension.

"I wish he was." Katy sounded wistful.

Was the problem between Katy and her husband? Or did the real source of tension lie between her brother and her husband? Pandora couldn't help wondering if Katy was caught between two dominant Greek men—the juicy bone between two alpha dogs. Katy clearly adored her brother and it was obvious she missed her absent husband.

Katy was fortunate. She was loved. For a moment Pandora felt envy blossom inside her, green and ugly. She thrust the unwelcome emotion away and ruthlessly suppressed a pang of self-pity.

"I'll call you in a week or so, we can meet for lunch," Katy was saying.

Pandora nodded. Her heart lifted. The lost feeling started to recede. "That will be lovely."

Katy patted her hand. "You looked so unhappy when you came in—don't let anyone spoil what you and my brother have."

Instantly reality came crashing back. What did they have? At worst, a sham of a marriage based on a pack of lies. At best, it was an illusion built on her naive assumption that Zac loved her.

What good would running do? She needed to find Zac. To get to the bottom of what she'd heard. To find out whether he'd married her because he loved her or because he needed a convenient virgin bride.

"No," Pandora said slowly. "I won't let anyone spoil what we have." But she couldn't help thinking it had been spoiled…ruined…already. By Zac's Academy Award-deserving deception.

The study was empty. Pandora found Zac in the elegant sitting room, reclining in the leather armchair positioned under the Chagall painting she'd admired when she'd first seen this room. With one knee crossed over the other, Zac perused the morning paper. Her heart started to thump.

"I need to talk to you."

He glanced up and a lazy, intimate smile softened his strong features. "Good morning, wife."

"Is it? A good morning?" She raised her brows and gave him a pointed little smile.

His mouth curved wider until white teeth flashed irresistibly against his tanned olive skin. Masculine satisfaction gleamed in his eyes. "You tell me."

"I'm not so sure."

"You're not sure? Come here, I'll show you. Last

night…" His voice trailed away as he leaned over and caught her behind the knees and swept her onto his lap. "Last night didn't convince you? I'll have to do something about that."

In his arms, Pandora turned to marshmallow. The sexy, suggestive timbre of his voice in her ear, the hard-muscled chest pressing against her side were almost enough to convince her to abandon the answers she sought. Almost.

"You are so beautiful." He pressed a kiss against her cheek and hugged her closer. "A good-morning kiss will have to do for now. We don't have enough time to make it to the bedroom, not with my family due to arrive any minute for lunch. Come closer, let me adore you with my lips, let me—"

"Stop it, Zac!" She turned her head away just before his lips landed on her mouth. "There's no need for such reverence."

He stilled. "What do you mean?"

She sat straight, no easy feat given that she sprawled across his lap, her colourful sundress bunched around his legs. "I know, Zac."

His eyes suddenly wary, he asked. "What do you know?"

Gauging his response, she peered at him from behind her fringe. "I know *everything*."

"Everything?"

"I know about the prophecy, about your need to marry a virgin bride."

"And?" He prompted, his astute eyes suddenly hooded. "What else do you know? Surely that can't be all."

She took a deep breath. "I know you don't love me."

He flicked her a quick upward glance. "And why do you think that?"

"Because you never told me. And I never realized…"

"But I—"

"Let me finish." She brushed her bangs back and glared at him. "You did such a great job of it that I never even realized you'd never told me you loved me. Jeez, I've been stupid."

"I told you—"

"Yes, let's revisit exactly what you told me. *You're so beautiful, Pandora. I love your hair. The pale gold reminds me of*—"

"Sea sand." Zac stretched out a hand and brushed the strands away from her face. "It does. It's so soft, so pale."

Pandora pushed his caressing hand away and stood. "Then what about *I love your energy—like quicksilver,* huh?"

"You never stop moving, it's intriguing. Your hands are so small, so fine-boned, yet they move so swiftly, even when you talk. Even now when you're mad."

She clenched her fists and put them behind her back. "And you love my laughter, too, huh?"

He nodded slowly, his eyes watchful. "A sense of humour is important in a marriage."

"And then there was *I love the way you make me feel.*"

"Definitely."

"But you know what? You never said *I love you, Pandora.* And given all these things you told me, I never thought anything of it." *Until now.* "It never crossed my mind that it was a clever way of getting out of—"

"Hey, wait a moment…" Zac straightened and pushed his hands through his hair. She'd never seen him look anything but coolly and good-humouredly in control. Now his hair stood up in all directions and a frown snaked across his forehead as he perched on the edge of the armchair.

"So say it, Zac."

He looked at her in disbelief. "You're kidding me, right?"

"I'm not kidding. I'm waiting, Zac."

He gave a short, unamused laugh and shrugged. "This is about three little words?"

"I overheard you talking. I heard that you need to marry a virgin. Right now I need those three little words."

"What the hell do they matter?" He stood, towering over her. "We're married. We're compatible. *On every level.* Do you know how rare that is? You understand my world—something that's very important to me. We share interests, a sense of humour. And as for sex…well—" he blew out "—that's better than I ever hoped for."

"Lucky you! Because I feel like I've been cheated." At her angry words, his head went back and his eyes flashed. "So when were you planning to tell me, Zac?"

His gaze dropped away.

"You weren't, were you? You were planning to let me live in the clouds, to think this was the love match of the century." She turned away, not wanting him to see what the realisation had cost her.

"Wait—"

"Wait?" She gave an angry laugh and spun to face him. *"Why?* For you to make a fool of me all over again?"

Zac stared into her furious countenance. Underneath the tight-lipped anger he thought he caught a glimpse of hurt in her stunning pale eyes. Those eyes that had held him entranced since the first moment he'd seen her.

She wanted him to say that he loved her.

He gulped in air. *God, what was he to do?*

"My family will be here soon. Let's discuss this later." And saw instantly it had been the wrong thing to say. Her fury grew until her eyes glimmered an angry incandescent silver.

"*Your family?* What do I care about your family? I've hardly even met them! For almost a week I've been trying to get you to introduce me to them. Every time you put me off. Stupid me, I was flattered. Thought it meant you wanted to spend all your free time alone with me. But I was deluding myself, wasn't I? You just didn't want me to meet them in case someone let slip that you needed to marry a virgin."

"It wasn't like that," he replied lamely.

"So what was it like? Explain to me, Zac. In little one-syllable words that even a fool like me can understand. Or are you incapable of using those one-syllable words like *I love you?*"

Zac blinked at the unexpected attack. "You're not a fool—"

"Oh, please! Don't give me that. You've played me like a master. Convinced me you loved me. Jeez, I can't believe how naive I've been. Why would you fall for me, a—"

"Because you're young, beautiful and—"

"And a stupid, pretty little virgin?" She gave him a tight smile. When he failed to respond, she added, "So what if I'm young and beautiful. What do appearances matter anyway? It doesn't say anything about the person I am inside. Good. Terrible. Or didn't you care as long as I was a pretty stupid little virgin?"

The urge to laugh in appreciation at the clever way she'd twisted her own words rose in him, but one glance at her face convinced him that she would not appreciate it. "Pandora." He took her hand. "I wasn't—"

The door swung open. "Zac, people are starting to arrive," Katy said anxiously, then put her hand over her mouth as she took in their obviously confrontational stances. "I'm out of here. But, brother, you need to get to the crowd downstairs."

"Katy, I want to introduce you to—"

But Katy was already gone.

"Don't worry, I introduced myself to your sister all by myself. Tell me, does she also know I'm a virgin?"

Zac took a deep breath and forced himself to ignore the inflammatory remark. "My family is here. I don't want them embarrassed. Humour me. I need you to pretend everything is fine between us. Please?"

"Pretend? You mean, like you *pretended* you loved me?"

Zac winced as her bitter words hit home. "My family mean a lot to me. I don't want them to see this discord between us—not when we only exchanged vows yesterday. We can talk it all out later, I promise you."

"Later?" She gave him a searing look of suspicion. "When?"

"As soon as my family are gone. Act out the charade for two hours, that's all I ask."

"Two hours?" Zac held his breath as she gave him a killing look. "Fine! I'll *pretend* for two hours and then we talk."

He let out a silent sigh of relief. "Thank you. You won't regret it."

"I hope not." There was a fevered glitter in Pandora's eyes that stirred remorse in him. Hurt sparkled in the clear depths—or were those tears? Hell, he'd *never* intended for her to find out.

Lunch was finally over. Pandora glared at the five-tier wedding cake, her fingers clenched around a large silver knife. Zac's hand, large and warm, rested over hers.

"Your hands are cold," he murmured in her ear.

Her hands? What about her heart? It thudded painfully, cold and bleak in her tight chest. Just thinking about Zac's betrayal made her poor heart splinter into tiny, painful little pieces. Zac didn't love her—had never loved her—had only married her because he thought her a perfect little virgin.

Perfect.

God, how she hated that word. How—

"Make a wish," Zac whispered, his breath curling into her ear. The familiar frisson of desire ran down her spine. His hand tightened around hers and pressed down.

Please, God, let this mess sort itself out, she prayed, and the knife sank through the pristine white wedding cake.

"Later I'll tell you what I wished for," Zac's voice was warm and husky against her ear.

Later? Jeez, but he was arrogant! He sounded so sincere, so loving. And there would be no later for them. Not anymore.

Pandora half wished she could go back to that blissful state of ignorance, before she'd learned the truth. Instead of this emptiness that filled her now. But what use would that be? She'd only be kidding herself. *Pretend,* Zac had said, and that's exactly what she was doing.

"Smile," his voice crept into her thoughts, and a second later a burst of silver-white light exploded in her face.

She looked wildly around at the throng, the people.

Katy grinned at her from behind an oversize camera. Pandora struggled to smile back.

No, this was not her life. *This public pretence.* The glimpse of what her life married to Zac would be like was devastatingly sad. Nothing more than a series of hollow pretences for public show from one day to the next—if she stayed. But she didn't have to stay trapped in a marriage to a man who wanted her only because she was a virgin.

Pretend?

Never. Zac was about to discover the extent of the error he'd made.

"Good, you are packed."

Pandora glanced to where Zac loomed in the doorway, immaculate in a lightweight suit over a white T-shirt worn with fashionable European aplomb. "I'm leaving, Zac. The fairy tale is over." She hefted a suitcase off the bed. "I think it would be best for all concerned if this marriage was annulled.

"Annulled?" Zac stared at her. "*Annulled?* This marriage can never be annulled. It's already been consummated."

Pandora raised her chin a notch. "Then I want a divorce. I'm not staying in a marriage with a man who doesn't love me."

A shadow moved across his face. "Pandora—"

She took a step toward the door…toward him. "No, I gave you the two hours of *pretend* you wanted. You're not going to sweet-talk me out of this—"

"There can be no divorce."

Stopping short of the threshold, she looked up at him. "What do you mean there can be no divorce? You're not the man I married. That man would never have pretended to love me. I want a divorce."

His face hardened. But instead of taking issue with her challenge, he spoke to the man behind him. "Take the bags, Aki."

"Hey, wait a minute. Those are my bags and my—"

"You said you were going. Aki will take your bags downstairs for you."

Was that all he was going to say? Pandora stared into his inscrutable face. Hard. Distant. A world apart from the man she'd married. Her mouth moved, but no words came out. She swallowed.

Was it over so easily?

She'd expected some resistance. A challenge. A huge wave of disappointment rocked her. Aki hoisted up her bags and headed down the stairs. Turning away from Zac, she moved back into the room and crossed to the dressing table to pick up the rainbow-hued silk scarf and designer handbag she'd so nearly left behind with all the turmoil stewing inside her. A quick check inside the bag revealed her wallet, her cell phone and her passport.

She tried not to let her shoulders sag. There was a thick knot at the back of her throat, but she wasn't going to let Zac see her cry.

The last thing she wanted was for him to know how much she cared—how much she'd loved him. How much his silent surrender to her demand for a divorce had devastated her. Fiercely she said, "I need to call the airport to book a seat."

There was a pause. Then Zac said, "Everything is being taken care of."

"Already?" She spun around to find him right behind her.

"I'll take you to the airport if that's what you want." His hand touched her elbow. "But first we talk. Alone, without interruption."

"We can talk on the way to the airport." She shrugged his hand off and glanced around the immense bedroom—the room where he'd made such devastating love to her and taught her about the power of being a woman. Stuff she'd never known.

Last night…no, she wasn't thinking about last night. About the tender passionate lover whom she'd *stupidly* believed loved her with all his heart.

With a jerky movement Pandora swung on her heel and made for the door. She charged through the sitting room in a blur of tears. Furiously she blinked them back.

Downstairs there was nobody to be seen. A sense of desolation overtook her. No one in the huge mansion cared that she was going, no one cared enough to say goodbye. She thought of asking to see Katy, then shook the thought away. What did it matter? She'd never see Zac's sister again.

Outside, the paved sweep of drive was empty. No one strolled in the parklike grounds, Mount Pendeli rising up in a solid mass of green beyond.

The only person to be seen was Aki crossing the driveway as he made his way to a circle of concrete set on the edge of the grassy park, where he deposited her bags.

"Where's the taxi?" She glared accusingly at Zac.

"*Christos.* Do you really think I'd see my wife off by taxi—like some common…" He paused, but she got the message. And then he reached out and grabbed her hand. "Come."

Almost running to keep up with his long, brisk stride,

she crossed the drive and then she was back on the grass. The sun blazed in the halcyon sky overhead. Pandora's heels sank into the perfectly manicured lawn. Aki had disappeared. Ahead lay the flat circle of concrete. A row of cypress trees lined the drive that led to the large electronic gates in the distance. Why had she not noticed how much those gates resembled prison bars before?

Surely he didn't mean to dump her outside the gates of his property? No, Zac would not do that to her. She was certain of that. He'd said he wanted to talk, so where was he taking her? She dug in her heels, dragging him to a stop. "Where are we going?"

"I'm taking you away. Where we can be alone, where we can sort this—this *misunderstanding*—out."

"Oh, no. I'm going to the airport. There's plenty of time to talk on the way."

"You're my wife, I am—" A deafening drone drowned out the rest of his reply. He grabbed her arm. Pandora resisted, determined not to let Zac dictate to her. Through the roaring noise she was aware that Zac was shouting at her.

She glared at him. "What?"

"Get down! Get back!" he yelled close to her ear.

The huge black shadow of a helicopter swept over them. Shuddering, finally comprehending, she let him pull her out of the path of the hovering machine.

Aki had returned with another batch of bags. These must belong to Zac, Pandora realised as the helicopter settled onto the concrete helipad and Aki started passing the bags—hers, too—up into the belly of the helicopter.

Zac's bags and her bags being loaded into the helicopter did not equate to her plan of going to the airport. She stared at the monstrous machine, its shiny white body bearing the royal-blue-and-yellow logo of Kyriakos Shipping. For the first time she saw the stylised feminine profile with long flying hair within the logo for what it was. A virgin. Then the slowing rotor blades grabbed her attention.

Pandora's stomach clenched and a fine attack of perspiration broke out along the back of her neck. "I'm not going anywhere with you. Especially not in that—" she stabbed a finger at the helicopter "—hellishly dangerous thing. I want a taxi to the airport. I'm leaving. I want a divorce."

"That's not going to happen."

Zac's bronzed face was hard. Inscrutable. This was not the man she'd fallen in love with. This was someone else altogether. A stranger, stripped of the indulgent, cherishing mask. A man so hard she feared he'd break her.

As he'd already broken her heart.

"How could I ever have agreed to marry you? I *hate* you."

Something moved across his face, a flash of darkness, and then it was gone. "That's too bad. Because we're going on honeymoon, to be alone—like you wanted."

"No way!"

There was a reckless gleam in his eyes. "Well, then, what have I got to lose?"

Picking her up, he hoisted her over his shoulder and tore across the grass to the open doors of the helicopter.

"No," she yelled, fear making her stiff.

He ignored her.

Each stride he took caused her to lurch against his shoulder, and with one hand she clung to her handbag while the other clutched his shirt.

"Put me down!" Pandora caught a glimpse of Aki's

startled face as Zac clambered into the helicopter, his arms tight as chains around her.

"Stop fighting me."

"Never," she vowed as she tumbled down onto his lap, her hair plastered to her face as tears clogged her eyes.

Zac shouted something at the pilot. The helicopter started to rise. Pandora hammered her fists against Zac's chest. "Let me out!"

She pushed back her streaming hair. In a blur of horror she stared out the window. Below, Zac's huge house was retreating, growing smaller. She let out a wail of disbelief, of sheer terror.

"Hush, you are making a scene."

Pandora realised she was sobbing. "That's all you can say? You kidnap me, then tell me to be quiet?"

"You're crying." His hand smoothed her hair.

"Of course I'm crying." She twisted her head away from his touch. "I don't believe you! Who the hell do you think you are?"

But she knew. He was Zac Kyriakos. One of the richest men in the world. So powerful that he could do what he liked with her. No one would stand in his way.

Four

When the descent started, Pandora lifted her face out of her hands and glimpsed the dark bronze disc of the sun glowing in the western sky against a fiery display of clouds. Out of the window she watched the darkening ground rushing up beneath the helicopter with a sense of frozen horror.

They were going to crash.

She was going to die. Panic bit into her and she struggled not to scream, knowing once she started she'd never stop.

Her fingers twisted around the soft, colourful scarf she'd rescued from her handbag and clung to like a talisman during the flight. She closed her eyes, hating the helplessness. And tried not to think about it. Not about what was happening to her now. And certainly not about the twisted metal wreck that burned in her darkest nightmares.

At last the helicopter rocked and settled on the ground.

A wave of uncontrollable anger swept her. How *dared* Zac do this to her?

Grabbing her handbag, she stormed to the door. The instant the pilot opened the door, she shot out, her legs almost collapsing under her as they met solid ground.

"Slow down." Zac was at her side, his hand under her elbow. She shrugged it off.

"Don't touch me," she snapped at him.

"You could've fallen."

"I would rather fall than have you touch me." Head bent to avoid the slowing rotor blades, she didn't look back as she scurried away. Once safe from the blades, she straightened. The rough fingers of the evening sea wind tugged her hair and the strands whipped across her eyes.

"That's not what you were saying last night. Then it was *Oh, Zac. Yes, Zac!* Last night you couldn't get enough of my touch."

At the taunting whisper, she turned and glared, brushing the hair out of her face with an impatient hand.

In the dusky light she could see the strange smile twisting his face, adding a cynical edge that caused her temper to flare higher.

"That was last night," she bit out. "Before I discovered that you'd misled me. Used me. I hate you, you know that? I've never said that to anyone in my life before. But I mean it—I really, *really* hate you."

The caustic, knowing smile vanished. For a second, stark shock flared in his eyes and he looked shaken by her response. A shadow fell across his face and all emotion leached out, leaving his gloriously sensual features hard and cold.

"Get a hold of yourself, Pandora. You're starting to sound hysterical."

The icy tone shook her. He spun away, and to her consternation Pandora watched as he strode across the flat rooftop, his suit jacket flapping in the wind. Anguish twisted inside her. How had it come to this? What had happened to the affinity, the sense of rightness between her and Zac?

Had he ever cared about her?

Or had it all been an elaborate charade?

Before they'd left Athens he'd said he was taking her somewhere they could talk. A quick look around the castellated parapets, sheer, steep white walls that ended on a slab of black rocks licked by the lazy sea far below revealed this was not quite the kind of venue she'd had in mind. Jeez, not even Rapunzel would've gotten out of here. *Where on earth were they?*

All she knew was that this godforsaken place was where Zac intended to have their showdown. She set her jaw and vowed not to let him walk all over her. She had some stuff to say to him, too. Her stomach turned over just thinking about that. But what choice did she have? Straight talk was all that was left.

And then she'd be off home to New Zealand on the very next flight. And Zac Kyriakos, his handsome face, gorgeous body and immense wealth could go to hell. She wasn't staying married to a man who didn't love her.

Ahead, Zac disappeared through an arch into the castle. Or eyrie. Or whatever this whitewashed structure was. Pandora was annoyed to find herself scurrying in his wake. She paused in the shadows at the top of a set of stone stairs that spiralled down into the heart of some kind of tower where wall sconces lit the whitewashed walls. Zac was already two levels down, his footfalls ringing against the hard stone.

"What about my luggage?" she called down.

"Georgios will attend to it," Zac tossed over his shoulder without slowing his pace.

"I hate you."

The staccato beat of his shoes against the stairs drummed the horrible words into a crazy kind of rhythm inside Zac's head and left him reeling.

I hate you. *I hate you.* The echo grew louder and louder until hc wanted to bang his forehead against the curving walls of the tower that surrounded him and watch the stone to crumble into dust…the way his dreams had.

But he couldn't. He was Zac Kyriakos. That kind of behaviour did not become him. So he squared his shoulders like the man he was, the man he'd been born and raised to be, and tried to convince himself that it wasn't relief that coursed through him when at last Pandora's footfalls sounded on the stone stair treads far above.

Good, she was following.

He slowed his pace a fraction. There'd been a moment after they'd disembarked from the helicopter when he'd wondered if she would. But she'd given in. He told himself that he'd never expected any other outcome, never doubted she would do exactly as he wanted.

Even though she hated him.

Zac was waiting when Pandora finally exited the stairwell onto a wide terra-cotta-tiled landing that branched off to a narrow kitchen on one side and a huge sitting area to the other. Pandora caught a glimpse of stainless steel and pale marble bench tops in the unexpectedly modern galley-style kitchen before Zac gestured her forward.

"This way." He spoke in a cold, distant tone, and nerves balled her stomach in a tight knot.

She followed him into a large, airy space—and gasped at the sight of the sunset-streaked sky. Glassed on three sides, the space gave an impression of height and light and freedom, of seeing the world from the perspective of a gull in the sky. A rapid scan of her surroundings revealed a pair of long ivory leather couches separated by a heavy bleached-wood coffee table. An immense cream flokati rug added softness to the room without breaking the mono-chromatic colour scheme. Like the stairwell, the walls in here were covered with rough plaster and washed with white. And nothing detracted from the incredible impact of the sky and sea turned gold by the setting sun.

Except the brooding man standing an arm's length from her.

Pandora gave him a quick glance and looked away, a frown pleating her brow. So he was affronted because she didn't want him near her? Because she'd lashed out that she hated him? What the hell did he expect given the way he'd behaved?

Kidnapping her.

Thrusting her into that flying monster.

Agitated, she brushed back the tendrils of hair that the buffeting wind on the rooftop had tousled. "You know, I haven't been up in a helicopter for years." Her voice shook with a mixture of anguish and rage and long-suppressed emotion.

He swivelled on his heel, arrogance in every line of that

hard, lean body, and balled his hands on his hips, watching her from behind inscrutable eyes. "I really don't care about the last time you went joyriding."

"God, I hate you!"

Pandora itched to smack that insolent, cold-as-marble mask. But her hands were trembling so much she doubted she would succeed. Where had she ever gotten the idea that his eyes were tender, loving? That the hard slash of his mouth revealed passion and humour? That this stranger *loved* her?

The urge for straight talk that had raised its head less than ten minutes ago vanished. He didn't deserve any explanation of her terror. He didn't deserve to hear about… about…about the other stuff she needed to tell him. His thuggish behaviour, his lack of consideration for her, had put him beyond the pale. She didn't owe him a thing. He could take his talk and stick it where it hurt most—she wasn't staying around.

Reaching for her handbag, Pandora struggled to unzip it. Her shaking fingers groped and encountered the smooth cover of her cell phone. She pulled the phone out, clutching it like a lifeline.

"I'm going to phone my father and then this nonsense is going to stop. He'll send someone to come fetch me."

Zac's gaze dropped to the phone in her hand. "There's no reception on the island."

"The island? *We're on an island?*" Pandora's voice rose until she could hear the shrill tinge of hysteria he'd mentioned so scathingly.

"Yes, Kiranos. My hideaway. Only my close family knows of its existence. It's where I come to unwind. No phones, no bodyguards—only the simple pleasures in life."

The gaze that rested on her face was filled with grim contemplation. "Just peace and quiet."

"I don't believe that!" She swept a quick look around and then out over the expanse of sea. And swallowed. "You're far too important to put yourself out of reach." Pandora hated the sliver of doubt that crept into her voice as she considered that this unknown Zac might well have set up this godforsaken place to be out of touch with the rest of the world.

"Believe it. Cell phones are useless on Kiranos."

Kiranos...an island. She struggled to come to terms with his unwelcome revelation. He'd brought her here to talk and be alone. Realisation dawned. He'd never intended to have a brief conversation and take her to the airport.

An island. Bang went her plan of getting on the next flight...unless she wanted to swim for it. Her gaze swept the vista ahead of her. No other landmasses. No ships.

A few quick steps took her to the wall of glass that translated into a set of sliding doors. Another step, and she stood on a narrow, windy deck suspended high above the rocky beach below. She stared over the glass balustrade at the endless stretch of water that gleamed like liquid gold far below. No, she'd never make the distance across the sea. She was trapped. Trapped with the formidable stranger who was her husband.

The only way she was going to get off this piece of rock with its moat of seawater was to convince him to release her. To *talk*—oh, God, that word again—her way out of it.

And she had to succeed.

With an impatient huff, she flipped the cover of the cell phone shut and stepped back inside to where Zac waited, unsmiling.

"So what am I supposed to do here?"

"Relax. Sunbathe. Gaze at your navel." He glanced at her from under those impossibly long lashes and added softly, "Make love…."

She flinched and dropped the phone. It thudded onto the floor. Zac bent to scoop it up.

Putting her hands on her hips, she faced him down. "You're mad, you know that? Totally psycho. You kidnap me, put me in a helicopter…now you expect me to make love? I hate—"

"You hate me. I know, I know. That refrain is becoming a bore." But a muscle worked in his cheek.

Emotion choked her, a painful knot in her throat. "You know nothing. But you think you know it all." To her horror, she felt the tightness of tears at the back of her throat. "Why, Zac? Why did you marry me? Obviously not because you loved me! Why did you bring me here with a drummed-up excuse that you wanted to talk? *Why can't you let me go?* What's so special about a virgin in this day and age, for goodness' sake?"

He stared at her, his eyes empty holes in that hard face.

Another swallow to ease the sudden dryness in her mouth. So perhaps it would be better to start the talk thing he'd been so hot on sooner rather than later. She didn't care for this silent, inscrutable Zac.

She tried another tack. "Tell me about this prophecy you and Dimitri were talking about. I deserve to know, don't you think?"

"Okay." Zac sighed and rubbed a hand over his face. His shoulders sagged and suddenly he looked so weary, so disillusioned, that Pandora was tempted to rush to him, throw her arms around him and comfort him. Then she came to her senses. Why on earth was she feeling sorry for him?

This was Zac.

Zac who'd laughed with her, hugged her and pretended to love her. Zac who'd lied to her. Zac whom she'd married yesterday in the wedding of the decade, promising never to forsake. Zac who'd brought her to this rock with a castle on it to *talk* to her. Well, now he could damn well talk.

"Go on," she invited with a barbed little smile.

He ignored the taunt.

"Let me get us something to drink." Moments later he was back with two short, squat glasses filled with blocks of ice and mineral water. He set them down on the wooden coffee table and shrugged off his jacket.

Pandora couldn't help noticing how the white T-shirt clung to his broad shoulders. Quickly she averted her gaze, picked up her glass and took a long sip. "You were going to tell me about this prophecy," she reminded.

He inclined his head. "It's a legend rather than a prophecy. Sit down, it will take time."

Pandora sank down onto the leather sofa and Zac settled himself opposite her. "I told you that my great-grandfather repaired the family fortunes after the first World War?"

Pandora nodded, her interest caught despite her resolve not to be sucked in by his explanations. "Orestes Kyriakos married a wealthy Russian princess and used some of her funds to rebuild the Kyriakos Shipping fleet."

"That's right. After the Suez Canal was opened, Orestes followed in the footsteps of Aristotle Onassis and Stavros Niarchos and built his first supertanker to transport crude oil. When my grandfather, Socrates, took over Kyriakos Shipping, he continued to commission more supertankers. And by the time the oil crisis hit in the early seventies, Socrates had gone into the production of crude oil. He established three refineries and he left those to my cousin, Tariq, whose mother—my aunt—married the Emir of Zayed."

"I didn't realise that."

"Socrates's remaining grandson, Angelo, inherited three islands and a string of resorts that Socrates owned." He paused. "But I digress. My father lacked the magic Kyriakos touch—he lost more money than he ever managed to make. My grandfather called him an idle playboy and took me out of his care when I was six years old. Said he didn't want my father's sloth rubbing off on me. He considered my father a disgrace to the Kyriakos name and disinherited him in his will. He raised me, didn't want me to be the failure my father was."

"Didn't your mother object when he took you away?"

Zac glanced at her sideways. "My mother had an addictive personality. She was in and out of rehab—she had enough alcohol problems without worrying about me. She was hardly more than a child when she married my father at seventeen and fell pregnant with me soon after."

Pandora's heart went out to the little boy he'd once been. But when she started to say something, Zac interrupted, "With the exception of my father, the Kyriakos men have always been associated with wealth and acumen. And beautiful women." He shot her a hooded look and Pandora bit back her instant derogatory response. "Orestes was rumoured to have rescued his princess from the Bolshevik revolution, although there were some who said he stole her from her father—she brought a fortune in jewels as her dowry."

"She was beautiful." Pandora had seen the painting that hung in the entrance hall to Zac's house.

"Before that there was an English heiress and a shah's daughter, as well as—"

"And were all these beautiful paragons virgins?" Pandora interrupted.

Zac gave her a long look. "Yes. It was their innocence that initially attracted a Kyriakos male and their purity of spirit that kept him faithful all the years of their marriage."

"Oh, please."

"It's true," he insisted. "Kyriakos men do not stray from the marriage bed."

"What about your playboy father?"

"He was an aberration. A disgrace to the Kyriakos name and my grandfather disowned him. But even my father never dared divorce my mother and he failed to live up to the family name. There is no divorce. Ever. The sacredness of the marriage lies at the heart of the prophecy. A woman pure of body and spirit means a faithful man, sufficient heirs and wealth forever."

"You believe all this?"

His eyes flickered. "It doesn't matter whether I believe it. It's the legend. It is what is expected. It's a self-fulfilling prophecy that no Kyriakos heir worthy of the name has seen fit to disturb for nearly a thousand years since the Fourth Crusade. That was when the first documentation appeared about the legend—in the journal of an ancestor who rescued the daughter of a silk merchant, a woman who was reputed to be as innocent as a lamb, more beautiful than Helen of Troy and more wealthy than Croesus."

"What happened to your ancestor during the Fourth Crusade?" Despite herself, Pandora's interest was tagged.

"He came to live in Athens—on the same piece of land where my home stands. Byzantium did not take part in the crusades. There were issues with Rome." Zac's jaw was tight. "War is a cynical business, and the lure of instant wealth in Byzantium caused a few of the Venetian noble-man to end their crusade long before they reached Syria. The pickings were easy, the people less fierce and the re-wards didn't mean facing an army. My ancestor saved the young woman from a marauding Venetian knight who treated her as little more than a slave—her only use to him was for ransom."

"So your ancestor stole her for her maidenhead and her wealth. What makes you think she grew to love him?"

"When he settled in Athens—a village then compared to Constantinople—he built her a castle. And beside the castle had a church erected. The castle no longer exists, but the church that he built for her in 1205, according to the family journal, still stands. It's now a national monument. And an inscription in the church records their love for each other."

Infuriated, Pandora cut across him. "And because your Kyriakos ancestors abducted their brides you think that gives you justification to kidnap me? Guess what? You're dead wrong about that. You had no right—"

"Pandora…" He moved to sit on the couch beside her. "You're right. This is not about my ancestors. We need to talk about us."

She froze as he came closer. Shaking her head so that her pale, long hair flew around her face, she said, "No, I don't want to talk about us. And it *is* about who you are, where you come from."

"Hell." He raked a hand through his hair and leaned back. "You make me sound like an alien from another universe."

"Perhaps you are." Annoyed and frustrated, she frowned at him. "I need to understand why a modern man gives credence to ancient superstition and waits years to find a virgin bride."

"I would never have married you if you weren't also—"

"Tell me one thing, Zac," Pandora interrupted him as she perched on the edge of the sofa, tension humming through her as she scanned his features. "Would I ever have merited a second look if I hadn't been a virgin?"

There was silence. "No." His reply was subdued. "I heard about this heiress who lived at the end of the world who was beautiful and innocent and I hoped—"

"That's why you came down to New Zealand instead of sending a minion? Not to see my father to broker some business deal?" Pandora could hear her voice rising again and she forced herself to speak calmly. "To look me over?"

Another hesitation. "I came to meet you, to get to know you."

"Oh, God!"

"But I would never have taken it to the next level, asked you to marry me, if I hadn't been sure—"

"I can't believe this!" Pandora threw her hands into the air. "It's the twenty-first century. Most people marry because they want to get married. For love, to have children—

for a whole host of reasons. And I manage to find the one guy on earth who's not after love. He's searching for a virgin bride because that's what his forebears did. You know what? It's downright archaic!"

"Stop." Zac held up a hand and straightened beside her.

Stop? She hadn't even begun. She opened her mouth to protest his high-handedness. "I—"

"Stop right there," he cut across her. "Let's talk about why you think I don't love you."

"Oh, come on, Zac." She pushed up off the sofa and took a couple of steps away. "There's no need to pretend anymore."

"Isn't there?" he asked enigmatically, watching her through half-closed eyes, his legs stretched out in front of him.

"No." She threw him an assessing look from under her eyelashes. Straight talk? It was now or never. He'd have no choice but to let her go. She drew a deep breath. "Anyway, it would appear that you've been under a misconception."

His gaze sharpened to a bright, brilliant green. "A misconception?"

"I was not a virgin on our wedding night." Raising her chin a notch, she met his gaze and held her breath.

He went white. The shock reflected in his eyes made Pandora's stomach clench. Any hope she'd had that he'd dismiss her lack of virginity with a wave of his hand disappeared.

No, Zac would never have married her if he'd known she wasn't a virgin. That much was clear from the accusing glitter in his eyes.

He uncoiled and rose in a smooth, swift movement. The anger in his gaze devastated her. Suddenly Pandora felt tired and old and thoroughly disillusioned. "So now you see why there's no point talking…or keeping me on this island."

Zac's jaw moved, but no words emerged from between his lips. And his face reverted to hard and blank. In his silence she had her answer.

"I'm right, then." Her shoulders hunched and she drew a protective shield around the hurt inside her heart. "You don't love me—you never did. You simply *pretended* that you did. You lied to me, Zac."

"This is where I get to tell you that you're not the only one who feels cheated." His mouth twisted. "You haven't been wholly truthful, either."

"Where did I lie to you?" Pandora demanded.

"You had me believe you'd led a sheltered life—"

"I have! I spent half my life in St. Catherine's—"

He rode over her. "And now you reveal you are not a virgin."

"Oh, for goodness' sake." Pandora rolled her eyes to the ceiling. "How many virgins have you known, Zac?"

His gaze slid away from her, toward the darkening sky outside the vast sheets of glass. "That is not a question I'm prepared to answer." A dark flush lay along his cheekbones.

"I'll tell you how many—none."

His head came around. "How did—" He paused, then shrugged.

"It's obvious." Pandora threw her arms wide. "That's what this is all about, isn't it? That's why you're in this fix. Because there aren't any suitable virgins out there. Not unless you want to marry a fifteen-year-old and look like an utter pervert because you married a schoolgirl less than half your age. That's why you picked me. For some reason, you thought I was the perfect candidate."

The flush of colour drained from his skin and the pale flesh stretched tautly across his cheeks like alabaster. He stood unmoving, like the marble statue at the Acropolis Museum she'd thought he'd resembled, staring at her with those disturbingly empty eyes.

She held up an index finger and noticed absently that it trembled. "One lover. That's all I've had before last night. One lover."

And it had been a stupid mistake.

She'd been innocent, a silly little fool. But how could she explain that to Zac? He would never understand. She'd been so young and so darn gullible. Seventeen—nearly eighteen—and madly in love for the first time in her life. Pandora felt a stir of guilt. She hadn't given a thought to what her crazy infatuation might one day cost her.

It was going to cost her Zac. What was the point of skirting around the issue? That was what was at stake here. Zac had expected to marry a virgin. And she bitterly resented that he couldn't see past her lack of virginity to the woman who loved him with her whole flawed heart.

So when he took a step toward her, she backed to the door. In case her resolve melted and she dissolved into his arms, yearning for his love.

Her hands warding him off, she warned, "Stay away from me. You're not touching me tonight. I don't want to be in the same room as you."

And then she spun away from Zac and hurried out of the room.

* * *

The gurgle of the last of the single-malt scotch running into his glass led Zac to the realisation that he'd drunk the whole bottle he'd unsealed several hours earlier. Lurching to his feet, he stumbled to the deck, where he hurled the contents of the glass far into the night, revolted by his excess.

His wife was driving him to drink.

But tonight there was no need for Dutch courage. Pandora would not be waiting for him in his bedroom. Hell, he didn't want to remember the look on Pandora's face when she'd rounded on him, making it more than clear he wasn't to go near her tonight. So he'd arranged for Maria to prepare her a smaller bedroom down the other side of the corridor.

But not even his wife's biting anger could stop him growing hard and hungry at the memory of their wedding night. Last night his beautiful bride had wanted, revelled in the passion he'd shown her.

Yet now she hated him. While he craved her.

He sank down onto the couch and shook his head to clear it of the alcoholic fog that hung over him.

His wife. He'd been so desperate to get his hands on Pandora in the lead-up to the wedding day, but he'd waited. Restrained himself because he'd wanted it to be perfect for his bride.

The wedding had been perfect. And his wedding night had been even more perfect. He dropped his hands into his head. Pandora had been so responsive to his touch but so obviously lacking experience. So tight when he'd penetrated her. There'd been no reason to doubt that she was a virgin. Hell, he hadn't expected an intact hymen, not with the active, sporty lifestyle a modern girl led.

But he'd been floored by her announcement that he wasn't her first lover. The whole dream had blown up in his face, scattering pieces of chaos everywhere. Zac gave a groan. And he didn't know how to put his orderly world back together again. No wave of a magic wand would turn Pandora back into a virgin.

There had never been a divorce in his family in a thousand years. Not even his failure of a father had committed that sin. Zac rubbed a hand over his face, mentally recoiling at the idea of all that ugliness.

His head ached thinking about the choice. A sullied bride? Never! The scandal of a divorce? He could not let Pandora go.

If he flew her to the airport tomorrow, he'd never see her again. Never hold her, never touch her. He closed his eyes at the wave of nausea that swept him at that thought. Pandora was not going anywhere. Not until…

Until…what? He shook his head and another wave of nausea swirled around him. Hell, he couldn't think straight. Couldn't think what to do next. The sheer lack of clarity shocked him. With a wretched sigh, Zac reached for his glass—then remembered he'd tossed the contents over the edge of the deck and groaned. Collapsing sideways, he slid full length onto the couch and closed his eyes.

And wished that the room would stop spinning around him.

Five

The following day, a tentative knock roused Pandora from the doze she'd floated in for ages since dawn. Instantly awake, she swung her legs over the side of the bed, intensely aware of the slither of the pale gold satin nightgown against her legs.

Could it be Zac? Her pulse picked up. Could he be coming to apologise for not loving her, for misleading her, for all the grief he'd caused her?

"Who is it?"

Her query was overridden by another—louder—knock.

Annoyed, she called, "Go away, Zac."

But the knocking continued to staccato against the door. Pandora leaped across the room, her heartbeat racing in anticipation of the battle to come. She turned the key in the lock and yanked the door open.

But it wasn't Zac who stood there. Instead, Pandora found herself facing an elderly woman balancing a breakfast tray on one hand, the other poised to knock again. Pandora recognised the bag and scarf slung over the woman's shoulder as her own.

This must be Maria, Georgios's wife. Pandora hid her exasperation and the twinge of disappointment that it wasn't Zac. "Oh, thank you. I must have left them downstairs last night."

Maria said nothing. Pandora tried not to let the woman's lack of welcome get to her. Instead, she scanned the teapot and cup, the bunch of dark purple grapes, the toast and conserve prettily arranged on the tray and said, "That looks delicious," before reaching for the tray.

Maria held on to it. For a moment Pandora thought the old woman intended to keep possession of it, then unexpectedly she relinquished it. Backing into the room clasping the tray, Pandora smiled her thanks.

Setting the tray on the chest of drawers beside the window, Pandora turned to find Maria in the room. The handbag had been set down on the bed. Pandora's silk scarf lay across Maria's hands, and the old woman's crooked fingers moved in little circles against the brightly hand-dyed silk.

Pandora warmed to her. "It's beautiful, isn't it? My favourite scarf."

Maria ignored her, her fingertips continuing to caress the fabric.

"Did Zac instruct you to give me the silent treatment? Is this another part of his kidnap plan? Isolate me? So that I fall into his arms?"

Nothing. Not even a glance from the other woman.

Pandora gave a sigh of impatience. "You know, a little politeness goes a long way."

At last Maria looked at her.

Pandora shook her head in disgust. "You're very rude," she said clearly. Shrugging when she didn't get a response, Pandora stalked to the door and pointedly opened it fully. There was no mistaking the message, and Maria's expression clouded over. She gave the scarf one last stroke before draping it on the post at the bottom of the bed. Then she shuffled past Pandora, her dark eyes veiled.

"Have a nice day." Pandora pinned on a wide smile.

But Maria didn't look at her again—nor did she deign to reply.

Shutting the door behind the rude old crone, Pandora locked it for good measure. Only then did she unzip her bag and realise that her cell phone was missing. She remembered Zac suggesting seductively that she spend her time on the island making love. She'd dropped the phone and he'd picked it up. The frustration simmering inside her notched up another degree.

Zac had kept her cell phone.

Seething, Pandora pushed open the curtains and blinked against the bright September sunlight. The absence of shadows made her glance at her watch. It was already midday, so she hastened to the en suite to wash and afterward pulled a floaty white sundress from the wardrobe where someone—Maria perhaps?—had hung her clothes.

Once dressed, she dragged an armchair from the corner of the room and placed it squarely in front of the window and settled down to tackle the fruit Maria had brought. She had just finished the grapes when a new volley of knocking thundered against the door. A moment later the doorknob rattled, but the lock held.

"Unlock the door." Zac's voice held a dangerous edge.

"Go away, Zac."

"Open it now," he demanded.

She stared mutinously at the door. A heavy thud rocked the door. But the wood held. His shoulder? Probably. She hoped it hurt like blazes. "Stop it, Zac."

"Open the damned door or I'll break it down."

At the thought of Zac's breaking the door down a forbidden flare of excitement stirred. *God, what was she becoming?* "If you use any force on that door, I'll lose the last tiny shred of respect I have for you."

There was silence. Then she heard him heave a heavy sigh. "You've hurt Maria's feelings."

The totally unexpected attack took her aback. "*I've* hurt Maria's feelings?" *What about her feelings?* Slowly she rose from the chair and went to unlock the door.

Her eyes widened as she took in Zac's appearance. He looked haggard. His normally tanned skin held an unhealthy yellow tinge, and his eyes were red-rimmed.

"Are you ill?" The words burst from her.

"Why?" he asked guardedly.

"You look terrible."

His gaze slid away from hers and he muttered something that sounded like, "I feel terrible."

"What?" she asked, frowning at him.

"It doesn't matter. What matters is that Maria is offended."

"I'm offended! That woman is rude."

"Don't talk so loudly." He flinched and half closed his eyes.

"You're hungover!" she accused.

He blinked but didn't deny it.

"You didn't see her. She was rude and insolent and ignored everything I said to her. She didn't even greet me."

"It's not her fault—"

"Of course it's her fault," Pandora cut in heatedly. She raised an eyebrow. "Unless you put her up to it?"

"I didn't put Maria up to anything. But I should've told—"

"You should tell her she needs to be more polite to me." Pandora cringed when she heard the self-righteous words and added lamely, "After all, I am your wife."

Zac stared at her as if he'd never seen her before. "Why do you deserve Maria's respect when you gave her none? She says that you opened the door, made her unwelcome in your room and slammed the door on her. That woman has been there all my life. She raised me when I lived with my grandfather at the house in Athens. She looked after me while my father went through dozens of floozies and my mother drank herself to death." Zac's eyes were flashing now. "One thing I never had you pegged for was a spoiled little rich girl."

"I'm not a spoiled little rich girl. She was damn rude to me. *She* ignored *me, she* turned *her* back on *me.*" It sounded so petty. It was obvious Zac cared about Maria. A lot. "Look, maybe she's worried now that you're married," Pandora conceded. "Maybe any woman you married would never be good enough in her eyes. But she didn't have to—".

"She's deaf."

"Deaf?" Pandora gaped at Zac. The scene in the bedroom ran through her head. "Oh, no! Now I feel terrible."

"It's my fault," Zac sighed. "I usually sign to her, although she can lip-read Greek fluently. I should have warned you to speak English very slowly and keep to a basic vocabulary. But I never even thought about it. I never think of her…disability."

"I'll tell her I'm sorry." Pandora lifted her chin. "But you're right—you should've told me. In fact, you should never have brought me here. What do you think Maria would think of the boy she raised abducting a woman?"

"You're not telling her that."

"I can't, can I? Not if she's deaf and can't lip-read English properly." She gave a mirthless laugh, furious with him, with her helplessness. "You've got it all sussed, right down to the deaf jailer."

"Kiranos is not a jail."

"It sure feels like one. Unless you're planning to take me to the airport?" Pandora sneaked him a look from under her bangs. But for the first time she wasn't so sure she wanted to go. Once she left, their marriage would be over. And Zac would never look at her with that glow in his eyes, never again touch her with fingers that reduced her to shivers—

God, she had to stop thinking about…about the sex side of their marriage.

Zac avoided her gaze. "I'll let you go when I'm good and ready."

His high-handedness caused another flare of annoyance. "And then you wonder why I say I hate you."

The eyes that met hers were a flat, expressionless green. "You don't hate me."

Before he could expose the ignominious desire she was trying to hide, Pandora retorted, "What's to like about you? You're arrogant, deceitful and sly. You talk about your noble ancestors and their chivalrous love for their brides, yet you abduct me and stop me from going home to my family. You are a man totally without honour."

Zac stared at her, his face ashen. Without a word, he swung on his heel and left her room, the door closing silently behind him.

Feeling no relief at her victory, only emptiness, Pandora slunk to the armchair and listened as his footsteps retreated. The tearing sense of loss splintered her soul, hurting deep within her psyche and leaving a void where her love for Zac had flourished. All that was left was the humiliating knowledge that she still wanted him. But after her last crack, he'd have to be made of steel to even think of touching her.

Dropping her head into her hands, she remembered Maria's sullen face when she'd left earlier…and just now Zac's face had been grey as a result of the words she'd hurled at him. Words that left the nasty, bitter taste of shame on her tongue. She'd always been kind and upbeat to everyone she'd met. At school, some of the girls had sniggered that she was a regular little Pollyanna. What the hell was happening to her? What was she becoming?

Yes, Zac's behaviour to her had been unacceptable. His actions had instilled a sense of confusion and powerlessness. And, yes, she'd been wallowed in her own misery. But there was no need to take it out on Maria.

Or even Zac. His shattered expression flashed through

her mind. She'd known that her words would hurt like poisoned arrows. Zac's sense of honour lay at the heart of the man he was—the man he believed himself to be. Her venomous attack had been small-minded, not like her at all. She'd behaved like a petulant child.

Remorse stabbed at her. And while a niggling voice said that he deserved it because he'd taken away her right of choice, her freedom, she suppressed it. She was not going to allow Zac's actions to destroy the person she'd always prided herself on being.

So when Maria arrived with her lunch tray, Pandora gave her a tentative smile and mouthed, "I'm sorry."

The Greek woman's face broke into a smile and she started to speak in very broken, very hesitant English. "Zac tell me you not know."

The knowledge that Zac had taken the blame for what had happened completely flummoxed her, and she stared after Maria openmouthed as she set the tray on the chest of drawers.

After Maria had gone, Pandora picked at the Greek salad with its red tomato quarters and fat olives before pushing the tray aside. Not hungry but not yet ready to venture out and face Zac, Pandora picked up a book. It was a mystery featuring a kick-ass heroine by a favourite author who usually held her entranced. But today the words on the pages aroused no interest.

The afternoon was hot. Even inside the thick whitewashed stone walls, Pandora could feel the temperature rising. The fine cotton dress clung to her body, so she turned up the air-conditioning. Thoroughly restless now, Pandora crossed to the window and pushed it open.

The villa—if one could call a structure with towers and parapets that—perched like an eyrie high above a sweeping cobbled terrace, and far below lay the stony beach. And beyond, the sea glittered in the sunlight. On the terrace, a thickset man with a head of unruly black hair—Georgios, Maria's husband, she supposed—was watering terra-cotta pots full of bright magenta geraniums.

The startling glare of the heat shimmered off the white walls of the villa. The sea looked blissfully tranquil. Incredibly tempting. Pandora stood there, her arms folded on the wide sill, for what seemed forever.

At last she acknowledged to herself that she was waiting for Zac to appear.

Turning away in disgust, she threw herself down on the bed and stared at the wooden door.

This time she hadn't locked it.

Because after her cruel words she knew Zac would not return.

Pandora spent the next three days closeted in her bedroom, avoiding Zac, full of remorse at the way she'd spoken to him the last time she'd seen him. But she couldn't help being a little irked that Zac hadn't bothered to check on her.

Yet beneath the conflicting emotions lay something more, an unsettling desire that was still very much alive. Despite everything he had done—and her own vehement demand for a divorce—what she really wanted was for Zac to apologise, preferably on his knees, for keeping her here against her will. It infuriated her to be so confused, at the mercy of a man and her own turbulent emotions.

The only respite from the quagmire of emotions, ironically enough, was Maria. Three times each day Maria brought her a tray heaped with delicious food. Swiss muesli and fruit and rich, creamy yogurt with honey for breakfast. Greek salads topped with chunks of crumbled feta cheese and glossy black kalamata olives, pita bread with *taramasalata* and hummus and slices of warm lamb seasoned with rosemary. Maria clucked like a concerned mother hen if she failed to finish meals and smiled her approval when the plate and bowl were clean of food. Any thought Pandora might've had to undertake a hunger strike to make Zac realise how seriously angry she was about what he had done was undermined even as it took root.

Maria brought Pandora a pile of outdated magazines. *Cosmopolitan, Harper's Bazaar* and *Town & Country,* as well as an assortment of Greek magazines, giving Pandora something to do. So one evening, when Maria arrived with a dinner tray, Pandora gave her the silk scarf she'd touched with such reverence that first morning.

Maria's eyes lit up. "Mine?"

Pandora nodded.

Maria took the scarf, holding it like some fragile piece of glass. Then she stood in front of the mirror and tied it around her neck.

"Here, like this." Pandora moved to Maria's side and fiddled with the ends until they were arranged to her satisfaction.

The smile of joy on Maria's face brought a lump to her throat. The old woman's wrinkled fingers kept going up to stroke the lustrous silk with reverent touches.

"Beau…beautiful." Maria struggled with the word.

Pandora dipped her head in acknowledgment. "It was

my mother's. She was an artist—she hand dyed the colours herself." She'd said too much—Maria's frown indicated she did not follow.

"Your mother…dead?" Maria asked finally.

"Ne." Yes. It was one of the Greek words she'd learned over the last few weeks.

Maria shook her head from side to side, muttering something in Greek, her hand going to where the knot sat at her shoulder.

"No." Stilling the older woman's hands, Pandora said, "It gives me pleasure to give it to you."

Maria seemed to get her meaning. *"Efgaristo."* And danced out the room on light feet.

Over the last three days Pandora had reread the meagre selection of books in her baggage, scanned the year-old magazines Maria had brought her until they were dog-eared, her heart stopping each time Zac stared unsmiling out of a photograph at her.

Now, as she readied herself for bed, Pandora finally admitted that she was bored out her skull.

So when she woke on Friday morning, Pandora stared out the window at the pebbled beach that edged the stony outcrop below the villa and decided she'd had enough of being cooped in her bedroom while the sun shone outside.

Quickly she donned a brief white-and-silver swimsuit and covered it with a white cheesecloth shirt that Zac had bought for her at the Plaka in Athens, then tied a yellow sarong around her waist and trod into a pair of metallic leather sandals. A slather of sunscreen, a hat, and she was ready to face the blistering Mediterranean sun.

She met no one as she crept down the spiral staircase and

bypassed the reception rooms. Outside, the beach was even more alluring than it had appeared from her window. The sea was a clear turquoise under the arch of cerulean sky. Round pebbles stretched into the water. Pandora found a flat rock and spread out her towel and stretched out in the morning sun.

What was Zac doing right now? Just thinking about him brought back the unresolved tension between them. She hadn't seen him since he'd left her room, white-faced, days ago. Where was he? She hadn't heard the helicopter depart, so she assumed he must still be on the island.

When was he going to release her?

Surely he'd need to return to the corporation he headed? Or did he maintain a makeshift office in the villa—despite his claim that Kiranos was his retreat from the frenzy that he existed in? From under the hat she risked a glance at the villa and scanned the windows overlooking the beach. Eventually she homed in on the three windows a level below the vast glassed living room. If an office existed, it made sense that there would be some sort of telephone, even a satellite phone—he couldn't be totally out of contact with the rest of the world.

With a sigh, she pushed the thought from her head and closed her eyes.

A little later, made lazy by the sun, she explored the beach, hopping along the pebbles to where a sheer wall of rock ended the curve of beach. Soothed by the gentle lap of the water against the pebbles, Pandora came back to where her towel waited and wedged herself in the shade of a large rock and closed her eyes.

That was where Maria found her when the sun was at its zenith. The tray of sliced fruit and fresh bread with slivers of smoked salmon and chunks of cheese looked delicious, and she thanked Maria. Made hungry by the salty air, Pandora ate with gusto. But she couldn't help wishing that Zac was here…to share the moment.

When she pushed her plate back onto the tray and pulled out the serviette wedged under a plate, a piece of folded paper fluttered onto the beach.

She bent down to pick it up.

Don't forget it is hot in the sun. Stay in the shade or come inside. Join me for a drink on the terrace this evening.

Pandora didn't need the slashed *Zac* to identify the writing.

At once a host of emotions shook her. Aggravation at his high-handedness. Regret for what might have been. And finally outrage.

How dared he leave her languishing for three days and now tell her what to do and demand her company? She ignored the twinge of fairness that admitted that staying in her room had been her choice. Deep down, she'd wanted him to come running after her, to placate her.

But he hadn't.

His failure to do so had both infuriated and frustrated her. Yet at the same time she was filled with a kind of relief. The past few days had given her much-needed breathing space and a chance to gain perspective.

She slopped on more sunscreen, telling herself it had nothing to do with Zac's directive about the heat of the sun, then lay down. But too soon she was hot and itchy. A sheen of perspiration dampened her skin. She wriggled and twisted. But the edgy feeling would not leave. Finally she rose and headed for the sparkling sea.

The water was cool against her heated body, the pebbles smooth under her toes as she edged carefully in. The water crept higher as she went deeper, and finally the unbearable frissons against her sun-warmed skin forced her to dive headlong into the calm water. She came up breathless from the mild shock of the saltwater. Swimming a little way, she turned onto her back and stared at the unfathomable blue of the sky overhead until the on-edge tightness subsided a little. She felt calmer, more able to deal with Zac.

Zac had been watching Pandora from his study on and off the whole morning—and it had shot his concentration to hell. Unsettled, he struggled to read the report his PA had e-mailed to him, a report that had to be finalized—he glanced at his watch—in the next half hour.

Pandora had called him a man without honour. And she was proving to be right. What did he care about a report deadline when Pandora floated on the sea in the tiniest wisps of white fabric bound with provocative silver bows that he itched to untie?

But her words rankled.

Because there was more than a hint of truth in them. Kidnapping her, bringing her to Kiranos when she'd clearly thought he was taking her somewhere to talk before allowing her to leave, had been devious.

He'd intended to talk her into staying married to him, to show her what they had going for them. And then she'd dropped her bombshell.

And it had all gone to hell.

Zac's gaze narrowed on the inert figure of his bride floating on the sea, only the occasional splash revealing she was awake. All his life he'd known he had a duty to fulfil. He was the Kyriakos heir. He would not fail the family as his father had. He would select a wife carefully when the time came. His bride's virginity was not negotiable.

Pandora had put her finger on the heart of his quandary: *That's why you're in this fix. Because there aren't any suitable virgins out there.*

He'd never been drawn to shy, simpering virgins. Since his twenty-first birthday, his family had paraded inexperienced sweet things in front of him—and none had stirred a response. It had taken Pandora, with her sharp wit and gentle beauty, to reach that part inside him that he'd always considered unassailable. He'd been so sure he'd found the answer to his prayers.

Except it had all been a cruel illusion.

He watched as Pandora rolled over in the sea and started to swim toward the shore.

Pandora was not pure in body. Telling himself that a sullied body didn't mean that her heart was any less pure did not help. He'd been misled. Although it was probable her father had believed his daughter to be untouched.

It was his own fault. He should have asked her outright before proposing. But he'd been too intent on getting her into his bed.

He'd been only too eager to accept she was a virgin.

So what if he'd known about her…flaw…from the outset, before he'd offered her marriage? Would it have changed anything? His head told him he would never have married her. Generations of Kyriakos men had married virgins. It was part of their identity, part of the rich heritage they stemmed from.

Part of the magic of the legend.

Yet his body was wired differently from his brain. Those few innocent kisses during their courtship had hooked him. Taking her to his bed and making love to her had been the most earth-shattering experience of his life.

How could he just let her walk away? Yet keeping her would rock the family to the roots and go against the tradition that his ancestors had established. A knot of pain formed under his heart.

Zac was surprised to discover that the thought of living without Pandora was more disturbing than her lack of maidenhead. Somewhere along the line, his priorities had shifted. He no longer really cared that he hadn't found the last virgin bride. He no longer cared about the Kyriakos legend. Not if it was about to cost him his wife.

He watched as she waded through the shallows, picking her way between the pebbles to where her towel lay. The sun glinted off her blond hair and turned her skin to a light bronze. Zac shoved his hands into his pockets.

What did his wife's lack of virginity matter? By marrying Pandora, he'd made her virginity a universal truth. The newspapers had speculated for years about whom he would eventually marry, running articles with accompanying photos of the young heiresses he might favour with a proposal and publicly knocking them off the list when they fell from grace.

He'd made damn sure that Pandora never saw the spate of stories that had followed his announcement of their marriage on her arrival in Athens. Stories headlining her purity to the public.

The tight knot in his chest started to subside. Her lack of maidenhead would be a secret he'd keep from his family—that way there would be no risk of the story leaking into the papers, making a mockery of who he was and destabilising the stock prices. No one else would ever know the truth.

Except…

He hesitated, watching as Pandora wrapped the towel around herself. Pandora had said she'd only ever had one lover. To date, the guy had not come forward—despite the enormous publicity of their marriage.

He'd find the man. Offer him enough money to silence him forever. He would do it for Pandora.

Yes, it was possible.

And he'd use this time on Kiranos to convince Pandora that they were perfect together. But first he had to overcome her fury and hatred. He just hoped he hadn't left it too late.

After the cooling swim, Pandora returned to her room and showered the last traces of saltwater from her body before slipping into a sleek white cotton sundress with a halter neckline. From her window she watched Georgios set two deck chairs out on the terrace. Zac appeared from the house, and her breathing quickened. He paused, said something to Georgios that made the old man laugh.

Pandora skittered back, not wanting Zac to see her. But he didn't glance up as he made for the steep stone stairs that led to the boathouse to the right of the beach.

Quickly she left her room and ran down the spiral stairway. She branched off on the level where she suspected Zac's study might be. Two doors opened off the small landing. Her heart in her throat, she opened the first and found a gym stocked with Nautilus equipment. The second door opened into a light, airy room that was clearly set up to be an office.

It was empty.

No sign of Maria cleaning…and she'd seen Zac heading for the boathouse.

Her gaze hurriedly scanned the desk, the bookshelves, taking in the bank of computer ware, the clean, organised surfaces…but no sign of her cell phone or Zac's.

About to leave, she noticed the flicker of the screen saver. Feeling like a thief, she scuttled around the desk and perched on the edge of Zac's big black leather chair. With a sense of nervous elation, she hit the enter button and waited.

A document opened. Zac had not logged out. Fingers shaking, she minimised the document and hit the Internet connection icon. A home page opened. Relief and a kind of shaky guilt made her sag. She cocked her head. Only silence. No sound of the pantherlike tread of Zac's returning footsteps.

She tapped in a Web-mail address and waited a moment before keying in her log-in and password.

Pandora stared at the screen. A list of unread messages sat in her in-box, several containing subject headers congratulating her on her marriage. No time to read them now.

Hurriedly, she clicked on the new message tab and typed in her father's e-mail address. After a moment's reflection, she filled *Need your help* into the subject line. It was much more difficult to find the words than she had expected. She wanted to tell her father that her marriage was over, that she needed him to rescue her from this mess.

But how to explain it all? She hesitated. How could she tell her father that she'd lost her virginity after some stupid visit to a nightclub with a man she'd barely known three years ago? Her father had trusted her to go stay with Nicoletta and to behave as he expected. How could she disappoint him?

And what would happen about the lucrative contract her father had signed with Zac? He'd walk away from it, putting her first.

No, she couldn't let her private failures screw up her father's business relationships. She had to sort this out herself. Her twenty-first birthday was less than a month away. She was an adult now, not a child who needed to run home to Daddy every time something went wrong.

Zac had brought her here against her will. To talk, he'd said. She'd been bitter, too angry to talk, and had flung her loss of virginity in his face. The diversion had worked. And she'd retreated to her room to sulk, wasting three days waiting for him to come seek her out.

It was way past time to grow up, to take control of her life and her future. She had to find Zac and have it out with him.

But first she owed her father a chatty, upbeat e-mail. He'd been so happy about her marriage. With a small sigh, she started to type.

"What the hell are you doing?"

Pandora jumped when Zac's voice exploded behind her. Spinning the high-backed leather chair around, she blurted out, "E-mailing my father. He'll be worried—and hurt— if I don't keep in touch."

"Daddy to the rescue," Zac said, but the deep lines of tension around his mouth receded.

"I don't need my father to fight my battles."

The glint in his eyes changed to something that she thought might be reluctant admiration. Then he spoiled it by saying, "I want to read what you have written."

Her chin went up. "Don't you trust me?"

His eyes flickered to the screen.

Pandora scooted the chair forward, blocking his view of the screen. "It's private, my communication to my father. I'm simply assuring him that I am well and that we are on an island—how do you spell Kiranos by the way? It would look strange if I didn't get it right."

After a fleeting hesitation Zac, spelled it out.

"Thanks." Pandora bent her head and continued to type. Tense now, she waited for Zac to move closer, to peer over her shoulder...to stop her sending the e-mail. But he didn't move. Finally she clicked the send button and looked up. "Done."

Zac was watching her, a bemused expression on his face. "I'm reputed to be a suspicious, hardheaded bastard. I can't believe that I trusted you to do that." He shook his head and held out a hand. "Come, let's go sit on the terrace and see the day out."

As Pandora rose and took his hand, a deep inner tension unwound and a delicious warmth spread through her. But she suppressed the treacherous want that unfurled inside her.

She and Zac needed to talk.

Six

"Zac, if you can trust me to e-mail my father, then surely there's no point in keeping me prisoner on this island?"

The sun was still hot on the terrace, but the shadows were starting to lengthen. For a moment Pandora thought Zac wasn't going to respond and that the words she'd flung at his broad back would be lost in the sea wind.

Then Zac swung around from where he'd been leaning against the white railing at the end of the cobbled terrace that overlooked the Ionian Sea and let the binoculars fall. "Kiranos is hardly a prison. You didn't enjoy your swim earlier today?"

Pandora slumped back in the deck chair Georgios had set out on the terrace along with a couple of side tables. If she were honest, she had to admit it was a pretty luxurious prison—her every whim catered for. Behind Zac, the sea lay blue and inviting. But it was a prison nonetheless. She lifted a shoulder and let it fall. "Swimming wouldn't have been my first choice of things to do."

"So what would have been your first choice of… things…to do?" The suggestiveness in his richly sensual tone made her flush.

"Certainly not *that*."

His gaze raked her, reminding her of the skimpiness of the fitted dress, with its shoestring halter neckline that left her shoulders bare and dipped to reveal a generous amount of curving breast. In the wake of his gaze, the heat ran riot.

He flashed her a grin. "Sure about that?"

"Yes," she bit out, resenting the effect he had on her body. She couldn't help noticing how cool and assured he looked in a pair of cargo shorts and a white Polo shirt. "I'm sure. There's lots better stuff I could be doing at High Ridge right now."

"You'd walk away from a stay on a Greek island, sunning yourself on a private beach, in favour of winter in New Zealand? Where it's bone-cold right now?"

Pandora hunted his face for signs of sarcasm but found none. "What good is a Greek island when you're only there as a hostage?" she said at last.

"You're not a hostage." Zac looked annoyed. The grin had disappeared. "Tell me, have I hurt you? Tortured you? Locked you in your room? Starved you?" With every word he came closer.

"No." She stared back at him, challenging him. "But keeping me here against my will—it's barbaric."

Zac shrugged. "So I'm a barbarian. Greek legends are full of tales of abduction. You need look no further than Orpheus—"

"Who took Persephone to hell!"

Zac gestured to the calm stretch of blue sea and the silver sunlight streaming down on to the water. "This is hell?"

"No. Yes. Whatever. It's not where I want to be. What you're doing is against the law. I'm going to report you to Interpol the first chance I get." He looked remarkably unconcerned about her threat, even though she knew it was an empty one. He hadn't hurt her, and she didn't really want him incarcerated for kidnapping.

"So where do you want to be, *agapi mou?*"

"Stop it! Don't call me *My love* in that phony way."

His jaw clenched. "I'm not going to argue with you in this mood." He lifted the strap from behind his head and held out the binoculars. "Here, take a look, there's a school of dolphins out there."

Anger forgotten, Pandora reached for the binoculars and came to her feet. "Where?"

"Under the swarm of seabirds."

"Oh, I see them. Five…seven…no, eight. I see about eight. There must be more underneath."

"It's a big school." Zac spoke from behind her, and she tried to ignore the fact that he stood so close that the scent of his skin enveloped her. "They've been frequenting the island for years. I recognise the big bull with the chip out his dorsal fin."

"This is wonderful. We get them at home. Whales, too. But it's lovely to see the dolphins here, as well. And such a big school. Oh—" she squealed. "Did you see? One just jumped out of the water."

"It's great to have them out there. That's why I pour

millions into coastal and ocean conservation each year. So that their survival is assured."

With the binoculars against her eyes, Pandora said, "But you own supertankers and transport crude oil. Isn't that a contradiction? What if there is an oil spill?"

"The Exxon *Valdez* incident was a tragedy. But it increased everyone's awareness of the danger to the environment. My supertankers are among the safest in the world. While all tankers are vulnerable to storms and human error and mechanical failure, mine are part of the new breed that are double-hulled for greater stability."

In the sea, two dolphins arched over the water. Zac watched her squeal with delight, his mouth curving into a smile—her pleasure was infectious.

"It gives me such a kick to know they're there." She lowered the binoculars and looked at him, the laughter fading from her eyes. "You know why that is, don't you?"

Zac didn't think he wanted to know what had caused the happiness to fade from her face, but he could see from the battle gleam in her eyes that she was intent on telling him. "Why?"

"Because they are free." She handed the binoculars back to him. "You need to let me go, Zac."

Zac looked away, unable to hold her defiant gaze. He didn't answer. If he let her go, would he ever see her again? Or would this consuming force between them be lost to him forever? How could he explain the corrosive fear that if she left, he'd be alone for the rest of his life?

He couldn't utter those words. Because she was all wrong for the man he'd been raised to be. So he swung around and strode away.

Five minutes later, his face annoyingly clear of expression, Zac returned from the villa carrying a tall frosted glass filled with amber liquid that looked like beer in one hand and a small sherry glass in his other hand.

Pandora eyed the tiny glass of sherry Zac held out to her and a surge of rebellion rose within her. A sudden urge of devilry prompted her to say, "That looks like something my great-aunt Ethel would drink on a cold winter's evening in front of the fireplace at High Ridge. I'd like a margarita, please, with crushed ice and lots of salt around the rim. And don't go too light on the tequila."

Zac did not look pleased. "Sherry is what the women in my family traditionally drink before dinner."

"Not this woman. Perhaps you should ask what I like to drink?" She cast him a quick look. His jaw was tight, his lips pressed in a thin line. "In fact, cancel the order for a margarita. Make it a Sex on the Beach. Please."

For a moment Zac looked stunned, then his eyes turned molten.

Pandora backtracked furiously. "It's a cocktail…made with vodka, peach schnapps, orange—"

"This is not funny," he interrupted. "My wife does not order such things to drink."

"It wasn't meant to be funny." From behind her fringe she tried to gauge his mood. "And I won't be your wife for much longer." Zac scowled and he loomed over her. She stuck her chin out, defensive now. Her attempt to put him in his place had backfired on her. Badly.

She tried to make amends. "Look, I can't drink wine. It gives me a headache. Spirits suit me better."

Some of the dark turbulence left his eyes. "Would a gin and tonic do?"

She nodded. "Even just tonic water with ice and some lime would be good." And she heaved a sigh of relief as he headed back to the house. She let her body sag in the deck chair and tried not to think about the sudden flare-up between them. Her resentment and ongoing urge to needle him weren't helping matters.

Zac returned with a long glass. She took a sip—it was cool and tasted of fresh lemons with the tiniest hint of juniper berries. "Thank you."

"Pandora…" Zac gave his head a shake and sank into the deck chair beside her, stretching his long, tanned legs out in front of him. "We've gotten off on the wrong foot. Believe me, I want this marriage to work." His eyes were intent, greener than she'd ever seen them and desperately serious. "I want it to be a real marriage, with you at my side."

"How can this be a real marriage if you won't let me go? If you stand over me when I e-mail my father? If you won't even give me my damn cell phone back?" She gave a sigh of exasperation when he didn't answer. "And all because of some random family legend, right?"

"It's not that random," he said, and she could feel the waves of tension coming off him from where she sat. "But you know what? Somehow the legend is not important anymore."

"Not important?" She set the glass down. "When you believed that I'd be the perfect patsy to marry?"

His brows drew together. "It wasn't like that."

"It was *exactly* like that. You convinced me that you

loved me. You married me because you thought I was a virgin. Who told you that, anyway?"

"Your father."

"My father?" She gaped at him in shock. "I don't believe you."

"I don't lie." The distaste in his tone quelled her instant response. "Your father wanted this marriage to happen. I was in Queenstown for an ecology conference. We met. He told me all about you—he's very proud of you. It was no secret that I needed a wife—the right wife."

"A virgin bride, you mean?"

He gave a slight nod.

How humiliating! The whole world knew Zac needed a virgin bride. No wonder he hadn't wanted her reading the newspapers after their engagement was announced. The tabloids' speculation must've been lewd. And her father had put her up as a pure-as-driven-snow candidate. Ack. Suddenly Pandora was fiercely glad she'd decided against e-mailing her father for help. Of course, her father didn't know about…the incident.

"So everyone knew about this…virgin deal…except me. I was stuck in the backcountry bush, looking after guests at High Ridge, while you guys plotted my fate. God, it sounds so feudal." She hauled in a deep breath and covered her eyes with her hands. "And I thought it was fate. True love. Jeez, you must have thought me a silly, gullible little fool."

"I thought you were exquisite. Sweet, charming, funny. I wanted to share my—"

"Stupid. That's what I was," she interrupted him, dropping

her hands and fixing him with a determined gaze. "A world-class idiot. So how are we going to fix this…this disaster?"

His eyes flashed. "It need not be a disaster. We can work it out. But first I want to hear about this man."

"What man?" But she had a horrible feeling she knew exactly what he was talking about.

Zac's deck chair scraped across the terra-cotta cobbles. He leaned toward her and held her gaze squarely. "The one who claimed your virginity."

"Zac!" Pandora gazed at him in fascinated horror. "You can't expect me to talk about that."

"Oh, yes, I can." His brows drew together, and the dusky evening light that fell across his face dusted his harsh features with gold. "You might not have lied to me intentionally, but you've put me in a situation I never anticipated. I need to know the full facts to put a game plan in place to cope with any possible fallout."

She stared blindly at the pink-and-orange clouds scattered across the western sky. This wasn't about her, about her dignity, about her future with him. This was about *him*. About *his* business. About a fortune in share losses. About how *he* was going to handle their divorce…except he'd said he wanted to stay married, hadn't he? She shook her head to clear it of the confusion and the ugliness.

Her relief when Georgios appeared to tell them dinner was ready was short-lived. No sooner had they made their way to the dining room and sat down at the table, where the silver cutlery glinted in the glow of half a dozen tall white candles, when Zac demanded, "Talk to me."

"Okay," she said in a flat little voice, and picked up her fork to toy with the seafood salad in front of her. "I'll tell you exactly what happened. His name was Steve. He was charming, fun, good-looking—"

"I don't want to hear that part," Zac growled, a muscle pulsing high on his lean, tanned jaw. "I want to know who his family is, where you met this man."

"I don't know anything about his family," Pandora said awkwardly, uncomfortable with the turn the conversation had taken.

"So how the hell did you meet him?"

She stopped picking at her food. "Sometimes my father allowed me to spend the August vacation with my best friend, Nicoletta. Her father was a very wealthy industrialist. They came from Milan, and a couple of times I stayed at their holiday home in Sardinia. A few times Nicoletta stayed with us. But High Ridge in winter isn't as much fun as Sardinia in summer, so that didn't happen often. She had an older brother—"

"Ah," said Zac.

Pandora glared at him. "Alberto was only interested in soccer. There was no time in his life for anything else."

"Then tell me about this man who—"

"I'm getting there."

"Too slowly."

"Zac! This is very difficult for me. Let me tell it my way, okay?"

Zac inclined his head. "I'll be quiet."

Pandora could see him visibly forcing himself to relax. It did nothing to calm her. She pushed her plate away and drew a steadying breath. "Nicoletta's parents told Alberto to escort us around, to be a good host. Nicoletta loved frequenting the fashionable beaches to work on her tan and flirt with Alberto's friends. I was horribly shy. But I went along with it because I wanted to fit in. Alberto tolerated the beach. In his view, it was better than taking us shopping. So each day Alberto would take us to play volleyball with a group of his friends—friends his parents approved of as fit company for Nicoletta—on the beach at Costa Smeralda. I started to come out my shell. It was fun."

"I'm sure it was," Zac growled.

"Zac, you said you'd be quiet!"

"I find it is impossible. What were your friend's parents thinking allowing you and their daughter to be exposed to all these young men?"

"They came from wealthy families, some had minders. Even Alberto and Nicoletta had a bodyguard. He was young—Alberto wouldn't tolerate an older guard—and just as mad about soccer and sports as Alberto. That's why Alberto put up with him."

"Don't tell me the bodyguard—"

"No, no, nothing like that! Give me a chance to finish, Zac." Pandora couldn't hold back her impatience any longer. "That's where I met Steve. On the beach, playing volleyball with Nicoletta, her brother and his friends. Alberto didn't know Steve, but they discovered they had an acquaintance in common."

"I bet they did."

"Zac! Anyway, Steve was good at volleyball. But he was different from the other guys—he talked to me and Nicoletta. He was interested in what we had to say."

Zac pushed his plate away. "I'm no longer hungry."

"Me, neither," Pandora muttered.

Zac let out his breath. The sound was loud in the silence

of the darkening room. "It couldn't have been hard to pick out a bunch of rich young kids. He must've had his eye on a rich wife."

"I didn't see it that way. He seemed so sophisticated. But, remember, I was not yet eighteen and he was twenty-five. He wore clothes with a cachet none of the guys I knew did. He drove a sporty red Alfa. He was very European, very cosmopolitan."

"I don't want to hear about your adolescent fantasy." Zac sounded fit to burst, and the muscle was back in play, working high on his jaw. "I want to hear what happened."

Pandora closed her eyes to avoid looking at him.

This was so much harder than she'd expected, reliving her stupidity, telling it all to Zac. "You have to understand…it happened precisely *because* he was an adolescent fantasy. I'd never dated. Goodness, I'd never been allowed to go anywhere with a boy. I didn't even get to meet any. I had no brothers. I was at a very strict girls' school. My father was very protective. Steve looked nothing like the kind of guy I'd been warned about. He was good-looking, obviously smart and successful and he wasn't a threat. I could lust after him to my little beating heart's content."

There was silence.

Pandora opened one eye, then the other, and slid Zac a sideways glance. He was glaring ferociously, his jaw working like mad. She took a deep breath and plunged on. "He was more interested in Nicoletta. She'd always been more sophisticated, more developed physically, too. But he was nice to me, polite."

"I'm sure he was." Zac snorted.

"He was! He was interested in what movies I liked, the books I'd read and in hearing about the kind of girl stuff guys usually ignore. He even knew how compatible our horoscopes were. We used to joke about it—especially because he fancied Nicoletta. And he took me and Nicoletta shopping. He knew all the best shops. He would give advice while we chose shoes and bags at Prada and clothes at Versace. He was fun." And she'd been enchanted.

"Sounds like a gigolo." Zac glared at her, the candle flame throwing his carved cheekbones into sharp relief.

"Zac, he wasn't. I certainly never gave him money." But she had bought him a pair of sunglasses he'd admired. And a wallet. Nicoletta had bought him a leather jacket—in spite of his protests—and some other frivolous items that had caught her eye. Pandora had signed some of the tabs when they'd gone to lunch, the three of them—she, Steve and Nicoletta—while Nicoletta had picked up others. They'd thought it empowering. Steve had joked how he liked twenty-first-century women.

"He talked us all into going clubbing." Pandora remembered her excitement, how it had felt to be seventeen and falling in love for the first time. This time it wasn't a crush based on a poster of a movie star or a photo of a school friend's brother. This time it was the real thing. Except she'd thought nothing would come of it because he'd so obviously preferred Nicoletta.

She'd been so naive.

"So he took you to a club and got you drunk." Zac made a growling sound. "Two young girls."

"We didn't go alone." She glared at him. "Let me finish. Alberto and the bodyguard came with. The first time we went, we only stayed for about an hour and we danced most of the time. But the next time we went, another friend of Alberto's arrived, a guy Nicoletta had always fancied. Steve was heartbroken."

"I'm sure he was," Zac muttered. "He must have been crying in his Jack Daniel's at the thought of the fortune slipping through his fingers."

"You're such a cynic. He wasn't like that!"

"Did he know how wealthy you were?"

"I don't think so. I was on the edge of the circle, the quiet, shy one."

But she hadn't been so shy that night that Nicoletta had gone off with Luigi. Then, she'd been animated—courtesy of the sweet, colourful cocktails with outrageous names she'd drunk to loosen her inhibitions. The excitement had carried her forward recklessly. When the seduction had come, she'd fallen into Steve's bed like a ripe plum.

"Afterward…" Even the memory of her enthusiasm was mortifying. Jeez, she'd even invited Steve to High Ridge. "I wanted him to meet my father. I started talking about how soon we could get married. I mean, that's what I thought love was about. I was so sheltered it was frightening. He couldn't get away fast enough. I went back to New Zealand with my tail between my legs."

"Idiot!" But Zac looked thoughtful now. "And that was the only time you slept together?"

She nodded miserably.

"Did he ever contact you again?" The intensity in Zac's voice told her this was important. She snuck him a look across the table. His face was tense, unsmiling.

She thought of the messages her father had passed on

to her when Steve had tracked her down and called her home in New Zealand a month later stating he needed to talk to her, that it had all been a misunderstanding.

Thank heavens her father had no idea what had really happened. She'd told him only that Steve was a friend of Nicoletta's brother, Alberto. That's when her father had told her that he'd had a trace done on Steve's number, had him checked out and had decided he was an unsuitable companion for his only child. That he wanted her to cut the connection. Pandora had agreed with alacrity—Steve had made it painfully clear that last time she'd seen him that he didn't feel anything like love for her. That her silly crush was not reciprocated. The last thing she'd wanted was her father to discover exactly how stupid she'd been, how she'd let him—and herself—down.

"No," she said, stretching the truth a little, justifying it to herself. After all, Steve had never actually spoken to her.

"And you never heard from him again?"

She fiddled with the corner of the linen napkin. "What's the point of all this? It's not going to change the fact that I'm not a virgin." Pandora wanted the inquisition to end. It achieved nothing except to stir up humiliating memories of the silly little goose she'd been.

"Humour me. Did you ever see him again?"

She shot Zac a quick glance. His face was set, his gaze persistent. He was not going to let it go. And she no longer wanted to talk about it.

"He's dead," she said very quickly, throwing the napkin down and crossing her fingers under the crumpled fabric.

Zac tensed, his body vibrating. "Are you sure about that?"

Pandora glanced away from his piercing gaze into the

blinding flicker of the candle flame. "I told you," she said tonelessly. "He had contact with Alberto through a friend. That's how I heard."

"I assumed his claim to know a friend was a con on the part of this Steve to gain access to Alberto's circle of friends."

She'd never thought of that at the time. How naive she'd been. No wonder her father worried about her.

"Okay," Zac said slowly. "So does anyone else know what happened that night?"

"I never told Nicoletta or Alberto…I was too ashamed." And racked with guilt because she'd coveted a man who fancied Nicoletta. "And I doubt Steve would've, either."

"No, he'd have wanted to keep open the chance to cement a relationship with your friend, Nicoletta, the wealthy industrialist's daughter," Zac remarked a trifle drily.

"Can we let it go now?" Pandora pleaded. "It was a mistake. I was so young, so romantic and so utterly stupid."

"The memory is painful—"

"*Yes*. I wish it had never happened. I moved on afterward—it was my mistake, my secret. I went to the doctor. That in itself was terrifying because I had to find a doctor that my father didn't know." It had involved deception and made her feel underhanded and defiled. "I confessed to the doctor that I'd had a one-night stand and that I was scared I might be pregnant. I was so naive I didn't even know if Steve had used protection that night."

She'd been distraught. The doctor had been sympathetic. She'd done a pregnancy test and sent away samples for tests for diseases that Pandora had never even heard of.

"I told myself that I'd been lucky. I'd made one mistake,

but I hadn't gotten pregnant, nor had I picked up any disease or infection. So I put the whole nasty experience behind me. I refused to let it wreck my life." Pandora blinked back the tears that filmed her eyes. "Yet now that night has come back to haunt me."

"Pandora," Zac's tone was urgent.

She met his gaze staunchly. Zac would not want her now. She would get her divorce and go home to High Ridge. *But at what cost?*

"That one night means I'm not fit to be your wife."

"Pandora!" Zac's hands reached across the table and closed over hers. The shadows from the candlelight played over his face, giving him a dark, mysterious edge. "There is a way. The only people who know about your… indiscretion…are you, me and the doctor who is bound to silence. The man involved is dead."

Something, some dangerous emotion, fluttered under Pandora's breastbone. "What are you saying?"

"I'm saying that we keep it a secret. The doctor's not going to tell nor will I. No one need know that you're not a virgin."

"Would you do that?" Did this sacrifice mean that Zac loved her? He was going against his entire upbringing— everything he'd believed in—to keep her with him. "Would you stay married to me? Keep the truth from everyone? Even your sister?"

Zac looked torn. "What choice do I have? It's too late to annul our marriage—it's already been consummated. If I walk away from you, the paparazzi will tear you apart. How can I do that to you? We have no option but to make this marriage work."

Her heart plummeted at his response. How wrong she'd been. He didn't love her at all. But his sense of honour wouldn't allow him to throw her to the news hounds.

How could she live with him for the rest of her life knowing her marriage was a sham?

"I don't know…" She hesitated.

If she left and returned to High Ridge, she'd never see him again. Never see that slow, sexy smile light up his eyes. Never experience the heart-twisting kisses again. Did she *really* want to walk away from him forever?

No.

"What have we got to lose?" Zac ran his thumb along the base of her palm, and tingles ran up her spine. "We have a certain chemistry between us already."

She blushed. "Marriage is about more than sex, Zac. It's about common goals and values." *And most of all, it was about love.* She'd always dreamed of marrying a man who loved her above all else.

"Sex is a damn good starting point." His slow, sizzling smile made her heart turn over and her pulse rush into overdrive.

How could she resist him in this mood? Did it matter that he didn't love her? Zac wasn't a fortune hunter. And, despite what she'd said, he wasn't cruel or barbaric. He loved his family. He was a good man, a man of principle, the kind of man she'd dreamed of marrying.

Could this simmering sexual connection between them be enough, as Zac had suggested? Should she take a chance and hope that he'd learn to love her?

"We'll take it slowly, one day at a time," Zac was saying. "And if you stay, let's get to know each other a little more. I don't expect you to share my bed right away." But his gaze had dimmed a little as he'd added the final words.

"You'd do that?"

"This is important to me. Give it two weeks here on Kiranos. At the end of that time, we talk again. Nothing is lost. If you still want to go, you can walk away and go back to your life in New Zealand. I'm offering you your freedom."

"You'd let me go?" Her heart sank. For some ridiculous reason, that wasn't what she'd wanted to hear; she wanted him to fight for her, convince her.

"I won't keep you against your will. I brought you here to talk, to ask if you would consider staying for a while so that we could get to know each other a little better. Unfortunately—"

"Unfortunately I told you I wasn't a virgin."

"That confession made things a little…difficult," Zac admitted, his eyes hooded from her gaze. "I needed time to come to terms with your revelations."

When his gaze met hers again, she thought she glimpsed something in the depths of his eyes, something vulnerable, uncertain. Then she dismissed it. Zac uncertain? Never!

"And what," she asked, "if after two weeks I decide I want to…to leave?"

"We go our separate ways for a year or so and then file for a quiet, low-profile divorce. I'll do my best to protect you from the media backlash that will follow. Being in New Zealand will help—it's a world away."

It sounded so simple. She could do that. Spend two weeks on Kiranos relaxing, enjoying Zac's company.

"You'll have no pressure of any kind. No lovemaking. Just the sun and the sea and spending some time getting to know each other all over again." Zac echoed her thoughts. "To see if it can work."

Except he omitted the one thing that she found herself thinking about most. His impact on her…

His touch.

His kisses.

And, above all, his lovemaking.

Disappointment curled inside Pandora. Their wedding night had been so exciting, a storm of passion. Nothing had prepared her for the wonder. The experience with Steve had not come close. Then, she'd been tipsy, filled with guilty excitement, and it had been over before it had started, leaving her feeling more than a little cheated. With Zac it had been different…

But Zac was right. A lot had passed between them. This was a chance to start over. To see what they had. All she had to do was sit it out on an island paradise and then she could walk away—if she chose to—without involving her father.

It wasn't even as if she was at any risk. Zac had made it clear he expected nothing from her—not even sex. Nothing except to give their marriage a chance.

"Okay," she said. "Now can I have my cell phone back?"

"Okay? Just like that?" He gave her a long look. "And why do you want your cell phone?"

She shrugged. "There's no reception, so it won't be much use to me. But think of it as a gesture of good faith."

"Agreed." A strange smile played around his mouth. He reached into his shorts pocket and drew out her small, shiny silver cell phone and held it out to her. "And now you can give me something."

Pandora hesitated, the glint in his eyes warning her. Then she took the phone. "What do you want?"

"A kiss." His smile widened. "Think of it as a gesture of good faith."

Seven

"A kiss?"

Zac didn't answer. But the teasing glint in his eyes challenged Pandora. He expected her to refuse. He was laughing at her, darn him.

Recklessly, she blew out the nearest candles, leaving only one fat white candle burning on the sideboard, then she rose and leaned over the table toward him. "All right."

Placing her hands on his shoulders, Pandora pressed her lips against his…and waited. He stayed motionless. Yet her own response flared wild and primal in her belly, and her breath came more quickly. The velvety darkness surrounding them intensified the sensual mood of the candlelight. Beneath her palms, his Polo shirt had become a barrier that prevented her from caressing his sleek skin.

She moved her hands in urgent little circles against the fabric.

Under her mouth, his lips moved. A sigh. His? Or hers? She didn't know...and didn't care.

His body heat rose through his shirt, warming her hands, and his scent was intoxicating.

Pandora's breathing became ragged. Parting her lips, her tongue stroked across the seal of his lips in a bold caress.

Zac's body tensed, coiling into a tight, expectant mass of bone and muscle and man.

She repeated the soft stroke.

He groaned and his mouth gave under hers. The only sound in the room was their ragged breathing. Her fingers tightened on his shoulders.

At last Zac pulled away. "You are so beautiful." The hand that stroked her hair away from her face shook. "You are kind to Maria—yes, she told me you gave her a silk scarf you valued. You think of your father worrying about you. Your heart is pure."

She thought of the lie she'd told him and her hands slipped from his shoulders. She forced a smile. "You're embarrassing me. I'm far from perfect. And I did consider asking my father for help. But I decided against it." And she squirmed inside.

"Pandora." Holding her a little distance away from him, he said, "Zeus, this is hard for me, but I'm not going to break my promise to give you time. I'm not going to make love to you."

His eyes were clear of everything except an intensity that drew her in, making her aware that he was male and she was his mate...and nothing else mattered.

"I'm not going to rush you into something that might be a mistake. I want you to be very, very sure. Understand one thing—I want this marriage to work, okay?"

Slowly she nodded.

The next week passed in a daze of sun and sea and sleep. As part of their two-week truce, they'd fallen into meeting before breakfast for a run along the footpath that wound past the pebbled beach in front of the villa and then curved away from the beach, between the olive trees up to the headland, before descending to a sandy cove on the other side. The sand in the secret cove was soft and silky, so different from the pebbled beach. Zac would strip off his singlet and charge into the water, and Pandora would drop her towel and follow at a more sedate pace.

Since kissing him at dinner, Pandora found it increasingly difficult to ignore the effect Zac's briefly clad body had on her. She seemed to have developed an inner sensitivity to his closeness. Each morning when they swam out and around the tall rock that jutted out from the sea, she was intensely aware of the smooth, easy stroke of his arms cutting through the water beside her.

Once back in the shallows, she struggled not to gawk at Zac as the droplets streamed off him, his broad muscled chest sheened by moisture and his skin golden in the sunlight. She was tempted to kiss that full, smiling and deliciously sensual mouth, but she didn't dare in case she unleashed a force that she could not control.

Instead, she would run up the beach, pull on her sneakers and grab her towel before tearing down the pathway. Zac would laugh, then she would hear the thud of his footsteps behind her. Eventually she would slow her pace to a jog through the olive grove, absorbing the clatter of the cicadas as the heat started to rise.

Back at the villa, she would veer off to her room for a cool shower, so that by the time she joined Zac for breakfast she was composed enough to face him with no sign of her craving hunger for him. After breakfast, Zac would disappear into his study, leaving Pandora to amuse herself for the rest of the day by listening to music, reading or sunbathing at the beach or watching DVDs from the huge collection Zac owned, while inside her the glow of desire smouldered unslaked.

By Friday Pandora had exhausted Zac's library of DVDs. It was after watching *Zorba* that afternoon that Pandora said rashly after dinner, while they were drinking strong Greek coffee in the glassed room, "Teach me to dance."

Zac got the reference instantly. "You've been watching *Zorba*."

"Yes, and that's not all. Although, I gave the soap operas a miss. Maria said she watches them."

"That's where she's learned the little English she knows. She loves them." Zac's eyes smiled as he spoke about the old woman. "So what else have you watched?"

"*Strictly Ballroom, Take the Lead* and *Shall We Dance?* You have an interesting selection."

"Katy loves dance movies." His gaze turned watchful. "Are you bored?"

"I'm not used to doing nothing," she said honestly.

"We'll remedy that. When we get back to Athens I'll introduce you to Pano, the CEO of Kyriakos Cruises, and perhaps you can develop an active role in the South Pacific region of our tourist-cruise program."

Pandora shot him a sideways look. He made it sound as if her agreement at the end of the two weeks was a foregone conclusion. Did Zac know how tempted she was to stay married to him? Even though he didn't love her?

But she wasn't ready to surrender quite yet. So she tracked the conversation back to dancing. "Remember at our wedding…you said you'd teach me to dance some of the more complicated dances?"

Zac pushed the coffee table back and moved to the bank of stereo equipment, and a few seconds later the sound of music filled the air.

"Come," he said.

Pandora rose. For a moment fear rode her and she wondered if she'd gone too far too fast. Then she stepped forward to where Zac waited and lifted her arms.

"The *hassipikos* is not like a lot of other Greek dances. We start slowly. Once the music speeds up do we change over to a faster, spiralling dance. Now, stand beside me. Here."

Pandora obeyed.

"Get ready to take a step forward. Left foot this time— not right, like most other Greek dances." The music changed. "Now."

Confidently, she stepped forward.

"Good," said Zac. "Two more steps, then we're going to move sideways. Watch my feet."

Pandora was laughing by the time they got through the next section of music, the sweeping arm movements, the complicated crossover steps.

"Let's try that again." Zac flipped the track back to the beginning. "Ready? Now wait for it, then the steps."

Pandora stood still, her arms stretched out and linked with his. She thought about what Zac had said during their wedding about listening to the music, about letting it take her. She heard the tempo change and started forward, the gliding, swaying steps with Zac beside her.

The music swelled, the singer's voice rose. Then she and Zac were moving sideways, their bodies perfectly in time, in tune, yet not touching. A sense of wild exhilaration filled her at the accomplishment.

"I did it! I can do it." She threw her arms around Zac. "Thank you." Her lips smacked his cheek. "I want to do it again."

Zac had gone utterly still.

Pandora pulled back. Too late. Emotion raged in Zac's eyes. Self-consciously she dropped her hands from his shoulders. Zac's hands shot out, circled her wrists and yanked her close.

"You're not going anywhere."

And then his head sank. His lips slanted across hers, hard and hungry. No longer gentle and exploratory, as on their wedding night. No longer immobile and waiting, as when she'd kissed him after dinner a week ago. Now his hips moved against her, his erection unhidden. This was the full masculine hunger unleashed. And it aroused her. Unbearably.

She gave a hot little moan into his mouth. The music was picking up, the rhythm quick, building to a climax.

It brought back the memories of their wedding night. Of the dancing. Of what had followed…his hands on her skin, her body writhing under his.

"No!" Zac tore his mouth from hers. "I gave you my word. Only another week still remains of the two weeks I promised you. Then I will demand my answer."

"You're refusing to make love to me unless I give you the answer you want?" She glared at him in mock outrage, her body objecting as he held her away.

A hard grin slashed his face. "Yes, I have to use every advantage at my disposal to get what I want. *You.*"

The days passed swiftly, and by the following Tuesday Pandora was the rich, golden colour of honey. A sensual glow filled her as she smiled across at Zac. They'd just completed their run to the sandy cove she'd begun to think of as their secret place.

Four days left. On Saturday morning Zac would demand his answer. And Pandora knew what she was going to tell him.

She watched him covertly as he shrugged off his singlet and waded out into the sea. When the water lapped the edges of his shorts, he dived forward and came up ten yards farther ahead. He flicked his wet hair away from his face and called out to her, "Aren't you coming in?"

What was the point of waiting? She knew what she wanted. She wanted Zac, inside her, here, now. Pandora's heart knocked against her ribs at what she was contemplating.

Before she could chicken out, she stripped off her T-shirt. Then slowly, with hands that shook, she tugged the bows that fastened her bikini bra loose. She let the skimpy top fall to the ground. Reaching up, she pulled out the hair tie that held her hair in a sleek ponytail. Bundling the mass together, she secured it with the stretchy tie on the top of her head, her breasts lifting pertly, the nipples tight from the excitement that pulsed inside her.

Finally she shot Zac a glance where he stood motionless in the sea. Pandora's nerve almost gave out. In the bright sunlight, his face was hard, the bones standing out in sharp relief under the taut tanned skin. She looked away and headed for the water, forcing herself not to hurry, aware of the undulating sway of her hips and the movement of her unrestrained breasts.

The sun was warm on her bare breasts, and the cool water rippled against her knees…rising higher as she walked steadily deeper…pooling between her legs… cooling her belly. With relief Pandora sank into the silky water and started to breaststroke into the deeper water, still refusing to look in Zac's direction.

But she could sense his stillness. Sense the tension winding tighter in him. So she stroked a little faster, her gaze fixed, unwavering, on the tall rock in the sea ahead. She heard the splash behind her and broke into freestyle. A quick glance over her shoulder showed her the flurry of Zac's arms powering through the sea, gaining on her, and she started to swim in earnest until her heartbeat resounded in her ears.

She didn't make it to the rock. It was still ten yards ahead of her when Zac's hand closed around her ankle. He yanked. She went under and surfaced a moment later, sputtering, as he forced her to the surface.

"What are you—" She didn't finish. His mouth covered hers, wet and cool and salty.

She gasped, her feet floundering, searching for the sea bottom, out of her depth in more ways than one.

Her legs brushed against his thighs, and desire bolted through her as she felt the hardness of his arousal.

He lifted his head and she gulped in air. "What are you doing?"

Pandora smiled into his eyes. By stripping off her brief swimsuit top and brazenly swimming past him she'd broken the pact between them and raised the stakes.

The days of inane chitchat had worn her down, and the egdy awareness under the banal social chatter had been rising, twisting higher and higher. She was tired of waiting.

"I want you." She moved against him.

He groaned. "Don't do that. We have an agreement."

"I know what I want. I want you. I want to stay married to you."

He stilled. "Are you sure you don't want to be free?"

"I want to be your wife."

Then his mouth took hers again, his hands framing her face. Tangling her legs with his, Pandora let her body go heavy and was rewarded as they sank, the water closing over their heads.

Zac worked his arms to take them to the surface, but Pandora countered by wrapping her arms around his upper arms. She opened her mouth. Her tongue slid into his mouth, her lips sealing against his to stop the water rushing in.

Zac had stopped beating his arms. The hair tie had worked loose and her hair spread around their faces as they spiralled lazily down, weightless in the current. Bubbles streamed past, diffusing through the blue-green world that encapsulated them.

The pressure started to build against Pandora's eardrums. She needed a breath, but she didn't want to leave the silent blue world where Zac floated warm and solid against her.

This must be what it felt like to be a mermaid, Pandora thought hazily and licked at the cavern of Zac's mouth. Then his legs kicked and they jetted upward. They broke the surface and broke apart, gasping for air.

"Are you trying to drown me?" He slicked his wet hair off his face.

For the first time since she'd met him she felt as if she had the upper hand. "I've never been kissed under water." A breathless exhilaration filled her and a reckless rush of adrenaline pumped through her. She grinned at him.

"Well, I'm glad there's something where I could be first."

Instantly the lighthearted euphoria evaporated. Was her youthful stupidity always going to come between them? Pandora turned away and struck out for the rock. She made it safely and pulled herself out, wishing desperately that she wore her swimsuit top. She folded her arms across her exposed chest.

When Zac reached the rock, he said, "I shouldn't have said that."

"No, you shouldn't." She pursed her lips and stared over his head at the white sandy beach.

"You look like a mermaid. A very beautiful, very sexy and, right now, mad-as-hell-at-me mermaid." The hand that he rested on her thigh made her jump. She struggled to ignore him.

"Look at me."

"Why?"

"I want you to see what you do to me."

"I felt…in the water." Pandora felt herself flush.

"I'm not talking about what you do to me physically. I want you to look into my eyes and tell me what you see."

She gazed into his upturned face. The reflected rays of the sun turned his eyes to jade, and a rivulet of water ran from his wet hair down the hard bones of his cheek.

"So what do you see?"

She shook her head.

"Tell me."

"I can't read you—you're too good at hiding what you feel."

"Then I'll show you," he said with a husky growl and dropped his head.

The sleek stroke of his tongue on the soft skin above her knee caused her to shriek, "Zac! Don't."

"Mmm, you taste of salt and sun and bright white heat."

Pandora shuddered but didn't object as his mouth touched her again.

Taking silence as assent, he moved higher.

She tensed…waiting. Her legs parted at his touch. He tugged at the little bows at her hips, and she sighed as the wet fabric gave and fell away. When his tongue touched her…there…she shut her eyes and her head fell back. She moaned, a hoarse, primal sound. She forgot about the hard rock under her bottom, forgot that she was naked, that he could see every intimate part of her, and her whole existence became focused on the sharp pulses of pleasure.

When the shudders came she gasped and tensed, then spun into a place that was hot and cold and the colour of silver. She opened her eyes, and his face, blazing with triumph, filled her vision.

"I could get addicted to watching you come."

She coloured, suddenly self-conscious, and shifted, closing herself to his gaze.

"Don't. You're beautiful. Like the heart of a flower."

"Zac, you're embarrassing me."

He rose up and with gentle care he lifted her off the rock, slid her slowly down his body until her thighs reached the water. She squealed at the cold and wrapped her legs around his thighs and buried her face in the arch where his neck joined his shoulder.

"What about you?" she whispered.

"What about me?" There was a hint of laughter in his voice, and Pandora was unbearably conscious of his hands cupping her bare bottom and holding her securely against him.

"Don't you want…to…to…" Her voice trailed away.

"Come?"

"Yes," she whispered, burying her face deeper against his skin and smelling the salt and residue of aftershave and pure male.

"We have the whole afternoon to make love."

That made her lift her head. "Here? On the beach?"

"Why not? We're all alone."

He bent and brushed a kiss over her mouth. Instantly her lips parted and his tongue sank into her. The kiss was deep. Intimate. Anticipation ratcheted up a notch and Pandora waited, her senses on fire. The hands on her buttocks tightened. She gasped and desire clawed its way up her spine. She wriggled against him, the hard stomach muscles rubbing the naked heat of her. He hoisted her a little higher so that the smoothness of his erection slid between them, sliding through the highly sensitive folds.

Shivers caught her.

The reckless desire soared.

"Now."

He laughed. "Be patient. We have all afternoon. We'll go back to the beach. I'll lay you down on it, then I'll kiss you here—" a touch that made her gasp "—and then you can have me."

Her head thrashed from side to side. "I don't want to wait. I want it now."

Zac's breathing grew ragged.

"Like this?" The blunt hardness probed her.

Pandora arched her back, sweat breaking out along her spine. "Yes," she hissed out. "Just like that."

He slid all the way in, and goose bumps of pleasure broke out over her skin at the intense sensation that swept her. She moaned and clutched at his shoulders.

He moved inside her. Pandora gasped. His hands relaxed a little, creating a space between them, and she felt him slide out, then he was pulling her close again, impaling her, the friction unbearable. Her pulse was hammering in her head, growing louder and louder until it became a roar.

Zac swore, harsh and succinct, and sank into the water, submersing them both below the surface. The sudden cold broke the daze of desire, and with a jerk Pandora realised the roar in her ears was real—not her heartbeat but the sound of a chopper. She yanked her arms from around his neck and crossed them over her breasts—way too late.

"Don't worry, they can't see us. We're in the lee of the rock." He held her locked against him, and the speed of his thrusts increased.

Pandora was torn between worry that they might be discovered—that the helicopter might sweep overhead—and the feverish escalating sensations that threatened to send her spinning into a climax.

"I can't hold back." His voice was hoarse. His hands tightened on her rear, pulling her closer still.

"Don't you dare—"

He was moving wildly against her, within her. "I can't hold anymore." And then he was shuddering, his large body trembling against her.

Pandora was aware of a terrible burning frustration before the sound of the beating rotors drowned out everything except the fear of discovery.

Zac swore. "Who the hell can that be?"

Pandora hoped frantically that Zac's assurance that no one except his family knew about his island hideaway was true. And that the paparazzi hadn't found them.

In silence they rapidly pulled on their clothes and jogged back to the villa. A helicopter bearing the logo of a commercial operator was partially visible on the helipad atop the flat roof by the time Pandora followed Zac up the stone stairs to the terrace and through the side door into the house.

She was excruciatingly conscious of her tousled hair and the wet patches where her T-shirt and shorts clung to her sea-dampened body, sure that anyone could see at once what they had been doing.

As the sound of a woman's voice reached them, Zac's pace increased. "What are you doing here, Katy?"

"Don't be so rude, brother dear." Katy shook her head. "Pandora, it's fabulous to see you again." Pandora was enfolded in a quick hug and an airy kiss landed on her cheek. Zac's sister stepped back. "Look at you, so tanned. You look wonderful." She drew a breath, bubbling with radiance. "I've picked up a little weight, can you see? The doctor said I was too thin—we're trying for a baby again."

Zac gave a sigh. "I suppose that means you won't come to your senses and leave Stavros?"

"Zac!" His sister pinched his arm. "Don't joke."

Pandora glanced from one to the other, trying to follow the byplay. She didn't think Zac was joking. He looked dead serious, his full mouth set in a hard line. What had Katy's husband done to deserve his ire?

"Where is Stavros? I don't suppose you left him behind in Monaco? Or at one of Angelo's resorts?"

"Zac! Don't be naughty. You know we've been in London."

Naughty? Pandora sputtered over Katy's choice of adjective. Zac was too male, too dangerous to ever be described as anything as boyish as *naughty.*

Katy was babbling on. "He's here. He's coming now. He wanted a quick shower. Be nice to him, Zac. For my sake. Please." Katy gazed up at her brother with soft, imploring green eyes. "He's trying really hard. He's promised me there won't be any more…slips at the casino tables."

"I'll believe that when I see it," Zac muttered sotto voce. Pandora glanced at Katy to assess her reaction to Zac's taunt. Either she hadn't heard the last comment or she'd chosen to ignore it. Deciding it was time to give Zac and his sister a little private family time, Pandora moved to the door.

"Where are you going?" Zac demanded.

"I thought Katy might appreciate something cold to drink in this heat."

"That would be lovely. Thank you, Pandora." Katy threw her a white smile.

"Maria will be up in a moment. Come sit down." But Pandora barely heard Zac. Her attention was riveted on the man walking through the door arch.

"Steve!" The strangled whisper died in her throat. No, it couldn't be. Not now. But the man looked horribly similar. Same curly black hair and brown eyes, same corded, lean body.

There was no doubt in her mind—it *was* Steve.

Older, a little softer, but still good-looking in an ivory-skinned, raven-haired, continental kind of way—and still very aware of the impact of his looks. He hadn't seen her yet; he was too busy directing that practised charming grin at Zac.

Of course, Zac didn't appear charmed at all. But then, Zac wasn't an impressionable almost-eighteen-year-old.

God, she'd landed in a nightmare.

She bent her head forward, hoping to remain unnoticed, peeping with fatalistic trepidation through her damp hair, her heart twisting in her chest, making her feel quite ill.

Zac had ironed the distaste out of his face. "Stavros, you missed my wedding. Let me introduce my wife, Pandora."

Finally Steve—Stavros, whatever his name was—looked at her. Pandora wanted to drop through the floor.

How could she have fallen so hard for this man? Next to Zac he looked so lightweight.

"Pandora?" Zac frowned at her.

"Oh, hi," she greeted breathlessly to make up for her lack of manners. *Please don't say anything,* she prayed.

Stavros was staring at her and she read the knowledge in his eyes. He remembered her. Damn. A quick brooding glance in Zac's direction, then his attention came back to her, a hint of malevolence in his smile. "It's been a long time. How are you, Pandora?"

The words were a death knell.

There was a horrid silence.

Then Katy said, "You know Pandora? What a coincidence. How nice for Pandora—she knows hardly anyone yet. Where did you guys meet?"

Pandora prayed harder.

Steve—Stavros, she amended—must have seen something of the desperation in her eyes, because he gave a dismissive laugh. "It was a very long time ago."

"It couldn't have been that long ago," Zac drawled. "My wife is not yet twenty-one and she was a schoolgirl not so long ago. Fill us in, Politsis. Please."

"Zac—" Pandora tugged at his sleeve. "Can I speak to you alone?"

"Now?"

"Yes." Pandora felt light-headed with shock. She must be white as a sheet.

A bride pure in mind. A bride pure of body.

God, why had she lied? She'd failed Zac on both counts. He would never forgive her, but she could try to explain….

Maria chose that moment to arrive with a tray of cold

drinks. Katy signed her thanks and took one off the tray with a big smile at the old woman.

Pandora edged to the door, dragging Zac with her.

Katy's glass clinked against the table as she set it down. "So where did you and Pandora meet? I can't remember you ever going to New Zealand?" Katy was asking her husband with interest.

Pandora quickened her pace, nerves balling her stomach into a tight knot.

"We met in Sardinia. Pandora was there with a group of friends."

Beside her, Zac halted, his biceps tense as steel under her fingertips.

"Zac, I need to talk to you," Pandora pleaded, desperation drumming inside her head.

"Wait."

Panic clamoured inside Pandora, cold and frightening. She tugged his arm again. "Zac, please…come."

"Oh?" Katy invited, sounding intrigued. "Did you know any of the girls? Anyone I know?"

"I'd become friendly with one of their brothers—we'd struck up an acquaintance on the beach playing volleyball."

Zac swung around. He shot Stavros a lethal narrow-eyed look and then the full weight of his attention descended on Pandora.

The green eyes were not warmly intent but slits of ice. She squirmed under his glacial gaze, then looked away, unable to handle the accusation there. She knew that she was flushed now, no longer pale. But the shocky feeling was growing worse. Anxiety and guilt must be written all over her.

"Pandora, look at me."

She shook her head.

"Look at me!" His voice was a whip crack.

She flinched. Her head shot up. There was distaste and rage and pain in his eyes. She swallowed and forced herself to maintain eye contact. *Zac knew.*

"You told me he was dead," he murmured through bloodless lips.

Eight

Pandora ran.

Locking herself into the guest bathroom, she bent over the basin, her temples throbbing. Not even the icy water she splashed on her face helped clear her head. At last the pulsing started to ease, and she straightened and stared at her wan reflection in the mirror.

She couldn't stay here all day. So after wiping her hands on a fleecy white towel, she moved to the door, pressed her ear against the dark-stained wood and listened.

Everything was silent. No shouting. But then, Zac was too civilised to ever do anything as uncouth as shout. Her heart hammering, Pandora opened the door a crack.

The sight of the man leaning against the wall made her start.

"Wait."

She relaxed a little when the figure morphed into Steve, not Zac. Warily she made her way out into the passage.

"You made a beautiful bride. The duckling has grown into a swan."

She was horribly conscious of her damp shorts, the clinging T-shirt and her hair hanging in rats' tails. "I didn't know Zac was your brother-in-law, Steve." *If I'd known, I'd never have married him.* But that didn't help an iota. Not now.

"It's Stavros, actually. Steve is the anglicised form of my name."

She ignored the explanation. "You weren't at the wedding. Did you know it was me?"

"How could I miss the photos plastered over every paper, in every magazine? Imagine my surprise at reading about my brother-in-law's luck at finding you—the rich, beautiful virgin who fulfilled the criteria of the Kyriakos legend."

Don't search for those photos in the newspapers tomorrow. The lies and half-truths that accompany them will upset you. Concentrate on us, on our future together. Zac's words came back to haunt her. And she'd thought them so romantic at the time, thought he was taking care of her... that he loved her. No wonder Zac hadn't wanted her reading the tabloids, hadn't wanted her to find out why he was marrying her. Another bit of her dream splintered.

"So you knew it was me." She eyed Stavros thoughtfully. He'd had the advantage of knowing they would meet eventually.

If only she'd had an inkling.

Fighting for composure, Pandora tried to get a handle on the queasy feeling in the pit of her stomach and cast around for a way to handle this gracefully. Right now she needed to get her mind together before the inevitable confrontation with Zac. "Look, I was very young then. It was over a long time ago."

"You wound me." His hand rested on his heart. "I tried to get in touch with you but your father—"

"Wouldn't let you contact me. I know. He told me. He thought you were an opportunist." She gave Steve a hard-eyed stare. Steve's mouth looked fleshy, self-indulgent, nothing like Zac's beautifully molded mouth. Had her father been correct? Had Steve been after her trust fund and her father's fortune?

Had Steve married Katy for her money?

"You mean nothing to me now, Stavros. You've got a wife, I've got a husband…" Her voice trailed away at the scornful look in Stavros's eyes.

"What?" she whispered. "Why are you looking at me like that?" The blood started to hammer in her head and she rubbed her temples.

"You won't have a husband for much longer. Zac's not going to want you now. You're soiled goods—and he's the Kyriakos heir. Your marriage is over, Pandora."

"What is going on here?" Zac came around the corner like a predatory cat hungry for prey, his eyes flashing accusingly as he took in how close Stavros stood to her. Pandora inched hastily away. "Is this a tender reunion of love rediscovered?"

The ache in her head intensified at the contempt in his voice. *Soiled goods.* She felt sick. "Excuse me."

"You're not going anywhere, wife of mine."

But Pandora had had enough. She plunged past Zac's outstretched arm and fled back into the bathroom and turned the key.

Pandora barely made it to the toilet before she started to retch, shock and horror causing her churning stomach to convulse.

When she opened the door again, Zac was waiting, his arms folded across his chest, his gaze hooded. Her heart sank like a stone. Of Stavros there was no sign.

Putting her head down, she brushed past him. Zac's hand caught her arm. "Pandora—"

"Not now, Zac." She wrenched away and broke into a run. By the time Pandora reached her bedroom, her heart was racing. But no footfalls followed.

Locking the door, Pandora ran a bath and added bath gel. But not even the frothy bubbles could lift her mood as, filled with self-recriminations, she sank back into the scented water.

What had made her lie to Zac?

Yes, that awful experience three years ago had been utterly humiliating. She'd wanted it erased from her life. Forever. And, yes, she'd sensed how important it was to Zac that Steve—Stavros, she had to get used to calling him that—was out of the picture.

Dead was as out of the picture as it got. It had seemed such a petty little white lie telling Zac that Stavros was dead.

As far as she was concerned, the damned man *was* dead. She'd never expected to see him again. So she'd lied on the spur of the moment. To make it all go away.

Not terribly clever. And now Zac would never forgive her. She'd lied to him, broken his trust. She had to come to terms with that. This time she'd gone beyond the pale.

The biggest irony was that more than anything in the world she wanted to stay married to Zac.

Oh, she'd been outraged that he'd brought her to Kiranos without her consent, angry that she'd been forced into a situation where she could not escape…where she'd been forced to listen to him. But none of that had stopped what she felt for him.

She loved him.

Pandora covered her face. *She loved him.* The past week and a half had been wonderful, the honeymoon of a lifetime.

Yet for Zac their marriage was one of convenience. Except, inconveniently, she wasn't the virgin he required. But against all odds he'd been adamant that he wanted her to stay, to give their marriage a chance, giving her a rock of hope to cling to that he might grow to love her. After all, he'd said he loved her sense of humour, loved her appearance, her intellect. That had to count for something.

Even though she'd failed him at every turn. *And how she'd failed him.* Pandora ran shaking fingers through her hair. He'd wanted a virgin. She'd slept with his brother-in-law. He'd wanted a wife he could trust. She'd lied to him.

Her loss of virginity was something she couldn't change, her maidenhood was gone forever. She didn't hanker after that. Her virginity—or lack thereof—didn't make her a worse or better person. *But she'd lied to Zac.* She'd told him that Stavros was dead. And that was something she could never forgive herself for.

She doubted he would, either.

It was hours before Pandora could bring herself to face Zac and the others again. Finally she went down to dinner, only to find that the meal was still half an hour from ready and that Katy and Stavros were already gone.

"I sent them away." Zac stood with his back to the wall of windows, a dark shadow against the waning light.

Pandora sank down onto the ivory leather and resisted the urge to burst into tears. "Your sister wanted to see you. Don't let this come between the two of you—I know how close you are."

"How can it not?" Zac didn't meet her eyes. His skin pulled taut across his slanted cheekbones. "Every time she comes to visit I will be forced to stare into the face of the man who took my wife's virginity."

"I'm sorry." It was a cry of despair.

He didn't respond.

"Do you want a divorce?"

Zac stared at his wife, shocked at the bald question. She was pale, her pink mouth the only hint of colour in a too-white face. The lower lip shook slightly, giving him some idea of how tough this was for her, but her remarkable silver eyes were steady as they held his.

She wasn't hiding from her lie. And she'd already realised the implications of it. He wanted to deny it, drum his fists against the wall, tell her that it didn't matter, because she was his wife, goddammit. That she'd always be his wife.

But it did matter. He was the eldest—the only—Kyriakos son. And he'd always known what his destiny had to be. Torn, he held her gaze, unable to utter the word that he knew had to be said. *Yes.*

But she must have read something in his eyes, because her teeth bit into her lip until he could see a white mark forming. He wanted to demand that she stop.

He moved. Instantly she drew her legs up until her feet perched on the edge of the seat and her knees formed a shield in front of her. "So Stavros was right. He told me that you'd want a divorce."

He wished he could get his brother-in-law's scrawny neck between his hands. Shake him. For the pain he'd caused Pandora.

He squared his shoulders. "I don't want a divorce."

"You don't have a choice. That's what Stavros said."

He hated that she'd been listening to Stavros. Hated that Stavros was right. Except he didn't want a divorce. He raked his fingers through his hair.

But how could he stay married to Pandora now, given the scandalous circumstances? If anyone ever found out…

Yet he'd wanted to stay married despite learning she wasn't the virgin he'd needed to marry, a little voice at the back of his head taunted. He'd been prepared to hide the truth of her lack of virginity then so that he could keep her. But that was before he'd discovered her relationship with Stavros. He sighed. "I need to think about this. I'm not going to make a hasty decision."

Her eyes widened. "You're not going to divorce me straightaway?"

"I'm not going to be rushed into a decision. I need time to absorb the fact that you had—" he paused "—intimate relations with my brother-in-law, to absorb that you lied about his death." He needed time to decide whether he could stay with a woman his brother-in-law had deflowered. Time to consider whether he could ever let her go. Time to calm down before he made the most important decision of his life. He dragged a ragged breath. "What else did Stavros say?"

"That—" She broke off.

The pain in her eyes damn near killed him. *"What?"*

"That I'm soiled goods."

"Damn him. I'm going to kill him."

"Zac! He's your sister's husband."

She was right. Yet the thought of Pandora with Stavros was driving him mad. He'd never felt like this about a woman. Possessive. Protective. "I can't believe you let Stavros—" He shook his head. "What is it about Stavros Politsis? My sister's so besotted with the bastard that I have no chance of convincing her to kick him out."

"You've tried?" she asked.

He nodded. "When they got engaged I tried to pay him off. He wouldn't take it. No doubt he rubbed his hands in anticipation of more to come down the road. He's not worthy of associating with our family." He pinned Pandora with his fiercest glare. "I want you to stay away from him from now on. I don't want you near him."

Pandora's shoulders stiffened and her eyes blazed. "Why would I want to go near him? He means nothing to me."

"Make sure it stays that way." Zac threw back his head and closed his eyes. "Tomorrow we return to London. Stavros's arrival has soured our stay here. I no longer have any taste to honeymoon."

The following afternoon Zac found himself glaring at Pandora where she'd curled up in the seat of the helicopter. The first he'd seen of her today had been after he'd sent Maria to summon her to the helipad.

Was she sulking? He couldn't forget the way her silver eyes had blazed at him yesterday after he'd commanded her to stay away from his sister's husband.

Zac slid into the seat beside her. "What the hell's the matter with you?" he said finally. "Why are you huddled up in a ball?"

"I don't like flying in these death traps."

"We'll be in Athens soon enough."

She raised her head and gave him a guarded look. "And what happens then?"

For a moment Zac said nothing. "I told you I need time. Don't force me to make a decision in haste about something as important as our marriage."

Her eyes widened in her ashen face. She looked even worse than she'd looked when she'd stepped onto the roof. Zac took in the trepidation in her eyes and for the first time started to wonder if she was afraid of heights—or flying. He pushed the notion away. No, it was unlikely. She'd flown all the way from New Zealand without a qualm. She was simply still angry with him.

He took his cell phone out of his pocket and pretended to be engrossed with the small screen.

But when she turned her head away and her shoulders started to shake, Zac felt something inside him give.

Pandora was crying.

"Pandora…" Her shoulders stiffened. "I know finding yourself face-to-face with Stavros could not have been easy for you—"

She swung around, her cheeks stained with tears. She swallowed visibly. "This—" she jabbed a finger at her eyes "—has nothing to do with Stavros, about what's happening between us. I hate flying, okay? It terrifies me."

Guilt spread through him. He remembered her hesitation on the roof, the bleak look she'd shot him before she'd clambered in. More guilt stabbed him as he thought back to her rage when he'd dumped her into the helicopter the day after their wedding. "You should've told me." He moved closer and brushed her silky hair off her face. She pulled away and he let his hand drop. "If you'd spoken up, I would've gotten you some medication to take the edge off the phobia."

"Drugged me, you mean? To make the kidnapping when you brought me to Kiranos easier?"

He felt his face grow tight at the barb. "You're deliberately misunderstanding me. I'm talking about now, not when I brought you here. A mild sedative would've made this flight easier."

"I don't need drugs. I shouldn't have had to make either flight—you should never have put me into a helicopter coming here, then I would never have had to endure it a second time." She felt so much better for chiding him. It helped take her mind off the fact that however long Zac took to think it through, there was only one outcome for their marriage: divorce.

"You need to get over this irrational fear."

She rounded on him. "My fear is *not* irrational. My mother died when one of these crashed."

He went still. "Dear God, when?"

"When I was seven." Zac had been sent away by his mother when he was six. Pandora resisted the burgeoning notion that he might understand a little of the loss and bewilderment her seven-year-old self had experienced.

"I didn't know," Zac murmured. "Neither you nor your father ever mention her."

"That's supposed to make me feel better? That you didn't dump me into a helicopter deliberately?"

"You should've told me."

"*When?* Do I need to remind you that I thought I was going to the airport to catch a plane? I can survive a trip in a jet."

"I'm glad to hear it. Because when we reach Athens we're going to transfer over to the Gulfstream to fly to London."

Pandora ignored him. "The first I knew of your intention was when I heard the damn thing hovering above me. I was slung over your shoulder at that point. Given the noise and my terror, I wasn't in the right frame of mind to give lengthy explanations. I begged you, damn you, to let me down."

"I thought that was because you didn't want to come with me."

"And that makes it better? You ignored my objections because you knew I didn't want to be kidnapped. Right?"

"Sarcasm doesn't become you."

She huffed out, "What do you expect? Submission? You've got the wrong woman. You know, I really should have you arrested. Think of what a juicy story that would make. I can already see the headlines. 'Desperate Tycoon Kidnaps Reluctant Bride.'"

He gave her a hard look. "You're joking, I hope."

She'd never have him arrested. *Never.* She loved him. She turned away from him—and found herself facing the window and the yawning emptiness tilting beyond.

"*Help.*" Covering her face, she fought the surge of panic.

"Come here." He pulled her into his arms. "I'm holding you and I will not let anything happen to you." The scent of his body filled her senses and slowly the panic subsided only to be replaced by something infinitely more dangerous—the lazy curl of desire.

As they hurried through Heathrow, Zac kept an eye on Pandora, his brows jerking together. No wonder she hated him. Her mother had died in a helicopter crash, and straight after the strain of their wedding he'd thrust her headlong into the capsule of her nightmares. He'd win the Bastard of the Year award hands down. He told himself he couldn't have known, that he'd make it up to her.

But would she let him?

A sideways glance revealed that with her black coat pulled around her and her long pale hair streaming down her back, she looked washed out. Her face was grey, her silver eyes dazed.

When a photographer slithered toward her, Zac barged the guy out of the way and slung a protective arm around his wife's shoulders, shepherding her to the chauffeur-driven Daimler waiting outside.

Once inside, she turned her face to the window, presenting him with the back of her head. Zac hated this unspeaking silence. He could sense her misery across the space separating them.

This was not the provocative mermaid he'd pleasured in the sea yesterday. Briefly he wished they could go back to that moment, when they were the only people in the deserted cove. Before reality had arrived in the form of his sister and Stavros and the scandalous revelation that had changed everything.

* * *

Zac's London town house was located close to Hyde Park, in the heart of the city. As they passed through electronic gates set in a solid fence of cast-iron pilings and huge white pillars, Pandora caught sight of window boxes planted with lavender, which softened the stark white lines of the architecture.

The phone was ringing when Zac and Pandora walked through the huge, imposing wooden door into the town house. A moment later Aki appeared, said something to Zac in Greek, his gaze sliding sideways to Pandora.

Zac strode away. Pandora followed more hesitantly across the glossy marble floor. She could hear him talking on the phone, his voice guarded, his replies terse, ending with an abrupt, "No comment."

Pandora tensed. *Why were the press calling?*

She forced one foot in front of the other and entered what was clearly the sitting room. A warm-hued kilim lay on the floor between a pair of rich brown chesterfield couches and what looked like a Magritte hung over the fireplace.

Zac was standing with his back to her in front of a wide television screen, the handset cradled in his hands revealing that the call had been terminated, and his shoulders were hunched. His reaction offered little comfort and the tension knotting her chest wound tighter.

"Zac?"

He turned and looked across to her, his eyes so dark, so full of turmoil that her heart missed a beat. "Zac, what is it?"

"They know."

"Know what?" But Pandora didn't need his answer—she read it in the starkness of his gaze, in the sallow shade of his skin. She sank down onto the nearest couch and dropped her head into her hands.

"The press know about Stavros…that he was your lover before you married me." Above her bowed head, the citation of facts continued relentlessly. "They know that you were not a virgin bride. The paparazzi are questioning whether I knew, too—and misled everyone—or whether I, the Kyriakos heir, was duped." And then she heard Zac tap out another number and speak to someone in rapid Greek.

This was it. *The end.* Zac must hate her.

"I'm so sorry." There was a deep, hoarse note in his voice that made her heart twist. "The tabloids are going to crucify you. It's going to be hell on earth for you."

She blinked, struggling to comprehend what he was saying. His shoes came into her line of vision and her head jerked up. "*For me?* What about you?"

He shrugged. "I will survive."

He would, too. Zac had that strong inner sense of self—it was what set him apart, what made him clearly a man among men. Here stood a man who all his life had been groomed for a position of power and followed the path that had been ordained for him from the minute he had been born. A man who had never set a foot wrong…until *she* had wrecked it all for him. Why should he pay the price for her mistakes?

She stared at his shoes, wishing a hole would open up in the carpet below through which she could sink. There was no doubt in her mind that Zac was going to pay the price, going to be humiliated in front of his peers, his business connections. The Kyriakos name was about to be dragged through the press.

It was all her fault.

At last she lifted her head and scanned his beloved features, taking in the harsh lines of strain around his mouth. The dark rings under his eyes only added to his appeal, giving him a dangerous glamour. "You must wish that you'd never set eyes on me."

Zac gave her a long, unfathomable look. "It is done."

He hadn't denied it. There was no doubt in her mind that he wished he'd never met her. Not that she could blame him. She'd brought him nothing but trouble. The thought hurt desperately.

Finally she asked, "Who leaked the story?"

Zac shook his head, and his eyes turned a dark, stormy green. "I don't know. I've already advised my security team of the breach. Believe me, I'll have the answer to your question very shortly. And when I get my hands on the bastard's wretched neck, his life will not be worth living."

The set of his mouth was grim.

A brief instant of pity for the culprit swept Pandora. It had to be an insider. Briefly she considered Stavros. She glanced at Zac, took in his fierce expression and decided against raising Stavros's name. Surely Stavros wouldn't be so stupid? He wouldn't risk his easy life married to Katy. She thought of the others she's come to know. Aki, Maria and Georgios and the rest of Zac's trusted staff and hoped none of them had betrayed him. Zac would be merciless in retribution.

The following morning Pandora wakened in the guest bedroom she'd chosen to sleep in to the sound of a commotion outside. Hurriedly, she slipped out of bed, pulled on a terry robe and crossed to the window.

Peering around the corner of the drawn drapes, she took in the photographers crowding the sidewalk and a security guard hanging out of a car, calling for the mass to disband through a loudspeaker.

Her heart sank and she ducked out of sight. So much for Zac's "No comment" yesterday.

They must be headline news this morning. Zac would be cursing her as he tried to control the notoriety the publicity must be causing him, his family and Kyriakos Shipping.

She showered and dressed hastily. The mirror revealed that she looked smart and composed in a pair of oyster trousers with a silver-blue silk blouse. By the time she'd slipped on a string of pearls, a pair of high heels and make-up, no one would detect the shame and misery beneath the mask.

Now she simply had to free Zac from the trouble she'd caused him.

Unzipping her purse, she pulled out her cell phone and perched herself on the corner of the bed.

"Daddy? Are you there?" Pandora asked as the line crackled.

There was brief silence, then her father's sigh came heavily over the line. "I've heard, Pandora. The story has already been picked up by the evening news down here. Is it true? Did you lose your virginity to Zac's brother-in-law?"

"Dad, I need to get out of Zac's life. I need to come home." Maybe if she hid at the end of the world and didn't have to meet Zac's angry gaze, she'd find the strength to cope with the horror of having her face infamously plastered over the world's newspapers. Of coming to terms with the fact that she was not the bride Zac Kyriakos needed—or loved.

"Is it true?"

What was the point in obfuscating? It had all happened so long ago. "Yes."

Even across the line she could hear her father release his breath. "You lost your virginity at seventeen to the man who is now your brother-in-law?"

It sounded so sordid. Pandora bit back a sob. "Yes."

"Poor Zac!"

Her father's exclamation cut her to the quick. She'd been worried about what it was all doing to Zac. Perhaps selfishly, she'd expected a little sympathy from her father.

"What about *me?* You and Zac cooked this marriage up between you. I didn't know I was supposed to be a virgin—not that the loss of my virginity was the kind of thing I would tell you about. *I fell in love with Zac.* Only to find out that he married me for my nonexistent virginity, that he didn't love me at all! I've been a silly little goose—twice over." All the disappointment of the past weeks spilled from her.

Silence met her outburst. Pandora could picture her father standing beside his leather-top desk at High Ridge, his face stern. A wave of longing swept her. "Daddy—"

"Pandora, I introduced Zac to you for the best reasons in the world. Zac needed a wife—he's a man I respect and admire. I leaped at the chance that you two might suit. You're my only child. I've always worried about you. About the unscrupulous men who might target you for your fortune. Your home is with Zac."

"How can Zac want me anymore? I've been nothing but trouble to him." A sob escaped her throat. "But you're right. I can't leave him to weather this crisis alone. Thank you, Daddy." Pandora said a subdued goodbye and made her way downstairs. From the windows beside the staircase it was clear that the town house was under siege, reporters thronging against the gate.

She shuddered in horror. They were after photos of the scandalous Kyriakos virgin bride. *Soiled goods.* Stavros's words taunted her. It was what the tabloids would be screaming, too.

Pausing in the archway to the sitting room, her heart missed a beat as she took in Zac's tall, lean frame. With a sense of inevitability, she saw the paper in his hands.

"Let me see that."

Poker-faced, he tried to hide it behind his back, but Pandora would have none of it. "I want to read what they say about me."

He handed it to her with a sigh. "Don't let it get to you. So much is lies."

The headlines were a thousand times worse than she'd anticipated, and for a moment Pandora wished she had fled back to her father, to the sanctuary of High Ridge.

"Zac duped by fake virgin," proclaimed one. And "Marriage turns tycoon into fool," screamed another.

"What impact is all this going to have on the company?" she asked, her hand over her mouth.

"The share price has already hiccupped." He must have read something of the devastation that ripped at her insides, because he said dismissively, "It will be a temporary thing. It will stabilise. We'll see what happens by the close of day on Wall Street."

"I'm so sorry," she said in a small voice.

"Try not to think about it," Zac advised. "We will get through this."

"I wish there was something I could do," she said.

But Zac had already picked up the remote and started flicking through the news channels, a frown on his face, and he didn't answer.

By the end of the day she was a wreck. She crawled into her bed—alone—unable to face Zac after the ignominy of the day's headlines.

She half hoped that Zac might come find her, make love to her, help her forget what was happening.

As she waited, tense and distressed, thoughts spun wildly inside her head. Finally, a long time later, she started to think clearly.

Zac would not come to her tonight. Zac could not stay married to her after this. He would have to divorce her. He had no choice.

And as she faced that truth, loss ripped through her. Despite the heat, she shivered against the cool sheets. The future that lay ahead would be bleak and a little scary without Zac.

But she still had tonight. And tomorrow night. And all the other nights until Zac asked her to release him from their vows. Those nights ahead offered a respite from the emptiness that she knew would dog her in the months to come. Could she do it? Could she climb into Zac's bed?

Was that something she could do for Zac—give him a few nights of mind-blowing pleasure? Would that go part of the way to easing the chaos she'd caused in his life?

Quaking a little with apprehension, she crawled out of bed and made her way to the cupboard into which a maid had unpacked her clothes. With trembling hands Pandora lifted out a wisp of pale silver silk that she'd bought for her honeymoon but never worn. It took less than a minute to shuck off her comfortable cotton nightie, brush her hair, spray on a little scent and don the silky garment that had been made for seduction. Her heart thudding against her ribs, she clicked off the bedroom light and stepped out into the moonlit corridor, her bare feet soundless against the thickly carpeted floor.

On reaching Zac's bedroom door she halted, her heart pounding. Could she do this? She turned the door handle and stepped into the room.

Zac was propped up against plump pillows. He glanced up, then froze. A lightning-swift look revealed his sleek, bare chest covered from the waist down by a white sheet.

"I came to say sorry." The expression on his face made Pandora conscious of exactly how little she wore, how skimpy the sexy little nightgown was and how provocative she must appear. She swallowed nervously. "Maybe this isn't such a good idea."

Zac's eyes flared, turning his face starkly male. "Come here."

Nine

For a moment Pandora looked as if she were about to flee, and Zac discovered that he was not going to let that happen.

Suddenly he didn't give a damn why she was here, that this might be about guilt for lying to him or penance for the headlines. It didn't matter. All he cared about was that she was here. That he would be able to kiss her, feel the touch of her skin against his, feel her silken walls closing against his hardening erection.

He lifted the covers. "Come," he said hoarsely.

She was across the room in a second and slid under the sheet, taking care not to touch him.

Rolling onto his side and raising himself onto an elbow, Zac faced his wife. She lay on her back, stiff and silent, staring at the ceiling. Her skin was luminous, her profile delicate and her pale hair gleamed against the snowy sheets. "You are the most beautiful woman in the whole world." Reaching out his hand, he stroked her shoulder. The shoelace tie of her nightgown fell away and she turned her head. Her eyes were wide and something sparked inside the silver depths as their gazes connected.

The heat started deep in Zac's stomach, spreading outward, pushing through his bloodstream…into his head. Never had he wanted a woman this much. Never had he felt the tenderness…the pain…that this woman roused in him.

Her lips parted. He dipped his head. Her mouth was warm and moist and so, so soft. His tongue touched hers, smooth and intoxicating, while his hand pushed the bit of silver silk down the length of her body, his fingers lingering against her skin. With a groan, Zac shifted closer, until his torso brushed her breasts.

Zac brought his hands up, spanned her rib cage, and his blunt fingertips sank into soft flesh. She moaned, stretched, and her breasts rose into proud, taut mounds, enticing him.

"You're beautiful." He reached out to touch. The peaks hardened, nudging his fingers, and he bent his head to take a pale pink tip into his mouth. Pandora gasped out loud and arched under him. His tongue flicked across the tight tip. She shuddered and moved restlessly against him.

His body responded, blood pumping through his veins in a hot rush. He could feel his erection pulsing, ready for her. Then her hand slipped between them, closed around him, holding him.

Zac raised his head. "Are you sure?" he gritted out.

"Oh, yes."

Her fingers started to caress him, sliding along his length, driving him wild.

His breath caught. "*Don't.* I can't hold back."

But she ignored him. Her hand moved. Zac didn't know whether to curse or kiss her.

She moved beneath him, positioning him so that he could feel the hot heat of her against him. He moaned, surged forward. And then he was inside her. Home, where he belonged. Clenching his teeth, forcing himself to slow down, Zac drew away and sank slowly back into her. Her body was tight and hot and utterly irresistible.

"Zeus, this is good."

He moved again.

And again.

She murmured something and wiggled her hips against him. He felt her tongue slick and smooth against his neck. The little licks sent shivers exploding through him. He drove his hips forward. Pandora responded instantly, her body arched against his, her breath ragged against his neck.

To slow the tightening tension, he slid out, waited a heartbeat and thrust back into her. She gave a little hoarse cry. Then her tongue was back, touching him, tantalising him, circling his earlobe, her hot breath sending adrenaline rocketing through him.

She whispered, "I'm almost there."

"Pandora!" The pressure spiralled up, pleasure and still more pressure until he could hold no longer, until it spun away. He let it all go and heard her gasp as he sank into her again and again, faster and faster until it all tore free.

"Now." His voice was hoarse. The spasms engulfed them, and he shuddered at the sensation.

Afterward, raising himself onto his elbows, he fought for breath. "Wow."

"Is that all you can say?" Her face glowed with desire and a hint of an emotion he'd never seen before.

He gave a broken, shaky laugh and smoothed a lock of her hair off her forehead.

"It's not over yet," she said.

But something in her tone caught his attention. Zac lifted his head. There was resignation in her eyes…and a hint of—what?—desperation? Zac's heart tightened into a band of pain inside his chest. He swallowed and stared down into her eyes, darkened to a cloudy grey and saddened by an emotion that looked suspiciously like regret.

No. She couldn't mean this to be goodbye.

"What do you mean it's not over yet?" He tried to hide his own desperation.

Her lips curved into a smile, but her eyes remained grave. "Tonight, we have tonight. And tomorrow night. And some nights beyond that. But sometime soon you're going to have to make that decision, Zac. About us. About our marriage. And I already know what it will be. Divorce. It can't be any other way."

Divorce.

The end of this magic sweetness between them. It was the last thing he wanted. He'd been raised to believe that a Kyriakos never divorced. The band inside him tightened. *It can't be any other way.* Anguish followed in the wake of her words.

Or could it? Deep inside the heart of him, something gave. For the first time in his life he didn't care about the future. About what people thought. Her past didn't matter any longer. More than anything in the world he wanted to banish the shadows from her eyes, to see her happy again.

What mattered most was that she was his. He no longer cared what people thought of the Kyriakos heir. He no longer cared about his dead grandfather's expectations—or that he might be considered a failure to the family name. He was not like his father. He would never fail his wife.

Because he had no intention of letting his bride go.

Ever.

Before he had time to ponder on the blindsiding discovery, Pandora touched him again.

"Are you ready? Or do you want to wait a while? We have all night."

Amazingly he found he was already hard again. Need surged through him and he pulled her toward him. "All night? Then let's not waste one minute." And he moved her warm, naked body over his.

When she awoke, it was morning. Zac stood beside the window, dressed in a suit, his back to her, his hands on his lean hips.

He must have heard her stir, because he turned.

"Pandora—" He started to say something, broke off. There was a sudden sense of awkwardness. "Did you have enough sleep?" he said at last. "You must be tired. It's Friday—take your time, relax, don't hurry to get up."

The memory of the night came to her. The things they'd done, the magic of their togetherness…the terrible sense of time running out. She searched his eyes, seeking answers to the questions she was too scared to ask. Is this the end? How many nights more? When do I go? Why did you have to be the man you are…and why could I not be the woman you needed?

Finally she said only, "I'm a little tired." Oh, dear God, why were they spouting banalities when she needed—

Zac's cell phone trilled.

He reached for it, glanced at the number and answered, keeping his responses short.

Pandora bit her lip. What had the press printed now?

Zac killed the line. "Katy is on her way over. She says she needs to see us. She sounded in a bad way." His gaze softened. "I'm sorry, Pandora, no chance for a lie in today. You'll need to get up and dressed."

Once downstairs, the tension in the sitting room was thick and palpable between them, the awkwardness of earlier undiminished. At last the sound of heels clicking on the marble entrance hall made Pandora look up from the book she'd been pretending to read.

Katy stood in the doorway, her face red and blotchy from crying, her heart-shaped face wearing a hurt, vulnerable expression.

Pandora shut her eyes. Katy had obviously been reading the papers. Pandora hadn't seen or spoken to Zac's sister since that awful moment on Kiranos. The last thing she needed was Katy's condemnation. Beside her she heard Zac rise to his feet. She opened her eyes to see him making his way across the room, intent on cutting Katy off.

Katy flung herself into her brother's arms. "It's terrible."

"I know." Over Katy's head Pandora read the pain in Zac's eyes. "But it will pass."

Poor Katy, having to read about her husband's lover along with everyone else. God, how many more people was that reckless one-night stand going to affect? If she could only have the time over, she'd never have done it. But she'd been seventeen, in love—or so she'd thought. Hardly surprising she'd had so little sense.

Zac had produced a hanky and was mopping up Katy's tears. But that only made Katy cry harder. "You're going to hate Stavros even more. But I *have* to tell you."

Zac froze. "What has that stupid bastard done now?"

"Zac!" Stepping back, Katy said, "Don't swear."

"Sorry, but he is a thorn in my side."

"I know," Katy wailed. "And now it will be even worse. I just found out today—a journalist called looking for him. Stavros contacted the papers, sold the story about him and Pandora."

"He did *what?*"

The fury in Zac's voice made Pandora cringe. At the expression on Katy's face, she leaped to her feet and rushed across the room. "Don't be mad at Katy. It's not her fault."

Katy fell into Pandora's arms. "I thought you'd never speak to me again. Stavros has done you such harm."

"But *you* haven't," Pandora pointed out gently. Over Katy's shoulder she caught a glimpse of Zac's stunned expression.

"I'm leaving him," Katy declared. "I never want to see him again. This time he's gone too far."

Zac closed his eyes. "I never thought you'd see sense."

"I can't believe he did this." Katy's eyes were full of bewilderment. "I knew he wasn't strong or invulnerable like you, but he's funny and he always makes me feel so… special."

"He's a lightweight, a fortune—"

Pandora shot Zac a warning look. For once he heeded it and broke off.

"I know what you think of him." Katy looked gutted. "But I thought you were wrong. I honestly, truly believed he loved me. That's why I never listened to you. And there's never been anyone else. If he'd been what you said, I thought he'd give himself away long ago."

"A bird in the hand is worth—"

"Zac," Pandora said quellingly. "Shut up."

To her amazement, he did.

Katy started to laugh—a touch hysterically. "Oh, Pandora, I love you. I don't think I've ever heard anyone tell Zac to shut up and live to tell the tale. Please never leave my brother. You're the only one who can keep him in line."

For a moment Zac looked as if he wanted to object, then he closed his mouth and shook his head. "Women," he muttered.

Pandora assessed Katy critically. It was obvious that Zac's sister had been through hell, but despite her tear-blotched face she looked composed. "Will you be okay staying alone, without Stavros? Or have you got a friend that can stay over for a few nights and keep you company? Do you want to stay here?"

"I'm staying with Stacy. She will handle my divorce. Stavros keeps calling me at home and I don't want to talk to him. Stacy's arranged for the number to be changed. But for the meantime the calls are being forwarded to her service. I've got a new cell-phone number, too. Stacy's taken my old cell phone and she's fielding the incoming calls."

"You're serious about this, aren't you?" Zac was looking at his sister as if he'd never seen her before.

"I have to be. It's going to be even harder when the baby comes."

"Baby?" Zac and Pandora spoke together.

"What baby?" Zac asked.

Katy's hand went to her mouth. "I haven't told anyone. I only found out today. We've been trying ever since that first miscarriage. I was so excited. But then I found out about Stavros selling that disgusting story—" she blinked as Pandora blanched "—sorry, Pandora. So I called Stavros and told him he shouldn't bother coming home. Not ever again."

"Did you tell Stavros about the baby?"

Katy glared at Zac. "Stavros doesn't need to know about the baby. I'm perfectly capable of raising her alone."

The eyes so like her brother's were flashing. Despite her own misery, Pandora suppressed the urge to cheer.

"You already know it's a girl?" Zac cast his sister a sharp look.

"I hope it is. I want a girl. I'm so sick of men."

Zac raised his eyebrows.

"Not you, of course—you're my brother. And I suppose once Stavros and I are divorced, the dislike of the species will fade."

Pandora suppressed the urge to laugh. It was not the right time. But Katy was on fire.

Katy sniffed and blew her nose. "I can't believe you're both being so nice to me. Stavros sold that exposé to cover gambling debts. I keep thinking I could've stopped it. He begged me to pay them. I refused. Last year, when you helped me get rid of those money lenders, Zac, I told him that it was the last time, that he needed help. I never thought my husband would stoop to this."

When Zac walked back into the sitting room after seeing Katy to the door, he found Pandora hunched over the tabloids, looking utterly wretched.

A twinge of pity, underscored by fury at his brother-in-law, shot through him. "Remember when you first came to Athens I said don't read the papers—they'll only upset you."

"You extracted that promise because you didn't want me reading about the speculation that you'd found a virgin bride in the remoteness of the New Zealand wilderness."

"Partly," he admitted. "But I also didn't want you reading the hurtful lies the scandal sheets print."

"Except this time it's true."

Zac blew out. "Thanks to my traitorous dog of a brother-in-law."

"And my lack of judgment three years ago. What did I ever see in Stavros?"

Zac's mouth kinked. "The impulsivity of youth." But his heart lightened. The fear that Pandora still fancied Stavros started to fade, leaving him surprisingly carefree.

"Oh, jeez!" She dropped the paper she'd been scanning. "That's disgusting."

"Don't read it." But the horror in her eyes had him reaching for the paper she'd dropped.

"They're saying that it's keeping love in the family, I'm the family whore. I feel like crawling into a hole and never coming out again. They've quoted Stavros—but it's all wrong. They're saying I met him in a scuzzy nightclub. They've even got a photo of it—it's called Wild Thing and it's famous for the wild swingers who hang out there, according to this article. But, I swear, I've never been there in my life."

Fury rose. "I'll sue. Put that rag out of business." He reached for the phone. After a short conversation with Dimitri, he dropped down on the couch beside her and gave her shoulder an awkward pat. "You're doing fine."

She buried her head in her hands. "I've besmirched your name. The sooner you get divorce proceedings under way, the better."

"I never said I wanted a divorce."

"You were thinking about it."

"I wanted time to work out what to do, how to cope with my feelings, the fact that you lied to me about your relationship with Stavros. With the story out, the damage is done. There will be no divorce."

Pandora grew still.

"It is Stavros who turned what was a private affair into a public scandal. Not you. My family has humiliated you. Believe me, I will not desert you."

Pandora peered at Zac through her laced fingers. He looked fierce and uncompromising.

"It is my responsibility to protect you." Zac sat straight and proud. If she hadn't loved him already, she would've fallen for him right that moment. This must be how his forefather's had looked when they'd ridden out and put the fear of death into the enemy while protecting those closest to them.

It shouldn't make her feel better that he was so protective of her. She was a modern woman. Feeling this way was positively archaic.

"After all that has happened, why do you feel the need to protect me?"

He looked trapped. "Because you are my wife."

"But why risk what it will do to you, to your profile?"

"I will survive." He smiled, then his eyes grew serious. "It will be better if we stay together. For appearances. My PR department will sell it to the media that we love each other, that our love is pure and that we respect the sanctity of our marriage. They will be convincing that your virginity is not an issue, the Kyriakos heir has found true love and will be married forever."

"But that's a lie. You don't love me," she objected, incredibly tempted to give in to the spin he was creating.

Zac shrugged. "My PR department will create the illusion of love."

His words brought her back to reality. Of course this wasn't about them, about true love. Last night's lovemaking would've made no difference to Zac. He was too in control for emotion to rule him. Her shoulders sagged, and instantly she forced herself to straighten her spine. Zac had analysed the situation and come up with a solution.

As little as she wanted such a marriage, how could she refuse? She owed Zac her support. Her place was by his side. After all, he was stuck in this quandary because of her.

"It sounds like it could work. Although it would've been easier if we'd really loved each other," she said a touch wistfully.

"Many marriages survive without love." Zac's expression revealed no emotion. "You've told me often enough you hate me. Love or hate, I married you—you are my responsibility. Especially now that my brother-in-law has defiled you in public."

Three things struck Pandora. First, Stavros had ensured that Zac would sacrifice himself, his name, because of his misguided all-important sense of honour. Secondly, Zac had already decided a marriage for the sake of appearances would take care of everything. And thirdly, Zac believed—wrongly—that she hated him.

Suddenly it was very important to rectify that misunderstanding. The trick was to do so without revealing what he meant to her. "I don't hate you," she said softly.

But Zac was already talking. "There are other things that are important—children, business, having someone to confide in."

"Children?" Pandora's heart started to ache. *Zac's children.* He would love his children, but not their mother. "So you intend us to have—" she swallowed "—children?"

"Of course." The searing look he gave her made her toes curl.

"Even though your nose will forever be rubbed in the fact that Stavros had me first?"

His jaw grew rock-hard. "We will not talk about that."

"But, Zac, the media will never let us forget it."

"I will take care of the media. We will fight fire with fire," he replied. "They are going to devour our story of true love."

Ten

The weekend passed in a haze of English drizzle, but even that did not deter the media siege outside the town house. Zac's security firm had brought in extra guards with fierce Dobermans on short leashes to patrol the fence perimeter, lest any story-driven newsperson venture onto the grounds.

A dinner out on Saturday night in a wildly popular restaurant where Pandora and Zac were snapped staring into each other's eyes and a supposedly spontaneous scoop while she and Zac strolled through Hyde Park tucked under one umbrella, their hands linked, were part of the PR plan to sow the seeds that this was a love match.

By Monday morning the tenor of the stories had started to change. Pandora no longer read them and tried to get on with her own life, but even she could not help being aware of the difference as the Kyriakos publicity machine started to take effect. She couldn't help thinking that Zac must be ecstatic that the blip in the Kyriakos share price had passed.

By the time Zac disappeared to the London office of Kyriakos Shipping, Pandora felt nothing but relief.

Determined to shake off the blues and make the best of her marriage, she arranged to meet Katy for lunch. Zac's chauffeur employed a range of offensive driving tactics to shake off the more persistent reporters and finally delivered Pandora to an exclusive department store where she was to join up with Katy. Hidden behind a disguise of overlarge sunglasses, with her giveaway pale hair firmly secured under a head scarf, Pandora helped Katy shop for some maternity blouses and dresses even though it was still too early in Katy's pregnancy for her to need them.

As they looked at baby clothes, Pandora couldn't help thinking about her discussion with Zac about children being a natural consequence of marriage. An unexpected pang of emotion floored her as she held up a tiny boys' T-shirt.

Her and Zac's baby.

Would her love be enough to hold them together? She didn't know. And he didn't even know she loved him. Should she tell him? One thing that had kept them apart had been her lie about Stavros. And deceiving Zac about the way she felt about him didn't seem like the right thing to do any longer. Not since she'd discovered he thought she hated him.

Biting her lip, she folded the little T-shirt up and put it back on the shelf and went in search of Katy.

By the time she arrived home she'd decided that it was vital for her to tell Zac the truth about how she felt about him. Even though he would never love her back, he deserved the truth.

But that evening Zac worked so late that Pandora was asleep by the time he came home. Tuesday came and her nerve gave out. She was dreading telling him how she felt about him, certain that it was going to be an exercise in humiliation. Not that Zac would intend it to be so, but how could he ever love her back?

On Wednesday morning, Pandora vowed she would tell Zac this evening. But when he called in the late afternoon to let her know that his meeting was running later than expected, the coward in her was relieved.

She was watching a video when the doorbell rang late that night.

The sound of male voices in the entrance hall drew her out of the sitting room, and she paused abruptly at the sight of Stavros arguing with Aki in the doorway, hands flying everywhere.

"Pandora." Stavros caught sight of her and shouldered Aki aside.

"Zac isn't here."

"Then I need to talk to you. Tell your guard dog it's okay."

Aki wore a disapproving expression. "*Kyria,* he should not be here. He's been drinking."

Raising a hand to silence Aki and frowning slightly, Pandora said, "Why don't you ring Zac in the morning? Set up a time to see him then?"

"It's about Katy."

The baby. Concern shot through Pandora. But Katey should be with Stacy. "Is Katy all right?"

"Can I at least come in?"

Ignoring Aki's disapproval, she nodded and motioned him through to the sitting room. Picking up the remote, she flicked off the television and positioned herself on the footrest in front of it.

Stavros collapsed onto one of the plump brown chesterfield sofas.

"What's the matter with Katy?" Pandora asked.

"She's booted me out. She wants a divorce."

Pandora gaped at him. "That's why you turn up here—" she glanced at her watch "—at ten o'clock on a Wednesday night? To tell me your wife's left you? It's hardly news that comes as any surprise."

"I can't reach my wife." He lurched to his feet. "Zac won't take my calls at his office. I want you to help me get Katy back."

"If Katy's left you, that's her decision. Nothing I can say will change it."

"Talk to your husband. He can influence Katy."

"Oh, no. I'm not getting in the middle of a marital quarrel. You got yourself into this by selling that damn story, you get yourself out." All her anger poured out in a torrent.

"You self-righteous little bitch. If you don't help me, I'm going to call up my reporter friend, tell him I've got another story for him."

"You wouldn't!" But fear burst inside her. She was never going to be free of Stavros's tentacles. He had a hold over her and he was never going to let go. Zac would be humiliated all over again. Would it never end?

Stavros came closer, triumph contorting his features. "He's eager for details. I'll tell him what you're wearing, how you lay down for me on—" he glanced around "—Zac's fancy rug beneath that painting he likes so much."

"I'm not listening to this." She jumped up. Aki was right—Stavros had been drinking. A lot. She could smell the alcohol fumes.

But before she got past, Stavros grabbed her. "I'll tell him how you squealed with passion as I—"

"Get away from me!"

"Didn't I warn you not to come near my wife?" The soft, dangerous lash of Zac's voice made Pandora jump. He stood on the threshold clad in a dark suit, holding a black briefcase, and his stillness was oddly threatening.

Instantly Stavros let her go and started backing away. "She asked me to touch her. She's hot for me."

Damn Stavros. Pandora knew she must look dishevelled. She pushed her fringe out of her eyes with shaking hands. "Zac—"

Zac's eyes had turned a flat, unforgiving green drained of all emotion. Ice. Cold and hard and freezingly remote. "You are no longer welcome in my home, Politsis. Get out. You'll find a cab waiting at the door. Be thankful that you are my sister's husband or I would call the police and lay charges of assault."

"I never touched you," Stavros spat out.

"But you touched my wife. And that is something I cannot forgive."

A flash of naked terror contorted Stavros's face. "I'm going." But as he reached the door, he turned. "But you're going to regret this."

Zac laughed, a chilling sound without amusement. "Do your worst, Politsis. You'll regret anything you do to harm any Kyriakos—and that includes my sister. Stay away from us. Get your own life. Or be ready to face the consequences."

* * *

Stavros departed in a screech of tires, ignoring the cab parked at the front door.

"I was so scared." Pandora decided to go for broke.

Zac came toward her, his arms outstretched. "I should have turned him to pulp for frightening you."

"I wasn't afraid of Stavros. Or, rather, I was terrified of what Stavros was threatening because I thought it meant the end of everything between us. But I was more afraid that you might believe Stavros when he said—" She broke off.

"When he said that you were hot for him?"

She nodded despairingly. "I was afraid you might think I'd betrayed you and considered sleeping with him."

Colour rushed into Zac's face. "Never. You're my wife."

Relief made Pandora go limp. "He came looking for you—apparently you wouldn't take his calls. He tried to force me to help him get Katy back. I'm worried for her."

Zac made for the phone, and Pandora heard him giving someone the address where Katy was staying, telling them to keep a look out for Stavros.

"So that's how you knew he was here. The security company called."

"Yes. They've been keeping close surveillance. But not because I didn't trust you with Stavros," he added hastily when he realised how she might construe his words. "I was worried some overzealous reporter might try get into the house."

Pandora knew that she and Zac needed to talk. Butterflies fluttered in her stomach. Finally she plucked up the courage to say, "Zac, there's something I need to tell you."

He turned to look at her. "What?"

"I've been thinking about why I married you." He looked startled and about to speak, but she held up a hand. "Wait, hear me out. A gorgeous, incredibly handsome guy who could have any woman in the world, and I was so dumb I never asked why you'd chosen *me*."

Zac opened his mouth.

"I'm not finished. I stayed married even when I discovered I wasn't the bride you needed because—" she hesitated "—because the biggest mistake I made was falling in love with you."

"You love me?"

"Of course I love you, Zac. And that's part of the problem. Because you're Zac Kyriakos. Too perfect to be true." More quietly she added, "The only mistake you've ever made in your perfect life was to marry me."

"I thought you hated me." He looked dazed.

"Zac? Are you listening?"

He simply stared at her, looking poleaxed. Pandora suppressed the urge to laugh at the ridiculous notion that any woman would hate him.

The phone shrilled into the charged silence. Zac didn't move. So Pandora started to rise to get it.

"It's almost midnight. Ignore it," Zac said urgently. "We need to finish this."

The ringing stopped. An awkward pause stretched between them. Before they could resume the conversation, a knock sounded on the door.

"Yes?" Zac demanded impatiently as Aki entered the room. "What is it?"

"It's your sister."

"Tell her I'm busy," Zac bit out. Then, softening his tone, he added, "I'll call her back. Later—much later."

Aki looked worried. "She says it's an emergency. Mr. Politsis has had an accident. He's in hospital, in a critical condition."

By the time Zac and Pandora arrived at the hospital, the news hounds, scenting a story, were already clustered outside the main entrance. His arm around her shoulder, Zac shouldered his way through the small crowd, while hospital security and Zac's bodyguards pushed the more aggressive reporters back.

Upstairs, Katy was pacing the plush carpet of the private waiting room, holding her stomach. Stavros was still in surgery, she told them in a thin voice.

"He arrived and started banging on Stacy's front door, yelling threats. We wouldn't let him in. Then two of your security guys arrived, told him to calm down. He stormed off." Katy swallowed visibly. "Next thing, the police called. Stavros had been speeding, driving recklessly. They gave chase. He ploughed his car into a wall. They said he was in hospital, that it was critical." Katy started to cry. "And now the doctors aren't telling me anything."

"I'll get some details." Zac patted her shoulder and disappeared out the door like a man on a mission.

"It's the waiting, it's killing me—" Katy stopped and looked horrified. "Oh, God, I don't mean that."

Pandora hastened to her side. Katy flung her arms around Pandora. "What's going to happen?"

"Hush." Pandora hugged Katy. "We'll stay with you for as long as you need us."

"I was so pleased about the baby. I wanted a baby so badly. I thought it would make everything right, force

Stavros to settle down even though he was never that keen on having kids. But then Stavros did that awful thing…" Katy covered her face with her hands and her shoulders started to shake. "I'm going to find a restroom. I need to wash my face."

Zac returned just after Katy had left, his face somber. "Where's Katy?"

"She's gone to freshen up." Pandora examined his face. "Is the news bad?"

He sank down on the chair beside her and took her hands. "Stavros has lost a lot of blood and the doctors are worried about the head injuries he sustained."

"Does that mean he's suffered brain damage?"

"They're not saying too much yet. Someone will be along as soon as they get out of surgery with an update." Zac sighed heavily. "All day I have wanted to be alone with you, and now that I am, I can only think that a couple of hours ago I wished that Stavros would disappear out of our lives. I didn't want to think about him…with you. Now he may die." His grip tightened on her hands. "And I can't stop thinking that I wished it on him."

"It's not your fault. You didn't cause his accident." Pandora slid her hands out of his hold and placed them around his shoulders, comforting him. "You didn't get him drunk or force him to drive like a delinquent. Jeez, you even ordered him a cab."

He turned into her arms and rested his head against her hair. "Thank you."

"You're too hard on yourself."

He took a deep breath. "I wanted you to be mine. Only mine."

"Zac—"

"I *am* a barbarian, you see. I'm not the perfect man you think I am—that I've always striven to be." His voice was full of torment.

"Zac, listen to me. I am yours. Only yours. And you're utterly perfect for me." Her arms crept around his neck and she held him tight. "You're not alone, you know."

"What do you mean?" Zac raised his head and stared at her.

"You weren't the only one who wished Stavros away— I told you he was dead. I think I hoped he was. It was far easier that way." Pandora gave him a shaky ghost of a smile.

Guilt. She felt guilty about sleeping with Stavros years ago. Zac looked at her carefully, saw the wariness in her eyes, the fine lines of strain around her mouth. No, he didn't want her experiencing guilt. Hell, she hadn't known him back then—hadn't known he even existed.

"I owe you an apology." He lifted his hand to cup her cheek. "I've never considered myself a possessive man, yet where you are concerned I find I am. I disliked the idea of you sleeping with Stavros—" he paused, searching for words, couldn't find any way to say it except for the truth "—because I was jealous."

"Jealous?" She stared at him. "But, for heaven's sake, Zac, why would you be jealous of Stavros? He isn't a patch of the man you are. You are so much more than Stavros could ever be."

So much more than Stavros could ever be. And just like that, the corrosive bitterness inside him evaporated.

He gave her cheek a last stroke and couldn't help marvelling at how fortunate he was to have Pandora. A few minutes later, when Katy came back looking a little more composed, he was doubly relieved to have Pandora at his side while he broke the news about Stavros to his sister.

Zac drew her into the circle. "You know, whatever happens, we'll be there for you and the baby."

Katy nodded. "That's what's keeping me strong."

It was six hours later before they heard that Stavros had survived the surgery and the internal bleeding had been stanched. He'd been moved to intensive care and would be monitored through the night. But the chances of permanent brain damage were looking increasingly likely.

Katy cried a little more, and Pandora and Zac did their best to support her as she started to come to terms with the shock.

"We're here for you," Zac said. "Whatever you want to do, we will support you."

Katy flung her arms around him. "You're the best brother in the world. What would I ever do without you?" She wanted to call Dimitri and Stacy with an update. Zac called his cousins, Tariq and Angelo, and informed them of the situation. Both insisted on speaking to Katy. Both men wanted to fly out immediately. Zac dissuaded them.

Stacy arrived and insisted on taking Katy back to her apartment. There was nothing left but for Zac and Pandora to go home.

Forty minutes later, Zac followed Pandora into the town house and bolted the front door.

Pandora yawned. "I'm tired. I'm going to bed."

"Oh, no, you're not. We have a discussion to finish." Zac caught her arm. She stiffened in his grasp, but he took heart from the fact that she didn't pull away.

"It's been a hell of a day." Then, after a beat, he added very quietly, "I need you."

"Why?"

He closed his eyes. He was going to have to lay himself bare.

"I love you." He made the mistake of opening his eyes. Pandora was shaking her head from side to side.

Zeus, had he made a huge, irrevocable mistake? Had she been joking earlier? Trying to teach him a lesson by pretending to love him? No. He dismissed his wild panic. Pandora would not do that. Not even to him.

"You love me?" she said slowly, disbelievingly, and came closer until she was standing in front of him, looking up at him.

"Yes." He waited, frozen, for her next move.

"*Yes.* That's all you can say?" Her voice rose and she jabbed him in the chest with her finger.

A huge wave of relief washed through him. She cared. "I thought *yes* was the most valued word in this kind of exchange."

Her silver eyes flashed. "Since when did you decide you loved me?"

"Pandora…" he said gently, putting his arms around her shoulders and leading her to the sitting room. He pulled her down on the sofa beside him and turned to face her. "I'm going to be honest with you. I struggled to find a bride. There were many candidates. But none of them were right."

"Why not?"

He shrugged. "I don't know how to explain it. But I kept putting marriage off. And then suddenly one day I realized that the years were passing and it was starting to look like

I would never find a suitable wife. I grew desperate. I met your father and he told me about you. You sounded perfect. Sweet and sheltered."

She made a growling sound.

He laughed, pulled her close and kissed her on the top of her head before setting her away from him. "Then I met you. You blew all my preconceptions away. You were so young. So beautiful with your pale hair and ethereal silver eyes. You looked like everything the Kyriakos virgin should be. But it wasn't just your looks. You were smart. Funny. And I wanted you."

"That's not love. That's lust at first sight."

"Maybe." Zac looked sheepish. "But you had my full attention. I left, but I couldn't stop thinking about you. I kept sneaking back to see you. I couldn't wait to have you. But you were a virgin—or so I believed, and I had no reason to doubt it—so I had to marry you first.

"When you came to Athens…that week was the week from hell. I couldn't touch you because I was terrified once I did, I wouldn't be able to stop. Our wedding night was my every fantasy come true."

"But the next morning…"

"I was furious that you wanted to leave me. I knew I couldn't let that happen. I had to convince you to stay."

"So you kidnapped me!"

"I'm sorry." Remorse darkened his eyes. "Then everything spun out of control. When I discovered you weren't a virgin…I still couldn't let you go. I was prepared to keep that our secret, anything to keep you. But even then I didn't realize what was happening. I thought it was just—" He broke off.

"Just sex?" A small smile played around her mouth.

He nodded. "That day in the sea, when you told me that you no longer wanted to leave…and what followed…I thought I was losing my mind. It was so good. But Katy and Stavros barged in and suddenly it looked like I was going to lose you anyway. I couldn't think straight. I'd never felt such fear. I still hadn't realized I loved you. All I knew was that something had changed. My head told me that the marriage couldn't survive, but my heart knew I couldn't bear to let you go. I didn't care what it would mean. I had to keep you by my side, but I needed you to *want* to stay. I needed you to love me."

"And you thought I hated you."

He sighed. "I could live with the fact that you weren't a virgin. I realised I was a man in my own right. It didn't matter who my ancestors were. It didn't matter why my grandfather's expectations were. What I couldn't live with was the fact that you hated me. That, I considered a failure."

"I'm sorry. That was not your failure. It was my own frustration and self-preservation. I loved you. I was torn apart when I discovered you'd only married me because you thought I was a virgin. And when you took me to Kiranos, I wanted to hurt you, make you pay. I acted like a brat." She peered at him from behind her hair. "Forgive me?"

He took her into his arms. "Will you forgive me for forcing you to come with me to Kiranos, for forcing you onto the helicopter? I felt terrible when I learned about your mother."

"I forgive you." She leaned forward and pressed a quick kiss against his mouth.

"It was after the story about you and Stavros broke in the papers and I saw your anguish at what was being said that I realized I loved you." His eyes held a glow. "I wanted to protect you, keep you safe from the scandal. When you came to me that night, I knew I loved you. It was a hell of a thing for me to come to terms with."

"What a lot of time we've wasted."

Could he expect Pandora to put up with the pressures of his world, the hunger of the press? They'd caused her so much harm already, made her so unhappy. He looked into her clear, silvery eyes, at the firm chin, and he knew that he had to give her a chance. It was her choice to make…not his.

"You have to be sure you can live with me."

"I am sure."

"You've seen what my life is like. How scary my family can be—even when they mean best. You've seen how obsessive the paparazzi can be. None of that is ever going to go away. Can you live with that?"

"You know, the first thing I ever noticed about you was how sexy your mouth is." Pandora touched his mouth with her fingertip. "Made for sin, I thought."

"Be serious." But Zac felt the heat uncoiling inside him.

"I am serious. Very serious." She drew a line across his lip. "You know what? I don't care about the family or the media. Nothing matters as long as I have you." But when she glanced at him, her eyes clouded. "But what are you going to do every time the papers run a story about my relationship with Stavros? Can you survive it?"

"In future I'll follow my own advice not to read the papers—except for the business pages." He licked at her tantalising finger, tasting the perfume of her skin. "And I'll have you. That makes up for whatever the media cares to throw at me. Which reminds me…I meant to tell you, the share price is up. It looks like everyone loves the idea of the Kyriakos heir finding true love."

"That's fantastic news." Pandora looked radiant. "Enough to make me consider forgiving the media for what I went through." She paused. "You did say you were going to buy a property in New Zealand, near High Ridge Station? We can always disappear down there. And when things get really bad, there's always Kiranos. I can cope with the helicopter ride as long as you are there to hold my hand. We can hide out there. No one will find us. I mean, there's not even cell-phone contact."

Zac started to smile. "You didn't try your cell phone on Kiranos, did you?"

"No. Why?"

"Because you would've found that it worked." Zac couldn't help laughing at her expression of outrage. "My wife says I've been wasting time." Hoisting her into his arms, he rose to his feet. "So I daren't waste a single moment more."

Pandora gave an unladylike snort. "Is this about getting me into bed?"

He kissed her nose. "Yes. But it's not only about making love, it's about holding you close to my side all through the night."

"Okay."

Zac's head reared back in disbelief. "*Okay?* No arguments? You accept the fact that I'm going to carry you away to my bed just like that?"

"Our bed," she corrected. "And there are conditions…."

"What?" Zac gazed at the woman he loved with a good

dose of wariness. She was no pushover, and he suspected she knew she had the upper hand, whatever she wanted. "What do you want?"

"When we get back to Greece, I want you to take me to meet that Pano guy who runs Kyriakos Cruises—I have some great ideas for the South Pacific route. And after that, you can show me that little church next door to your house that your ancestor built, and I want to renew our vows. On my birthday in ten days' time. Just you and me. This time I want to be sure that our love for each other is out in the open. No more secrets between us."

He tightened his arms and made for the door, heading for the stairs. "Anything. Anything you want, *agapi*." And there was no hint of mockery in his voice as he added, "You are my bride, my true and only love, for all my life."

Stop Press

Kyriakos Heir Finds True Love

Zac Kyriakos announced today that both his marriage and the Kyriakos Shipping Corporation are stronger than ever. "The secret is true love," he told reporters, holding his new bride close. "I love my wife. The prophecy that the Kyriakos heir requires a virgin bride to find true love has been proved false. This marriage will last forever."

* * * * *

THE APOLLONIDES MISTRESS SCANDAL

BY
TESSA RADLEY

Dear Reader,

As a teenager I read romances that I discovered in the garage…and later in the library and bookshops. There were all sorts of stories. Reunion stories, stranded at sea stories, secret baby stories…some of them seemed quite far-fetched to me. But it didn't matter how unrealistic a story might be, I finished it to discover the happy ending.

In those days I used to horse ride a lot. I'm told one day I fell off a horse—I don't remember. Or rather I remember getting onto the nag early that morning. It had been giving me a little bit of trouble and I was supposed to sort it out—well, three hours later I was in hospital, lights out. I came round the next morning with a killer headache. The funny part of it all is that the guy who saw me fall off and who called my mom, summoned help and did all the things a hero should is now my husband—and I don't remember the first time we ever met.

Every time I fell off a horse afterwards, I waited for the jolt to bring my memory back, like in romances I'd read—it never did. But I still got my happy ending!

I hope you enjoy *The Apollonides Mistress Scandal*.

Take care,

Tessa

ACKNOWLEDGEMENTS

To the readers on the eHarlequin.com
10,000 Book Challenge boards. You blew my annual
book budget in about a month!:-) But I thank each one
of you for the great recommendations and lots of fun.

To Melissa Jeglinski, my thanks for valued advice
and thanks to Karen Solem for always being there for
me. And Abby, Karina and Sandra, what would
I do without you?

To my family—
Tony, Alex and Andrew, you guys are simply the best!

One

Gemma Allen was back.

Forcing himself to snap out of the shock that held him rigid, Angelo Apollonides strode across the pale sand towards the woman who had betrayed him.

His staff had not lied. The nasty truth was that his beautiful former mistress stood on *his* beach, on *his* island admiring one of *his* sleek, double-hulled catamarans. And Angelo intended to find out precisely why she had chosen to return.

"What are you doing here?" Angelo fought to keep his voice even, to keep the string of ugly curses from escaping. "I never expected to see you again. Particularly not here on Strathmos."

She turned, her tawny eyes wide and startled. The first week of November had passed, the evenings on

Strathmos had begun to cool. The sea wind caught at Gemma's dark red hair, whipping it across her face, hiding her expression for a beat of time. When she brushed it back, she'd recovered her equilibrium and her eyes were wary.

"Angelo." Gemma's voice was cool, composed. A world away from the alarm that had flickered in her eyes only seconds before. "How are you?"

"Forget the pleasantries. You have nerve showing up at the Palace of Poseidon." Angelo pressed his mouth into a tight, forbidding line. "I couldn't believe it when I was told you are performing in the Electra Theatre."

She shrugged. "It's a free world. I can work where I want."

"Anywhere except on Strathmos. This is my world, run by my rules." The island was more than his world; it was his home. The resort had been created from his dreams. Today he'd returned after a hectic month away to find that Gemma had already been working here for over a week.

"Do you really want to be faced with an unfair-dismissal action?" Her wariness had been replaced with attitude.

Angelo froze. He was known to be a fair employer, hard but just. He didn't need the headache of an industrial action—and there was a good chance she'd succeed. Frustrated, he stared at the face that had grown more beautiful in the years since they'd been apart. Her hair was longer…wilder, her eyes glowed brighter and as for her mouth…that lush red mouth taunted him with fighting words. He jerked his attention away from her provocative mouth and gave her slender body an insultingly slow once-over. "Singer is certainly a step up from exotic dancer."

"It's been three years. Things change," she pointed out.

"*I* haven't changed." He widened his stance and put his hands on his hips.

"No, you haven't changed one little bit," she agreed.

He assessed her through slitted eyes, not liking the bite in her tone. "So what do you want, Gemma? A second chance?"

An emotion he couldn't decipher flitted across her stunning features. Gemma gave a brittle laugh. "A second chance? With you? You must be mad!"

He frowned, not liking the fact that he couldn't read her any longer. "Why are you here?"

"I'm here to work…it's a free world." With a sweeping hand she gestured to the blue stretch of the Aegean Sea beyond the beach where the catamarans rested. "You—or rather your minions—gave me the job. The money was too good to pass up."

"Aah. Money."

"Don't scorn the lack of it so easily." Her eyes were flashing now. "Just because you inherited an empire of resorts that stretch across the Greek isles before you turned twenty-one doesn't give you the right to look down your nose at me. I need the money."

Angelo felt himself bristle. Her tongue had developed a razor-sharp edge since their last unforgettable encounter. "I worked damn hard to build a chain of family hotels into world-class resorts. And you never objected to the funds it gave you access to in the past."

He felt her withdraw, even before her eyes went blank. Then she murmured, "If the recent tabloids are to be believed, you're so far removed from us ordinary working mortals, you might as well inhabit Mount Olympus."

"You should know better than to believe everything you read in the newspapers," he snapped, shuddering at the memory of the latest batch of headlines about his breakup with Melina.

"Really?" She raised an eyebrow. "You're not the playboy they portray you to be? You don't wear a different rising starlet or supermodel on your arm every month?"

He glared at her, his frustration increasing to a rising inferno, fanned by her sharp words. "The media exposure is advantageous to both the women and myself."

"So it's all about glamour? About creating an illusion about the rich and famous, then? Nothing more?"

His brows jerked together. "Why are you so interested—unless you do want a chance to get back into my bed?"

She snorted. "I don't want you back."

His mouth slanted. "Didn't anyone tell you that you should be nice to the boss? Three years ago you would've never dared speak to me as you just did."

"Three years ago, I was a silly little goose."

She shifted and her tank top rode up, revealing a strip of tanned midriff. Every male instinct went on alert. "But you don't deny that you are interested?" Angelo moved closer.

Gemma glanced at her watch. "I can't deny you're a fascinating man."

The bite was back. He gave a surprised laugh. "You don't want me back…but you're interested enough to admit you find me fascinating? What message are you trying to send me?"

For an instant she looked rattled. He noticed that goose bumps had risen on her arms. "Are you cold?"

"No." She rubbed her arms briskly, not meeting his eyes.

He touched her arm where the fine hairs stood on end. Gently. With a fingertip. "If you are not cold, then what is this?"

She jerked away. Her gaze swung up to meet his. He read bewilderment…and something more. A stark, turbulent emotion. Fear?

Gemma stepped away. "Excuse me." The smile she gave him didn't reach the eyes that were stretched wide. "But I need to go. It's nearly time for the show. I've got to get ready. Maybe you can come watch." She flung the invitation over her shoulder. As she brushed past him, Angelo let the weight of his hand land on her arm, stilling her.

She turned. This time, he was certain of the emotion that darkened her eyes from tawny to a deep sherry-brown.

It *was* fear. Powerful and totally overwhelming. He inspected her. From close-up he took in her darkened eyes, the taut tension in her face, the tiny shivers that rippled across her skin. He could smell the saltiness of the sea in her hair and feel the cool edge of the wind on her skin.

Why was she here? She'd implied she needed money. Was that the only reason? Or, despite her denial, did she hope to rekindle the burnt-out embers of their affair?

"Let me go." Her voice was toneless. Pointedly, she stared at his long, tanned fingers lying against her skin.

He removed them, taking his time and watching intently as she hauled in a steadying breath.

The nagging wind tugged at her wayward hair as she gave a hurried glance at her watch and scooped up the sandals lying in the sand. "I suppose I should say it's been nice seeing you—"

"But you'd be lying."

"I didn't say that." She stilled. There was chagrin in her eyes. "Don't put words in my mouth."

Her mouth. His gaze dropped to her rosy lips. Full and lush. The sudden surge of desire was unexpected. It left him reeling. He clenched his fists. How could he want Gemma Allen? After everything she'd done?

How the hell could he have forgotten how sexy she was? The lush bee-stung lips, the sinuous curves of her sleek body, the cloud of dark red hair…how could he have let those details slide from his consciousness?

Reluctant to examine the discovery that he still desired her, he said softly between his teeth. "From exotic dancer into singer…I want to see this transformation. I'll be at your show."

Half an hour later, wearing only lacy briefs and a silky black halter-neck slip, Gemma sat alone in front of the mirror in the dressing room she shared with Lucie LaVie, a likeable comedienne who did a very funny routine in the bar adjacent to the Electra Theatre.

Meeting Angelo on the beach so unexpectedly had been a shock. Dammit, she hadn't even known he was back. She'd been on Strathmos for just over a week, waiting for him, half-dreading their first encounter. She'd planned to be prepared…to be dressed to the nines…to show him what he was missing when they met again. Instead she'd been wearing shorts, no make-up and her legs had been covered in sand. She certainly hadn't expected the curious numbness that had enveloped her.

Staring into the mirror, Gemma couldn't help wondering what Angelo would make of the transformation. The heavy stage makeup gave her skin an unnatural perfection, blotting out the light sprinkle of freckles across her nose and cheeks. Eyeliner accentuated her tawny eyes and dark ruby lipstick added lushness to her lips that gave her an in-your-face sensuality.

Angelo liked his women beautiful and flamboyant. His most recent mistresses had all been actresses or famous models. And, according to the recent tabloids she'd studied, he still showed no sign of settling down. She examined herself in the mirror. She looked beautiful…flamboyant. And Angelo would be out there tonight watching her.

Her plan had to—

A rap on the door broke into her desperate thoughts. "Ten minutes to showtime, Gemma."

"Won't be long," she called back, and ran her fingers through her hair in an effort to tame the wild auburn curls. She couldn't remember the last time a man's fingers had stroked through them. A vivid image of Angelo's hand on her arm, his long fingers and buffed square nails, flashed into her mind and she swore softly.

An instant later the door burst open and Angelo entered with all the force and energy of a hurricane.

"Hey. You can't come in here!" After the initial shock, Gemma resisted the urge to cross her hands over her breasts. Despite the skimpy fabric and the low dip in the front, the slip covered all the strategic places.

Angelo shut the door and, folding his arms, leaned against it. "There's nothing to see that I haven't seen before."

Right. Gemma swallowed. Then she let her gaze run over him. He looked magnificent. The white dinner jacket must've been tailored to fit his tall body. Under the lights, his hair gleamed like old gold and his startling turquoise eyes blazed. He looked assured, wealthy, powerful.

And this was the man she intended to teach a lesson he'd never forget.

"What do you want?"

"Join me in the theatre for a drink after the show."

Gemma hid her exultation. It had been worth coming all the way to Strathmos. A few years ago he would've impressed her—with his Greek-god looks and the sheer force of his personality. But these days she didn't go for the domineering masterful type.

She dared not give in too quickly. She didn't want to lose his interest. Nor could she let herself forget for one moment why she was doing this.

"Don't you think you should wait outside until I am dressed?" Gemma waited a beat then added delicately, "Boss…"

Angelo's brows jerked into a frown at her disparaging tone and Gemma felt a fierce rush of pleasure. Of course, he was accustomed to admiration…adulation… women falling all over him. But not her.

"You—" He broke off and sucked in a deep breath. Then in a soft, dangerous tone, he said, "Do not presume on our past relationship."

"I would never do that." In the mirror, she slanted him a small smile. "I came to Palace of Poseidon to sing."

"Precisely." He didn't smile back. His eyes were bright and ruthless. "Or were you lying earlier? Perhaps you *were* hoping I'd want you back in my bed?"

Annoyance swarmed through Gemma. Quickly, she veiled her gaze before he glimpsed her ire. "I never imagined you'd want that. And nor do I. I've told you that already." Gemma drew a steadying breath. She had to be very careful; she could mess it all up with one careless mistake.

"I thought you might be hankering after the style to which you'd become accustomed."

God, he was arrogant. Gemma spun around on the plastic stool and glared up at Angelo. He was so tall, he positively loomed over her. "You make me sound like a sycophant. I worked for you, as well."

"You consider sharing my bed for half a year work?" The look he gave her stripped her naked of the silky slip and told exactly how little respect Angelo had for her.

Again, she fought the urge to cover her breasts, to check that the silky material didn't reveal the outline of her dark nipples. Supremely self-conscious now, she rose and crossed to the corner of the room where a small closet held several outfits.

Gemma peeled the dress she intended wearing tonight off its hanger. Keeping her back firmly to Angelo, she slid on the sleek crimson tube covered with winking sequins that should have clashed terribly with her hair but didn't.

The electrifying quality of the silence behind her flustered her. Gemma swivelled. The expression in Angelo's eyes made her breath catch. She became aware that the dress hugged her curves like a lover, that the neckline was low, provocative. That she and Angelo were totally alone.

Hurriedly she said, "My career has always been important to me." And fame had been important, too, she supposed.

"If you say so." He gave her a strange, intent look. "I say that changed once you got what you wanted…"

"And what do you think I wanted?" Then wished the words unsaid as tension sparked in the air between them. Suddenly Gemma didn't want to know the answer.

A frown drew his surprisingly dark brows together. "A man wealthy enough to pander to your every whim. A gold card with no ceiling…clothes, jewellery…" His gaze dropped pointedly to the gold ring set with a large showy topaz on the little finger of her left hand. "You chose that after we visited Monaco for a weekend. Remember?"

"I'm afraid I don't." She grabbed a pair of gloves out the closet and, with an ease born of practice, pulled on the long, black lace gloves embroidered with dark red roses and covered the ring. Outside the door, Mark Lyme, the manager of the entertainment centre called her name. Gemma moved towards the door. "I must go, I'm due on stage."

"Wait, you're not running out on this conversation." Angelo flung his hands out wide. "Of course you remember. That night we attended the Rose Ball, and you wanted to go partying afterwards. You flirted with every man who glanced your way."

Men? She hesitated. *What men?* "No—"

"Were there so many men that you cannot remember the one from the other?" Angelo's eyes glittered.

"I don't remember—"

"Oh, please, don't feed me that. You're wearing that ring *I* bought and paid for. Did I buy you so much jewellery that you can no longer remember the occasion of each purchase? I'm sure you remember every moment of the time we spent in bed afterwards."

Gemma's stomach turned. Outside, Mark called again. Gemma wrenched open the dressing-room door. "That's just it," she cut in before Angelo could interrupt again. "I don't remember. Nothing about that night at the Rose Ball. Nothing about you. Nothing about our time together. I've lost my memory."

Gemma bolted out onto the dimly lit stage, the vision of Angelo's stunned expression imprinted on her mind. She stared blindly out at the audience. She had to get a grip. She had to thrust the disturbing scene in the dressing room with Angelo out of her mind.

The chatter stilled and the cutlery stopped clinking. By now most of the patrons had finished their meal. Being Friday night, the supper theatre was packed. Gemma paused. Clouds from the smoke machine swirled around her, coloured by red and blue lighting and adding to the moodiness.

For a moment the familiar nervousness swept her. Then she embraced it and stepped forward to the waiting crowd. This was a space she cherished, a special place where her voice and mind and body all flowed into the music.

It was at the close of the second song that she spotted Angelo through the feathers of smoke. He sat alone at a table, casually propped against the wall, his arm along the back of the chair. The narrowed gaze focused on her revealed nothing. And the table in front of him was empty of food or drink.

Gemma quaked at the prospect of joining him for the drink he'd invited her for. The memory of how her skin had prickled when he'd touched her and the blind fear that had followed, swept over her.

Ripping her attention away from him, Gemma worked to make the crowd smile…and sigh. As her voice died after the final held note of the last song there was a moment's silence, then clapping thundered through the theatre. Gemma blew them two-handed kisses and sank into a bow, her unruly hair sweeping forward. She straightened and flicked her hair back and the clapping evolved into stamps and whistles.

"All right, one more, an Andrew Lloyd Webber composition, a personal favourite," she agreed. Her voice reverberated and the cacophony subsided. "If you've ever lost a loved one, this one is for you."

Gemma launched into "Memory." Her voice cut through the theatre, sharp and pure. She barely noticed that the audience seemed to hold its collective breath and when she reached the last line she let the final notes slide into silence.

This time the crowd went mad.

Smiling, Gemma waved to them. But she couldn't stop her gaze seeking Angelo's. The lyrics lingered in her mind. *A new day.* For a long moment their eyes held, the connection taut, and her smile faded.

There would be no new day for them. The past lay between them like an unassailable barrier.

Gemma was trembling with reaction by the time she reached the dressing room. She felt as if she'd been two rounds with Rocky Balboa. Lucie had returned from her act and lay sprawled along the length of the two-seater couch, dressed in funky street clothes that suited her spiky blonde hair and wide eyes.

"Boss wants to see you," she said, tossing a slip of paper into the trash basket as Gemma sat down.

"Mark?"

"No, the big fish, Angelo Apollonides." Lucie's green eyes were curious. "A reminder that you're to join him for a drink at his table. You didn't say anything about that invitation."

Gemma should have known that he wouldn't let her get away. That he'd want to know more about the bombshell she'd dropped before she had rushed out.

"It happened just before the show." Gemma wasn't confessing that Angelo had been here, in the dressing room. And she'd never told Lucie anything—thankfully no one had commented on the past affair. Perhaps most of the entertainment staff had only been there less than two years. "I'm too dog-tired to cope with Mr. Apollonides," Gemma muttered. The fatigue was not physical. It went soul-deep. She felt raw and emotionally drained. And she couldn't face Angelo right now.

The memory of how she'd reacted to his touch had spooked her. The last thing she needed was to feel desire for Angelo Apollonides. She needed time to come to terms with that unexpected complication. When she confronted Angelo it would be in her space, on her terms, not in the dark smoky intimacy of the supper theatre.

At Lucie's look of blatant disbelief, Gemma added, "And you can tell him that I'm passing for now." Rejection would do Angelo the world of good. Make him more eager to see her again.

"Gemma, you're being stupid. In the eight months I've been working on Strathmos he's never once invited an employee for a drink. And you refuse?" Lucie jumped up and started pacing the small space. "I just don't get you. He didn't even bring a woman with him to Strathmos this time, rumour has it that he ended it with—" she named a well-known model "—last month. Why not try your luck?"

Gemma didn't answer. She picked up a bottle of makeup remover and a packet of face wipes and started to clean her face with quick, practised moves. Soon Angelo would come looking for her, and she had no intention of being here.

After a moment Lucie gave a snort of disgust and stalked out of the room, muttering something about being the messenger of bad tidings and that some people had all the luck.

But Gemma knew Angelo's demand to join him had nothing to do with luck. His reaction on the beach had made it clear he was less than happy about her appearance on Strathmos.

She had to play this very, very carefully. For a year she'd been trying to get close to him. She'd finally been granted a four-week chance when the performer who was originally booked had pulled out. Gemma's agent had scrambled for the booking. With only eighteen days

left to discover what she wanted and find a way to make
Angelo pay for the grief he'd caused her, she couldn't
chicken out just because her senses had been set on fire
by the touch of a single finger.

Two

Gemma had stood him up!

And she hadn't even bothered to tell him herself, she'd sent a messenger to deliver the unwelcome news. The anger that had simmered within Angelo since he'd that discovered Gemma was on Strathmos, living and working in *his* resort, took on a new edge.

Gemma claimed that she'd lost her memory. How had that happened and what did it have to do with him? And why had she returned to Strathmos?

Angelo found himself glaring in the direction where the maddeningly capricious Gemma had vanished from the stage, while the bare skin of her back and that provocative red dress remained imprinted on his vision. He hated the sneaky realisation that he hadn't stopped thinking about her since he'd arrived back on

Strathmos. And now she'd deliberately left him cooling his heels.

Angelo rose to his feet, abandoning the bottle of Bollinger he'd ordered—Gemma had always had a taste for champagne—and, jaw set, stalked out to find her.

She was not in the dressing room. But a comprehensive scan took in the red dress hanging in the closet. Clearly, she'd already been and gone. Nor was she to be found in the row of bars and coffee shops that flanked the theatre. Angelo barely slowed his long strides as Mark Lyme hurried over. Two minutes later, with the next potential crisis averted, he exited the entertainment complex, searching for Gemma's distinctive dark flame hair under the lamps in the wide paved piazza.

About to veer off to where the staff units were located, he spotted a lone figure walking towards the deserted beach. Hunching his shoulders against the rising wind, Angelo quickened his pace. With her give-away hair, not even the fact that she wore jeans and a bulky sweater could hide that it was Gemma.

He came up behind her. "If I give an employee an order I expect it to be obeyed." The deceptive softness of his tone didn't hide his anger—or his frustration.

Gemma's shoulders tensed and she came to a halt. Then she turned. In the dim light of the lanterns that lined the promenade, he saw her eyebrow arch. "I thought it was an invitation," she said with soft irony. "One that I never accepted."

"Or refused."

She considered him, her head on one side. "Give me one good reason why I should have joined you."

He blinked. Women usually thronged to his side.

Hell, he didn't need to issue invitations. Women gate-crashed celebrity functions to meet him. "Because I wanted to speak to you."

"What about?" Her tension was tangible.

"Your memory loss."

"Not true. You invited me for a drink before you knew about that."

She had him there. What he really wanted to know was why she had come back to Strathmos. It had to be about more than money. His gut told him it had something to do with her amnesia. He wasn't about to admit that what pricked his ego was the fact that she didn't remember him. Or was it a ploy? Was her amnesia nothing more than a sham designed to avoid facing up to her treachery three years ago? Or a last-ditch effort to recapture his interest? At last he said, "You've forgotten carrying on with every male under the age of eighty at the Rose Ball? You don't remember about me…us?"

She closed her eyes at the sheer incredulity in his voice. "Is that so hard to accept?" she asked warily. "I have amnesia."

"How convenient."

Gemma opened her eyes and met his narrowed gaze. She tried to speak but her voice wouldn't work. So she simply shrugged and let her arms fall uselessly by her side.

"What kind of amnesia?"

"Does it matter?" The sick feeling in the pit of her stomach tightened. Couldn't he see how much she hated this? "Fact is, I can't remember anything about what happened here three years ago. It's just…one vast blank."

"It certainly explains how you have the gall to come back."

She let that barb go. "It's not easy being here. But I need to find out about my life. What it was like… well…before." She slid him a sideways look. The anger had faded, but his eyes still glittered with suspicion. "It's really strange, because I remember lots of stuff before I met you. Most of it, I think. And I know what happened…afterwards. It's the time in the middle that's gone."

He loomed over her. "How did it happen? Did you fall? Did you hit your head? What do the doctors say about the prognosis? Will you ever get that part of your memory back?"

"I don't know. I don't want to talk about it." Gemma's voice sounded thin and thready even to her own ears. "It upsets me."

Angelo gave a harsh sigh. "I suppose I can understand that. It must be scary."

Not as scary as Angelo. Even when he was being nice—like now, when his eyes were full of sympathy—there was a taut purpose to his body, an air of danger and tension. Gemma shuddered. Nice wouldn't last. Not with Angelo Apollonides. He hadn't transformed a string of family resorts into modern extravaganzas built for year-round entertainment by being a nice, sympathetic kind of guy. He was tough, decisive and ruthless. A man who worked hard—and played harder. A Greek success legend.

His gaze was direct. "Have dinner with me."

The unexpected request startled her. She chewed her lip. It was what she ought to do.

"Is it such a difficult decision? Do I scare you so much?" His hands came down on her shoulders and the touch scorched straight through her lamb's-wool sweater.

She went very still. "You don't scare me at all," Gemma said with false bravado.

His hands tightened. "Prove it by having dinner with me."

A dare. How infantile. She froze under his touch. A hint of stubble darkened his jaw and the hard line of his mouth had relaxed into a sensual curve. The dark intensity of his gaze and the way her flesh reacted to his touch told her that he was way out of her league. She wasn't ready to have dinner with him, to be the sole focus of his attention. He was so much more than she'd expected. But she had no choice. Not if she wanted to learn what she needed. "Not tonight. It's been a long day. And it's late."

He was about to say something, to argue, when his cell phone trilled. He mouthed an apology and turned away, talking rapidly in Greek, and Gemma realised she'd lost his attention.

Gemma wanted to kick something—preferably herself—and she wished desperately she'd accepted his invitation. Even though the prickles of excitement his touch had generated terrified her.

He hit a button and slid the phone into his pants pocket. "Tomorrow night?"

Relief overwhelmed her. She hadn't blown it. She drew a deep, shuddering breath. "Okay, I'll have dinner with you."

"So how did we meet?" The following evening Gemma sat across from Angelo in a secluded corner of the Golden

Fleece restaurant, her half-eaten meal of grilled calamari garnished with sliced lemon in front of her.

"At the film festival in Cannes." Angelo set down his knife. His plate was empty. "I thought you were an actress."

That would explain some of it. Angelo had never been linked with a dancer previously.

"Oh? What happened next?" She speared another tube of calamari and popped it into her mouth.

"You were beautiful—and funny. I enjoyed your company so I invited you to spend a weekend at Poseidon's Cavern." He named one of the famous resorts that he owned. "You accepted. And, when business called, you came back to Strathmos with me—it's where I live, after all." He gave her a grin that transformed his face, the harsh line of his mouth softening into a passionate curve.

Gemma set her knife and fork together and shifted in her chair, uncomfortable with the notion that it had been so easy for him. "And then I got a job in the resort? Right?"

"Do you want desert?"

"No, thanks."

"Coffee?"

She shook her head, impatient for his answer to her questions.

He came around and pulled out her chair. Close to her ear he murmured, "There was so much more glamour in being the boss's girlfriend than working." His voice was loaded with cynicism. "And you'd led me to believe you were taking a break from stage work. I had no idea you were an exotic dancer until about a month later."

"Oh." Gemma rose and shot him a wary glance. "I never wanted to…leave?"

He gave a hard-edged grin. "Why should you have? You had it all. Great resorts to live in, an unending credit line and good sex."

That was supposed to be funny? Gemma had never felt less like laughing in her life. She walked quickly ahead, not noticing the attractive man with long dark hair who waved to her. She smouldered silently until they exited the restaurant.

"So I no longer had a career—" She squawked in shock as Angelo pulled her into an alcove behind an immense bronze statue of Hephaestus. The sconce of fire that burned in the statue's raised hand cast leaping shadows against the walls. Gemma opened her mouth to protest.

"If you mean, you no longer danced half naked in an upmarket bar, then no, you no longer had a career. Instead you had me." In the close confines of the alcove his face had changed, toughened. He looked hard and ruthless and suddenly Gemma could see exactly why he was such a successful businessman and commanded so much respect. She had to take care not to provoke him.

"I had you." Gemma struggled to keep the anger at his arrogance out of her voice. "And what did you get out of this deal?"

"A beautiful woman in my bed."

"I don't suppose it occurred to you I might've wanted more?"

"More?"

"A career—"

He gave a snort. "You scored by being my live-in

lover. Travel to different resorts. A-list parties. No need to work. Believe me, it was better for you my way."

His way. Gemma had a feeling that most things ended up his way. The alternative would be for his kept mistress to hit the highway. "Did you love *me?*"

"Love you?" His head went back and she could see she'd surprised him.

"Yes, did you love me?" She pressed. "With all this good sex, did you feel anything for me at all?"

"Look, Gemma, this wasn't about love. It was about two consenting adults who met and enjoyed time together." He spread his hands sideways. "Hell, we were hardly Romeo and Juliet."

"If we had been Romeo and Juliet, you'd have been dead by the end," Gemma said through gritted teeth.

"Hey," he objected, "what are you getting so worked up about? All I meant was that we weren't young lovers, dizzy from an attack of first-time love."

"Did *I* love *you?*"

He gave an astonished laugh. "What's the fixation with love? You certainly never told me you loved me. But then you weren't in it for love. And nor was I."

Gemma bit her lip, thinking furiously. "I can't believe I would've lived the kind of life you've painted for any other reason than because I loved you more than anything in the world. It's so against everything I believe in."

"Well, you showed no sign of loving me...and if that's what you believe now, then you've changed."

She stilled. "Maybe I have."

His eyes darkened. "Gemma." He stretched out a hand and stroked her arm. "You should—"

"What am I doing?" She dropped her face into her hands, then raked her fingers back through her hair.

"Trying to regain your memory? Maybe this will help you remember." There was a huskiness to his voice that caught her attention.

Slowly she raised her head. He was close, far closer than she'd realised and in the flickering light his gaze was intent. Her heart started to pound. She swallowed and the sudden ringing silence stretched between them.

"Yes?" The sound was little more than a croak. But Angelo understood. It meant yes to so much more. Even to that which she most feared.

The instant his lips brushed hers Gemma knew her life would never be the same again. Every preconception she had of what it might've been like to be kissed by him vanished.

It was fire and light. Energy and emotion. Then his tongue touched hers and sparks shot through her. Adrenaline. And something magical.

She held her breath, didn't move in case the magic vanished. Then his tongue swept her mouth and the fire leapt inside her. Gemma groaned, closed her eyes and abandoned herself to the wonder.

When his fingers stroked the naked skin of her shoulder, every nerve ending went crazy. Frissons rippled down her spine and a reckless want followed. She moved closer, pressing herself up against him, until she felt the unmistakable ridge of his erection through the soft silk of her dress. It was a shock…a sign of how out of control this had become…but it was also incredibly satisfying.

Whatever the past held, Angelo wanted her. Now.

She sighed into his mouth, he deepened the kiss and

his breathing grew ragged. His hand closed on her shoulder and he pulled her against him.

At last he raised his head. "Do you remember that?"

Gemma stared at him, then regretfully shook her head.

He put her away from him, his hands shaking a little. "*Thiavlo*. I think we both need to cool down. Let's visit the casino—you always enjoyed that."

"Okay," she managed as he led her out from behind the inscrutable Hephaestus. Her knees shook. She had never felt less like gambling in her life.

Large double doors opened into the Apollo Club, the casino reserved for A-list clientele. Crystal chandeliers hung from the domed ceiling painted with beasts and heroes from myths Gemma knew well. The ambience in the room warned her that the stakes would be frighteningly high.

Angelo led her to a table with a group of men in tuxedos and two women—a blonde and a brunette—in evening gowns, jewels glittering at their necks and wrists. No voices hummed in here. Only the clatter of chips broke the solemn silence.

Murmuring an order, Angelo placed a wad of notes on the table. An elegant croupier in a long black dress slid several stacks of chips across the baize. Angelo passed the stacks to her, and Gemma realised he'd spent a small fortune for her to fritter away. She started to feel ill. "I can't gamble that kind of money."

The look he gave her was more than a little pointed. "It never troubled you in the past."

Gemma bit her lip. "What if I lose it all?"

Angelo shrugged. "Then I'll buy more."

And what would he expect from her then? Sex? Obviously that had happened in the past. Something within her shrivelled at the thought.

"No!" She shoved the chips back at him. "I might have forgotten how to do this, forgotten the rules."

"Try and we'll see."

"Angelo, I don't want to do this."

His gaze held hers. After a long moment he said, "All right. We'll see if we can penetrate that memory another way. Keep these—" he separated a small heap of chips "—in case you decide you want to play later."

She shook her head and pushed the chips away. "I don't feel like gambling tonight."

"Would you like to go for a drink?"

She nodded. This close she could see the laugh lines around his eyes, the glitter in his compelling eyes. He stilled in the act of gathering the chips and stared down at her.

"Gemma?"

With a start, she looked away, breaking the tenuous thread that linked them, and turned her head, searching for the source of the call that cut through the hush of the huge room.

"I *thought* it was you." The guy coming towards her was darkly tanned with Gallic features and carefully styled shaggy black hair. Gemma stared at him blankly.

The blonde at their table squealed in delight and grabbed his arm. He bent to kiss her cheek. Her much older companion didn't look happy.

The hand cupping Gemma's elbow tensed. "Did you invite him?" Angelo murmured in her ear.

"Invite him?" She swung around to cast Angelo a frown. "What are you talking about? I don't even know—" She broke off.

"Who he is," Angelo finished smoothly, and started to laugh, but Gemma noticed his eyes were devoid of humour. "I don't think Jean-Paul will appreciate being forgotten so soon."

"Who is he?" Gemma hissed.

"Jean-Paul Moreau." From Angelo's air of expectancy Gemma suspected the name was supposed to mean something to her. It didn't.

She lifted her shoulders and let them drop. "So…" she prompted.

"Your lover." Some ugly emotion flashed over Angelo's face then his features turned wooden. "The man I threw naked out of my—our—bed three years ago."

Three

Gemma stared.

Angelo's shocking revelation was the last thing she'd expected. Yet, judging by his narrow-eyed expression, he clearly believed it to be true.

She tested the discovery against her own belief. No, she couldn't accept it. Angelo must've made some awful mistake.

But before she could question him further, a mist of designer aftershave surrounded her. Then came a whisper of "*Cherie,* you are more beautiful than ever," and male lips nudged her cheek.

"Hello—" she tried frantically to remember his name "—Jean-Paul."

"I thought you were ignoring me, *cherie.* You stared straight through me earlier. I'm glad to know you remember your old friends."

Beside her Angelo snorted. Gemma shot him a warning look. She didn't want Jean-Paul knowing about the amnesia.

At least not yet.

Coming face-to-face with a man Angelo considered her lover had taken her aback. Much as she disliked Angelo, he had no reason to lie to her about the past. She needed to learn more.

With an extravagant flourish Jean-Paul produced a roll of euro notes from inside his jacket and signalled to the croupier. When the chips came, he slipped one pile across to Gemma. "For you, *cherie*."

The smile Jean-Paul gave her was disconcertingly intimate. The secretive smile of a man to a woman he knew very, very well.

Gemma could sense Angelo's silent tension. Her stomach rolled over. "Thanks," she said stiltedly. Realising that she sounded terse she pointed to the unused chips on the table that Angelo had been in the process of gathering up before Jean-Paul's arrival. "But I have enough—and we're going for a drink."

Jean-Paul's gaze swept over her, explicit, knowing. Leaning towards her, he whispered, "*Cherie,* you're not the kind of woman ever to have enough. Here—" he slid a handful of chips towards her "—have a bet on me."

"Enough!" Angelo said harshly. A tanned arm hooked around Gemma's waist from behind, his other hand pushed his chips towards the croupier. "The lady doesn't want your chips." Against the length of her spine Gemma could feel Angelo's body through the thin silk of her dress. It was at once comforting and vaguely threatening. His arm lay coiled around her, under her breasts like a hard band, and awareness of his strength, his power, shivered through her.

It was the sudden ratcheting tension in his body that made her realise that Jean-Paul had moved. Within Angelo's hold, she twisted around on her stool. The two men faced each other like duelling adversaries.

Jean-Paul's gaze shifted from Angelo to Gemma and his mouth twisted. "It's like that, is it? *Cherie,* don't be fooled. Apollonides is the same man as three years ago. Work will always be his first mistress. Will that be enough for you this time around? Or will you come searching for warm arms, words of lo—"

"I said *enough.*" Even Jean-Paul heard the suppressed violence in the whip-crack sound and took a hasty step back. "You go too far, Moreau. If I catch you near Gemma I will have you thrown off the island. Do you understand?"

A Gallic shrug and Jean-Paul smiled. "Keep cool, man. It doesn't mean a thing—it never did." But there was a wariness in his dark eyes that hadn't been there seconds before.

The last thing Gemma wanted was a scene. Already they were attracting the glances of people alerted by the bristling men and hissed words. The two women at their table were staring openly, while the croupier called for bets with a touch of desperation.

"Angelo—"

The arm tightened, cutting off her protest. "Gemma, you will not encourage this man. Moreau, you will keep your distance from Gemma. I've told you both before, I don't share my woman. Understand that." Releasing his hold on her, Angelo moved between her and Jean-Paul and with a hard glance at her, he added, "Both of you."

Then, in a swift movement, he swept the euro notes off the table and nodded at the croupier. "Come, Gemma. Let's go."

Without a glance in Jean-Paul's direction, Gemma slid from the stool.

The hand that came down on her shoulder was possessive, a warning. *His woman.* Angelo had warned Jean-Paul—and her—that he had no intention of sharing his woman, clearly not for the first time. Did that mean he still considered her his woman?

A frisson of dark emotion speared her. Gemma wasn't sure what to make of his claim and kept silent as they left the gaming room.

By the time they exited the elevator a floor down and walked out the hotel into the starry night, the anger inside Angelo was still simmering. Maintaining a terse silence, he strode along the path lit by decorative Victorian-style lamps. He was aware of the anxious glances Gemma kept casting him as she hurried along beside him, her high heels clicking against the terra-cotta flagstones.

"I'm sorry about what happened."

He shrugged. "It had to happen sooner or later. And it's only a matter of time before it happens again...before another man rises from the ashes of your past."

"I don't remember him," she said quickly.

Too quickly? "Meaning, you won't remember the others, either?" He shot her a derisive smile. "Poor bastard. I can almost feel pity for him."

Yet he had to admit he found it immensely satisfying that she didn't remember the Frenchman. Especially after...

Hell!

"I knew about Jean-Paul, saw you both in my bed with my own eyes." His tone took on a dark edge. "I can give you details of how you were straddling him, your knees around his hips, your bare breasts bouncing and the satin sheets—*my* satin sheets—crumpled around you. Your skin like a pearl against—"

"Stop." Gemma came to a jarring halt. "I don't want to hear this." Her head bent, she stared at the shadowy footpath and tension hunched her bare shoulders. She shivered as a sharp gust of sea-wind cut through the night.

"If I tell you what I saw, what I can still see so clearly, it might help you remember." He knew his bitterness was showing. But he wanted to hurt her, cut to the heart of her. Humiliate her as he'd been humiliated. "How many more men like Jean-Paul will there be? Men that I don't know of? Men that you don't remember?"

Gemma shivered again.

Angered by her lack of response, he said, "Tell me, Gemma, how many more?"

"I don't know," she said in a very small voice.

"Look at me." His hands closed on her shoulders. Her skin was like ice. He swung her round and her eyes snapped open revealing her bewilderment as she stumbled on her high heels.

"Careful!" He tightened his grip and couldn't help noticing how soft her skin felt.

She ducked away. Her heel gave and she almost fell.

With an exasperated imprecation he yanked her upright. "Are you okay?"

"No thanks to you." She wrenched herself free. "If

you hadn't grabbed me like some Neanderthal I'd have been fine."

"Neanderthal?" He didn't know whether to laugh or to swear at the crack. *"Neanderthal?"*

Gemma's heart sank as she absorbed his outrage. Then she stiffened as her own indignation kicked in. It *was* his doing that she'd nearly fallen. He'd spun her round. Ever since Jean-Paul's arrival he'd been acting like a jealous jerk. She didn't have to put up with it.

Tossing back her hair, she lifted her chin. "Yes. Neanderthal. You know—some primitive three-hundred pound gorilla type." Her heart was galloping as she stared at him defiantly, waiting for his response.

For a moment he simply stood there. Then he gurgled something that sounded like *gorilla* and his arms shot out.

She gave a squeak. And then it was too late.

He had her in a hard hold, his fingers imprinted on her shoulders, and his lips slanted across hers, grinding down against the softness cooled by the night breeze. She wriggled and murmured a protest.

He raised his head, and she gulped a much-needed breath. "So I'm a gorilla, am I?"

Hastily she shook her head. A mad urge to laugh bubbled through Gemma. Then his mouth was back, open and hungry on hers, and all coherent thought left her. His tongue stroked the soft, tender skin inside her cheeks. Heat sliced through her, a restless yearning started to build. The desire he'd ignited when he'd kissed her in the alcove returned in full force. Gemma's head spun. What the hell was happening to her?

His arms tightened, drawing her up against him. He was already aroused.

The realisation sent a wave of reckless euphoria coursing through her. Her bones softened, and in her lower body the heat started to spread. Her hips seemed to have developed a life of their own and moved in slow circles against him. Angelo groaned.

His hot breath rushed into her mouth and the intimacy turned her knees to liquid. Gemma staggered backward, her heels digging into the turf, and Angelo followed, his thighs moving against hers in an erotic dance, their mouths devouring each other.

The roughness of a tree trunk stopped Gemma backing up. Angelo didn't pause until he had her plastered against the trunk, his body reamed up against hers in the dark space under the wide canopy of branches, his hands twisted in the tangled mass of her hair. Her nipples pebbled, aching under the press of his body. Here, in the silent darkness, the golden glow of the lamplight seemed far away.

The pressure on her mouth gave a little and then the tip of his tongue started to outline her lips, slowly, deliberately, his hands holding her head, positioning her for maximum impact.

It was teasing, frustrating. She wanted him to kiss her. Intimately. *"More."* The demand was torn from her. She butted her hips forward, finding the length of his erection and started to rock back and forth. She wanted more of his mouth, more of his touch…more… of the intense want ripping through her.

But he kept the tongue strokes light and toying and she writhed against him.

When Angelo finally lifted his head, Gemma moaned a protest. In the stillness of the night the sound of their breathing was hoarse and ragged. His fingers fiddled at her nape and a moment later she felt the straps of her halter dress and the bra beneath give.

A warm hand slipped under the fabric and stroked the bare flesh of her breast. His fingers brushed the nub; sensation shot through her and she gasped, arching against the tree. He repeated the motion. She tensed as a rush of heat pooled beneath her panties.

"Ghhh." The sound that escaped her was foreign, incomprehensible even to her own ears. Rising on tiptoe, Gemma rocked harder, rubbing herself against his solid flesh, concentrating on that sensitive part of her—the part that touched him, aroused him, despite the rasp of the fabric that separated them. Then his leg moved, bracing his weight, so that the hardness in the front of his trousers fitted in the space between her legs.

Her eyes tightly closed, her head flung back, Gemma focused on the fingertips massaging her nipple, on the sensation spreading out hotter and hotter from the junction between her legs.

She started to pant and the desperate heat climbed higher…higher…within her. She rocked faster still, rubbing against him, and he responded, his hips moving back and forth, the friction building—building until Gemma knew that she was poised on the lip of the void.

The taunting, teasing touch on her nipples tightened. And when his tongue entered her mouth in wild, consuming thrusts a bolt of electric sensation shot through Gemma.

Turned on beyond belief, Gemma gasped, a wild, keening sound. Her body tightened, the sensitive point at the apex of her legs caught fire and the convulsions began.

She sagged against the tree, spent and dizzy, her pulse pumping furiously through her head. Her legs had turned to water, and she suspected that had the tree not supported her she would've collapsed.

Angelo lifted his head and withdrew his hand from her breast. Her body cooled as he stepped away, his expression unfathomable in the criss-cross shadows of the branches.

"Maybe that will help you remember!"

God, how she hated him. At his awful words she fumbled for the straps behind her neck, but her fingers were shaking so much she couldn't tie them. Finally, with an impatient mutter Angelo stepped forward. But this time he kept his body from touching hers, and unexpectedly Gemma ached for the loss. The pull of the straps tightening as he knotted them was unbearably intimate and Gemma searched desperately for something to say to break the ghastly, growing silence.

What was there to say to the man who'd pleasured her so thoroughly without taking the time to remove her dress or her panties? Hell, despite her dislike and distrust, she'd let him do what he wanted, touch where he wanted without a murmur.

She shuddered with shame.

Telling herself she despised him didn't help. She'd driven him on, rubbing herself against him like… Oh, God! She flushed at the memory of what she'd done… her lack of restraint. Fully clad, Angelo had touched her with only with his mouth and the fingertips of one hand and brought her more ecstasy than she could ever remember experiencing.

She wanted to run. To hide. Before her composure gave way.

"I'll find my way from here. You don't have to come any farther." Then she closed her eyes as she replayed her own words and waited for him to point out that he hadn't come. Yet.

"I will walk you to your unit." His voice was colder than winter. "The sooner your contract ends and you leave Strathmos, the better for both of us."

"I'll leave tomorrow," Gemma blurted out, her eyes stinging. "Leave me alone. I don't want your company."

Once inside her unit, Gemma flipped the kettle on with hands that trembled, and blinked away the tears that blurred her vision. Feeling utterly wretched, she craved a mug of camomile tea to soothe her shattered nerves while the aftershocks of their terrifyingly passionate encounter quaked through her.

She couldn't stay.

She would leave Strathmos tomorrow, catch the first ferry out—even if it meant breaking her contract and putting her professional reputation on the line. She could not do this.

Never had it crossed her mind that she would melt under Angelo Apollonides's touch, press her body up against his, encourage his kisses. He was a suave playboy. No one knew better than she.

Oh, God. How had she gotten herself into this fix? Distraught, Gemma speared her shaky fingers through her hair.

She needed to get a grip. Fighting for control, she tried to think analytically about what had happened out there, under the cold stars. Okay, so she'd provoked him. Intentionally. But she hadn't expected him to react so fiercely, to move so quickly. His cool eyes, his mocking smile, his legion of beautiful cookie-cutter lovers had indicated Angelo wasn't a man given to impulse. That devastating kiss—and what had followed—stunned her.

He was far more dangerous than she'd ever known.

When the kettle clicked off, she reached into the cupboard for a mug and poured boiling water over the teabag. *Why had she risked all the ground she'd made by provoking him?* What had she hoped to gain? What was it about Angelo that made her itch to disconcert him? To prove to him she wasn't the woman he thought he was?

Cradling the mug between her hands, she propped her elbows on the bench top. The photo at the end of the bench top mocked her.

Setting her tea down, she picked up the photo. It looked like such an idyllic family. Mum and Dad flanking their smiling, all-grown-up daughter against a backdrop of lovingly tended rosebushes. Tears pricked again. Gemma craved a dose of her mother's kind common sense. Checking her watch she calculated that in New Zealand it would be morning. She picked up the handset from the wall and punched in the familiar number of her childhood home.

"Hello?"

Despite the distance her mother's voice was clear and familiar.

Gemma swallowed the lump in her throat. "It's me, Mum."

"Sweetheart, I'm so glad you've called. I've been worried sick about you!"

"I should've called sooner." Gemma had known her parents were worried. She'd been avoiding their concern. "But you know I had to come."

"Yes." Her mother's voice held a touch of resignation. "Has it helped?"

The grief counsellor had supported Gemma's determination in the face of her parents' objections. Closure came in strange ways. And that's what this trip was about, closure. "I don't know. Mum, I'm so confused." Gemma thought of Angelo's effect on her, how he only had to touch her to send her up in flames and gulped. "Sometimes I feel like I'm losing my mind." But tomorrow that would end. She would leave…and never see Angelo Apollonides again. It was for the best—even if it meant she'd never know the truth…

"How is Dad?"

"Fine."

"No, I mean, how is he handling my coming to Strathmos? He was very upset when I left."

Her mother sighed. "He's worried. And it's opened up the memories about your sister's death. He's afraid of what might happen to you."

"Tell him I'm fine…and I love him."

"He's gone back to therapy. The doctor says he's over the worst of the depression. For him, like you, the hardest part was not knowing why Mandy died."

"Double trouble, that's what Dad used to call us." Staring at the photo, Gemma searched the face of her twin for answers. Mandy had died, unhappy and lost. But no one knew why. Only Angelo could provide the answers that would let her father—and Gemma herself—find a little peace.

Closure.

That's what they all needed.

And that was why she could not tell Angelo to go to hell and walk away. Cold seeped in, chilling her all the way to her soul.

She could not leave tomorrow.

"Oh, *sweetheart*. Come home."

"I can't." Her lips barely moved. "I have to find out what happened to Mandy. For all our sakes. Then we can get on with our lives."

"Oh, Gemma. Your sister wouldn't want you to suffer like this, she'd want you to remember the special times you had together."

"I know. But I need to understand what happened to her…what this bastard did to her and why she reacted like she did. Dad and you need to know, too."

"Your father and I don't want you meddling with this man." Her mother's voice was anxious. "He's wealthy, powerful. He could hurt you."

Like he hurt Mandy.

Gemma knew what her mother was thinking. But the words remained unspoken.

"Mum…" Gemma's voice trailed away. She thought of what had just happened between her and Angelo. If her parents knew about that…they'd be on the next flight out to rescue her.

"Have you spoken to him? What did he say?"

Reluctant to admit that she hadn't confronted Angelo about Mandy's death, and even more loath for her mother to discover that Angelo believed she was Mandy, Gemma spoke in a rush. "I wanted to find out what kind of man he is first."

"And what kind of man is he?"

Compelling. Passionate. "It's difficult to explain."

"Gemma, be careful." The sigh came over the miles. "You're not Mandy. Chasing after trouble was her speciality, not yours. You were always the sensible one, Gemma."

Her mother was right, Mandy had always been a little…wild. Taking Gemma's passport and credit card to Strathmos and assuming Gemma's identity was only one of the pranks Mandy had played.

Oh, Mandy, what happened on Strathmos?

Gemma couldn't help thinking about the familiarity in the Frenchman's tone earlier, his easy kiss. She remembered Angelo's hard gaze, the coiled tension in his muscled body. She remembered the taste of his mouth—hot and seductive against hers—the thrill of his body pressing into hers and her pleasure as she came apart under his touch.

Once again confusion and turmoil wrestled within her. God! How could she teach the bastard the lesson he deserved if she desired him?

And how could she face him again?

Gemma squeezed her eyes shut. How on earth could she have reacted like that to the man who had destroyed her sister?

Four

Gemma tossed and turned for most of the night. Several times she jerked awake from confusing dreams of what had happened in her sister's life. Beneath it all festered an uneasiness about the disturbing passion that had flared between herself and Angelo. Just before dawn the pitter-patter of rain against the window pane lulled her into a restless sleep.

In the morning she clambered out of bed, crossed to the window and hitched the curtain back. No sun peeked through the cloud cover. The trees outside swayed in the wind. But at least the rain had subsided. With her morning free of rehearsals and her next show scheduled for later that evening, Gemma decided to make for the beach to go windsurfing. That was one place where wet and wind wouldn't matter. And it would certainly shake the dark mood that gripped her and take her mind off Mandy, Jean-Paul and... Angelo.

Pulling on a sleek black maillot, she called reception to check that no storms were forecasted, then grabbed her wet suit out of the cupboard and trod into a pair of ancient sneakers. A couple of bananas, a bottle of water and a towel, and she was ready to go.

The beach was deserted. To Gemma's relief, there were no whitecaps on the water. A gust of wind tugged at her hair as she hauled a windsurfing board out of the stack. Dragging the board into the sea, she waded calf-deep into the water and waited with both hands on the boom. When a puff of wind came, she pushed the mast straight up and stepped onto the centre of the board. Shifting her feet, Gemma adjusted the sail and, looking upwind, she turned the board to the open sea.

The sail filled and she took off, the wind rushing past her ears. She barely noticed the rain and her worries evaporated as she raced across the water.

She welcomed the freedom.

A couple of hours later Gemma became aware of another windsurfer on the water, coming towards her through the rain. Leaning her mast back, the nose of her board started to turn upwind across the face of the wind, away from the intruder. But the other windsurfer gained on her, trespassing on her solitude.

A quick glance at her watch showed that she still had lots of time before her show. It wasn't often that she had the sea to herself. Why would she go in simply because someone was crowding her? There was a whole sea for the two of them. If she tacked away, perhaps the other windsurfer would get the hint.

But the larger black-and-white sail continued to bear down on her. Glaring at him—it was undoubtedly a male figure—Gemma's annoyance grew when she recognised the windsurfer.

Angelo.

Setting a course upwind, Gemma decided to force him to yield to her. A glint of white as his teeth flashed. *He knew what she was up to.*

Determined to get ahead, she started to work every ounce of speed out of her rig. The board responded willingly and elation swept through her.

Then she saw that Angelo had taken up her challenge.

For a moment she thought that they might collide. She faltered, her board wobbled and her nerve almost gave in, before he gave way, falling back to sail in her wake. Her sail shivering under the pressure of the wind, she skimmed across the water, while her heart beat rapidly at the near miss—and the euphoria that came from racing the wind…and besting Angelo.

Angelo stared after Gemma not sure whether to whistle in admiration or holler at her recklessness. She was going full tilt, not giving an inch. He pointed his board to a destination upwind of where she was headed, and he set off after her.

The breeze blew on his face, lighter on the inside near the shore. He came down the line he'd planned, unfazed by the rain, tacking with speed and closing his distance on Gemma.

She turned, glancing over her shoulder as he gained on her. He could see the determination in her stance. This was no beginner. She was going to give him a good run.

They battled it out downwind. Her jaw was set. She wasn't giving an inch. She wanted to win. Despite the rain, her hair streamed behind her like a bright banner, a lithe graceful figure in tune with the elements.

Never had he wanted her as much as he did at the moment. She looked elemental and a little elusive. Not the sure thing he'd always considered her.

Working furiously, Angelo finally notched ahead and threw a triumphant smile over his shoulder, confident that the race was done.

The next instant the wind dropped and the rain eased. Both boards slowed. Angelo bit back a curse at being deprived of a clear victory. He dropped down to straddle the board and, glancing sideways, saw that Gemma had dropped onto her stomach and was already paddling with her arms and making for the shore.

Pacing himself, he kept abreast of her, his powerful arms stroking through the water. But she didn't look at him, she kept her gaze firmly ahead.

In the shallows, keeping her face averted, Gemma leapt off the board, dragging it in behind her, intensely conscious of Angelo following close behind.

Flutters of apprehension started deep in her stomach, and the battle of the last half hour between them was forgotten as the memory of what had happened between them last night rose in her mind.

She didn't know how she was going to face him.

The attendant, now at his post, came running to take the board. She gave a brief, abstracted smile of thanks. Her saturated sneakers squishing with water, she hurried to where she'd dropped her towel and water bottle earlier. Collapsing onto a damp wooden bench, she uncapped the bottle and took a long sip, her heart banging against her ribs as Angelo approached.

He stopped beside her. She stilled, then took another sip, pretending to ignore him, while every nerve ending quivered warily at his closeness.

"You never told me you could windsurf."

The rasp of the zip sounded loud in the silence. Gemma was achingly aware of his peeling off his wet suit and slinging it over the back of the bench. Underneath he wore a pair of boardshorts that rode low on his hips. The unwelcome memory of last night clear in her mind, Gemma tried not to notice that his stomach was taut and tanned, the defined muscles revealing that he worked out regularly—or led a very active lifestyle.

Gemma whipped her gaze away and shrugged. "I don't know why I didn't tell you. I would've thought I had." Why had Mandy not told him? Especially as it was clear it was something Angelo excelled at. Her parents had paid for lessons for both her and Mandy to learn to windsurf down at Buckland's Beach, near their childhood home. Mandy had been more interested in flirting with the youths in the class than learning to sail. Deciding to distract him with flattery Gemma added, "You're good. Those were some great moves out there."

But Angelo didn't bite. "So, when are you leaving?"

Gemma drew a deep, shuddering breath. "I'm not." His expression never altered, but she sensed his sudden tension.

"Last night you said you were going, why have you changed your mind?"

Even though his tone remained even, his eyes told a different story. Her gaze fell before his challenging stare, landing on his legs. His thighs were solid, the skin darkened to a deep bronze by the Greek sun. She felt herself flush and quickly looked away over the sea. She didn't want this awful awareness of this man. "Because my reputation would be mud in entertainment circles if I walked away from my contract."

"I would see to it that didn't happen."

He wanted her gone that much? Gemma swallowed, then said baldly, "I can't go, I need the money."

A coolness entered his voice. "Is this where I'm supposed to offer to pay you to leave?"

"No!" Gemma jerked her head up to stare at him, horrified by the conclusion he'd drawn. "But I've got a contract and I'm entitled to payment for doing my job. I need it."

"What do you need the money for?" Angelo dropped down beside her and his arm stretched along the back of the bench, so that it rested behind her head.

She thought furiously. "Medical expenses," she said at last, trying to ignore his arm. It wasn't easy. "From the…er…car accident." She swallowed again and stared out over the sea.

"That's what caused your amnesia?"

Damn. What to say now?

The silence stretched. He was waiting for her reply. Gemma discovered she wasn't crazy about lying to him. Strange, because she'd never thought it would worry her in the least. Not after what he'd done.

"Witnesses say it was a hit and run," she expanded, sticking to the story she'd originally planned. "Luckily when I came round in hospital I remembered who I was. But I don't remember anything about you, about Strathmos…or anything that happened for a while after I left Strathmos."

"So you're suffering from retrograde amnesia. You lost the events immediately before the accident."

Retrograde amnesia? Gemma blinked. "Uh…yes." His interest took her aback. She gave him a weak smile. "Have you been doing research?"

"A little. Did you experience any memory loss after the accident?"

This time she was prepared. "Yes. There was some anterograde amnesia. I remember waking up in hospital. I don't remember the accident itself—or getting to the hospital. The specialists did say that the events I could no longer recall before the accident might return as time passed. But to date they haven't. I lost several weeks of my life." She delivered the explanation as she'd prepared it.

"Was there any other damage?" His fingers brushed her shoulder. Despite the thick protection of the Neoprene wet suit, Gemma felt as though she'd been scorched.

"No, I was fortunate," she said a trifle huskily as shivers coursed through her.

"Nothing lucky about it," he said abruptly. "Such an accident should never have happened. Did the police catch the perpetrator?"

"No." Gemma fidgeted. She hadn't expected his concern and outrage on her behalf. She folded her arms across her stomach, feeling terrible. Then she recalled her father's depression, her mother's tears after Mandy's unnecessary death. Instantly her heart hardened. "Now can you understand why I need money?"

"What will you do when you finish here?"

"My agent is looking for something for me." There had been offers, but Gemma hadn't been in a hurry to take another booking. She hadn't been sure how long she needed on Strathmos to learn the truth.

"So long as you know that your contract to sing here will not be extended. I don't want you here."

Gemma gulped. That was pretty direct. It also meant that she had less than three weeks to find out the truth. "I understand."

Two days passed without catching sight of Angelo. On Wednesday morning Gemma lounged beside the resort's heated outdoor pool, soaking up the mild early morning sunshine. She'd heard that Angelo sometimes swam laps after breakfast before the resort guests started to congregate.

Huge sheets of glass shut out the unpredictable autumn wind without obscuring the view of the Aegean. In the centre of the pool a marble quartet of golden winged horses danced under the spray that jetted from three tall fountains. Through half-closed eyes, Gemma could almost imagine the mythical beasts thundering across the heavens, steered by the sun god.

A young poolside waiter had just delivered a tall glass topped with a pink umbrella and a row of cherries on a swizzle stick when a familiar voice shattered the fantasy.

"So this is where you've been hiding."

Tensing, Gemma wished she was wearing more than

the tiny bikini with the skimpy bandana top. Hidden behind sunglasses, she said, "Don't you have more important things to do than look for me?"

Angelo waved his hand dismissively. "You told me you are here for the money. Right?"

"Y-es," she stretched the word out, waiting, wondering why his eyes had turned as hard as stone.

He dropped down on the lounger beside hers; only a low glass-topped table on which her drink stood separated them. Uncomfortably conscious of his closeness, Gemma pushed her sunglasses firmly up her nose, grateful for the protection they offered from his icy scrutiny.

"I've just learned you wanted this contract badly enough to take a drop in pay." His voice was edged in steel. "I want to know why. How could you afford to do that with the medical expenses you cried about only a couple of days ago?"

Raising her shoulder, Gemma dropped it with false aplomb. "I took the drop because I was desperate for money. I needed an income—I haven't been getting regular work."

His gaze glittered with suspicion. "You once told me that one of the joys of being an exotic dancer is that there's always work. So if you were short of work why sing? Why not dance?"

Gemma forced herself not to shudder. She'd never understood why Mandy danced or how she put up with the hoards of leering men—even if the money was good. "Uh—I don't do that anymore. I love singing." That, at least, was true. "And singing pays more when I get the right spots, which I'm getting more often. I'm on the rise."

"What's this?"

Something in his sharp tone turned her head. He was scowling at the glass the waiter had brought. She frowned, puzzled at his ferocity.

"You can't drink before you sing."

"Not even fruit juice?" she asked tartly. He looked unconvinced, so Gemma picked the glass up and thrust it at him. "Here, sniff it."

"Very clever." At her baffled frown, he added. "Given that your preferred drink is vodka, sniffing won't help much. Not with the overpowering flavour of pineapple."

Of course! Mandy had always been partial to vodka. "My only vice," Gemma said at last.

"*Only* vice?" His smile was sharklike. Setting the glass down, he leaned closer.

This close up his eyes were mesmerizing. The vibrant turquoise irises were surrounded by a row of lashes too long for a man. Dark brows arched over the top. No question about it, Angelo Apollonides was the most gorgeous male she had ever set eyes on. Pity he was not her type.

"It's the only one I can think of right now," she said carelessly. "If I thought about it very hard, I might discover one or two more."

His mouth flattened. "Try. I'm sure you will find there are more vices that you will remember. Like lying."

Gemma's breath left her in a rush.

"When did I lie?" Did he know? She gave him a searching look as adrenaline started to pump through her. *God.* What would he do if he discovered—

"When I discovered you'd taken a drop in pay, I thought you lied to me. That you had another agenda. Don't ever lie to me."

She almost collapsed from relief. So she glared at him. "I'm *not* lying. I do need money. My credit card is a little over-extended." The thirty-thousand dollar debt merited a bigger description than *little*.

"Too much shopping and partying?"

If he only knew. While Mandy had been a party animal, Gemma preferred spending her spare time outdoors. Walking. Windsurfing. Or simply attending concerts in parks. Simple pleasures, not the sophisticated pursuits his mistresses would enjoy.

She pursed her lips. How could she admit how much money had vanished, and that she had no idea where it had gone? The large cash withdrawals her credit-card statements reflected told her nothing.

"You had no debt three years ago. And some nice pieces of jewellery." He gave a pointed stare at the ring she wore. The ring Mandy had given her just before she had died and Angelo had claimed to have bought for Mandy in Monaco.

"I don't know what happened to all that," she said honestly.

He gave her a searching look. "You don't remember?"

She nodded.

"I was more than generous," he said. "I indulged your desire to party, to shop until your cupboards were overflowing. If you'd behaved better, you might not be in this predicament."

Surely Angelo wasn't suggesting they might still be together? Not when she knew the kind of man he was. A playboy. A man who traded one beautiful woman for another, as soon as their temporary sell-by date was over.

Her lip curled. "You mean, if I was still your mistress? Putting up with your demands, your—"

"I thought you'd forgotten everything. So how do you remember how demanding I was?" His tone held a sensual rasp, belied by his shrewd gaze.

"I read gossip cuttings. How do you think I learned about our affair?"

He reached out and put finger a finger under her chin. He put enough pressure to tilt her head up, so that he could stare down into her eyes. "So you came here not only to earn money and regain your memory, but to learn more about us?"

The sudden flare of heat that followed in the wake of the touch of that one finger shocked her. *No.* She was not going to respond to his very obvious attraction. He was the last man on earth to whom she could afford to be attracted.

A spoilt playboy who'd had a fortune handed to him on a plate. A dilettante who destroyed people without compunction. Keeping her voice level she said, "I know exactly what kind of man you are."

"Do you really?" He raised a dark eyebrow, looming over her.

Too close. Too male. Too…everything.

She backpedaled. "I don't remember anything, but I know how you make me feel."

"And how is that?" The pressure of the pad of his index finger lessened. The tip trailed down her throat and settled just below the tender hollow at the base of her neck. The touch felt like a brand.

Oh, no. She spotted the trap too late. She swallowed. "Repelled."

He bared his teeth in triumph at the tiny give away as her throat moved. "Ah, you tempt me to prove you a liar."

Gemma gave an uneasy laugh. "Perhaps I haven't been completely honest with you."

His pupils expanded. "Go on."

"I came here to ask for your help." She sucked in a breath. "I woke alone in a hospital in London with no memory of how I got there, who I'd been with at the time of the accident or where I'd been."

His hand dropped away.

Gemma could breathe again.

Until he spoke. "You weren't able to track down information from the people with you at the time of the accident?"

She had to be careful. She couldn't afford to trip herself up. "The only clue about where I'd been was a bunch of old pay slips from Palace of Poseidon." She'd found them in her sister's things. "Later I found out that I'd worked here…that we'd had an affair."

More lies. It hadn't been later. Mandy had e-mailed her from Strathmos, crowing about the fabulously wealthy man she'd landed.

Gemma stared at him defiantly. "That's why I'm here. I thought if I came…back…met you, I might re-member something about—" she paused "—my past."

His expression altered subtly. He came closer. "Is it working?"

"No." Her voice turned husky. She picked up a towel and draped it over her bare, exposed tummy. "I had hoped by staying on Strathmos some things might come back to me. But they haven't." She paused for a beat, peered up at him over the top of her sunglasses. "But perhaps if you helped, if you let me ask you some questions, maybe something you say might act as a trigger. And the past might come back to me."

She waited, holding her breath, her blood hammering in her head, causing it to ache with tension. What had Angelo done to reduce Mandy from a confident, somewhat reckless party girl to a pale, shaking ghost of her former self?

She *had* to find out.

At last he gave a curt nod. "But if it doesn't work, that's it. Okay? You leave as soon as your contract is complete." He rose to his feet. "We'll start tonight, after your show."

"I'd rather meet in the mornings."

"I'm a busy man. If you want my help then you'll have to meet me tonight. In my suite."

"No." Gemma shook her head emphatically, her hair swirling around her face. The last thing she wanted was to be alone with him. The attraction he held terrified her. While she desperately wanted to know what he'd done to her twin, she was not about to let him destroy her in the process. "I'll meet you after the show in the Dionysus bar."

For a moment Gemma thought she'd lost him. Then he said, "You're on."

Five

When Gemma hurried into the Dionysus bar later that night it was buzzing. She hesitated, scanning the press of people, until Angelo rose from a table near the window. Outside, the resort's landscaped gardens were lit by floodlights. Beyond them she could see the lights of vessels winking out on the dark sea.

"Sorry I'm late," she gasped. "I had to shower and change." She indicated to the shimmery wraparound dress that she'd slipped on.

"No problem." He pulled out a chair for her. "How did the performance go?"

"Good. It never fails to put me on a high."

Angelo beckoned to a waiter. "What can I order for you to drink?"

"A white-wine cooler would be good—with lots of sparkling water, ice and a little lime, please."

He gave her a long look. "Are you sure that's what you want? Your performance is over. You can have something more…robust if you want."

The euphoria left her. She sagged into the chair. "I don't drink much of the hard stuff. But thanks."

Gemma watched him as he spoke to the waiter. What had his relationship with her sister been like? Mandy had always loved to party…and the kind of men she'd picked tended to have no problem with that. But Angelo seemed almost disapproving. Not what she'd expected from his playboy personna at all.

When he turned back, Gemma—unable to let his comment pass—said, "Strange for an hotelier to be watching his guests' liquor consumption." With a sweep of her arm, she encompassed the full-to-capacity bar. "Can't be good for business."

"You're not a guest, you're an employee," he said quellingly. "And you don't have a great track record."

"What do you mean?"

He shook his head. "Be grateful that you don't remember."

"But I *want* to know."

"You're better served moving on from those events. It's enough for you to know that you had a…problem."

A problem that he had exacerbated?

Gemma studied his expression. To be fair, it didn't look like he'd approved of Mandy's antics…whatever they had been. Was it possible that he'd had nothing to do with Mandy's slide from grace?

He forced me. I loved him. I wanted to please him. I was ready to do whatever he wanted. And it made me feel good. I'm so sorry for failing you all.

The memory of Mandy's words caused Gemma to steel herself. No. Angelo was *not* uninvolved. He'd destroyed her twin.

But before she could tell him what a low-life skunk she considered him, their drinks arrived.

Angelo passed a long glass to her. "So what do you want to ask me?"

She stared at him blankly.

"That's why we're here, remember?" His smiled was sardonic. "So that you can ask me questions, to try and jolt your memory."

Oh, yes. She gave herself a gentle shake. Nothing would be served by telling him what she thought of him. Better to focus on what she'd come here for—to learn what had happened to Mandy…to find a way to make Angelo pay.

Gemma took a sip of her drink. It was cool and refreshing. "You wanted to know why I need money. In addition to the medical expenses—" she broke off, reluctant to perpetuate that lie, then blurted out, "I want to know why there was thirty thousand owing on my credit card. Do you know where it went?"

"I have no idea."

"I drew cash out with my credit card and ran through it in your casinos, didn't I?" She was pushing him now, but she wanted answers. She wanted him to confess what he'd gotten Mandy into. "*Your* casinos. *Your* fault I'm thirty-thousand in the red."

"You liked to gamble…I didn't force you. But I wouldn't call you an addict."

Gemma flinched. "But it would've been more than I could afford."

"Your chips went on my account. It didn't cost you a euro. You must have accumulated your debts—" he picked the word with fastidious care "—after you left me."

"So where I did I go from Strathmos?"

He lifted a negligent shoulder. "I have no idea."

"Nor did you care—certainly not enough to buy me a ticket to make sure I reached home safely."

A frown creased his brow, he picked up his drink and leaned back. "I'm a generous man. I gave you a more than a plentiful allowance while you lived with me. Gold cards, a supply of cash that you ran through like water." There was distaste in his tone now. "You could have saved that for a rainy day."

Gemma opened her mouth to argue, then shut it again. His words held the unmistakeable ring of truth.

"I regret the hit-and-run left you floundering for your memory." The sympathy in his eyes faded as he continued, "But you're an adult. You've worked in nightclubs in London, Paris. You considered New Zealand a backwater. I assumed you'd simply find another big city, another big-spending benefactor to fund your love of the high life."

She blinked. While he'd clearly enjoyed having Mandy in his bed, it didn't sound like he'd held her twin in high regard. Poor Mandy.

He set his glass down. "After I found you with Moreau I didn't give a damn where you were going. Right then I hoped you'd drown in the sea. You'd betrayed me, in the worst way that a woman can betray a man. I couldn't wait to see the back of you."

Gemma flinched at his bitter words. Yet under the white-hot anger she suspected that Angelo was telling the truth. He *didn't* know where Mandy had gone after leaving him. Could that mean that she'd misjudged him? Had he had nothing to do with Mandy's problems? Had they only started after her sister left Strathmos?

Her shoulders sagged. She'd had such high hopes that Angelo would provide the key to the puzzle. Then she thought about what he'd said, and lifted her head. "Did I leave the island with Jean-Paul?"

He shrugged. "It's possible. I wanted him out my sight, too."

Perhaps the Frenchman could provide a clue to what had happened. Angelo's face had tightened at the mention of the other man. She changed the subject. "You said that you inherited a string of family hotels from your grandfather. How did they transform into this?" Gemma gestured to the bar and, beyond it, the resort.

"On my twenty-first birthday, I inherited three islands and a chain of three-star holiday hotels geared to foreign budget tourists. My grandfather had been ill for a while. The hotels were shabby, showing their age. While they were well booked over the summer months, they were deserted in winter. I knew I could do more. I wanted resorts where occupancy was guaranteed all year round."

"That's why you went for casinos?"

He nodded. "But I wanted more than glamorous casinos. I wanted places where everyone in the family would have a good time. That meant themed resorts, cinemas, a variety of shows that would draw people back again."

"You achieved everything you set out to do."

He nodded. "It took a while. I first worked at upgrading the hotels I had. I knew the first spectacular resort had to be built here at Strathmos. It was my dream. I hadn't been back to the island since I left as an eighteen-year-old. Once I got it up, Poseidon was born."

"And now Poseidon's resorts are associated with worlds of fantasy." She tried to hide her admiration by giving the words a bite. "The Golden Cavern. The Never-Ending River." She named some famous drawcards.

His gaze narrowed. "You remember? You remember visiting them with me?"

The damned amnesia. She'd nearly given herself away. Slowly she shook her head. "I told you, I tried to put together the missing parts of my memory so I read up about our relationship in the tabloids. There were bits about Poseidon's Resorts, too. Like their fantasy themes and what they're worth today. About how innovative you were." And on the Internet there had been endless details about the wealthy, powerful and good-looking Angelo Apollonides, Mr. Eligible Bachelor Billionaire of the Year. But she wasn't telling him any of that. The last thing she wanted was for him to think he interested her. Gemma shifted, uncomfortable with where this conversation was heading.

She could barely hide her relief when the duty manager arrived and whispered into Angelo's ear.

"I'm sorry," he apologised. "I am needed. And we've barely gotten started."

"Don't worry. We can talk again some other time."

"Shall I order you another drink?"

"No, I'm done." She pushed the empty glass aside. "I might wander over to one of the coffee bars. And then I'll make my way back to my room. I can use an early night. Don't worry about me."

He rose and gave her a slow smile. "I find that I can't help worrying about you." And her heart twisted.

And then he was gone.

Still thinking about that delicious smile—and her reaction to it—Gemma picked up her purse and threaded her way through the packed bar to the exit—where she almost ran into Jean-Paul.

"Steady, *cherie*." He caught her by the elbows. "Can I buy you a drink?" His dark eyes lingered on her appreciatively.

Sensitive to Angelo's accusation that Mandy had cheated on him with the Frenchman, and Angelo had warned her in no uncertain terms to stay away from him, Gemma's first response was to refuse. But what if Mandy had left Strathmos with Jean-Paul? Gemma hesitated, then thrust her scruples aside.

She needed to talk to this man.

"I'd love a drink." She gave him a bright smile to make up for her hesitation. He was back in minutes with two glasses.

"What is it?" she asked, eyeing the clear liquid uneasily.

"Surely you didn't think I could forget, *cherie*? You're the only woman I ever knew who drank triple vodka and tonic like water." He gave her a very knowing smile. "The secret of your success, you called it. And what made you so exciting."

Angelo strode out of the Apollo Club. It hadn't taken long to calm two furious patrons after an accusation of cheating in the discreet back room where a poker game with extremely high stakes was being played.

In the elevator he greeted an American IT billionaire and his wife who came to the Palace every few months.

Hurrying out the elevator, he glanced at his watch. Gemma should be back in her unit by now. Downstairs, he stopped beside a porter kiosk and called reception requesting to be put through to her room. It rang unanswered.

Perhaps she was still in one of the coffee shops.

He made his way to the entertainment complex. He didn't find her in the first coffee shop. Nor in large alcove with soft armchairs where a pianist played Chopin. But as he passed the Dionysus Bar he caught a glimpse of copper flame.

Gemma.

Frowning, he ground to a halt and looked again.

It *was* Gemma. And she was not alone. Jean-Paul Moreau was standing beside her barstool, his arm resting on the bar beside his drink, looking utterly enthralled by her.

What the hell was she doing with Moreau?

He'd warned her to keep away from the man. The silver dress she wore showed off her curves and her hair was a vivid flag of colour against the pale fabric. Seated on the barstool, her sleek legs were shown off to maximum advantage.

Three years ago he'd felt nothing except anger and disgust for Gemma and he'd hardly thought of her in the intervening years. So what the hell had changed? Why could he not stop noticing every detail about her? Especially given that it was clear that nothing had changed—she still hankered after Moreau.

He gave a grim smile when she jumped as he stopped beside her.

"Angelo! I thought you were—"

"Busy?" he finished, and gave Moreau a cool nod.

"Well…yes."

"I sorted the problem out and came back to finish our conversation."

"Oh." Her eyes went round. She glanced in Moreau's direction.

Trying to work out how to dump the Frenchman, Angelo suspected.

"Another vodka?" Moreau offered.

Vodka? Angelo narrowed his gaze. A flush rose in her cheeks. *Guilt.* "I thought you didn't drink much of the hard stuff any more? In fact, I seem to remember mention of a hot drink in a coffee shop after I left you earlier."

"Gemma is of age," Moreau interjected. "She can drink whatever she desires."

"I told her to stay away from you." Angelo shot the Frenchman a killing look. Then he said to Gemma, "What the hell does it matter? Have another goddamned vodka with him."

Deeply disappointed he turned and walked away. He told himself he didn't care what she did. Gemma Allen was bad news. A liar. A faithless little cheat. The anger she'd ultimately caused him three years ago had not been worth the pleasure she'd given him in bed.

And she hadn't changed. The sooner he put her out of mind the better.

"Angelo…"

His long, angry strides had already carried him out

the bar, across the entertainment complex and he was headed for the lobby to the elevators that would take him to his penthouse.

"What?" He swung around, glaring down at her as a bolt of sensation shook him as she caught his sleeve. He didn't want this attraction. Not to this woman.

She released him. "Forget it."

"No, you're here now. So talk."

"I wanted to explain why I had a drink with Jean-Paul."

Her eyes were wide and dark. Gentle and pleading. He looked past her, clenching his jaw. All she wanted was his help to regain her memory. Nothing more. Better he remember that. "Drink with whom you please."

"I wanted to find out if he knew anything about the thirty thousand—"

"Forget about trying to find out what happened to the damned money. It's gone. Put your stupidity behind you. So you have some debt, so what? You're young, you can work it off." A pause, then he added softly, "On your back if need be."

Gemma's expression changed. He saw the fury, the darkness in her eyes as she registered the taunt. Her hand came up. She swung wildly. Angelo ducked, she missed. A glass vase from the glass table beside the elevator crashed to the ground. A party of guests took one horrified look at them and hurried past. Gemma barely noticed. Angelo knew he should rush after them, offer them a free night, gambling chips. Damage control.

But he didn't.

Right now Gemma had his full attention.

"How dare you?" She hissed. "How dare you say that, you…you…"

"Gorilla? Neanderthal?" Behind him the elevator opened. He took a deft step backward. "Who knows, I might even be convinced to consider taking you back to my bed and if you're very, very good—maybe I'll help clear that debt." And he hit the button for the roof garden.

She rushed forward, balling her fists and swung again. "I wouldn't sleep with you if you were the last—"

"Neanderthal in the world?" he finished with a hard laugh, and caught her flailing hands. "You might not be so lucky then. You've done it before, why the scruples now?"

He felt her stiffen with outrage. He secured her arms behind her back and pulled her up against him and his mouth slanted across hers.

She tensed.

The elevator shot upward. As his tongue delved into her mouth, Angelo felt her give and lean into him and the familiar arousal shafted through his lower body.

How could he have forgotten how soft her skin was? How full of life her red hair was? Or the little moaning noises she made into his mouth as she pressed against him? He couldn't remember her feeling…tasting…this good.

Hell, so maybe he had amnesia, too.

Distantly he heard the ping of the elevator door opening and the sound of talking and laughter. The rooftop garden was occupied.

Releasing her hands he pressed the ground-floor button and then they were sinking. Her tongue stroked against his, hot and deliberate. The fire inside went wild. He released her hands and cupped her buttocks, pulling her towards him. She came eagerly, rising on tiptoe, her body soft, melting against him like warm golden honey, and he ached with want.

He was tempted to yank open the bow on that wrap-around dress, unfurl her, rub his hand between her legs to check if she was damp enough to take him and slide into her slippery warmth. Only the knowledge of where they were stopped him.

An elevator. *Hell.* Given how annoyed she'd been minutes ago, she'd slap him for sure. Hard. Even if only after he'd driven them both to completion, tasted her satisfied sighs. No, better to take it slow.

Instead he slid his hands up…over the feminine curves of her bottom to her waist and back down again tracing the tiny string of an excuse for underwear she wore. Heard her breath catch…and hold. Taking advantage of her expectancy, he fingered the thong through her dress.

She wriggled against him, and he drove his tongue deep into her mouth, giving her a taste of what he wanted, what he really craved. She arched against him and he felt his erection leap.

The car shuddered to a stop. He lifted his head. "Carry on like that and I'll forget my good intentions. I'll hit the button for my suite. Three steps and we'll be in the dining room. Three minutes and we can both be naked. Is that what you want?"

"No." She shook her head wildly, her face shocked and pale. "I don't want this…you." She stumbled backwards out of the confined space, her hands covering her eyes. "God, what am I *doing?*"

He followed more slowly. Putting an arm around

her shoulder he guided her away from the public lobby. Out of sight. "What we've done many times before?" he said helpfully. Her hands dropped away from her face and she bit her lip, her teeth white against the bee-stung bottom lip as she glared at him. But something in her eyes, a deep agonised confusion made him stretch his hand out. "Hey, it's okay, I know you don't remember. But it doesn't matter."

"It matters." It was a wail. Then her head was back in her hands, her fingers knotting through the long dark red curls. "It matters more than I can tell you."

"It doesn't." He stroked her shoulder and noticed absently that his hand was trembling. "I'll tell you something, it's even better now than it ever was in the past. It's more…I can't explain. But I can't seem to get enough of you. The taste of you, the feel of your body up against mine. I want you, Gemma. Badly."

"Believe me, that's not good." The smile she gave him was wan.

"It will be very good," he promised, "you'll see."

"I can't." Her expression grew resolute. "Angelo, I can't make love to you—"

Irritation twisted inside Angelo. He wanted her. He wasn't accustomed to women saying no. "Why? You want to."

"That's arrogant." *But true.* She was terrified she was going to cave in to his demand. She drew a ragged breath. There was one thing he would understand. "I can't make love with you until my memory returns."

He cursed.

"Who knows," she added, "there might be someone else—"

"Someone so important that you don't remember him?" he sneered. "Someone like Jean-Paul Moreau?"

That only made her expression harden. "That's it. Good night. I'm finished with trying to talk to you. I'm going to bed. Alone."

Six

The ringing of the phone woke Gemma. Any plans she'd harboured to sleep late on Thursday—her day off—fell apart when Mark Lyme, the manager of the entertainment complex, told her that Lucie had come down with a flu-like virus. Immediately Gemma offered to take over some of Lucie's performances and arranged a time to meet with Mark to discuss a suitable program.

The Dionysus was a very different set-up to the Electra Theatre, and it had been years since she'd worked in a bar environment. Most of the day was spent putting together the program with Mark and Denny, another performer, for the first fill-in performance early that evening.

The substitute show was rough and ready but it was enough to satisfy the crowd. They sang a couple of duets, Denny told some jokes and they invited some of tourists to sing along karaoke-style.

Gemma caught a brief glimpse of Angelo in the back of the bar halfway through the evening. He was waiting for her and she found herself accepting his invitation to dinner. At first she fretted that he might try to kiss her…seduce her…but her worries proved to be unfounded. Angelo behaved like the perfect gentleman.

Lying in bed that night, Gemma covered her eyes and moaned out loud. *She was so confused.* Who was the real Angelo Apollonides?

By Friday Lucie's temperature was raging and Dr. Natos, the resort doctor, had prescribed bed and rest.

Gemma and Denny met for another rehearsal. During a brief break, she found Angelo at her elbow, holding two paper cups. "Coffee? I'm sure you could use it."

"What's that saying about not trusting Greeks who come bearing gifts?" She slanted him a provocative glance.

"Hardly a gift. Consider it an apology."

After a moment's pause she took the paper cup. "An apology?"

He looked abashed. "For my behaviour the other night. I should have apologised over dinner yesterday. But I didn't."

"Oh." She took a sip. It was strong and sweet and pungent.

He frowned. "I'm confused."

That made two of them! She slanted him a wary glance. "Why?"

"I had no intention of having anything to do with you. But I keep thinking you've changed. Then something happens—like seeing you with Jean-Paul—and I think I'm wrong. You're still the same." He raked his fingers through his golden hair. "Have you changed?"

She shut her eyes. *God.* How on earth was she supposed to respond to that? Not honestly. It was too late for that. She had to soldier on. And then there was the fact that she wasn't ready to face the rage and scorn in his eyes when he discovered her treachery. Not yet.

She'd tell him when she was about to leave. When her contract had ended. And she had uncovered the truth about Mandy. Whatever that might be.

He waved a hand. "Forget it. That's a stupid question. Sit down, you could probably use the break."

Gemma followed him dragging her feet as he led her to the cluster of seating in a small lobby.

His cell phone rang. Fishing it out his pocket, he studied the caller ID. "My mother," he said. "Excuse me."

Angelo could feel Gemma's eyes resting on him as he responded to his mother's well wishes. He listened with half an ear to a story about the car her latest husband had bought, laughed when expected. Conscious of keeping Gemma waiting, he cut the conversation short.

"For a playboy, you have a good relationship with your mother," Gemma said, her eyes curious.

He didn't rise to the bait. "Even playboys have mothers. And, despite all the wealth in the world, her life has not been easy," he answered guardedly. "She fell pregnant with me when she was very young. The man abandoned her. I never met him."

Not *my father,* but *the man,* Gemma noticed.

"Oh."

It must have been hell for a young boy.

"So is today your birthday?"

"Yes—I'm blessed with two celebrations in one month. Last week it was my name day."

"Name day? What's that?"

"A day all people bearing the name of a particular saint celebrate. So on the eighth of November anyone called Angelo celebrates. My mother thought I was an angel when I was born." He gave her a sardonic smile.

She laughed. "Did you get gifts?"

"Most people simply called to send greetings—that's what my cousins, Tariq, Zac and Katy did. My mother sent a gift. Some of the villagers who've known me all my life baked for me."

"O-kay." She suppressed a smile. From what she'd seen of him so far, he'd struck her as a jet-set prince. "I didn't have you pegged for the kind of guy who received home baking."

"I love home baking. But you didn't—too fattening, you said. In fact, you hardly used to eat at all. Your appetite is better now. You've stopped all those diet pills." He gave her a frank, appreciative look. "Now that I think about it, you've picked up a couple of pounds. It suits you. Makes you sexier than ever."

The air sizzled between them.

When she saw Mark waving, Gemma wanted to swear. Angelo had been opening up. She drained the cup and threw it in a trash can. "I have to go," she said to Angelo.

"I'll see you later." He gave her a wry smile. "And I

won't try to seduce you. At least not until your memory returns—unless you ask me very nicely."

That night Gemma and Denny delivered a far more polished show. Her own Friday night show in the Electra Theatre followed, and Gemma returned to her unit exhausted but more than satisfied with how the evening had gone. Kicking off her shoes, she switched on the kettle and made for the loveseat in the sitting area.

The knock on the door came as a total surprise. More surprise followed when the handle rattled and Angelo walked in, clad in dark trousers and a white dress shirt with black snaps. "You've forgotten to lock your door."

"Good evening," she said. "Shouldn't you be partying?" Surely there was no shortage of supermodels or starlets who he could've flown in to help him celebrate.

His gaze went past her to the bare table and neat kitchenette. "I take it you haven't had a chance to eat since your show?"

"No." She liked to wind down first. Then realization dawned. "I'm not having dinner with you. I'm tired."

"You need to eat."

"It's too late to go out."

"Who said anything about going out? We can eat right here, have a picnic on the bed, just like old times. I've ordered some of your favourites from room service. Bollinger, caviar, some crackers." He flashed her a triumphant smile, his teeth white and even against his tanned skin. "And you can't refuse—it's my birthday."

Her favourites.

Mandy's favourites. Suddenly she was wide-awake

and very, very edgy. A picnic on a double bed with Angelo sounded lethal. Even more dangerous than going to dinner with him in one of the resort's restaurants. Given her deception, spending time here in this small, intimate space would be stupid. "I'd rather go out."

Her unease was interrupted by another knock, softer this time.

Angelo's gaze locked with hers. "Too late. Dinner has arrived. No need to do anything. Just relax and enjoy. Nothing is going to happen between us. Not until your memory returns. I promised, remember? And I don't break my word."

But she had no intention of keeping hers.

There would be no return of her rogue memory. *Damn.* How had it ever gotten to the stage that Angelo Apollonides was starting to look like he had more honour than she did?

In the end, Angelo's impromptu birthday supper proved to be a lot of fun. They sat thigh to thigh on the loveseat and ate gourmet food off utilitarian white crockery.

Gemma was under no illusion that Angelo had set out to make her relax. And it was working. She found herself laughing at a story he told about capsizing a catamaran—and liking him more and more as the evening wore on.

On some level a hum of awareness vibrated between them. But it never surfaced enough to make Gemma jumpy and set her on edge. She believed Angelo's promise that he would not try make love to her…and she allowed herself to chill out.

At last the meal was finished. Even the rich chocolate cake, with a single candle on it that Angelo had blown out.

And, seeing that she had no gift, Gemma had insisted on singing "Happy Birthday." For the first time she had seen Angelo flush awkwardly.

After she'd finished giggling at his embarrassment, she'd risen to make coffee and Angelo had followed to help. Only to discover that tiny kitchen area was too cramped for two. So he settled for propping himself up against the counter and watching her prepare the blend. When the coffee was ready, she bustled around, tidying up and they chatted drinking the rich dark brew.

The mug clattered on the countertop as he set it down. When he commented, "Your hair suits you like it is now." She turned from packing away the crockery she'd rinsed off to smile at him, only to find him holding the framed photo of Mandy with their parents.

Gemma's heart came to a standstill. And then it started to race. After the rush of adrenaline came relief. Now he would discover the truth. With a shock Gemma realised that she wanted this masquerade to end. She was not cut out for deception.

His glance shifted between the photo and Gemma. "This must have been taken around the time I—" he hesitated "—knew you."

Her eyes narrowed. He hadn't realised the truth. He'd put the small external differences between her and Mandy down to the passing of time and superficial changes. As his gaze lingered on her, Gemma suspected he was considering the changes that lay below the all-covering jeans and shirt. As he'd noticed, she'd never been as thin as Mandy.

His eyes kindled an urge within her. The flame flickered, danced. Slowly. Sensuously. A womanly desire that refused to be banished.

"I like the curls more than the straight style you wore back then." He glanced down at the photo and back to her and his mouth softened into a smile that she suspected was supposed to melt her innards.

A hint of annoyance doused the desire. How could he not tell the difference between her and Mandy? Suddenly, perversely, she wanted to be found out. "My hair has always been wild," she said, a little tersely. "Curls are much less work."

"So why straighten it?"

She shrugged. "That was the fashion then."

"And you always do as fashion dictates, do you, Gemma?" Suddenly there was an edge in his voice. An edge she didn't understand.

"Excuse me?"

But his attention had returned to the frame cupped in his hands. "Are these your parents?"

"Yes." Gemma moved closer until she could also see the three figures in the photo. Dad was staring sideways at Mandy, while Mum smiled into the camera.

"Your mother's pretty. I can see her resemblance to you—and where the red hair comes from."

"Her name is Beth. She's really easygoing, despite the red hair." Yet despite Mum's normal placidity she'd been vocal in her opposition to Gemma coming back to Strathmos to confront Angelo. Mum had been worried, had begged Gemma to leave the past behind. But Gemma couldn't. She *had* to know…

"And your father looks so proud of you. Who's your mother smiling at?"

Gemma closed her eyes as a sharp burst of memory slivered through her of that sunny day in her parents' suburban garden against the foot of Pigeon Mountain in Auckland. She could remember the scent of the damask roses. She could feel the warmth of the sun on her back. She could remember Mandy laughing—

"I don't remember," she said tonelessly.

Something in her eyes must have alerted him to her confusion and pain because he came swiftly towards her. "Hell, of course you don't. And I'm a stupid idiot to ask such questions."

He was so close that Gemma could smell the scent of his skin overlaid with a tangy aftershave. A hint of amber, of musk…and something else.

Arousal.

A chill shot through her. No! She scuttled backward and collided with a chair jutting out from under the bench top and would have tripped if Angelo's hand hadn't shot out and stopped her from falling.

"Hey!" He yanked her upright. "Are you okay?"

His eyes were a rich turquoise, the colour of the sun-lit sea with no hint of black or grey. The thick brows above were pulled into a frown and Gemma read concern.

She could almost believe—

Damn! She broke free with a sharp twist. She recognized the sensation that unexpectedly flooded her. Recognized its warmth, its seductive danger—and it scared her spitless.

She swallowed, her mouth dry.

She'd been convinced that her hatred would fortify her against this attraction, like a talisman against evil.

So how was she supposed to deal with an Angelo she was beginning to like? Underneath the playboy exterior lay a complex man who was so much more than the media portrayed. She was even starting to doubt that he was the selfish manipulative lover Mandy had described.

"Are you okay?" he repeated.

"I'm fine," she said, and gave an elaborate yawn. "Just tired."

He got the hint but after he'd left, she felt more alone than she'd ever felt in her life.

Gemma was surprised when she looked out into the audience on Saturday night to see Angelo seated with a crowd of people at a table in the front of the Electra Theatre. Three women, all beautiful, and two men.

None of them were eating.

They must be here only for the show. She almost stumbled over her next line, recovered and then sang on, trying very hard not to look in their direction again.

She made it through the show without another stumble. By the time she got to the dressing room, Angelo was waiting.

"Come, there are people I want you to meet."

"I'm tired." It was an excuse. A lie. She was too wired to sleep.

In the end she convinced Angelo to let her shower and change and agreed to meet him at his penthouse—a huge space with black leather furniture and modern artwork and an endless expanse of glass that Gemma realised must showcase fabulous seaviews in the daytime.

The crowd turned out to be Angelo's cousins Zac Kyriakos and Tariq bin Rachid al Zayed and three women; Zac's new wife, Pandora, and Zac's sister, Katy, and their cousin, Stacy.

"We thought we'd surprise Angelo," Zac explained. "His birthday needed celebrating."

"You should feel honoured, Angelo," Pandora said darkly, "I braved a helicopter flight for you."

Angelo gave her a hug. "Thank you for coming. All of you."

A late-night meal had been arranged buffet-style on the sideboard. Grilled calamari, prawns on long elegant skewers and oysters on the shell. Spears of asparagus, slivers of capsicum, sticks of cucumber and sliced fruit added colour beside the seafood.

"Help yourself," Angelo told Gemma, setting down a glass of white wine on the low table beside the sofa on which she sat.

"I will." She threw him a smile and he surprised her by leaning over and brushing a kiss across her brow.

"A toast." Zac raised his wineglass. "To Angelo and many more birthdays."

They all echoed it and Angelo reciprocated by lazily raising his glass and proposing a toast to Pandora and Zac. Which led to Pandora suggesting that it was time for another wedding. A horrible silence followed.

"Don't look at me," Tariq grated. "I'm no advertisement for marriage."

Gemma assessed him. He stared back. She detected suspicion in his golden gaze. He was gorgeous in a stern, hawk-eyed kind of way and wore a long, flowing thobe—although his head was bare—that suited his air of command. She couldn't help wondering what had happened with his wife.

After dinner there was a large marzipan-iced cake, with candles for Angelo to blow out. Gemma grinned at him and decided to spare him another rendition of "Happy Birthday."

"Speech, speech," called Pandora. "Zac, *agapi mou,* come and sit." Pandora patted the cushion beside her. She was blonde and beautiful in a wistful kind of way.

Zac landed beside her and, pulling her onto his lap, he growled. "Don't call me *my love* in that fake way."

"Phony was what I said. Not fake." Pandora started to giggle and gave him a look brimming with love and humour, telling Gemma this was a very private joke.

"Ignore them," Katy advised, rolling her eyes to the ceiling. Gemma noticed that Katy had lines of strain around her eyes. "Pandora is the only person I've ever met who can put my overbearing brother in his place." Katy looked around with a frown. "Now, where is Angelo? Ah, getting out of making his speech and catching up with Tariq in the kitchen. Look at them, they must be talking about women."

Gemma noticed how close the men stood, both serious, their heads together. "I take it Tariq's marriage is unhappy," she murmured softly.

"They're separated. I think the experience totally put him off women," Katy confided.·

Gemma started to wonder what these forthright women would say about her later.

Katy seemed to read her mind. "Relax, we like you. Almost as much as Angelo does. Otherwise you wouldn't be getting the inside gossip."

"Angelo doesn't like me," Gemma protested.

"Mmm…maybe *like* isn't a strong enough word. We're not going to ask what happened between the two of you in the past—"

Pandora clambered off Zac's lap and came to stand beside Gemma. "Except that we hope you had a damn good reason for two-timing—"

"Hush. We agreed that was none of our business."

"It is none of your business," Stacy said, entering the conversation. She glared at the other two women.

Gemma stared at the three of them, bemused.

And then Angelo was beside her. "Are you okay?"

She turned her head. "Shouldn't I be?"

He perched beside her and slung an arm around her shoulder. "My family can be a little overwhelming at times."

Pandora and Katy started to laugh. "Come," said Stacy, "give them a break."

Later Angelo saw her back to her unit. The night was cool but there was no rain. The fact that the wind had died down meant that they could hear the hiss of the sea. "I think your family may have the wrong impression about us…me," Gemma said.

The lamps that edged the walkway shed enough light for her to see his eyebrows jerk up. "Why?"

"They seem to think that we're an item. And Katy didn't even seem worried that we'd broken off in the past. Although, I did detect some reserve from Tariq."

"He thinks I'd be mad to take up with you again."

"Oh?" The image of their heads close together in the kitchen came back to her. "You talked about me?"

"Tariq talked. He thinks you'll betray me again. Break my heart."

Gemma wanted to object. To deny that she'd ever do such a thing. Just in time she remembered that he thought she was Mandy. And Mandy had always been a flirt, a heartbreaker. So she drew a deep, steadying breath and asked, "So what did you say?"

In the shadows she could feel the force of his regard. "That I never loved you, so you never broke my heart. And it won't happen this time around, either."

Seven

Angelo and his family all left Strathmos on Sunday. Gemma heard the beat of the blades of the helicopter departing just after noon, but didn't realise that Angelo had gone until she found the note in the backstage pigeon hole where her mail was delivered.

Back next Sunday. See you then.

That was all. He hadn't even signed it. But she knew without doubt who had sent it.

Later she heard that he'd gone to Athens, that he'd be flying on to the resort at Kalos for a series of hush-hush meetings about a new opportunity he was investigating. Gemma had expected to feel relief at his absence, a cessation of the tension that twisted within her. But instead there was only an unfamiliar emptiness inside her.

Gemma suspected she was headed for heartbreak. Angelo had made it clear last night that there was no chance that he would ever love her. So she'd better take care to guard her hollow heart.

Gemma took one of the bicycles that the resort made available to the staff and guests and cycled down to Nexos, the small fishing village or *xorio,* not far from the resort.

The tables outside the local *taverna* were all taken. Most by locals playing *tavli,* backgammon. At one end, a fashionably dressed couple, clearly from the resort, shared a platter of *mezze* with olives and pita and a selection of spreads. Another young couple sat holding hands across a table. And a pang shot through Gemma.

There was no chance that she and Angelo would ever resemble these lover-like couples.

She turned away from the tables and chairs and wandered into the bakery beside the taverna, spoiling herself to a couple of *tiropites*—triangles of phyllo pastry filled with cheese—and a bottle of mineral water. She wheeled the bicycle across the cobbles and settled herself on the seawall to watch the fishermen spreading the nets in the sun and eat her impromptu lunch.

All around her, village life carried on. Across the road, two elderly widows dressed from head to toe in black were shuffling into the churchyard of the quaint white-washed church with its domed bright blue roof.

The church reminded her of Pandora's talk about weddings yesterday and Tariq's bitterness. Had he loved his wife? Why had his marriage fallen apart?

Of course, love was not strictly necessary for a marriage—or even for a relationship. Angelo had confessed last night that he'd never loved Mandy. What was it with these men?

Then she thought of the loving tenderness Zac demonstrated to Pandora and an ache settled in the region of Gemma's heart.

Unscrewing the top off the mineral water, she took a swig. She doubted Angelo would ever love anyone like that, without reserve. He was so self-contained, he didn't seem to need anyone.

For a fleeting instant Gemma couldn't help wondering whether he was alone now. His little black book would have no shortage of numbers of beautiful women to call on. If he chose to…

The thought depressed her.

Last night he'd made it clear that he was in no danger of falling for her. So much for her wild idea of making him pay.

She'd fantasised about proving to him that he wasn't irresistible to every woman in the world. That she held him in disdain. And she'd contemplated seducing him, making him fall for her, then rejecting him. But now she'd met him and found that he was so far out of her league that her half-baked plans were absurd.

She didn't dare seduce him. Because she suspected that once she'd made love with him, she would never be able to walk away. That she would be marked as Angelo Apollonides's woman for life.

She brushed the crumbs off her fingers and screwed the cap back onto the empty bottle. Sleeping with Angelo was not going to answer all her answers about why Mandy had died. And she could not betray her sister's memory in that fashion. Or risk her heart for a man who would never feel a thing for her.

In a little over a week it would be time to leave Strathmos…and Angelo. And move on. Strathmos was a foreign world, exotic and removed.

Angelo's world.

The empty place in her chest expanded, chilling her. Gemma took a last look at the fishermen on the beach. They looked so unhurried, so content.

Unlike her.

Biting her lip to stop the tears of loneliness that threatened, she rose to her feet and made her way to her bike. She would return to Auckland and get on with her life as her mother had suggested. Perhaps the familiar warmth of her family and friends would bring comfort. Tonight she would call her agent to line up the next gig.

The time had come to lay Mandy to rest.

With Lucie back at work on Monday, Gemma's frenzied schedule returned to normal. Yet she was restless. And her mood was mirrored by the unpredictable weather. Gusts of wind and bursts of hard rain shook the island. Gemma threw herself into her show and a couple of days passed before she had time to draw breath.

Weather allowing, she'd intended to spend her day off on Thursday windsurfing. The morning dawned clear and sunny with enough wind for a good run across the chop. But Gemma's heart wasn't in it. In less than thirty minutes she was back on shore, refusing to admit to herself that windsurfing alone was no longer what she desired.

She missed Angelo.

Blocking out that traitorous thought, she spent the afternoon in the entertainment centre. The resort staff had started erecting a giant Christmas tree and, with nothing else to do, Gemma stayed to help.

It was bittersweet hanging the decorations. It had been a while since she'd celebrated Christmas. Her family had avoided it…Christmas Day had become a time of grief.

As she reached up to hang a silver ball on a branch, her cell phone trilled.

It was Angelo.

Immediately her pulse quickened; the tree seemed greener, the lights around her brighter. For the first time since he'd departed she felt truly alive.

"Missing me?" he asked, humour in his voice.

"Of course not," she lied. "I've been too busy to think about you."

There was a little flat silence. Then he asked what she'd been doing. Gemma told him about the awful weather, the winds and the rain. He laughed a little when she commented that this was not what she expected of life on a Greek island.

"Christmas is coming," he said, "expect more rain."

"Oh, no." Then she told him about the Christmas tree that she was decorating. "It's always strange to see decorations out in November. I can see why your grandfather's tourists came only in the summer months. And I can understand why you've created the casinos and laid on all the entertainment you do. The resort is seething with people."

"Good." He sounded distracted. There was a short silence. Then he said, "I will be back early on Sunday morning. I always attend the Sunday service in the village when I am on Strathmos. Will you come with me this Sunday?"

Spend time with Angelo?

"Of course. But I need to be back for a rehearsal afterward." Even though she knew she was setting herself up for heartbreak by continuing to see him, Gemma simply couldn't resist.

The rest of the week dragged past.

Gemma had just taken a call from her agent on Sunday morning with an offer to sing in a popular Sydney club where Gemma had sung before, when a dull, droning noise interrupted their discussion.

Clutching the cell phone, Gemma rushed out of her unit. A moment later a huge shadow passed over her. Glancing up, she squinted into the sun and made out the dark shape a helicopter.

Angelo was back.

A thread of dark, forbidden excitement shivered through her. "I have to go, Macy."

"Wait, I need to know what—"

"I can't give you an answer. Not now. I'll call you tomorrow." She wasn't aware of Macy's mutterings; all she could think about was that soon she would see Angelo again.

By the time he arrived to collect her, she'd managed to get her pleasure at his return under control.

A rapid glance showed that he was dressed in a beautifully cut designer suit. She wore a smart sleeveless black dress and her hair had been confined into a French braid. Gemma knew she looked elegant and restrained...no hint of her wild excitement showed.

He didn't kiss her, not even a light buss on the cheek. Instead he stared at her for a long moment, his expression unreadable, and her pulse raced. Gemma got the feeling he'd been about to say something momentous.

At last he held out his hand, and said, "Come."

She took it. His clasp was warm and firm, his hand strong. And her heartbeat steadied.

Once they reached the church, she looked around with interest. Despite the white exterior, inside the church, colours ran riot. Just inside the tall double wooden doors, almost a hundred slim white candles flickered. Bowls of bright pink and red cyclamens and a huge vase of crocus added more colour. On the walls, saints with gold-leaf halos looked down on the packed pews.

They found seats near the front. A large woman beckoned to them, gave a very brief smile to Gemma and spoke rapidly to Angelo in Greek as she shifted along the wooden pew. Trapped between the older woman and Angelo, Gemma was very aware of the warmth of his thigh pressing against hers. When the priest appeared, she forced herself to concentrate.

The service was long and unlike any service Gemma had ever attended. Villagers wandered in and out in an ever-changing stream. Children played on the floor beside the windows. And the priest chanted in ancient Greek, while rich incense filled the church.

Afterwards people spilled out into the churchyard, congregating in small groups under a vine-covered pergola. Angelo kept her close to his side, his arm around her waist. A cat sat on the low wall not far from them; Gemma gave the animal a wary look.

The strange juxtaposition of the exotic resort, the simple church with its ancient ceremonial customs struck Gemma. Had Mandy seen this side of Angelo's world?

Gemma tilted her head to Angelo. "Have I been here before?"

"I asked you to come with me often enough in the past, but you didn't want to."

So Mandy had never been to the church with him. Given her twin's love of sleeping late and her preference for the good life, the refusal made sense. "Do you come often?" Gemma changed the subject.

He propped a foot up on the low wall beside her. The cat saw it as an invitation and came closer, purring and rubbing against his legs. Angelo bent to stroke the appreciative feline. Gemma backed away.

"Are you frightened of cats?" he asked.

"No, allergic," she replied. "I don't need red eyes or a fit of nonstop sneezing."

"Then let's move along." They found a new spot and watched as two girls came to play with the cat. "I come to this church every Sunday morning when I'm on Strathmos. I was baptised here."

"Oh. I didn't know that."

"It's not the kind of thing we usually talk about, is it?" His mouth kinked up. "In fact, we never spoke much at all in the past. I didn't even know you were allergic to cats.

We've talked more in the last couple of weeks than ever before. Maybe it has something to do with the amnesia."

That brought back her deception. Mandy had never been allergic to cats. Gemma certainly didn't want to talk about how she'd deceived him. Even though she knew that she would have to. Soon. On Tuesday she would be giving her last show. And then she'd be leaving. For good.

To distract herself, she asked, "Who was the woman who made space for us in the church?" Then added hastily, to justify her curiosity, "She looked familiar. Does she work at the resort?"

"That's Penelope." He pronounced it Pen-e-lop-i with the stress on the *O*. "You met her, when you were here before. Perhaps your memory is starting to return. You should let Dr. Natos check you out at the resort."

That was the last thing she wanted. "Maybe my head is getting better." He didn't look convinced. "Who is Penelope?" She asked again. "In case we bump into each other—she'd think me rude if I didn't know."

He shot her a strange look. "That didn't worry you much in the past. You never had much time for her. She was my governess when I was a child."

"A governess?" It accentuated the divide between them. She hadn't been deprived, but hers hadn't been an upbringing populated with governesses and servants and limitless privilege.

"Someone had to teach me to read and write. I didn't get sent to school in England until I was ten."

"You went to school in England?" That would account for his flawless English—no hint of an accent, no misuse of idiom.

"Yes, my mother thought it was for the best. My grandfather couldn't sway her."

"Did you enjoy it?"

"Not at first," he admitted. "It was a long way from home. I didn't speak good English. Initially I felt so isolated. I wanted to come home."

"Home? Here? To the resort?"

"No, there was no resort. There used to be a house on the island."

Gemma gave the hill behind the village a sweeping look. "A house?"

"I pulled it down and built the resort on the site of the wreckage."

Something in his voice gave her reason to pause. The tanned skin had stretched tautly across the high, flat cheekbones. He looked remote and ruthless.

Gemma shivered. There was so much she still didn't know about him. And now it was too late. She would be leaving soon.

After they got back to the resort, Gemma hurried to the entertainment centre to help Mark with the Christmas show rehearsal. She wouldn't perform in that. Tomorrow would be her last appearance. In a couple of days, she'd be back in Auckland. And she'd have to put the pieces of her life back together again.

"Gemma." She started when she heard her name called. Mark and Lucie were watching her with quizzical expressions.

"Wakey, wakey," Lucie called. "You look like you're off in dreamworld."

Gemma felt herself flush. Nightmare world, more like. "Okay, where are we?"

"In the Apollodrome," said Lucie with a cheeky smile. "Rehearsing for the Christmas spectacular."

"I remember." Gemma flinched the instant the words left her mouth. Lucie and Mark wouldn't realise the savage irony of that.

"Can you sing the Christmas medley?"

"I don't know the words," Gemma called back. "I'll sing something else to give everyone a chance to do the movements."

"Gemma's not booked to sing in the Christmas Eve spectacular." Angelo's voice broke in as she strode forward. "Stella Argyris will be performing."

Gemma stiffened.

"I asked Gemma if she would stand in for Stella," Mark moved forward and gestured to Gemma to get into position. "Stella's not due to arrive for another ten days but many of the other performers are here. I want to get the show on the road, so to speak."

"I've worked with the divine Stella before," Lucie murmured to Gemma. "She's a cat. A man's kind of woman. She'll be itching to get her claws into our gorgeous Greek boss."

Gemma's heart splintered. "Lucie, hush. He might hear you."

Lucie shrugged. "So what?"

Gemma wished she had a fraction of the other girl's insouciance. "Tomorrow is my last day. I want to leave on a good note."

"Judging by the way he's looking at you, I'd say you've hit the highest note already. Stella's gonna hate you."

Gemma whipped around to see what Lucie was on about and encountered Angelo's intimate gaze. "Hurry up—I've got plans for the afternoon."

Gemma turned scarlet. She launched into "O Holy Night." The instant she started to sing "the stars are brightly shining," she knew she'd made a mistake. She'd always loved this carol on a deep, emotional level, but now as she sang the image that came to mind were the silver-white stars in the sky over Strathmos. Why couldn't she've chosen to sing "Away in a Manager," she wondered frantically, at least that would've had no deep, soul-rending connotations.

Angelo seemed to have turned to stone. He was staring at her like he'd never seen her before.

Gemma's lashes feathered down, blocking him out her line of sight. The next line poured from her, her voice swelling, her throat thickened with emotion and her smoky voice became even more husky than normal. The climax came too soon and by the time the last words left her, Gemma was spent.

There was a moment of silence.

"Wow," Lucie broke it, sounding awed. Gemma opened her eyes and blinked. Behind Lucie, Mark had started to clap and one by one the dancers joined in. Only Angelo stood unmoving. Gemma started to feel a little ridiculous; she clambered down the stairs, off the stage.

Finally, Angelo shook himself. He headed off her escape route. "You sing like an angel."

With shock Gemma realised that his voice was hoarse. As if he'd been as moved as she'd been.

"I love that carol," she said, and thought how trite it sounded.

"You sang 'Happy Birthday' to me the other night, but this…this…is something else." He sounded awed. "To think I never even knew you could sing when you were with me. What the hell else did I not know about you?"

At his words Gemma came crashing back to earth. The magic vanished. She was Gemma Allen. Not the Gemma Allen Angelo believed her to be—that was Mandy—but another creature all together. The tangle of deceit she'd created had spun out of control.

After the rehearsal Angelo and Gemma had a light lunch and after she'd changed, he took her sailing. The afternoon passed in rush of wind and laughter.

That evening the applause after her show was even more fervent than usual. And Gemma knew that the audience had sensed the energy and emotion that the day spent with Angelo had unleashed inside her.

She was aware that this could not go on, would soon be over. She still hadn't phoned back Macy about the offer of work in Sydney. By now the job would be taken. Gemma knew she was living for the moment, until it all came crashing down on her head. As it must.

So when Angelo took her back to his penthouse for a late dinner after the show, she didn't protest. This was it. Her last chance to spend time with Angelo in the bubble that she'd created.

During dinner, they spoke of mundane matters, the candles on the table creating a golden haze around them. But beneath the everyday words, something buzzed, vibrating between them, an inexorable force. By the stillness of his body, the light in his eyes, Gemma knew he was aware of it, too.

Setting his knife and fork down, Angelo said, "I haven't helped you regain your memory at all, have I?" His eyes were dark with emotion. "Your return to Strathmos has been in vain."

She should confess now. But she didn't. She didn't want to extinguish that glow on his face that existed for her alone. She wanted to bask in it—for just a little longer. Once the bubble world was gone, it would be burst forever. There'd be no going back.

"Not in vain," she said finally. "The job has been great. And…I met you." Then she hastily tacked on. "Again."

An unmistakable passion flared in his eyes. He pushed back his chair and stood. "Come here."

Gemma knew what he was asking. If she went, everything would change. A moment of fear flickered in her chest. If she went to him…she would have to accept that she no longer believed he had destroyed Mandy and caused her to self-destruct.

That he was not the utter bastard Mandy had painted. That, for her own reasons, Mandy had lied.

"Come," he said again.

Slowly she rose to her feet and started to move around the dinner table. He met her halfway. Took her hand and dropped down onto the long leather couch and pulled her onto his lap.

Need uncoiled within Angelo. A need to see her smile again, to banish the shadows from her eyes, a need for her to be happy, a need to touch her…a need that grew and grew.

What the hell was happening to him? How could he care so little about Gemma's past betrayal? All he knew was that the whole week he'd been away from her had dragged like a prison sentence.

Experience had taught him that Gemma was treacherous, faithless. One side of him craved her, wanted to believe her promise that Jean-Paul meant nothing to her, wanted to believe it could be different this time… and fought to convince that other, more cynical side of Angelo that she had changed.

Her head was turned away from him. From this angle he could see the rise of her cheekbone, the straight line of her nose. He raised his hand, smoothed the wild tangles back to reveal the soft creamy skin at her neck.

"Ask me to make love to you," he breathed. "So that I don't break my promise to you."

He watched her throat move as she swallowed. When she turned her head, he met her gaze and he read the same desire that consumed him, as strong as a relentless tide.

"Please make love to me, Angelo."

A slow sensation rumbled like liquid thunder in his chest and, leaning forward, he brushed his lips across her silken skin. Her mouth opened. She tasted soft and sweet.

A long time later, she gave a breathy gasp and shifted, so that she knelt across his lap, her body tight and expectant.

His hands came up to her shoulders, dislodged the thin shoestring straps and eased the top of the dress down. She wore no bra. One glance revealed that her breasts were high and firm, the nipples dark and his heart began to pound.

He pulled her up…towards him…took the waiting nipple and surrounding flesh into his mouth. The nipple peaked under the stroke of his tongue.

Angelo pursed his lips, sucked, felt her body jerk and wrapped his arms tightly around her.

Her still-clothed belly moved in slow, insistent motions against him. In one swift movement he peeled the Lycra dress off and revelled in the sensation of her naked skin beneath his hands. He stroked her back, the sleek, rounded globes of her tight buttocks; the piece of stretchy lace that qualified for underwear was no barrier to his touch. His fingers slid beneath the thong.

She was warm and wet and his fingers moved effortlessly in the sleek furrow. He could tell by her ragged breathing that she was hot, that she wanted this as much as he did.

As his fingers moved back and forth, his mouth echoed the rhythm against her breast, until she gasped out loud and he felt the suppressed shudder that shook her.

Then she pushed away.

"I can't take more."

Before he could object, she'd slid off his lap, knelt between his thighs. He felt her fingers at the zipper of his trousers. A rush of want surged through him. He grabbed her head between his hands.

"No."

She tipped her head up, her eyes glazed with emotion.

"Yes."

"No." His control was slipping. He had a turbulent sense that if he let this happen his world would never be the same. That he was poised at a doorway to an undiscovered universe.

He heard the zipper give. Her hands brought him out, hard and potent.

"Gemma."

She ignored his desperate croak, her fingertips soft against his sensitive skin.

Giving in, he flung his head back against the sofa and groaned as she stroked him.

When the warmth of her mouth closed over him, he squeezed his eyes shut at the unbearably sweet heat. *"Gemma!"*

The slow sucking started, driving him to the edge of a dark, unfamiliar abyss where he could hold on no more. Shadows started to dance against his eyelids. His thighs began to tremble and then he was convulsing again and again, trapped in pleasure beyond what he'd ever experienced.

Eight

He carried Gemma through to the bedroom, laid her down on his bed. "My turn," he growled.

He stripped the thong off and started to stroke her with fingers that possessed a magic touch. A fine tension tightened in Gemma's belly. She shifted, the raw silk of the bedcover creating a delicious friction against her back, her thighs.

He touched the little button, her knees came off the cover. She moaned. He moved his fingers and her breath left her. Closing her eyes, she shut out everything. Nothing existed, except this room, this man…and his touch.

And then the heat of his mouth was against her. Slick. Teasing. His tongue probed. She gasped. He licked again. Gemma locked her fingers in his golden hair and pulled him away.

"I can't…"

He lifted his head. His eyes gleamed. "You can."

"I want…more."

He must've understood her incoherent mumbles. There was the sound of foil tearing and a moment later he'd crawled over her, his chest hard and sleek against her taut, aching breasts. Then his mouth was over hers, his tongue hungry and plundering as he took her mouth in a kiss so hot, so wild, that her hips bucked under him. Impatient. Desperate.

His hand closed on her breast. Heat seared through her, stabbing between her legs. She bent her knees up, tilted her hips, hinting, clamouring for more.

Angelo moved against her. She could feel his erection, the blunt tip sliding against her. She was ready for him.

He pushed forward and slid all the way in. Gemma moaned, a hoarse primal sound, as pleasure shafted her. Her arms went round his neck, tightening. And her legs wrapped round him, locking him to her.

There was a moment when he lay utterly still, filling her, and then he pulled back a little, and sank forward again. The friction was intense. The pace ratcheted up.

Gemma's breathing quickened, shallow gasps that sounded overloud in the quiet room.

She squeezed her eyes even more tightly shut, focusing on the friction, the sensation that arced through her, from between her legs, through her belly, to her nipples, to her tongue that slid wildly against his.

There was an instant of darkness, the world went black and then she was shivering into a void of light.

Angelo groaned, and she felt him pulsing deep inside her. "Hell, it's never been like that," he muttered hoarsely. *"Never."*

As his words registered, the brightness faded, and a shiver of apprehension shook her.

Her final show had arrived. Tonight Gemma wore a black dress with spaghetti straps that made her dark red hair appear redder than ever. The low scooped back revealed her carefully cultivated tan and Gemma took her time applying makeup to emphasize her eyes and lips. By the time she was finished, she knew she looked good.

Her time on stage passed in a blur. She squinted past the lights but couldn't locate Angelo at any of the tables. At last she gave up and tried to concentrate on the words she was singing, on communicating the meaning of the song to the audience, but some of the lustre had gone.

She left the stage with a sinking heart. Her time on Strathmos was over.

On the way to her dressing room, Denny waved and Gemma gave him a half-hearted smile.

Pushing the door open, her eyes widened at the unexpected sight of Angelo reclining in her dressing room. Gemma hesitated on the threshold.

He should've looked out of place surrounded by the heap of glittery clothes that Lucie had abandoned on the floor. But he didn't. Instead he looked unfairly at ease as he dwarfed the couch, his long legs stretched out in front of him.

She averted her eyes from his gold hair and bright, piercing eyes and the taut body encased in the beautifully fitting dark suit. Warily, she entered the dressing room and closed the door. "What are you doing here?"

"Waiting for you. Since this morning, you've been impossible to find. I don't intend to let you run out on me tonight."

Last night had been so special…earth shattering… she hadn't been able to face him this morning. She'd needed time alone to come to terms with it.

"I wouldn't have run out on you." They needed to talk. He was going to be furious with her. Her heart clenched at the thought of the coming confrontation.

"Join me for dinner?"

Dark and deep, that voice did stuff to her that should be declared illegal. "Anywhere except your penthouse." She didn't want to make love, it would distract her from what she had to say.

The smile he gave her was irresistible. "*Endaxi.* Okay."

He took her to the Golden Fleece. The decor was rich and warm with exquisitely painted murals on the walls of Jason and the Argonauts performing daring deeds. The high-backed chairs, white table linen and dim lighting, together with the hushed service gave it an outrageously exclusive ambience. As the meal progressed, and the conversation topics remained general, the tension that grasped Gemma started to unwind.

Gemma declined desert in favour of coffee and while they were waiting for it to arrive, she examined a mural depicting Jason with a woman who must be Medea. Angelo followed her gaze. "She was hard work, a sorceress and a witch."

"Yes, but he didn't do right by her. She helped him gain the fleece, he took her back to Corinth and married her. But then decided it was too tough to be married to a woman who was a witch—and a foreigner to boot. So he planned to dump her and marry another woman."

"Except Medea spiked that plan rather dramatically." Angelo's lips curved in a wry smile.

"Poor Glauce," Gemma agreed. "She certainly didn't deserve what she got. Medea's sending a robe steeped in poison as a wedding gift was downright evil."

"You know your Greek mythology pretty well."

"I should do. My father lectured classics. I grew up on the ancient myths. Greek and Roman."

Angelo shot her a surprised stare. "You never told me that."

Uh-oh. Gemma wished she'd kept her mouth shut. Mandy had never been much of a reader, she'd hated what she called "Dad's boring tales."

"So how did you end up a singer?"

"My mother could play the piano reasonably well, so I learned to play, too. I loved to sing, so it wasn't long before I started going for specialist lessons."

"And dancing…what did your mother say about your dance career?"

She drew a deep breath. Should she tell him now? He was smiling at her, his eyes warm. No. In a little while. She wanted just a little longer. "Actually Mum was responsible for that. She was a professional ballet dancer. After w— I…" she broke off at the near give away "…I was born, she opened a dance school and taught lots of little girls instead of performing live—she wanted to spend time with—" *us* "—me. What about you?" She shifted the focus of the conversation to him. "When did you know what you were going to do?"

"On my thirteenth birthday my grandfather took me

out for lunch and told me that one day I would inherit the chain of hotels he owned, and to prepare myself to look after them. My cousin Zac bore the family name, so he would inherit the Kyriakos Shipping Corporation. Tariq was to inherit the oil refineries.

"My grandfather also promised me I'd inherit the three islands he owned—Strathmos, Kalos and Delinos. I'd spent the first years of my life on Strathmos, so I knew it well. After that day I absorbed everything I could about the hospitality industry, about business, that I could lay my hands on."

There was a pause when the coffee arrived. Gemma reflected on the single-mindedness of the man sitting opposite. He'd known what he wanted and gone after it. He been responsible for a large part of his success. There was a lot more to him than the playboy image he projected to the media.

After they'd finished their coffees Angelo walked back to her unit. At the door he took the key from her and unlocked the door before following her in.

Gemma's heart started to knock against her ribs.

"Another coffee?" she asked, desperate for something to do while he stood in her space. Her voice was several notches higher than usual.

"Why not?" Mercifully, he moved away, and Gemma was able to breathe again. He picked up the photo on the bench top and instantly the tension was back, turning her rigid with anxiety. Her breath ragged, she said, "No sugar, right?"

"Black. No sugar."

It figured he wouldn't share her lethally sweet tooth. She emptied sweetener into her coffee and hoped she'd be able to sleep tonight given all the caffeine she was consuming.

"You're holding a cat."

"What?" She stared at him trying to make sense of the comment, to reconcile it with the rising tension that incapacitated her, numbed her ability to think straight.

"In the photo, you're holding a cat." His voice was endlessly patient.

Her brow wrinkled. "Yes, Snuggles."

"You told me you were allergic to cats."

Uh-huh. Gemma stiffened, wary of a trap. "I am," she said slowly. "Snuggles belongs to my parents."

"So why are you holding him? In the churchyard you told me how cats affect you."

Tell him.

She stared at him, her mind went blank. Her tongue felt thick, she scratched for words. "Because he always comes to me. He likes to see me red-eyed and sneezy."

That, at least, was true. Snuggles, the darn cat, had a wicked sense of the misery he caused her. But of course, the real truth was that *she* wasn't holding Snuggles in the photo. Mandy was. And Mandy had no allergy to felines of any description.

The tightrope of lies she was balancing upon became ever more precarious. And when Angelo put the photo down, she said a prayer of thanks and placed the two mugs on the coffee table in front of the loveseat.

Appearing satisfied with her explanation, he sank onto the plump seat. "When are you thinking of leaving?"

"Tomorrow. I'll catch the midday ferry, spend a couple of days in Athens sightseeing and then I'll fly back to Auckland."

"It's too soon." His eyes turned to flame. "Come here."

Tell him. "Angelo—" Gemma backed up at the intent in his brilliant eyes "—I'm *not* going to sleep with you."

"Who said anything about sleeping?" There was an intimacy in his gaze that did dangerous things to her equilibrium. "I just want a kiss."

A kiss…one final kiss… She went into his arms. It felt like she was coming home. And that created a maelstrom of emotions churning within her. Guilt. Confusion. Regret that she hadn't met him long before Mandy.

But it didn't stop her responding to him.

When he lifted his head they were both breathing fast.

"Some kiss," she said.

He didn't smile. Eyes intent, he said, "I have to leave for Kalos tomorrow. I have a series of meetings there. Come with me."

She started to shake her head.

"Please, come. You can stay as long as you like. I don't want you to leave again."

He still thought she was Mandy. But Mandy was dead. And *she* was alive.

Disturbed by the direction her thoughts were taking, she rose. She needed to tell him the truth. And leave. She couldn't allow herself to be tempted to stay. Even though she wanted to. More than anything.

He grasped her hand and pulled her back. She landed on his lap. With an embarrassed laugh she struggled to extricate herself. He wouldn't let her.

Face close to hers, he said, "I want to spend time with you—more than I want you in my bed." There was a hint of bewilderment in his eyes.

And that was when Gemma knew he felt it, too. This strong, enduring bond between them that was turning her life upside down, forcing her to reevaluate who she was and what she wanted from her life.

"Okay, I'll come."

His eyes lit up. He raised her hand to his lips, turned it over and placed a soft, seductive kiss inside her wrist. "You won't regret it."

Gemma gave him a look of disbelief. Of course she was going to regret it. But she couldn't let the chance to spend a few more days with him pass.

Poseidon's Cavern, the resort on Kalos, was magnificent. At the centre of the main resort complex Angelo had installed a giant tank filled with sea creatures and fish. Walking through the lobby, she was drawn to the tank to stare at the rays flapping past the viewing windows.

"This is fantastic." She turned to Angelo. "I've never seen anything like it."

"I brought you here before. Doesn't it stir any memories?"

Gemma's excitement dimmed and she shook her head, hating the lie that she'd trapped herself in.

"Don't worry. Later I'll show the rest of the complex. There's a bar and a restaurant with a fabulous view of the tank. They were designed to feel like part of an underwater grotto. Aside from the theatre and cinemas, there's a water theme park to keep you busy. On the south side of the island we've used the underwater caves in the theme park and we'll take a ride through them tomorrow. It will be a little cool this time of the year, but it's spectacular down there and it's something that we hadn't completed last time you were here."

"That's sounds lovely." But the best part was that it was an experience where she wasn't following in Mandy's footsteps. She wouldn't have to worry about how her twin had reacted.

Not that she was worried about Angelo working the truth out any more. If he hadn't twigged by now that she wasn't Mandy, but her twin sister, it was unlikely that he was going to discover the truth. But she couldn't allow this to go on.

A week, she decided. She'd give herself a week. And then she'd tell him. That night she made love to him with the fervour of the damned. Afterwards he looked at her with a question in his eyes.

When Angelo disappeared the following morning to his all-day meeting, Gemma took one look at the overcast sky, then spent a couple of hours examining the enormous tank inside the resort and reading the plaques about the occupants. Later in the morning she made her way to the heated conservatory pool where she was stunned by the sight of Jean-Paul tanning himself beside a svelte blonde.

"Cherie." He leapt up when he saw her. Gemma turned her head, and the kiss intended for her mouth landed on her cheek.

"Has Apollonides allowed you out your cage, pet?"

His words riled her. "Looks like you've acquired a pet of your own." Gemma gave the blonde a meaningful look.

"She is nothing. I'd drop her like a hot potato if you showed any interest."

His faked heartbroken expression made Gemma glare at him. "You're a wicked man."

"Who loves to do wicked things, remember?" His voice dropped to husky intimacy.

She didn't want to go there. "I don't want to remember."

"Ah, the big fish pays better. How can I blame you?" Jean-Paul sounded philosophical. A waiter materialised at his elbow. "Ah, pull up a lounger for the lady. Gemma, let me order you something to drink and we can catch up on old times."

Gemma wasn't that keen to catch up on old times but she badly wanted to quiz him about Mandy. So she opted for a coffee—and so did Jean-Paul's companion whom he introduced as Birgitte. She turned out to be Swedish and, besides having a wonderful figure, appeared to be thoroughly nice. Gemma couldn't help regretting her *pet* crack. After they'd finished their coffees Birgitte took off to the nearby spa.

"Are you ready for a swim?" Jean-Paul asked.

"In a while."

"I'm sure it won't be long before Apollonides arrives—and he won't like finding you in my company." Jean-Paul looked pleased at the prospect.

Men! Gemma gave a mental headshake. "Angelo doesn't own me. He said I could drink with whom I liked." But apprehension shivered through her.

"If he pays your bills, he owns you. That's how a man thinks."

"How awful." Gemma took the gap he unwittingly provided. "Speaking of bills, after my last encounter with you three years ago my credit card suffered more damage than I expected. I must have gambled more than I'd intended."

"You're calling it *gambling* now?" Moreau shot her guarded look and Gemma's interest picked up. *He knew.*

She gave him an enticing smile. "What would you prefer me to call my little secret, hmm?"

"*Cherie,* better to keep quiet about that. Apollonides might not be happy about your little habit."

So Angelo hadn't known. Or at least that was what Jean-Paul believed. Gemma frowned. That was not the impression Mandy had given Gemma before her death. *I loved him, he ruined me.*

"Did you share my little secret?" It was a shot in the dark. The memory of her sister's wan, sunken face, her listless eyes, her shaking hands still haunted Gemma.

Jean-Paul's gaze sharpened. "Why are you asking me these questions?" His eyes dropped to the shirt over her swimsuit. He pushed the buttons aside.

"Hey, what are you doing? Take your hands off me!"

"Sorry…I thought…it doesn't matter."

But Gemma put it together. "It was you. You introduced her to the drugs that killed her."

"What do you mean *her?* And what are you talking about, saying I introduced *her* to drugs?" Jean-Paul's gaze darted around, examining everyone in the immediate surround.

Gemma realised her indiscretion. She'd nearly given away the fact that she was not the woman he thought she was. She couldn't afford another slip like that. "You were the source, the supplier."

"But, *cherie.*" He stroked his hand along her thigh. "You know all—"

"I don't remember. I had an accident, I lost my memory. So don't *cherie* me." She smacked his hand away. The way he'd touched her chest made sense. "You thought I was wearing a wire. You're scared of being arrested."

A flash of fear flitted through his eyes. "I'll deny it. Everything. You'd be stupid to start this. You've got Apollonides eating out of your hand." He gave an acid laugh. "I never thought I'd see the day that he took you back into his bed. Not after what he saw. He must want you badly. Funny, I didn't think you were that special myself."

Gemma's stomach turned. She felt ill.

Oh, Mandy…how could you?

As Gemma had gotten to know Angelo, she'd come to wonder how Mandy could have cheated on him. Jean-Paul's words made it clear that her sister *had* climbed out of Angelo's arms into the Frenchman's. Angelo was convinced there'd been other men, too. Maybe he was right. And he believed she was Mandy.

Pain twisted deep inside her. Well, she could hardly object. She'd led him to believe she was her twin. She couldn't blame him for that. But she hadn't given a damn about Angelo at the start of her deception, when she'd arrived on Strathmos. She'd believed him to be the bastard who'd gotten Mandy hooked on hard drugs.

But she'd been mistaken.

It wasn't Angelo who started Mandy down her path to destruction…it was Jean-Paul.

Revulsion swept her as Jean-Paul smiled at her, over-familiar and over-expectant. She had to get away from him. He'd ruined her sister's life, caused her death. Mumbling an excuse, Gemma hoisted her tote over her shoulder and scooted off the lounger, desperate to find a place where she could be alone to think about what she had discovered.

One thought kept festering: how could she ever set her relationship with Angelo right?

Nine

Standing outside one of the boardrooms in the high-tech conference centre, Angelo shook hands with Basil Makrides. "I am pleased you are satisfied with our agreement."

The older man nodded. "I want to spend time with Daphne, with our sons. Too much of my life has been lost on building an empire." There was sadness in his eyes.

Angelo was privy to the tragic situation of Basil's younger son. "I am sorry about Chris. I hope he will recover."

Basil sighed. "We will give him all the support we can. At present he's getting the best care in the world. And Daphne and I will be there at his side when he comes out."

Angelo's step was light as he went to find Gemma. The negotiations with Makrides had ended sooner than he'd expected. He now owned a group of small but exclusive resorts in Australia that he was keen to bring in line with the rest of the Poseidon ventures. He was looking forward to taking a couple of days off and relaxing with Gemma.

She delighted him, enthralled him.

Each day, he grew more intrigued by her, discovered yet another facet of her character. Gemma had changed, more than he could ever believe possible. They meshed in a way that they had never done in the past, in a way that he had never fit with any other woman. He was prepared to let the past go...to start over with her.

He didn't want to think too much about what was happening to him. He simply wanted to enjoy Gemma...her company...and her sexy body.

When he saw her ahead of him, clad in one of the pool's cover-ups, a tote slung over her shoulder, he lengthened his stride.

"Gemma." He snagged her elbow, and she jumped. "Sorry, I didn't mean to startle you."

She turned, her tawny eyes widening when she saw him. Something shifted in the depths, then vanished. "I thought you were busy with a meeting."

"I finished early. And seeing that the squall that threatened this morning has blown away, I wanted to show you the underwater caverns."

Fifteen minutes later, clad in wet suits to minimize the coolness of the subterranean winter water, they each hopped into a giant yellow inner tube that would float them through the honeycomb of tunnels. Because of the cold, there weren't many others in the dimly lit caves, so Gemma pushed off from the wall and scooted across the black water before rebounding off the opposite wall of the tunnel. She gave a squeal of laughter. "This is fun."

"The current will move us along." Angelo's tube bumped into hers, and she laughed again. His gaze lingered on her white smile and pleasure surged within him. "Not scared?"

"Not at all."

"It gets dark a little farther on," he warned.

"Ooh, spooky." She bumped her tube into his, and he rebounded into the wall. Trapped between the cavern wall and her tube, Angelo watched her approach with a wicked smile. Before he could move, she leaned over and scooped some of the dark water into her hand and flung it at him.

Angelo spluttered as the cold spray hit the side of his head. "Is that the way you want to play it?" He growled, using his hands to paddle closer.

"No." Gemma started to giggle helplessly. "Don't wet me more. The water is freezing."

His arm snaked out and hooked around her waist. She shrieked as she slipped off her tube. "Don't dump me in this water, I'm sorry. I won't do it again."

Angelo swept her over the divide between the two tubes. She landed, sprawled across him, her front plastered against his. Instantly he was aware of the softness of her body outlined by the Neoprene suit. The tangle of her wet hair brushed his cheek.

She shifted, twisting away. "My tube!" Her bright

yellow tube bobbed along in the distance, moving fast without a passenger.

"Hold still. You're going to capsize us," he warned, dragging her closer.

She froze. "That's the last thing I want."

"Don't worry, it's only about a metre deep."

"I don't care about the depth. It's the freezing, dark water I want to avoid."

"Be adventurous." Angelo settled her against him. "Live dangerously."

"This is more dangerous than it looks." She sounded breathless.

His arm shifted, he could feel her heart beating wildly. From the exertion? The thrill of the ride? Or something else?

He pulled her closer with one arm, the other holding onto the ring moulded to the tube. "Feel safer now?"

"No," she moaned.

Angelo was smiling when he kissed her. Her lips were cold and wet, but they parted the instant the tip of his tongue stroked hers. The kiss grew wild...deep. He'd never felt this kind of insatiable hunger for a woman before.

Then everything went dark.

He raised his head. "It's the Midnight Bend. We'll round the corner and then there'll be light."

"You think I'm scared?" There was amusement in her voice.

He kissed her again. But she'd moved so he missed the lips he was aiming for in the pitch black, and had to make do with kissing her neck, the softness behind her ears.

"That's so good," she groaned.

He tongued her skin, unbearably aroused.

The tube swung around a curve and they were back in the dim, ghostly light. He pulled away. "Want more?"

"Mmm," she murmured.

This time he made sure he got her lips. The kiss was deep and very, very hungry. Her hand crept up, caressing his nape, then spearing into his hair and pulling him closer still.

Finally he pulled away, breathing hard. "Hold tight," he gasped.

Her hands tightened against his head.

"I mean, hold the tube, hold me. There's a bit of a rapid ahead." He saw her eyes widen, then she was shrieking as the tube started to speed up and go downhill. The tube jerked and shook as the current swept it forward. Angelo braced himself, holding her close against him.

Faster and faster they went.

The last part of the descent was the steepest. Gemma was shaking under the weight of his arm.

"It's okay."

"It's great!"

She gave a whoop of excitement. And that's when he realized she was laughing, that she was high on enjoyment, not shaking with fear. They came careening down the final slide and surfed onto the wide pool at the bottom.

Gemma shifted in his grip, twisted her head around and beamed incandescently up at him. "That was fantastic! Can we do it again?"

And right then Angelo knew why she was different

from every woman he'd ever known. She was so transparent, so intensely warm and joyous.

Gemma was one of a kind.

The next day passed in surges of adrenaline, moments of apprehension and utter pleasure in Angelo's company.

In the morning they spent time feeding the fish in the huge tank and then they went for a walk marked along the island. After lunch, Gemma insisted on trying out ride after ride in the theme park. Protected by the wet suit and high on excitement, Gemma didn't feel cold until several hours later, when Angelo said, "Time to call it a day. We've got guests coming for dinner. You'll like them—the Makrideses are nice people."

Wet and suddenly weary, Gemma allowed Angelo to drape an oversized towel around her and usher her back to the resort.

Back in his penthouse, she stepped gratefully into the shower and let the heat beat against her skin. She lathered her hair, combing the tangles out with her fingers, and afterwards she took her time blow-drying the curls before pinning them up into a sophisticated twist. An easy-to-wear stretchy Lyrca dress followed. A careful application of light makeup and a pair of gold hoop earings, and she was ready to face Angelo and his guests.

She waltzed into the open-plan seating area, only to find the laughing man of earlier gone. Angelo stood with his back to the view over the island, impeccably dressed in black trousers and a black T-shirt, but his jaw was set. "You didn't mention that you had an intimate little tete-a-tete with your former lover at the pool yesterday."

Gemma's heart sank at the coldness in his eyes. She stared at him through her lashes, not knowing quite what to say. She'd wanted to forget about Jean-Paul. Escape. And, to be truthful, she hadn't wanted any mention of the Frenchman to wreck the burgeoning relationship between herself and Angelo.

"Nothing to say? Did you know that Jean-Paul would be here? Is that why you agreed to come?"

"No! Jean-Paul means nothing to me." Angelo's suspicion threw her. She should've expected it. After what Mandy had done, it wasn't surprising. And with that came a further revelation. His opinion mattered because she was starting to have real feelings for him. He was the worst man in the world for her to fall for— Hell, he didn't even know who she was.

The time had come to tell him the truth.

Scanning the piercing eyes, the mouth pulled into a tight line, she knew there would be no forgiveness.

It was way too late.

The elevator pinged, breaking Angelo's fixed, angry stare and Gemma felt weak with relief. Coward, she admonished herself, as he moved fluidly towards the elevator and greeted the man and woman stepping out.

Gemma followed more slowly, wishing the evening was already over. She needed to talk to Angelo alone. For her own peace of mind, she had to come clean. She could delay no longer, however much she wanted to spend time with him.

She forced a smile to her lips as Angelo performed the introductions. She couldn't tell Angelo now, not with his guests here. Later, after they'd gone.

Daphne and Basil Makrides were a reserved couple, both with worry lines around their eyes, though they grew less reserved as the evening wore on. But Angelo remained cool, and Gemma found it increasingly distressing.

Two members of his staff poured them cocktails and served a selection of mezze-style starters. Gemma chatted to Daphne about the resort, about the excitement of the wild ride through the underground caverns, and Daphne smiled.

The conversation moved on to food. Basil and Daphne were well-travelled, and Angelo contributed to the conversation, although Gemma couldn't help being aware of the dark glances he shot her from time to time. She tried to ignore it, chattering gaily and soon all four of them were talking of favourite spots they'd visited.

But the unbearable tension between herself and Angelo caused Gemma's stomach to knot up. When he moved to change the music, she followed him. "I honestly didn't know Jean-Paul would be on the island," Gemma murmured in a low voice that would not reach his guests. "I was surprised when I met him at the pool."

"Maybe not such an accident on Jean-Paul's part."

"For goodness' sake." Gemma rolled her eyes. "He was with a stunning Swede by the name of Birgitte."

Angelo looked surprised.

"Obviously your informant failed to mention that," she said, a touch acerbically. "Although, to be fair, Birgitte did leave to go to the spa for a while. But I also left not long after that. I had no desire to share Jean-Paul's company." She'd stayed only as long as had been necessary to learn what she needed.

Her distaste must have been clear, because his hand covered hers. "I'm sorry."

She jerked under his touch. "Why?"

"For misjudging you. I thought—" There was confusion in his eyes. Pain, and a hint of vulnerability.

He thought she'd been ready to betray him with Jean-Paul. For a second time. *She had to tell him the truth.* A glance in the Makrideses' direction showed her that they were hovering near the dining table. No time now. So she said, "I won't see him again. I promise."

Angelo inclined his head. "Thank you." The liquid voice of Andrea Bocelli swelled through the room. Angelo started to speak, but then he shook his head. "Later."

Later. Apprehension knotted in her stomach. There would be lots to talk about later.

Gemma followed Angelo slowly towards the table where two waiters in waistcoats and bowties were setting out plates with polished-silver covers to keep the food hot.

"Do you have any children?" Gemma asked Daphne after the meal and they'd returned to the comfortable sofas to drink rich coffee from tiny Greek coffee cups. The staff had left, and the four of them were alone.

Daphne stilled. There was an uncomfortable silence and Gemma had the horrible premonition that she'd put her foot squarely in it. Then Daphne replied, "Yes, two sons, Chris and Marco."

Gemma changed the subject and started to talk frantically of the cooling weather and how different it was from Auckland where the weather would now be humid with less than four weeks to go until Christmas.

Gemma chattering on with increasing desperation about Christmas decorations and shopping habits until Daphne said suddenly, "Whenever I try to talk about Chris everyone smiles and talks about something else. It's like he has an unspeakable disease."

"He's ill?" Gemma asked carefully.

"No, not ill, not in the way you mean. He has a… problem."

"Oh." Gemma wasn't sure what more to say. So she said nothing and waited.

"He's in rehabilitation." Daphne named a famous French drug-and-alcohol rehabilitation centre. "It's his third attempt, we're hoping that this time it will work."

Gemma placed her suddenly cold hands over the other woman's. "I'm so sorry."

Daphne's eyes glinted with moisture. "No one lets me talk about it. It's like Chris no longer exists."

"I understand."

"How can you possibly understand?" There was a tinge of anger in the woman's question.

Gemma drew a deep breath. "My sister died of a drug overdose."

Daphne gasped. "I am so sorry. I didn't realise."

"The worst was not realizing she'd been an addict—for some time." Gemma blinked back the familiar tears. "The last couple of months of her life were awful. She self-destructed before my eyes. I was so furious with her." And with her sister's billionaire boyfriend who had gotten her hooked on drugs. *That* anger had been misplaced. "I miss her desperately."

"There are times when I'm so cross with Chris I want to shake him, ask him why he's doing this…and

most of all I wonder where Basil and I went wrong."
The words burst from Daphne. "We gave him everything we thought he wanted."

"It's not your fault."

Daphne looked at her, her eyes sunken in their
sockets, haunted by unhappiness.

"You can't blame yourself. We always try to blame
someone in these situations. It's human nature to try
find an excuse for terrible things that happen."

She had blamed Angelo. Wrongly. Unfairly. It
wasn't his fault Mandy had died. He wasn't the ogre
she'd imagined.

Gemma shot him a glance. He was talking to Basil,
as if aware of her every move, he glanced up, their eyes
tangled…and held. Her heart shifted.

At that moment, Gemma realised she loved him.

She stilled in shock. Then he was in front of her.
"Can I get either of you ladies a nightcap?" Gemma and
Daphne shook their heads.

"The coffee is good," Daphne said.

Angelo slid into the space beside Gemma on the
sofa and his thigh pressed against hers, sending sharp
slivers of desire splintering through her. Wrapping his
arm around her shoulder, he placed a kiss on her brow.
The bold claim took her by surprise, she saw the astonishment in Daphne's eyes as Basil came to stand beside
her.

Twenty minutes later the evening was over and, as
they walked to the door, Daphne swung around and unexpectedly hugged Gemma.

"Thank you for sharing how you feel about your
sister's death, it helped me more than you'll ever know.

At least Chris is still alive, still has a chance to recover. And I've made a decision. I am going to fund a foundation to help warn young people about the dangers of drugs. Basil has spoken about doing something like that in the past. But I was simply too listless to do anything."

Basil threw Gemma a surprised look. It was clear that the topic of Chris and his addiction was not something he was accustomed to his wife discussing. Gemma didn't dare look at Angelo.

Then she told herself he couldn't possibly guess her secret. She forced herself to smile calmly as they said goodbye to the Makrideses.

Angelo locked the elevator with a click. "I didn't know you had a sister."

Gemma's throat closed in apprehension. "Yes."

A frown furrowed his brow. "You told me you were an only child, I never realized you'd lost a sister."

Mandy had denied her existence? Was that what her twin had secretly always wanted? To be the only child, the centre of attention? Did she feel cheated by having to share the limelight with a sister—or worse than that, did she resent the interest that came from being a twin? Something inside Gemma withered at her sister's rejection.

Angelo was speaking again. "What was her name?"

"Mandy." Her answer was terse.

"Is it still painful to talk about her?"

"Very."

"I'm sorry."

His sympathy and tenderness worsened the ache in her heart. His grip on her hand tightened and Gemma's throat tightened. *She loved him.* Her deception pressed in on her. How could she ever tell him? She turned into his arms and lifted her face. His arms tightened around her and his breathing grew heavy.

She wanted to be close to him. Naked. For the last time. Then she'd tell him. And it would all be over.

Ten

In the bedroom they undressed quickly and collapsed onto the bed in a tangle of limbs. A lamp in the corner of the room, between the wide bed and the wall of drawn drapes, cast a pale glow over them.

Angelo moved a little closer. "How did I ever let you go?"

A moment of darkness disturbed the passion that had overtaken her. *He thought she was her sister.* And she had to set him right.

"Angelo—"

His hand trailed across her breast, across the curve, brushing the delicate tip. Gemma sighed as frissons of delight followed beneath his fingertips. She lost track of what she had to say.

Then his tongue came out, probing, tasting the dark

nipple and heat splintered in her belly. Gemma fought a groan as that maddening mouth feasted on her.

He paid homage to the other breast, and when he'd finished Gemma stared at her taut quivering nipples with a sense of shock.

What was it about Angelo that stripped her of all her inhibitions? She wanted him…but there was more. There was a sense of belonging together, a deep-rooted understanding between them that she'd never experienced with anyone else.

It overwhelmed her. It scared her. Because it couldn't possibly survive what she had to confess.

"What are you thinking?" Angelo pulled her against him.

"Nothing." Her voice cracked on the lie. "Nothing," she said again, trying to make it sound convincing to her own ears.

"Then I'll have to give you something to think about." He stretched out a hand to stroke her naked flesh. "You're trembling."

"Yes."

Her breathy reply made Angelo grow harder in anticipation. His every nerve seemed to be on edge, suspended on the razor-edge of pleasure. By contrast, her body was soft, her skin silky under his hand and a wave of tremors shook her.

"Are you all right?"

She nodded, her eyes wide. He paused, determined to take it slow. Then her lips parted, her tongue tip slicked across that luscious lower lip and his control shredded.

A rush of heat seared him. He moved over her, chest

to her breast, his legs sliding along the length of hers, and bent to take that tantalising mouth.

Lower down he was aware of his body pressing into her. Her thighs parted and he tilted his hips forward until no space remained between them.

This close, her eyes were velvety with desire and he was supremely conscious of his strength, the power of his arms braced on each side of her upper arms, the weight of his torso brushing her breasts and the muscles shifting in his thighs. In contrast, she was so feminine, her long legs flexing subtly against him.

Breathing harshly, Angelo lifted his mouth and shifted his weight. Supporting himself on one elbow, he rapidly readied himself with the other hand, hoping he wouldn't erupt before he'd even entered her. The sheath of rubber rolled onto him. She shifted underneath him, tempting, impatient.

As he penetrated her, stretching her, she lay motionless. Finally sheathed deep within her, he lay against her—head bowed, eyes clenched shut—inhaling the sweet fragrance of her skin.

She moved and her inner muscles tightened on him, demanding a response. Pleasure streaked through him and his relentless control frayed. He began the slow sweeps that would take them towards a place he'd never known.

As the pace quickened so did the intensity. His hands cupped her hips, pulling her closer as he drove harder and harder into her. She echoed his ferocity.

When he thought he could take no more, when the pleasure was so great he felt that he would explode if it didn't end, he felt her contract against him, once, twice, and it was enough to tip him over the edge, into the fire that threatened to consume him. And then he pulled her into the curve of his arm, his body warm and relaxed against hers. "Look at me."

Gemma avoided his gaze, simply dropping her head against his chest, nuzzling his skin, breathing in his hot male scent.

She was here now. In his bed. In his life. Did it matter who he thought she was?

She stroked his stomach, let a finger trace the indent between the muscle definition. A wicked temptation called to her. *Kiss him.* He need never know she wasn't Mandy.

After all, if she never told him would he ever learn the truth? Probably not. He'd had many mistresses and none lasted. Their relationship would run its course, too. This sweet madness between them would not last.

But what if it did? What then? Could she keep this secret forever?

No. She didn't want to live with a past that Mandy had already stained with betrayal. She had to tell him. *Now.* While they were immersed in this special, loving glow. Acid ate the back of her throat. She swallowed. He would understand why she'd done what she had. *He had to.*

She pulled away a little, to give herself some breathing space, to gather her courage—and so that she could look into his face, the face she'd come to love so much.

"Hey, come back here, I want to hold you."

Gemma propped a cushion behind her back. "Angelo—" It came out a croak. She tried again. "I need to tell you something." She stroked his cheek with trembling fingers.

"Yes? What's wrong?"

She bit her lip. How…where…to start? She drew a deep breath. "I told you my sister died…"

He nodded.

"She was my twin."

"I'm so sorry. I've heard that twins are very close. It must have been hard. You said her name was Mandy?"

It was Gemma's turn to nod. "She died on Christmas Eve nearly three years ago."

"Three years ago?" Then he snapped his mouth shut.

Gemma could see his resolve not to interrupt, to support her, let her explain. Her love for him swelled.

For the first time she started to hope that he might be able to accept what she was about to tell him.

"Mandy was…well, Mandy. She made me laugh, she loved practical jokes when we were kids. She knew no fear and would try anything." Except Mandy had been terrified of being unpopular. She'd always wanted to be the ahead of the peer group, the first to swear, the first to smoke.

Gemma moved away from him and crossed her legs. "When we were kids we both loved to create shows. I'd sing and she'd dance." She recognized that she was rambling, trying to delay that moment of terrible truth.

"A talented duo. What did Mandy grow up into?"

Gemma hauled in a deep breath, met his gaze squarely. "She became a dancer, an exotic dancer."

Angelo stilled. "So both of you worked as exotic dancers? Did you ever work together? Identical twins… that would've been a card to play." He paused. "Or were you very different from each other?"

"We were nothing alike—even though we looked very similar."

"How similar?"

"Practically identical." The confession was dragged from Gemma. "At school our teachers struggled to tell us apart." Mandy had traded classes with Gemma to avoid those she hated. "And I'm not an exotic dancer, I've only ever sung."

There. She held her breath.

"What do you mean you—" He broke off. A horrible, tense silence followed. He shook his head, his eyes dazed like a fighter reeling from a blow. "What are you saying?"

"You knew Mandy, Angelo," Gemma confirmed. "Three years ago—"

"I knew Gemma." His voice was hard, definite. "Who the hell are you?"

"*I* am Gemma."

"Gemma worked for me, I have a copy of her work permit, her passport, to prove it."

Gemma uncrossed her legs and slung them over the edge of the bed, her back to Angelo. "Mandy didn't have a work permit. She was convicted for shoplifting with a group of friends a teenager. So her application for a work permit was declined."

"*Look at me.*" She heard him move, then he was standing, looming over her. "I want to see your face. We would not give anyone a job without their paperwork being in order."

Gemma took a deep breath. "She had a work permit. She applied for it in my name, without my knowledge. She took my passport and my credit card when she left." And Gemma had never told a soul. When her father surmised that Mandy had been lucky to get a work permit, Gemma had remained silent. She'd been stranded in New Zealand, her career options curtailed—with no chance of working in Australian or Pacific island resorts, furious with her twin, waiting for Mandy to return. She bowed her head, covering her face.

"Didn't you tell the authorities?"

"You have to understand, all our lives we covered for each other. It was a hard habit to break. But I never thought that Mandy would come to any harm, not on a Greek island." Although she had experienced some qualms when Mandy had e-mailed to tell her about the fabulous man she'd hooked up with. Handsome. A billionaire. She'd been even more worried when Mandy had sent her press cuttings and photos of Angelo, whom Gemma had dismissed as a dashing sophisticated playboy. She'd begged Mandy to come home. But Mandy had been in heaven living out her fantasy lifestyle.

Gemma let her hands drop and glanced up at him. "I was more worried that you'd break her heart. You had a reputation as a playboy who went through beautiful woman like a hot knife through butter."

"A lot of that is PR. For show, to attract the jet set." His face darkened. "I'm very generous to my girlfriends. All the women I've been involved with know the score."

Except for her. She'd fallen in love with him. And, at the start, she'd believed Mandy had been in love with him, too. It had never crossed her mind that there'd been someone else in her sister's life.

"So why did you come here?" He flung his arms out wide. "Why the whole elaborate charade of pretending to be your sister?"

"I wanted to get close to you."

He stared at her in disbelief. "You certainly managed that. Did you plan to sleep with me?" There was a cynicism in the lines around his mouth and his bright eyes were dull.

She blinked.

"You did plan this!" He looked at her like she was something nasty.

Gemma swallowed. "In the beginning, I had some stupid half-baked idea that I might seduce you. But I abandoned it." She had to make him believe her. "I thought that you were responsible for Mandy's death."

"What about the amnesia? You told me about a hit-and-run in London. Was that true? Or another lie?"

Gemma looked away and shook her head. "There was no accident. I don't know where Mandy went after leaving here, but by the time she returned to New Zealand she was a pitiful, broken creature. She suffered from moodswings and had muttered wildly about the glamorous man she'd loved…and lost to another woman. I thought that was you."

"Nice to know that you hold me in such high regard," he bit out sardonically. He stalked away, pressed a switch and the wall of curtains started to open. He looked out into the darkness. "When your sister stayed with me, I caught her once using cocaine at a party and I made it clear that I wouldn't tolerate it," he said in a flat monotone. "That if it ever happened again, our relationship was over. She said it was a mistake…that she'd never done it before and wouldn't do it again. I believed her.

"I suspected she had a drinking…problem. I'd tried to convince her that she needed help after she'd had a little too much to drink at a party, stripped her clothes off and started to can-can. She argued that she was fine, it was just a bit of fun…that I was too staid. I broke it off that night, but she was so apologetic, said she wanted another chance. I gave it to her." He turned around, his eyes angry. Unforgiving. "And you thought I was responsible for her addictions? Did she tell you that? Mention my name?"

"No." Gemma felt awful. "I assumed. But I knew she'd had a relationship with you—she was so proud of it."

"So you never read about our affair in the scandal-sheets?" he said sardonically.

Gemma shook her head. "Mandy was in a bad way. We didn't have much time with her once she returned home. She took an overdose and then she was dead."

"Was it deliberate?" His voice softened.

For a wild moment Gemma thought he was about to reach for her, but then his eyes iced over.

Her throat thickened. "I thought so. I thought that you'd driven her away after getting her hooked on drugs, that she coped by turning to the drugs for solace. I thought she didn't want to live without you."

He paced along the length of the window, a dark shape against the night. "No wonder you hated me. No wonder you wanted revenge. But do you have any conception of the kind of danger that you put yourself in? What if I'd been the kind of man you thought?"

"I *had* to do it. She was my twin sister. My other half." And then she realized that was wrong. *He* was her other half. The bond, the empathy, that had been growing between them was stronger than anything she'd ever shared with her sister. She rose to her feet, took a step towards him. "Angelo—"

"Even though she lied to you, stole from you, defrauded you?" He was angry, she saw. "Mandy used the credit card that you told me you'd mysteriously maxed out and couldn't remember how, didn't she?"

"Yes. But from what you told me, the dates correlate with after she left Kalos, while she must've been with Jean-Paul. And he supplied drugs to her…he admitted that much to me."

Angelo's gaze narrowed. "I'm not having a dealer on my island. I will take care of him. It makes sense. If Mandy no longer had the allowance I gave her at her disposal, then she must have pawned the jewellery I bought her for a fraction of its value." He glared at her. "Why didn't you stop the card when you discovered it missing?"

She shrugged. "I couldn't leave her stranded overseas with no money if she needed it. I simply never expected her to run up that kind of debt. She knew I'd have to repay it. It must have been for drugs."

"Well, I won't leave *you* stranded." There was a note of finality in his voice. "I will book you a ticket to take you back to New Zealand safely."

It was over. He was dumping her. Gemma lifted her chin. "That is not necessary. I can make my own way home."

"I can't believe what you did." Anger and a mist of complex emotions clouded his gaze.

"I'm sorry," she whispered.

He turned away, stared out into the night. "I told myself you had changed. I thought I had found a woman who was special…one of a kind. But you are even more treacherous than your sister. Your betrayal was calculated to—"

"No, I didn't mean—"

"Be silent." He cut her off. Moving to the door, he added, "I will find somewhere to spend the night. By morning I want you gone. And don't return. Because I never want to see you again."

In the slanting morning light Gemma packed her bags, her heart aching, but she had a frightening suspicion that her heartbreak served her right. She'd called reception and been told that a ferry would be leaving in twenty minutes. If she hurried she could catch the boat to the mainland.

Angelo had not come back to the room since their awful confrontation. She'd waited, huddled on his bed, for him to return.

But he hadn't.

The message was clear. She had to accept that it was over. He did not want to see her. That to him her betrayal was worse than Mandy's had been.

Downstairs, the reception lobby was bustling. Gemma waited in an alcove for the shuttle to the ferry to arrive. The mural of a golden-haired sun god driving his fiery horses across the sky brought a bittersweet lump to her throat. She'd ventured too close to the heat and been badly burned.

But she would survive.

"Gemma?"

She turned at the sound of her name and her heart sank when she saw Jean-Paul. He examined her, his eyes searching for she knew not what, while a frown creased his brow.

"What?"

"You are Gemma?" It was the question that only yesterday she would've dreaded.

"Yes, I am Gemma."

"But you are not the woman I—" he paused "—once knew intimately."

Jean-Paul had worked it out. Probably as a result of her slip the other day. She released the breath she hadn't even known she was holding. "No."

"You're a dead ringer for her. She has to be your twin."

Rage surged through the pain. "Dead is what she is. And it's all your fault."

An ugly expression came over his face. "You breathe one word to Apollonides and I'll tell him the truth. That you've been deceiving him, laughing behind his back. You said that you've forgotten the past. That's how you've explained away not knowing things you should."

Behind him Gemma glimpsed the doorman who had offered to call her when the shuttle came, coming towards them. It was time. She rose. "Do your worst, Jean-Paul. Angelo already knows."

And she walked away leaving Jean-Paul staring after her, his jaw slack.

From the hilltop above the resort Angelo watched the ferry pull away, white water churning in its wake. He shoved his hands deeper into the pockets of his windbreaker.

Gemma was gone.

His mouth twisted. He'd told her to leave, and she'd obeyed. So why did he feel no better?

The wind caught at the windbreaker and ruffled at

his hair. He didn't notice. He narrowed his eyes against the sun and followed the course of the ferry until, a long time later, it disappeared from sight.

Then he started down the hill. A police helicopter approached from the mainland, making for the heliport.

Good. The police had organised a search warrant after his tip-off. Angelo couldn't wait for them to search the man's room and arrest Moreau. He suspected it would be a long, long time before the man frequented any resorts.

Just as it would be a long time before *he* forgot about Gemma.

Eleven

It was humid in Auckland in December. Gemma returned to her parents' home after a morning's Christmas shopping with her mother and made for the bathroom clutching the box she'd bought at the pharmacy. In less than five minutes she had the answer she'd dreaded.

"Mum," she staggered out the bathroom. "This is going to be a shock."

"What's wrong, darling?"

"I'm pregnant."

"Are you sure?"

Gemma nodded and held up the indicator stick.

"Oh." Her mother looked like she wanted to say something. Finally she asked, "Do you know who the father is?"

"Of course I do."

"But you're not telling?"

Gemma gave a laugh. To her own ears it sounded hysterical. "I will when I'm ready." She wrapped her arms around her mother. "You shouldn't be so understanding."

Her mother hugged her back. "How can I not be? Do you know how far along you are?"

"Not far at all. I missed a period, that's what clued me in. I've always been so regular."

"Go see your doctor. You may not be pregnant at all. Perhaps your body is just playing tricks on you after the long flight."

"I've been back almost two weeks—it's unlikely to be the flight."

Beth Allen shook her head. "But the pill makes the chance of it happening so remote."

"Except I haven't been on the pill for a while. There was no one in my life, so there seemed little point. He used protection. Something must have gone wrong. I'll go see the doctor, but I doubt it will change things." Deep in her heart Gemma was already sure. "Mum, I should tell you. The father is—" She broke off.

"Yes, darling?"

Gemma swallowed. "It's Angelo Apollonides."

Her mother's hand came up to cover her mouth, but no sound escaped. But her eyes were wide and dismayed as she stared at Gemma. Then she stepped forward and hugged Gemma. "You can tell how it came to pass when you're ready."

They stood like that for a long while, holding one another, and Gemma drew support from her mother's warmth. At last she said, "Thanks, Mum, for your support."

"Your father and I will always be there for you and the baby."

"I know. But I need to you to understand one thing, Mum. Angelo wasn't responsible for what happened to Mandy. It was another guy, Jean-Paul Moreau. I think Mandy loved him, and he rewarded her by making her into an addict. I hope he burns in hell."

"Oh, sweetheart, I have to tell you that is a relief to hear it wasn't your Angelo."

Later Gemma went home to the apartment she'd rented out while she went to Greece. It seemed strange to be living in the middle of the city after the time she'd spent on Strathmos.

Gemma made a pot of weak herbal tea and poured herself a mug. She intended to cut down on caffeine for the next nine months, that meant less tea and coffee.

Taking the mug she made her way to the dining-room table. She lay her hand on her flat stomach and thought about the baby. About the future. And about Angelo.

The phone interrupted her thoughts. It was her agent, thrilled with an offer for Gemma to perform at a brand-new Australian resort.

"It's the chance of a lifetime," Macy was gabbling. "The money is great and it's for six months. You get star billing. You'd be mad to let this pass."

Gemma considered it. The sum would wipe out the debt on her credit card; help her start the baby's life on much more stable footing. She could sublet the apart-ment while she was gone, that would give her a nest egg. But she couldn't take the job for the full six months. She'd be showing by then and she'd want to slow down.

"Macy, see if they'll do a deal for three months. I'll take that. I'll be ready to start in the new year. But get me the best money that you can."

She set the phone down, feeling a lot better now that she had a plan to get the burden of the debt Mandy had run up under control.

Now she'd have to call Angelo and let him know about the baby. He deserved that much.

Macy called back two days later, ecstatic with the deal she'd managed to secure Gemma. The contract was for four months and would start in the new year, and she'd managed to better the money, as well.

As for telling Angelo about her pregnancy, in the end Gemma's parents convinced her that it would be better to tell Angelo face to face. Her father was quite forceful about it, and was ready to come along, too, until Gemma talked him out of it. But she was pleased to see that he was looking a lot happier. Her pregnancy had given him a new interest in life.

Gemma had argued at first that flying to Strathmos was an expense she couldn't afford, particularly with the costs that the baby would incur, but in the end they'd convinced her.

So a week later Gemma found herself across the world again on Strathmos. She called ahead to make sure Angelo was in residence. The first person Gemma saw when she reached the resort was Lucie.

"Gemma—" the slight blonde threw her arms around her "—you're back."

"Not to stay, I'm looking for Angelo."

Lucie stepped back, her eyes curious. "He's around

somewhere. But it's the Christmas show tomorrow night, you must come watch. Even though Stella Argyris is the star of the show—and she never lets anyone forget it. She's even more of a pain in the butt than I remembered." Lucie rolled her eyes.

"I will." If she was here that long. If Angelo didn't kick her off the island the moment she delivered her news. And that reminded her, she'd need to book accommodation in the village later so that she'd have somewhere to stay for the night. Although, if the worse came to the worse, she had no doubt that Lucie would let her use the sofa in her unit.

"Any idea where I can find Angelo?"

Lucie shook her head. "He was talking to Mark earlier outside Dionysus's—but that was a while ago. Have him paged," she suggested.

"Thanks." Gemma had no intention of forewarning Angelo about her presence.

She wandered around, Angelo wasn't on the overcast beach where the westerly wind blew the sand up in gusts. Nor was he in the entertainment complex, although Mark greeted her eagerly. She didn't catch a glimpse of him in the lobby so she made her way to the casino. The gaming rooms were already occupied by some of the more hardened gamblers and she smiled at the bouncers as she made her way into the Apollo Club, but there was no sign of Angelo there, either.

She'd just about given up, deciding he must be in his penthouse and that she'd have to have herself announced, when she saw him seated in one of the many coffee bars, with a woman who was making every effort to keep his attention, flicking her long dark hair from her face, thrusting her chest forward to show off a superb stretch of cleavage.

Gemma turned away, her heart constricting. What had she expected? He'd told her he intended to forget her, and what better way than with a beautiful woman?

Angelo was gorgeous, wealthy…of course women would throw themselves at him. She'd never expected him to hanker after her. Yet seeing him with someone else hurt. Horribly. She made blindly for the exit. Outside the air was cool, the wintery edge of the wind cutting through her cardigan.

Gemma headed for the entertainment centre. As she rounded a bend, she saw Mark approaching from the opposite direction. She had no desire to talk to anyone so she slipped through a door into the massive Apollodrome super bowl where the Christmas extravaganza would be held.

She slipped into a seat and fought to blink back the tears that threatened. People came in and out, a couple of guys shifted props across the stage, but in the huge space she remained unnoticed.

It was a while before she gained sufficient control over her emotions to feel up to venturing out. The people had started to buzz in and out and she didn't particularly want to bump into anyone she knew. So she stayed where she was and realised the final dress rehearsal must be about to start. Squinting, she recognised several of the dancers in their workout gear, a couple of the backing singers. Just as she was about to stand to leave, all the lights came up and she saw Angelo walk up the centre aisle.

But he was not alone.

The beautiful brunette clung on to his arm, talking

vivaciously, her fingers tapping against his arm, demanding his attention. Angelo bent his head.

Gemma shrank back and felt a searing stab of jealousy.

When Mark came across the stage, the brunette rose onto her tiptoes, kissed Angelo's cheek and made for the stage stairs. It was then that Gemma realised that this must be Stella Argyris.

Clearly, Angelo already had a new mistress.

She rose clumsily to her feet, intent on getting out of here. She saw Angelo turn as if drawn by some sixth sense and freeze.

Then she was plunging out of the row of red seats, her heart tearing with pain, desperate to get to the exit, to get away from the sight of them…of him.

Why had she come back to Strathmos?

She should have called him, told him about the baby over the phone. She should never have let her parents talk her into doing the right thing.

But her reluctance to lie to herself made her face the truth.

It wasn't because of the baby that she was here. She'd come because she'd hoped that there was a chance to salvage something between them. That Angelo would take one look at her and know that he wanted her forever.

No chance of that. She'd deluded herself. Angelo had already found a new bed partner. Moved on. He wasn't the kind of guy to fall in love with someone like her. So what had she been thinking?

A hand closed around her arm. "I heard you were here, asking for me. What do you want?"

Affronted and upset, she yanked out of Angelo's

grasp. "I made a mistake. I should never have come back." And then she tried to move past him.

He blocked her path, his body broad and intimidating. "So why are you here?"

She shook her head. "It doesn't matter."

His fabulous eyes glinted. "I will decide if it matters. Something brought you a long way back. What?" There was an intensity in his tone that she didn't understand.

She shrugged, ducked around him and started to walk quickly, her head down, intent on getting away from him.

He kept up with her. "We need to talk."

"No, we don't." She rushed down a flight of stairs, her sights fixed on the exit to the Apollodrome. A vision of Stella Argyris kissing him filled her mind. "There's nothing to say."

She reached the exit and broke into a run, desperate to get out of the entertainment complex, to get away from him, before she started to cry.

She could hear his footsteps behind her. She ran faster, dimly aware that people—performers and tourists—were staring at her as she bolted past.

They'd reached the exit doors. Gemma plunged through them, into the salty windy air. She veered away, heading for the pathway to the village.

He caught her arm. "Slow down."

"Let me go."

He ignored her. Pulling her around to face him, he said, "You wanted to see me, now you've nothing to say?"

"Exactly."

"We need to talk."

She stuck her jaw out. "We don't."

"Okay, I'll talk, you can listen. But I suggest we do

this in the privacy of my suite—unless of course you like the idea of public scrutiny."

Gemma looked around. A group of gardeners was staring at them, talking. One laughed and Gemma flushed.

"No, not a good look for the boss to be arguing with his former mistress in public."

Her chest constricted.

"I don't care what people say about me, but I thought it might worry you."

She glanced up. His eyes were hard, his jaw set. Her breath caught. He was so utterly gorgeous. And she loved him desperately…was carrying his baby. She gave in. "Okay, we'll talk."

Except for the addition of a Christmas tree decorated with gold and red balls, his suite was unchanged from the night weeks ago when she'd carried out a vigil waiting for him to return to her. Gemma wasn't sure why she'd expected it to look different. Probably because, for her, everything had changed that night.

And now she carried Angelo's baby.

"Have a seat."

She took her cardigan off, dropped it on the floor beside the sofa and sat. Then gulped when he moved to stand in front of her. "So, tell me why did you come back? What was so important to come all the way across the world?" His eyes were guarded, but she got a sense that his body was wound tight.

She bit her lip. How was he going to react? Would he be angry? See it as an obstruction to his relationship with Stella?

"I'm waiting."

"I'm pregnant."

Whatever he'd expected, clearly, that wasn't it. His head went back, his eyes flaring with shock…and something else.

"Run that by me again?" he said very, very softly.

"I'm pregnant." Tremors of tension shimmered through Gemma as she waited for his reaction.

His eyes narrowed. "You're pregnant. Did you do it deliberately?"

Twelve

"*What?*" Gemma didn't try to hide her shock.

Angelo's handsome features could have been carved out of marble. "Is this your idea of revenge? Your way of punishing me for your belief that I'd caused your sister's death? Did you plan all along to fall into my bed, to get pregnant?"

"*No.*"

His tension uncoiled infinitesimally. "So why *did* you let me make love to you, knowing I thought you were *Mandy?*"

Oh, dear God, this was the one question she could not answer. Not without giving herself away. Irretrievably.

So she said with a touch of mockery, "Because you turn me on. More than any man I've ever met."

His voice held an edge. "Oh, that's the only reason?"

She shrugged. "Well, yes. What more could there be?"

"What more could there be?" he repeated savagely. Then he landed on the arm of the sofa and slid in behind her. "What more could there be?" A feather light kiss landed on her cheek. "This…" He pulled her across his lap, angled his head and his tongue stroked across her bottom lip, igniting a well of longing within her. "Someone who turned you on. That's all I was?" There was affront beneath the annoyance.

"Well, that's pretty much why you slept with me, wasn't it?"

"Maybe I thought I'd found my dream woman." His voice was ironic. Before Gemma could respond, his hand slid under her T-shirt, found the bud of her breast. "I was wrong. But we still have this, don't we?"

Gemma shoved his hand away. She felt a tearing ache of loss. He *didn't* love her. He could never love her. "I just wanted to tell you that the baby existed. You have a right to know. I won't even put your name on the birth certificate."

"Why not?"

"You want to be listed as the father?" She'd never expected that.

"Of course. No child of mine will grow up with the slur of *father unknown*."

She took a deep breath. "What will you tell people? What about Stella?"

"Stella?" He frowned, bewilderment clouding his features. "Why are you asking about Stella?"

"I saw you. I saw you kissing her."

The frown deepened and his eyes grew cool. "You saw Stella kissing *me*."

She folded her arms across her breasts. "And I saw

you having an intimate little conversation in the coffee shop," she plunged on.

He shrugged. "Stella wanted something."

Stella wanted something. That was for sure. Stella wanted Angelo Apollonides. "Are you trying to tell me that there is nothing between you and her?"

"That's exactly what I'm telling you."

"That you haven't slept with her since I left?"

"I shouldn't need to answer that. Especially since your only reason for sleeping with me was because I was a warm body." The savagery was back, and his lip curled into a snarl.

Doubts swirled through Gemma. What did Angelo want of her? Did he mean that he hadn't had another woman since she left? And given his reputation, could she believe that?

He was moving away. "And you won't need to worry about other women—because we're getting married."

Gemma froze. "Why should I marry you?"

His eyes grew wary. "I would never knowingly allow a child of mine to be raised with the slur of illegitimacy."

She didn't want Angelo marrying her only for the sake of the baby. "But lots of couples have children without the blessing of marriage."

"Not me." Angelo was unequivocal. "I grew up in a time when the world was more harshly critical. I lived with the sharp edge of the slurs. Even if the world has changed, I don't want that for my child."

Any romantic hopes Gemma may have harboured about his proposal died. He didn't love her, this was all about making sure his child had parents who were married.

* * *

Gemma was still trying to fathom how to react to Angelo's bombshell when they made their way to the Apollodrome for the Christmas Eve show the following evening.

Angelo had insisted Gemma stay in the penthouse, in the spare bedroom. And, with nothing suitable in her luggage, she'd been grateful to Angelo when a box emblazoned with the fancy logo of one of the exclusive boutiques in the lobby arrived at the door.

Opening the box, she glimpsed a fabric that glowed like crystal between layers of tissue paper. The dress was soft and clingy and fitted as though it had been made for her. The fabric changed colour from snowy white through to sparkling silver. A pair of silver heels and a tiny silver bag completed the outfit.

Now, as she glided backstage beside Angelo, Gemma felt anything but pregnant and ungainly.

Until she looked into a pair of enraged jet-black eyes and read the malevolence there.

"Angelo," Stella croaked, "my throat is in agony."

Mark rushed up and paled with dismay. "My God, Stella, you should've told us earlier. The show is sold out, ready to go."

"I didn't want to be a bother." Stella lowered her eyelashes. "I thought it would pass."

Gemma gave the woman a hard stare. She looked stunning, her black sheath made the most of her curves and her makeup hid any pallor that might reveal that she was unwell. But with a throat infection, she would not be able to sing.

"Angelo, maybe if I sit down a little while, it might

ease." Stella's hands fluttered at Angelo's sleeve, but he was already turning away.

"Mark, where's the program?"

It materialized with a flourish. Angelo pulled out a pen. "We'll cancel the solo that Stella was going to do, replace it with an item by Lucie LaVie—I'm sure she'll have a hilarious Santa story to share."

"But—" Stella's eyes widened with horror.

"And Aletha—" Mark named one of the other singers "—has been working as understudy. She can sing 'Oh, Christmas Tree' and 'Kalanda, Kalanda'—" he named the Greek version of "Jingle Bells" "—but that still leaves a hole where Stella was going to sing an encore all by herself, we'll just have to scrap that."

"But I can—" Stella interrupted frantically.

"Gemma," Angelo touched her arm. "Would you very much mind singing 'O Holy Night' as the encore? Please? I know you're not booked for this, that you were expecting to enjoy the performance as a guest. But would you do it? For me?"

She'd do just about anything for him. Singing her favourite carol was a cinch.

"Of course." She didn't dare look in Stella's direction.

"Brilliant idea," Mark said. "Gemma stood in for Stella in several of the early rehearsals."

"Gemma doesn't need to—"

"Stella, don't worry yourself about it. You're ill. I know that you would not have jeopardized such a show unless you were very sick."

Gemma whipped around to stare at Angelo in astonishment. *He knew.* He knew that Stella had been after the limelight and he'd dealt with her ruthlessly.

She shivered, suddenly feeling sorry for the other woman.

"Now, go." It was an order. "You need to be in bed, taking care of that throat so that you're well enough to perform for your next obligation." Even Stella caught the not-very-subtle warning and she slunk away without a word.

"Gemma, you'll need stage makeup." Mark was shepherding her to the dressing room. "Sorry to spoil your evening, you're a sport to help out when you must have been looking forward to watching the show from the front row."

"But what's everyone going to say when they find out they're not seeing Stella? She's a well-known singer. She'll have fans that came to see her."

Mark shrugged. "Too late to worry about that. At least they get to see a spectacular show, better than a cancellation."

In the wings Gemma waited. She'd also be singing a duet with Denny. She watched as a fire-eater gave a spectacular performance juggling torches and a whole lot of stunts that had the crowd gasping, then she and Denny were on.

The next ten minutes passed in a rush, she could barely remember what had happened. On the way off the stage, she passed a group of Christmas elves going on, a Russian troupe of acrobats that had the audience "oohing" and "aahing."

The carols sounded wonderful. Gemma started to relax. The finale came, everyone was on stage and the chorus voices were rising. Gemma felt the performers' excitement mirrored back by the audience.

Her hand brushed her stomach. *Hear that, baby? Next year you'll see the show, too.* So hard to believe.

The choir sashayed off, the dancers did a last sequence and with a wave they were gone. The curtains fell and applause followed.

Then Gemma was on the stage all alone. The audience lay like a vast sea of darkness ahead of her as a single spotlight lit her.

She searched the front row. And found Angelo through the bright beam of the spotlight.

She launched into "O Holy Night." She sang it for him…as he'd requested. No one else existed.

Only Angelo.

Afterwards she felt drained, but curiously exhilarated as clapping swept the showroom. She waved her hands in thanks, smiled and bowed. When she looked for Angelo again, he was gone and her heart sank.

An expectant hush fell over the crowd. Gemma started to walk to the wings, still facing the audience, waving, smiling until her cheeks hurt. The crowd started to buzz.

She turned to see what had caught their attention.

Angelo was on stage, coming towards her, his arms filled with a huge bouquet of red roses.

Joy twisted through her.

And then she remembered. This tribute was meant for Stella. Not her.

Stella's red roses.

Meaningless. Nothing to do with love. Nothing more than a goodwill gesture of appreciation.

Angelo reached her. He held a microphone in one hand. "That was a marvellous performance." The audience erupted into a burst of clapping. "Yesterday, I asked Gemma Allen to be my wife. Now, I'd like you all to celebrate her answer with me."

He held the microphone towards her.

The silence was absolute. The audience waited. Angelo, waited, his body taut.

Gemma gave him a despairing glance. What was she to say? How could she marry a man who took mistresses rather than a wife? A man who didn't—would never—love her?

Then a woman in the front row jumped up. "Say yes, Gemma."

Startled Gemma squinted into the lights. The woman was unfamiliar, blonde. She smiled, gave her a little wave.

"Ignore my mother," Angelo murmured.

"Your mother?"

Her voice boomed out over the microphone. Gemma blushed as the audience tittered. Out of the darkness came an indecipherable bit of advice.

Gemma ignored it.

She knew what she was going to do.

She was going to marry Angelo. For the sake of her baby. And for her sake…because she loved him.

"Yes." Her voice was strong and clear and the crowd whooped.

Then the roses fell from her grasp as Angelo swept her up into his arms, his mouth meeting hers in a kiss that held hunger and a touch of desperation.

Gemma wasn't acting as she grasped his shoulders and gave the best—and most public—performance of her life.

* * *

There was a Christmas party after the show. Lucie came rushing over with a tray of glasses filled with champagne as soon as she and Angelo arrived. Gemma laughed. "You're making me feel quite the celebrity."

"You are! You are! How could you keep—" Lucie flashed a sideways glance at Angelo "—such a secret from me?"

Angelo grinned. "I only asked her to marry me yesterday. I wasn't going to give her a chance to say no."

"Really? You railroaded her in front of all those people. Oh, naughty man."

Even Gemma laughed at Lucie's antics. And Angelo held her close to his side, his grip possessive, his hand heavy on her hip. For a while Gemma started to think that this could work, that even though he didn't love her, her love…and the baby…would be enough to meld them together.

Angelo went to fetch her a drink and Mark materialized at her side. "Your worry that the crowd would be disappointed by Stella's absence was all for nothing. Angelo's proposal gave them a once-in-a-lifetime show."

Gemma smiled at him. "At least the fans weren't disappointed." But it set her thinking. Had Angelo thought of it as a publicity stunt? She didn't think so. Her experience of him revealed an intensely private man, who as much as he liked a gorgeous woman by his side, treated that woman like a goddess. He was far kinder, far more complex than she'd expected.

The Angelo she'd read about in the gossip columns

was not the kind of man who would've married his pregnant mistress, and she struggled a little with the vast dichotomy between the playboy public profile and the complex man she'd come to love.

It wasn't long before he returned. But he wasn't alone. "My mother, Connie."

Gemma's eyes widened as she took in the slim, tanned woman. Connie looked liked she'd just stepped out of a beauty salon. Immaculate. Tanned. Not a hair out of place. And she certainly didn't look old enough to be Angelo's mother.

"Hello." Gemma smiled uncertainly.

"I am thrilled to meet you. Angelo told me all about you."

Gemma shot Angelo a questioning look. How much had he told his mother? Not everything, she hoped.

"I met your sister, once, briefly. The resemblance is remarkable."

So Angelo must have told his mother about her deception. "We were very close—even though we had little in common."

"Except my son."

"Mamma." Angelo's tone was furious. Gemma was too embarrassed to even look at him.

"I'm sorry. I'm sorry." Connie's hand covered her mouth, her nails perfectly manicured. "I can't ever seem to keep my thoughts to myself."

Angelo's eyes were clouded as he said, "But you can try. At least until Gemma gets to know you a little better."

"I'm sorry, Gemma. Forgive me?" Connie's long manicured nails rested against her arm. "Come, let's sit down somewhere, the three of us. You can tell me about the names you are thinking of for the baby."

So Angelo had told his mother about the pregnancy, as well. His mother seemed to have taken it well. No drama about a grandchild ageing her. Gemma let out a sigh of relief. On the plus side it looked like her future mother-in-law was totally without guile.

"Angelo, a glass of champagne for me please, and—" she turned "—what would you like, Gemma?"

"Water would be fine."

"Make it Perrier, my son." When Angelo wound his way into the throng she said, "Tell me about New Zealand. I have never been there. Are the men good-looking?"

Gemma laughed. They chatted for a while, Angelo brought their drinks and joined them for a while before he was dragged away by a staff member to welcome a big spender who had flown in to try out the Apollo Club and heard about the Christmas party.

"I'm thrilled Angelo is getting married. He always said he never would."

"It's the baby—I don't think he would've married me otherwise." What was the point of hiding why Angelo had proposed?

"So you are aware that Angelo is illegitimate?"

"Yes." Gemma reached out to touch Connie's hand. "But you don't have to—"

"I do. You need to understand the man you're marrying." Connie sighed. "His father was a handsome man, an entertainer, a singer of love songs. I fell in love with him. He was charming…a show man. I was eighteen. An heiress. Too sheltered. I became his mistress. Within the first month I was pregnant. The relationship did not last. I came home to Athens, to my disappointed parents.

"My father arranged a marriage for me to Mario Apollonides. To give the baby a name. My father built the house on Strathmos for me and my son and my new husband. The truth was hushed up. But, of course, there were rumours and lots of speculation. Too many people knew about my passion for Angelo's real father. Needless to say, the marriage lasted less than five years. So you see, my dear, why my son would never marry a woman just to give a baby a name."

Gemma stared at Connie. What was Connie telling her? Was there another reason why Angelo had proposed? He'd insisted that no child of his would grow up a bastard. Was Connie mistaken? Why would Angelo lie?

"Nor did my staying secluded on the island work," Connie continued. "Before long, I'd met another man— a business associate of my father, a millionaire. I became his mistress."

"And what of Angelo?"

"He stayed on the island…with his governess. When he was old enough I sent him to an English boarding school to get him out of the fishbowl that Greek society is. My father wanted Angelo to live with him, in Athens. But he already had another boy in his care, Zac. I was afraid that Angelo would grow up in his shadow."

Gemma remembered Angelo speaking of school, of the isolation. "He was a long way from home."

"Yes. It was hard for him, of course, coming from such a prominent family. I was linked through his school years with quite a few high-profile men."

Angelo would've hated that. But it explained his

attraction to glamourous, sophisticated women who wouldn't demand more than he was prepared to give. Emotionally or by way of permanent commitment.

And his love-them-leave-them image was born.

"And being illegitimate made it worse. Once, when he was about six he asked me why I hadn't married his real father. I told him I'd made a mistake, met the wrong man. But that I needed to get married, because society demanded it. He told me that he wouldn't make a mistake like that, he would never marry the wrong person."

Gemma stared at his mother.

So why had Angelo told her he wanted to marry her for the sake of the baby? Angelo was so self-contained, how was she going to find out?

Gemma was no closer to an answer when Christmas Day finally dawned.

By the time she'd dressed, the rain had set in, echoing her pensive mood, bringing back memories of Mandy's tragic death. She made her way through to the kitchen and stopped in astonishment at the sight of Angelo preparing breakfast.

"Merry Christmas." He grinned at her and leaned over to kiss her cheek. He looked so happy and relaxed that her own mood started to lift. "My mother called, she will join us for lunch—that gives us some time alone. The coffee is already on the go and the table has been laid."

They ate a breakfast of thick Greek yogurt and honey and fruit topped off with fried eggs and bacon. Afterwards they took their coffee mugs through to the lounge and settled beside the Christmas lights. Christmas…Gemma closed her eyes and thought briefly of Mandy.

Be happy for me, sister.

When she opened them, the lights on the tree winked at her, as if to say Mandy had heard her plea. *Thank you.*

When she looked up Angelo stood in front of her holding a gaily wrapped parcel. Gemma was relieved that she'd had the foresight to purchase a book on Greek legends for Angelo for Christmas.

She unwrapped his gift and took out the beautiful silk sarong. "It's beautiful," she mouthed.

He tore the wrappings off his gift and a smile lit his face. "I haven't read this. I'll look forward to it."

Then he took a little parcel out his pocket and tossed it to her.

"What's this?"

He shrugged. But his bright eyes were darker than usual and he looked almost hesitant. "Open it."

The removal of the gold paper revealed a black velvet box. Her heart stopped.

"Do you like it?" he asked softly.

Speechless Gemma stared at the elegant ring, a row of baguette diamonds vertically positioned in a channel setting.

"If you don't like it, we can change it."

His voice sounded far away.

Time seemed to hang suspended. Gemma couldn't stop staring at the ring. What if he never grew to love her? How would she survive being married for the sake of his child? Finally she looked up. "I don't think I can do it."

He stiffened and his gaze grew guarded. "What? Marry me?"

"You're only marrying me because of the baby."

"I want to be part of my child's life."

Gemma stared at him. "You're a high-powered businessman, you flit from resort to resort. You don't really want a family to drag you down." She tried to sound reasonable.

Angelo walked to the window. For a long moment he stood staring out. Then he swung around to face her. "I've been thinking about what Basil said. I'm going to delegate a lot of what I do. Family is important. I want to be part of my son's life. I want us to be married, to bring him up together."

"It won't work." She bit her lip. He sounded so convincing.

His gaze sharpened. "What are you frightened of?"

That you'll never love me. God, he was intuitive. "I'm not frightened. I just don't think—"

"—you can do it." He came towards her and took her hands in his. "You've said that already. But I think you're scared. What are you afraid of?"

Gemma swallowed. "Nothing."

"Then why is your pulse erratic." His fingertips stroked the delicate blue-veined skin inside her wrists. "Why is your breathing so shallow?"

"You know why." She watched him from under her eyelashes. "It's this overwhelming attraction between us."

He shook his head. "If that was all it was you wouldn't be trying to back out, you'd be bright-eyed and eager. No, this is something else." He scanned her face.

She could see that razor-sharp mind thinking. Would he guess the truth?

That she loved him?

"Are you worried that I still have you confused with your sister?"

"No." Strangely that didn't worry her at all.

Some of the tension went out of Angelo. "Good. I'm glad we've got that out the way because the two of you are really not alike at all. I knew you had changed. It simply never crossed my mind there were two of you. I thought you were one of a kind. Now, what are you afraid of?"

Gemma swallowed again. "I don't want to be married to someone who—" She broke off.

"Who what?"

Who didn't love her.

That was the simple truth of it. She'd been contemplating marrying one of the most desirable men on the planet. A man who didn't love her. For the sake of her child.

She must be mad.

"Who what?" he prompted again.

"A man who a zillion other woman are going to find as a hot as I do," she replied after a pause made it clear that he would remain silent until she answered.

"Ah—" he stroked her hand "—now it gets interesting. You'd only need to be concerned if those gazillion women interested me," he said quietly.

She thought about what he'd said. Her stomach rolled over. Could he possibly mean… "So why wouldn't you be interested in any of those zillions of woman?"

"Why did you really agree to marry me?"

There was a burning intensity in his question. Their eyes duelled, held. Indecisively, Gemma gazed into his turquoise depths.

"I'm scared," she confessed.

"Of what?"

"That if I tell you, you'll—" She broke off and shook her head. She couldn't bear it if he laughed…or worse, looked at her with pity in his eyes.

"Would it help if I told you why I asked you to marry me?"

"Because of the baby?"

He drew a deep shuddering breath. "Not because of the baby. For me." His grip tightened on her hands. He leaned closer. "After you left, it wasn't the same. My life was empty. I need you to complete me. I love you."

Her breath caught.

His eyes were bright, unguarded. The love shone from them. "The baby was an excuse, a way of getting what I really wanted. You."

Gemma's breath left her in an audible whoosh. Warmth filled her, her body softened, leaning into him. He felt warm and solid against her. Permanent. "I love you, too."

"At last!" He yanked her into his arms. The kiss that landed on her mouth held a touch of desperation.

And she realised that Angelo had been nervous. He hadn't been sure of her at all. "I was getting cold feet at the idea of being married to someone who didn't love me."

"And I have to admit I wasn't thrilled at marrying someone who wanted me only for my body. Wench." He sat up and grabbed her hand and slid the ring onto her finger. It fit perfectly.

Gemma giggled. "It could've been worse. I could've told you that I was marrying you for your money. To settle my credit-card debt."

"I knew that wasn't a factor."

"How?"

"The offer of the contract to sing in Australia would have taken care of your debt." He slanted her a look. "That's a resort I've recently acquired. I wasn't intending to let you get too far away. Once I got over the shock of your revelation that you weren't Mandy…and the even bigger shock that I wanted you back. I had to make a plan to get you back."

"I should've known!" Gemma laughed with joy. "I almost turned it down. Because I'd discovered I was pregnant. I wanted to work in New Zealand so I could be close to my parents. But the chance to get rid of that debt was too good."

A kiss landed on the top of her head. "Now we'll spend our honeymoon there and I'll spend the four months I have you under contract overseeing the developments I have planned for those resorts."

She cuddled closer. "And speaking of work. I still want to sing. But something Daphne said struck a chord with me. She's talked about starting a foundation to educate young people about the dangers of drugs. I'd like to get involved with that."

"Do anything you want. I will support your decision."

No longer his way. But their way. Gemma smiled to herself. "I'd like to feel that someone like Mandy could be saved. Or someone like Daphne's son, Chris."

He hugged tightly to him. "You have my support, on one condition: we get married before the new year."

She lifted her face to his, hooked her arm around the back of his head and pulled his mouth down to hers. "Deal!"

* * *

Angelo had one final surprise for Gemma. He flew her parents out to Strathmos for the wedding and watched her stunned delight as they walked into the penthouse to surprise her.

He put himself out to charm her parents. Two nights before the wedding the four of them had dinner in the Golden Fleece and afterwards they strolled down to the Apollo Club.

Later they shared a nightcap in the penthouse. By the time her parents were ready to call it a night, it was ten o'clock. After kissing her mother good-night and giving her father a hug and seeing them to the door, Gemma turned to Angelo with a gleam in her eyes that made his throat tighten and said, "I fancy a long, hot soak."

They wallowed in the huge spa tub in his bathroom. Angelo lounged across from her, his damp hair had darkened to bronze but his eyes were as startling, as vivid, as ever.

"Tired?" Angelo's tone was gentle.

She opened her eyes. His gaze held a tenderness she'd never seen before. "More like lazy. I feel like I never want to get out the water."

He smiled. "Oh, I guarantee you'll want to."

Her heartbeat bumped up. Her skin prickled, every inch of her instantly awake and energized.

"Angelo—"

Under the water his hand slid over her belly. "Our baby."

She smiled at him. "Our baby."

His gaze very intent, he said, "I love you, Gemma. Only ever you."

"I know," she murmured. "And for me there will only ever be you."

His eyes started to smoulder. "I believe you. I know you will never betray me.

"Come." He pulled her over him and water washed around them both at the sudden movement.

Gemma became intensely aware of the supple strength of his chest against her back, the hard length of his erection against her buttocks, ready and waiting.

Her head fell back into the crook of his shoulder where it joined his jaw, uncaring that her hair would be soaked.

When his other hand came up to play with her nipple, locking her in the circle of his arms, Gemma made a frantic, keening noise in the back of her throat and bucked her hips.

Angelo laughed softly in her ear. "More?"

The sound she made was barely coherent. One of his hands left her breast, snaked downward and slipped between her thighs.

There was something so intimate about being spread over Angelo's body, unable to see him, but aware of every arch and muscle of his flesh. She felt surrounded by him. He was under her, his arms around her, and all the while the wild flames licked between her legs.

She started to pant. She closed her eyes, focusing on the desire that burned through her.

When Angelo moved, her eyes snapped open. The next instant he hoisted her up onto the lip of the bath, parted her knees and knelt in front of her. She cried out as he entered her.

Heat ripped through her, wild and ferocious.

He moved again, Gemma's hands closed around his head, her fingers digging into the dark gold hair, and then she felt herself give.

"Angelo!" It was a cry of desperation, of satiation.

Angelo stood at the door of the church he'd been baptised in, waiting for his bride.

Connie, along with her latest husband and Gemma's parents, sat in the front row. From where he stood he could see Penelope dabbing the tears of happiness from her eyes. Tariq sat beside Connie, looking very grave, his white robes flowing behind him.

At the altar stood Zac and Pandora who'd agreed to be *koumbaro* and *koumbara* and crown him and Gemma in the wedding ceremony.

At last Angelo heard the drone of a motor and moved towards the entrance. A white limousine emblazoned with the resort's crest came down the winding road and slowed as it reached the church. He narrowed his eyes against the light, trying to catch a glimpse of Gemma.

The village priest materialized beside him. "It looks like your bride has arrived, my son."

Angelo started to move.

The priest's hand caught his arm. "Wait, let her alight."

The driver came around and opened the door.

One taut, elegant leg appeared. Then the other. Finally his bride emerged in a dress so white it dazzled him. He stepped forward, and barely noticed the priest's hand falling away, all his attention focused on the woman ahead.

She smiled at him and offered him her hand. He took it in both of his and raised it to his lips.

"I love you. I honestly do."

She rewarded him with that radiant smile that he knew would brighten the rest of his life.

* * * * *

STOP PRESS

The wedding of playboy hotelier Angelo Apollonides to songbird Gemma Allen was celebrated on the Greek island of Strathmos. When asked for comment, Apollonides stated that he and his wife would be honeymooning in Australia where he has recently acquired a string of brand-new resorts. "I will be taking it easier in the future, and I intend to learn to delegate and spend time with my wife and family."

Rumour has it that, having shaken off the title of the Most Eligible Bachelor in the Universe, Apollonides intends to waste no time in starting a family.

* * * * *

THE DESERT BRIDE
OF AL ZAYED

BY
TESSA RADLEY

Dear Reader,

I found it very hard to write this letter—mostly because I've reached the end of the BILLIONAIRE HEIRS trilogy about cousins Zac, Angelo and Tariq. And I don't really want to say goodbye to these gorgeous men. Not yet. Nor do I want to say goodbye to Pandora, Gemma and Jayne. I've spent so much time with these people over the past months that they've become a part of my life.

But now it's time to go out and meet—even embrace— new characters. Learn about them. What they like. What they loathe. And most importantly what happens to them when they fall in love…

Because at the heart of it all it's fabulous to create people who, after a rocky beginning, end up falling in love—and convincing readers that their love will last a lifetime. And sometimes, like Jayne and Tariq, they don't get it right the first time around. In *The Desert Bride of Al Zayed* Jayne and Tariq have a second chance at love…and a chance to get it right.

Take care,

Tessa

I grew up surrounded by inspiring women.
My mother, Ria, who always stays true to herself.
As well as Sophie and Esme who give so generously
of themselves. Thank you all for your love.

Much thanks to Melissa Jeglinski and Karen Solem
for giving me the freedom to write.

And Abby Gaines, Karina Bliss and Sandra Hyatt—
thank you for never being farther than a call away!

One

"I want a divorce."

The moment she'd blurted the words out, Jayne felt her pulse quicken. She squeezed her eyes shut…and waited. The silence on the other end of the line was absolute.

"No."

The answer rang with finality over the vast distance that separated Zayed from New Zealand. Tariq's voice was smooth and deep and very, very cool. Like ice. Tingling shivers of apprehension started to dance along Jayne's spine. She recognised that sensation. It meant trouble.

Jayne gripped the handset until her fingers hurt. "But we've been separated for over five years. I thought you'd be jumping for joy at the prospect of a divorce." *And your father, too.* She refrained from adding the dig. Mention of his father, the Emir of Zayed, tended to result in arguments—she'd learned that a long time ago. And she didn't want a battle with no ceasefire in sight, she simply wanted a divorce.

But this was not going quite as she'd planned. From the outset Jayne had intended avoiding any direct contact with Tariq—or his father. She'd phoned the Emir's chief aide, Hadi al Ebrahim, and had bluntly stated that more than five years had passed since Tariq had banished her from Zayed. Tariq was a citizen of Zayed and their marriage had been conducted in accordance with the laws of his country. According to the laws of Zayed, parties had to be separated for five years before a divorce could be petitioned.

The legal waiting time was over. She wanted to set divorce proceedings in motion. The excruciatingly polite aide had taken her number and promised to call her back.

But the aide's promised call hadn't come. Instead Sheikh Tariq bin Rashid al Zayed, her husband—no, her hopefully soon-to-be-ex-husband—had called.

Only to refuse her request.

No. No explanation. No softening the blow. Just a very blunt, very final *"No."*

Jayne resisted the urge to stamp her foot. Instead she tried for her most reasonable teacher's voice, and said, "You haven't seen me for years, Tariq. Don't you think it's time for us both to move on?" From a past that had brought her more pain and anguish than she'd ever anticipated.

"It's not yet time."

Jayne's heart skipped a beat. She sensed all her well-laid plans to start a new degree with the new year, to start dating again, to come out of hibernation and start living a life, unravelling. "Not time? What do you mean it's not yet time? Of course it's time. All you need to do is sign—"

"Come to Zayed and we'll talk about it, Jayne."

Even over the distance between them the husky sound of her very ordinary name on his tongue sounded sensual and intimate and had the power to make her shiver. It was madness.

"I don't want to talk. I just want a divorce." Jayne heard the touch of shrillness in her voice. She could see her brand-new life, her well-laid plans going up in smoke. Damn Tariq.

"Why?" His voice changed, became harsh and abrupt. "Why are you suddenly so desperate for a divorce, my faithless woman? Is there finally a man who objects to having a woman with a husband?"

A brief hesitation. She thought about Neil, the nice accountant her brother-in-law had introduced her to three months ago. He'd asked her out, but she hadn't accepted. Yet. "No! You've got it all—"

"We will meet in Zayed," her husband decreed. "There will be no divorce. Not yet. But it is possible that the time will come soon. Very soon. We will talk."

"Tariq—"

But he was already firing information about dates and flights and visas at her. Belatedly Jayne realised that she no longer held her Zayedi passport, she'd left it behind in the bedroom she'd shared with Tariq on that terrible last day. She'd had no intention of ever returning. She'd have to apply for a visa to go to Zayed, which meant at least a week of delay.

"Tariq." It was a desperate call.

He paused and the sudden silence that stretched between them was shattering.

Jayne swallowed, her mouth dry. Then, more quietly, she said, "Can't we meet somewhere— *neutral* "—else?" Tariq would not come to New Zealand; it was too far. He was a busy man. And she didn't want him here, destroying her safe haven.

But there had to be other options. Somewhere where she wouldn't need to revisit those traumatic weeks before the end of their marriage, somewhere she wouldn't have to walk through the corridors of the lavish palace that had stifled her dreams, or confront the two men who had killed her soul. "What about London?"

"There are…problems…in Zayed. I cannot leave."

She thought about that for a long moment. "I *can't* come to Zayed," she said at last.

"Can't or won't?"

She didn't answer.

"Then let me make it easy for you. If you don't come to Zayed, Jayne, I will oppose any application you make for a divorce."

The words were chilling, even though the tone that delivered them was rich and lingering. The laws of Zayed stated that no divorce could be granted unless the husband consented. As much as it riled her, she needed Tariq's consent.

Unless she went to Zayed, Tariq would deny her the one thing she wanted above all else: her freedom.

"Don't forget to send me photos of Zayed."

Jayne had almost reached the front door of her sister's house, the Louis Vuitton bag clutched in her hand, when the request caused her to pause. She turned to look at the three people gathered in a huddle to see her off, the three people she loved most in the world—her sister and her two nieces. Raising an eyebrow at her elder niece, Jayne asked, "What kind of photos?"

"Of the desert…the palace—anything cool."

"It's very hot in the desert, not cool at all. Certainly not as cool as anything here in Auckland." Jayne kept a straight face as she referred to her older niece's active social life, then broke into a smile when Samantha poked a pink tongue out. "What do you want the photos for?"

Samantha moved closer. "I'm doing a PowerPoint project on Zayed. Most of my class has never heard of it."

"I'm sure I can dig up some really up-to-date information while I'm there," Jayne promised, setting the heavy bag down for a moment and flexing her fingers. Samantha flashed a pleased grin and Jayne restrained herself from rumpling her niece's sleekly gelled hair. The style was so much more so-phisticated than the ponytail Samantha had worn last year. It was hard to believe that in less than a month Samantha would turn thirteen. A teenager.

"Great." Samantha beamed. "If I can wow my teacher, I might even get an A."

"Do you really have to go?"

A small hand tugged at her arm. Jayne looked down into the hazel eyes of her younger niece—her goddaughter—and her heart twisted.

"I really have to go, Amy, my sweet."

"Why?"

Jayne hesitated. *Why?* She thought of the abortive conver-sation with Tariq. How to even start to explain? "Because…" Her voice trailed away.

"'Because' is not an answer," Amy replied, her freckled face solemn.

"Quite frankly, I can't understand why you're going, either," Helen chipped in with typical older-sister impatience.

"After everything that happened in that godforsaken country, what Tariq and his horrid father did to you, why on earth would you contemplate going back?"

Jayne recognised her sister's impatience for what it was—concern. "Because I want a divorce—and it looks like going to Zayed is the only way I can get it."

Tariq had made that clear enough.

"Why Zayed?" Helen asked, her lips tight. "Why couldn't you have met in London?"

"It wasn't an option I was given." Jayne shrugged her shoulders. "That's Tariq. His way. Or no way."

"Are you sure he isn't up to something?" Helen fretted. "I don't trust him one bit."

"Hush, don't work yourself up." Jayne moved closer to her sister. Helen had never understood the attraction, the fascination that Tariq had held right from the moment that Jayne had walked into him in the Tate Gallery in London and landed ignominiously at his feet. How could she explain the untamed attraction Tariq had held? "There's no reason to be suspicious. Tariq wouldn't take me back if I came coated in twenty-four carat gold."

Helen's eyes sparked with indignation. In a low voice she murmured so that only Jayne could hear, "He never deserved you."

Emotion surged through Jayne. She slung an arm around her sister's shoulder and pulled her close. Helen smelled of talc and roses and the familiar comfort of home. "Thank you. And thank you for all the support you've given me. For everything."

"I don't want to see you in that state again." Helen hugged her back fiercely. "Five and a half years ago you were a mess."

"It won't happen again," Jayne vowed, suppressing the

sudden stab of apprehension. "I'm no longer nineteen. I'm older now, able to take care of myself."

"Famous last words. And it better not happen again, because this time I'll tell Tariq what a—" Helen cast a glance at the girls and lowered her voice "—*jerk* he is."

Her sister sounded so ferocious that Jayne couldn't help the giggle that escaped her. For the first time in a week, the tension that had been winding up in her chest subsided. Her sister would always be there for her. Family. Sisters. A sacred bond.

"I suggest you don't say that to Tariq's face." Just the thought of his freezing expression, the way he would look coldly down his elegant bladed nose, was enough to make Jayne chuckle again.

"You won't be here for my first day of school." Amy's desolate wail cut into Jayne's moment of good humour. Instantly all laughter dried up. Bending down, she swept Amy up until the little girl's eyes were level with hers.

"But I'll be thinking of you," Jayne promised. "I'll even know where you'll be sitting. Remember? You, mom and I went together to check your new school out?"

"I s'pose," Amy said reflectively. "And I'll have the pencils you bought me." She already sounded more cheerful. Jayne smiled at her sister over Amy's head, her throat tight.

A hoot sounded.

"Daddy's ready." Amy wriggled out of Jayne's arms.

Helen rushed over and then Jayne was wrapped in her sister's warm arms. "Take care, Jayne."

"I will." Jayne held on for a moment. A kiss on her sister's cheek and then she freed herself and picked up her bag. "I'd better not keep Nigel waiting. Look after yourself—and the girls. I'll e-mail photos, I promise," she called to Helen and Samantha as she hurried out the door. From beside the car, Jayne gave them a last wave before getting into the idling car where her brother-in-law waited to take her to the airport.

Finally Jayne let herself admit she wasn't looking forward to the long flight that lay ahead. And she dreaded the coming confrontation with the man who waited for her at the journey's end.

The chilly air-conditioning in the international airport at Jazirah, the capital of Zayed, took the edge off the searing heat that shimmered over the runways outside the terminal building. A deferential official took charge of Jayne the instant she presented her passport and whisked her through customs. He retrieved her luggage and showed her to a plush seat in a sheltered alcove off the arrivals concourse, murmuring that he'd be back shortly.

Jayne attempted to assure him that she was quite capable of organising her own transport, but he grew increasingly agitated. He was obviously concerned by the fact that she was travelling alone. Zayedi men could be extremely protective, to the point of being overbearing. So Jayne subsided with a shrug and watched him scurry away.

Pulling the white chiffon scarf out the side pocket of her handbag where she'd tucked it in before leaving Auckland, Jayne looped it around her neck. It wasn't a *hijab*, but it would do. Zayed was more modern than its neighbouring states, some of the youth even wore jeans, but most women still adopted conservative dress. Jayne knew that the narrow black trousers and casual geometric patterns of the black and white shift dress she wore over them were acceptably modest…even if they were straight out of this season's budget fashions in Auckland, a far cry from the traditional jilbab and colourful kaftans so many older married Zayedi women wore.

From where she sat, Jayne could see the long wall of glass that separated the airport from the drop-off zone outside. A fleet of shiny black Mercedeses were parked there, reminding her of the extent of the wealth in this desert sheikhdom.

A commotion a way down the concourse attracted her attention. Jayne rose to her feet to get a better look. A knot of uniformed men were causing a stir. Her gaze narrowed. She recognized those uniforms, they belonged to the Emir of Zayed's palace guard. They held some very unpleasant associations. The last time she'd seen the red and khaki colours had been here, at this airport, when the men wearing them had been charged with making sure she left Zayed.

Behind them she caught a glimpse of a tall man in a dark suit. His sheer imposing height and the familiar tilt of his head caused her heart to leap. *Tariq*. Jayne froze, her muscles tight, and her head swam with the sudden light-headedness caused by the panic that swirled through her.

He was coming closer. Her pulse grew choppy, loud in her ears. His head turned and their eyes connected. The first thing that struck her was that his eyes were still the colour of pure, molten gold. The second was that they were not the least bit welcoming.

Tariq raked her from head to toe, and his lip curled. Instantly all the old insecurities crashed back. She was plain Jayne Jones, in the everyday chain-store shift dress that she'd worn over her most comfortable black trousers for the flight.

The antipathy directed at her caused Jayne to stumble backward. Nothing had changed. Her husband detested her.

The earth rocked under her feet and she glanced away, disconcerted. And caught sight of the red carpet. Of the trio of little girls holding posies. But it took the black print on the brightly coloured banner two women were unfurling to jolt her into disbelief. Welcome Back Sheikhah, it read.

This dog-and-pony show was intended for her.

In a flash the reason for the official's agitation became clear. Her first meeting with Tariq was going to be conducted under public scrutiny. Jayne's palms grew clammy and her pulse started to race.

No.

She gave the gathering crowd a wild glance, took in the scaffolding with the mounted television cameras, clearly here to film her return. She was so not prepared for this hullabaloo. She'd come to meet Tariq, to talk in private about their divorce.

Tariq was walking with purpose. Backed by the squad of the palace guard, he looked dangerous, resolute. But Jayne knew that whatever the reason he'd demanded her return to Zayed, it had nothing to do with the love they had once shared.

She cast a frantic gaze around. People were milling forward, crowding around the red carpet, the guards and the powerful, commanding man in the heart of all the fuss. No, she hadn't come to be part of this…circus.

She wanted to meet Tariq on her terms. In private. Without an audience.

Two cameramen with huge cameras mounted on their shoulders that sported the local TV network logo rushed ahead of Tariq to capture the moment for the news. They blocked Tariq from her view.

Cautiously Jayne edged forward. No one was looking in her direction. With a surreptitious movement, she hitched the sheer scarf off her shoulders and draped it across her hair, then hoisted up the Louis Vuitton bag, a legacy from her past life with Tariq. Keeping her head down, she made quickly for the double sliding doors that led out of the airport. They hissed open and she escaped through.

The heat hit her like a wall. Oppressive. An inferno compared to the coolness in the airport and the temperate weather she'd left behind in Auckland. Jayne thought she heard a shout. She didn't look back. Instead she kept her head down and increased her pace. A taxi was parked behind the string of Mercedeses.

As she broke into a run a taxi driver straightened from the low railing he'd been leaning against and parted his lips into a smile that revealed stained yellow teeth separated with chunks of gold. "Taxi?" He opened the rear door and music blared out.

"Yes," she gasped, deafened as she fell into the backseat. When she didn't bother to haggle over the rate, his smile grew wider still. "Take me to the palace. Please."

The smile withered and he shot her a lightning-fast once-over glance, before climbing into the driver's seat and turning the radio down a notch.

"Hurry," she said, peering anxiously out the window beside her.

The motor roared, drowning out the radio for a moment, and her unsuspecting rescuer swerved out onto the strip of concrete road.

Driven by an impulse she could not explain, Jayne turned back to stare through the rear window at the glass doors through which she'd escaped.

His tie flapping with his stride, Tariq strode through the glass doors. Behind him followed the pack of palace guards. Jayne shrank back into her seat. Even from this distance she could tell that Tariq did not look pleased. The angle of his broad shoulders, the set of his head, the impatience in his long stride all showed his fury.

Trepidation coursed through her. This was no longer the young man she'd fallen in love with. This was a different Tariq. Older. Regal. The only son of the Emir of Zayed. A man accustomed to having his orders obeyed.

Jayne closed her eyes in relief at having gotten away. The taxi rocked from side to side as the driver darted through the traffic. Afraid that the roller-coaster motion might make her queasy, Jayne opened her eyes.

"Hey, slow down."

Jayne sighed in exasperation when her demand met no response, and leaned back into her seat to brace herself for the ride.

The airport was located a distance away from the city. On the left side of the car, the stony desert stretched away as far as the eye could see. On the other side, a narrow strip of land separated the six-lane highway from the azure sea. A couple of minutes later they passed the desalination plant that Jayne knew had cost millions to set up ten years ago.

The taxi driver swerved past a tourist camper van and cut across to the exit. Once away from the highway, they wove through the city streets between old historic buildings and modern glass skyscrapers.

"Are we being followed?" Clutching at the seat belt as they hurtled through an older section of the city between ancient mosques and colourful *souqs,* Jayne voiced her worst fear.

But the taxi driver didn't answer. Could he even hear her with the radio blaring? Jayne wished she'd sat up front. But this was Zayed, not New Zealand. Women didn't sit up front. Not unless they wanted the taxi driver to construe the move as flirtation. While Zayed was a safe country, a woman travelling alone had to take care not to attract unwelcome attention. She shouted the question more loudly.

The taxi driver glanced in the rear mirror. "No one is following."

But Jayne's apprehension didn't ease and the knot in her stomach grew tighter. Tariq was going to be fit to be tied. She shivered, then reason set in.

It was his own fault. He should have warned her. He should never have sprung that spectacle back at the airport on her. She gave her casual outfit a quick once-over. At least then she would've had the chance to dress up a little. Make the best of the little she had. Not that clothes and a little bit of makeup could bridge the gulf between them. They were too far apart. In every way.

She tried to set the worry aside, tried to tell herself that the sooner she met with Tariq in private and got it over with the better. But even that didn't help. Jayne's fingernails bit into her palms. She'd explain. She'd tell him that—

The sudden swerve of the taxi threw Jayne against the door, and she gave a shriek of fright. The driver leapt out of the car and Jayne could hear shouting.

When she emerged from the back of the car, her heart pounding, a shocking sight met her eyes. A youth was sprawled on the road, his bicycle lying on its side. He was groaning.

"Oh, my heavens." Jayne moved toward the victim but the taxi driver grabbed her arm.

"Wait, it could be a set-up…"

"How can it be a set-up? He's hurt!"

The youth was screaming now. A basket, its lid off, lay on the road and a clutch of ginger chickens were clucking in terror.

"Is he okay?" Jayne's first concern was for the youngster. "Did we hit him?"

"No, no. The idiot—"

The youth interrupted with a deluge in Arabic. Jayne held up her hand. "Is he hurt?"

The taxi driver rattled off and the boy muttered, shaking his head. Relieved Jayne said, "What about his bike?"

"No problem."

A crowd had started to gather. Quickly Jayne peeled some notes out of her bag.

"U.S. dollars." The youth's eyes lit up as he reached for them.

The taxi driver started to protest, Jayne handed him the next set of notes. "You can leave me here." She'd had enough of his driving.

"But the palace?" He looked suddenly nervous.

Jayne waved a hand. "Don't worry about taking me to the palace." She'd have a better chance of surviving on her own. Jayne looked left and right, hitched her handbag over her shoulder and grabbed the handle of her suitcase.

Down the street she could see the flower *souq,* the market where blooms were brought early each morning. Across the road a pension-style hotel attracted her eye. It looked modest and unassuming, the kind of place where a woman alone would be safe from unwelcome attention. She could stay there for the night. And tomorrow she'd be better prepared to face Tariq, rested and refreshed. She started to feel better.

A hand brushed her arm. Jayne tensed and spun around,

then relaxed. The taxi driver thrust a grimy square of cardboard at her. Jayne glanced down. Mohammed al Dubarik and a scrawl of Arabic characters followed by some numbers that clearly belonged to his cell phone. With a final flash of yellowed teeth and bright gold, he departed in a roar of dust.

Jayne shoved the card into her bag and looked both ways then hefted up her bag to cross the street. The curious crowd, sensing the drama was played out, started to disperse. Pulling the chiffon scarf more securely over her head she made for the door of the pension. She'd almost reached it when a touch on her shoulder startled her.

At first she thought the taxi driver had returned.

She turned her head…and saw the youth who had fallen off the bicycle. Standing, he looked a whole lot bigger. And far more threatening with the gang of faces that loomed behind him. With no chickens and no bike, he suddenly didn't look so young and vulnerable. In fact, he looked downright menacing.

And then she saw the knife.

Jayne screamed. The sound was cut off midutterance as the biggest youth moved with the speed of a striking snake and shoved her up against the rough plaster wall of the pension. Through the tinted glass door, Jayne glimpsed an elderly man inside the pension, behind the reception desk, he caught her eye and looked away.

No help from that quarter.

Fear set in like a bird fluttering frantically within her chest. "Please, don't hurt—"

A screech of brakes. A shout of a familiar voice in Arabic. Then she was free.

Jayne heard the sound of feet rushing along the sun-baked sidewalk, caught a glimpse of khaki and red uniforms giving chase.

"Jayne!"

She knew that voice. Recalled it from her most shattering dreams…and her worst nightmares. She sagged against the rough plastered wall of the pension as Tariq leapt from the Mercedes, shutting her eyes, blocking him out. *All of him.* The lithe body that moved with the fluidity of a big cat, the hawk-like features that had hardened with the passage of the years, the golden eyes that were molten with a terrible anger.

"Get in."

"I want—"

"I don't care what you want." The molten eyes turned to flame. *"Get into the car."*

To her astonishment, Jayne found herself obeying. The Mercedes smelled of leather, of wealth and a hint of the spicy aftershave that Tariq wore—had always worn. The scent wove memories of Tariq close to her, holding her, of his skin under her lips. She shrank into the corner and curled away from the unwelcome memories. Memories that she had come here to excise forever. By getting a divorce.

"Look at me."

She turned her head. His face was set in stone. Hard. Bleak as the desert. Until she detected a tangle of swirling emotions in his eyes. Not all of which she could identify. There was anger. Frustration. And other emotions, too. Dark emotions that she'd hoped never to see again.

Two

"So, you decided to avoid the welcome I had planned for you." As the Mercedes pulled away, Tariq delivered the statement in a flat, emotionless tone, despite the rage that seethed inside him at what had nearly happened to her.

"Welcome?" Jayne laughed. It was not a happy sound. Annoyingly, she looked away from him again and he couldn't read her eyes—the eyes that had always given away her every emotion. "You would be the last person I'd expect to welcome me anywhere."

"I am your husband. It is my duty to welcome you to Zayed."

Jayne didn't respond.

"Why did you run?" He didn't like the fact that she had taken one look at him in the airport and fled. Whatever else lay between them in the past, Jayne had never feared him. Nor was he happy with the notion that the only reason she was in the car was because he was the lesser of two evils. The thought that she considered his company only a notch above that of the youths who had assaulted her turned his mouth sour.

"I wasn't dressed for the occasion."

Anger rose at her flippant response and he pressed his lips into a thin line. Was she so unmoved by the attack? He knew that it would prey on his mind for a long time to come. He had thought that he had no feeling left for his errant wife, that her actions had killed every feeling he'd ever nurtured for her. But the instant he had seen that young dog lay his hand on Jayne, rage—and something else—had rushed through him. He could rationalise the anger, the blind red mist of rage.

She was his woman.

No other man had any right to touch her. Ever.

What he couldn't understand was his concern for Jayne, the woman who had behaved so atrociously in the past. He couldn't understand this urge to make such a woman feel safe, to assure her that what had happened out there in the back-streets of Jazirah wasn't her fault. Even though it would never have happened if she had graciously accepted the welcome he'd arranged.

Before he could work through the confusing threads, Jayne was speaking again, "I don't intend to stay long. A big welcome like the one you arranged would give the wrong impression and suggest that I've returned to stay." She shrugged. "I thought it for the best to leave."

"The best for whom? You? It certainly did me no good to be left standing there looking like a fool."

"You would never look like a fool. But I would've. I was

ill prepared for the occasion. How do you think I would've looked…sounded…on national television?"

Tariq swept his gaze over her, taking in the tension in every line of her body, the way the cheap clothes stuck to her in the heat, the dishevelled hair revealed under the scanty *hijab* that had fallen away and the white-knuckled hands clasped on her lap. Perhaps she wasn't as composed as she sounded. Perhaps the attack had shaken her. In the old days she would've come apart, started to cry, she'd been so gentle, with her huge, adoring, doelike brown eyes. It had been her gentleness that had caused him to love her. There had been so little tenderness in his own life.

"What are you looking at? I'm sorry if I'm not wearing haute couture. I'm sorry if you think I'm unfit for your company."

There was an unfamiliar note of annoyance in her voice, and resentment flashed in her eyes. Tariq blinked in astonishment. Where had this come from? Jayne had always been easygoing and eager to please, hero-worshipping him. "Unfit for my company?" he repeated. "I have never thought that. I married you, didn't I?"

She ran a hand over her face. "Look, I feel like I've been flying forever. I'm tired, cranky. The last thing I wanted was a welcome reception with TV cameras, for heaven's sake."

"Your apology is accepted."

He waited and watched the wide brown eyes flash again. He almost smiled. Yes, he could get used to this.

"It wasn't an apology, it was an explanation why I am less civil than normal." Her voice was curt. "You should not have sprung that surprise on me. And as for what's best for me, yes, in the past our relationship was always about what you and your fa—family wanted. I didn't need that circus back there at the airport. I came here for one reason only, to talk. With you. Alone. To get a divorce. I didn't want to be welcomed back as your sheikhah. That would be a lie, because I have no intention of staying."

Tariq gave her a long, level glance. She wanted a divorce. Three months ago he'd have been too eager to grant her that, he would have been grateful to have the gentle, malleable wife, who he tried so hard never to think about, out of his life. But then everything had changed. His father was far from well. He needed her in Zayed at his side. And after his response to her attack and seeing the new flash of fire in her, he was not sure that he'd be letting her go too quickly.

For the first time in his life he was confused. And he didn't like that bewildering sensation at all.

The palace lay ahead of them, dazzling, stupendous. The sandstone had been bleached over the centuries to a warm and inviting shade of gold. A mirage. Because Jayne knew that behind the walls lay a world of intrigue, politics…and the cold heart of the Emir who had destroyed her.

They drove around the side and under the rising wrought-iron portcullis into a large courtyard paved with cobbles where the Mercedes slowed to a stop. The driver opened her door and Jayne alighted.

Even now, with her confidence rebuilt after more than five long years away, she felt apprehensive as she entered the immense vaulted hallway through the side door.

"I'd like to call my sister to let her know I arrived safely." Jayne craved the reassurance of Helen's no-nonsense voice.

"Of course."

She thought of Samantha's request for photos. "And is there somewhere I can use for e-mail?"

"Yes, my study is available to you at any time."

"Thank you." She directed a small smile up at him.

Tariq went still. His eyes glinted as he came closer. "Jayne—"

"Excellency, it is good that you are back." The interruption came from an aide wearing a worried frown. "Sheikh Tariq, there is need for your presence. Sheikh Ali has arrived demanding an audience. He has brought Sheikh Mahood, and they have been waiting for you." The aide was wringing his hands.

Tariq moved away. Jayne felt his withdrawal, and it left a chill, cold feeling in her chest. Her heart sank further at the mention of Sheikh Ali. That was another name she would never have regretted not hearing in her lifetime again. She sneaked a sideways glance at Tariq.

His face had darkened. "Tell them that I will be with them shortly."

"I've already told them that you were welcoming the sheikhah back after a long absence. They do not care about that, they are only concerned about the issue of grazing rights in the northern territories."

Jayne flinched at Tariq's short, sharp curse. Then he turned to her. "I need to go. I will see you at dinner." Tariq's voice was brisk, businesslike. "We will talk further then. In the meantime, Latifa will show you to your apartments."

Jayne hadn't heard the woman's silent approach. Her face was round with the plumpness of youth, her eyes wide and respectful as she gazed at Jayne, waiting for instruction.

"Wait—" Jayne called after Tariq, but he didn't hear, because his pace picked up as he strode away to attend to the latest crisis in Zayed, his head bent to listen to the aide beside him.

A sense of loss ebbed through Jayne. She forced it back with effort and turned to the young woman who waited respectfully. "Thank you, Latifa. I'd appreciate it if you showed me to my room. I'm looking forward to freshening up."

It turned out to be a vast boudoir with stone arched windows that looked out onto the lush palace gardens filled with date palms, fountains and the clinging fragrance of honeysuckle and gardenia.

Jayne kicked off her shoes and toured around the rooms, exploring the crannies before making her way to the large bathroom where Latifa had filled the enormous spa bath. The sweet scent of the crushed rose petals was inviting…intoxicating. One of those little luxuries that seeped the ache out of the soul, made the daily misery of life in Zayed seem bearable.

Ten minutes later, lying back in the sleek, scented water, the realisation that she was back here in Tariq's world, where she'd sworn never to return, sank in.

Jayne wondered whether there would be chance to talk with Tariq later. Her husband was an important man. He was no figurehead sheikh. His father had always demanded his full involvement in the affairs of the state that he would one day head. Not that the Emir would be in any hurry to relinquish control of his rule.

In the past the demands on Tariq's time had driven a wedge between them. And Jayne was relieved that on this visit it was not her problem. She no longer needed Tariq to fulfil the role of husband and lover. All she required was sufficient time to discuss his enigmatic statement:

"There will be no divorce. Not yet. But it is possible that the time will come soon. Very soon. We will talk."

She wasn't accepting that kiss-off. She had come to Zayed for a divorce. The time was here. She would not allow Tariq to dominate her as he had done in the past. She'd grown up; she was no longer in awe of her powerful husband.

A long soak left her body feeling heavy and languid. At last Jayne summoned the energy to get out of the bath and, wrapped in a soft ivory towel, she made her way back to the sumptuous bedroom where her meagre selection of clothing had been packed into the cupboard by Latifa.

Mindful of the conservative nature of the palace, Jayne chose a long black skirt that clung to her hips before falling to just above her ankles and teamed it with a black top with a vee-neck and long, trumpet-shaped sheer chiffon sleeves. A pair of ballet-style black pumps and she was as ready as she'd ever be to face Tariq.

Downstairs she was surprised to find only Tariq waiting for her in the small salon. He'd shed the dark designer suit and wore a traditional white *thobe*. It added to his height, emphasised his dark, hawklike features and made him appear more imposing than ever. Jayne hesitated in the doorway. "Where is everyone?"

In the past, facing a room full of strangers she barely knew at the end of the day over the long dinner table had been one of the major strains of life in the palace. Aides and distant family members of the Emir, members of desert clans, all came to the palace to seek advice from the Emir or one of the senior members of the ruling family. And she'd expected the delegation Tariq had met with about the grazing rights earlier today to be here.

· "My father is…not well. Many are keeping vigil in the courtyard and antechamber outside his rooms."

"Oh." For a brief moment Jayne considered asking what was wrong with the Emir, then she decided against it. It would be too direct a question. Too impolite. And then there was the fact that she was reluctant to become embroiled in an argument with Tariq about his father. Which was where any innocent, well-meaning query would end. Instead she focused on what she'd come for. "Can we talk about finalising the divorce?"

"After dinner," Tariq said. "You have been travelling, you will need sustenance."

"I'll be fine, this won't take long." She glanced at him with a frown. He was prevaricating. That was a palace etiquette rule, if it would raise conflict, a matter could not be aired during a meal. "I can't believe you forced me to fly across the world to talk about a divorce to which I am entitled."

His expression became distant. "You are not entitled to it, not until I give my consent."

She gave a snort of disgust. "Surely you're not going to take that line. It's antiquated. If this is about your male pride, then *you* may divorce *me*. I don't care. You needn't have dragged me across the world for this."

His eyes were hooded. "You will be recompensed for any…inconvenience."

"That's not necessary." She raised her chin. She didn't need his money. "All I want is the divorce. That will be worth every cent of the trip."

His brows jerked together. "You will get your divorce. When I am ready. But now we eat."

Jayne found herself bristling at the command. But she forced herself to take a deep breath and follow him through the French doors onto the terrace outside. Stairs cut into a wall of stone, lined with flaming sconces, led to a secret garden where white flowers bloomed in the waning light. In the arbour, surrounded with white roses, a table had been laid and an array of food spread out.

Nearby a fountain tinkled, the sound of water calming Jayne's frazzled nerves.

There was huge platter of fruit with dates and wedges of crumbly white cheese that resembled *haloumi.* Another plate held a selection of flatbreads with hummus, fried *kibbe,* the spicy meatballs with pine nuts, and a dish of tabbouleh salad. Eyeing the spread, Jayne discovered that she was hungrier than she'd thought.

"Is that falafel?" she pointed to a plate of patties.

"*Ta'amiyya.* It's made with fava beans, but it's not dissimilar to falafel. Try some."

Jayne did. She selected a little of everything and let Tariq pour her a glass of icy water. After she'd finished eating, Tariq selected two peaches from the fruit bowl to the side of the table. Picking up a sharp knife he deftly cut the peaches into slices. The inner flesh was a ripe golden orange and the juice dripped from his fingertips.

He offered her the plate.

"Oh, I couldn't, I pigged out."

"Try them. The taste is sweet, the flesh of the fruit soft and succulent. They were flown in from Damascus today."

He made them sound utterly irresistible. Against her better judgment, Jayne reached out and took a sliver. Tasted it. The peach lived up to everything he had promised.

"Like it?"

"Mmm."

His eyes grew darker at her throaty murmur. "You used to make delighted sounds like that when we made love."

"I don't remember."

"Of course you do." Tariq's eyes were hooded, but his voice was softer than velvet and caused little shivers to spread through her.

The meal was over. She no longer had to observe social niceties. It was time for a little directness. "I don't *want* to remember. I want to go back home, to move on with my life."

"There was a time when your home was with me—"

She waved a hand, dismissing his claim. "That was another life."

"So, there is another man…at this new home?"

"I didn't say that." But Jayne couldn't help thinking of Neil, who had waited so patiently, asking her out every couple of weeks, taking her refusals stoically. He was so safe. So different from her overwhelming husband—and that was precisely what made Neil so attractive. He wouldn't take her to the highs or the lows that Tariq had. He wouldn't crush her love and her trust and rip her heart out.

"I have no doubt that the sudden urge for the divorce is linked to a man." Tariq's savage cynicism took her aback.

"Why does it have to be about a man? I want to move on, get a life." Jayne swallowed under his quelling gaze. "I want my identity as Jayne Jones back. I no longer want to be associated with you, Sheikh Tariq bin Rashid al Zayed, son of the Emir of Zayed."

The look he shot her was deadly. "I hadn't realised I was such a liability."

"Surely you want to move on, too? Get married? Have children?"

"Maybe." His face gave nothing away.

A sharp stab of emotion pierced her. His father had wanted Tariq to marry Leila, the daughter of one of the sheikhs who had arrived at the palace earlier today. Both men were counted amongst the Emir's closest friends. Sheikh Ali was a power in the north of the country. He owned extensive land, controlled oil leases and governed several, at times, unruly clans. And Leila's uncle, Sheikh Mahood, was related by marriage to a sultan who ruled a bordering state that put out a massive amount of barrels of oil per day. Tariq's marriage to Leila would solidify the fate of Zayed, making the tiny country more powerful and strategic in the region.

No doubt that marriage would take place once their divorce was final.

"On the way from the airport you said that in the past our relationship was always about what I wanted, about what my family wanted. That it wasn't about you. I don't remember it that way." His voice lowered to throb a little above a murmur. "In fact, I remember sitting on a hard park bench in London, not far from that awful one-bedroom flat we rented, and staring into your eyes while we talked about the future and shared our dreams. It was about us. Not me. Not my family."

How dare he remind her of those long-ago days? She'd been so young, so in love with the gorgeous student she'd met at the Tate Gallery. Too soon they'd been married. A mad, later regretted, impulse. "Our marriage was a mistake."

Before his world and the reality of who he was—the Emir of Zayed's only son—had come crashing in on them. Memories of the bittersweet days when he'd loved her—and she'd loved him—with youthful joyfulness haunted her. Then the long shadow of his father, the Emir of Zayed, had raised its head. Tariq had been summoned back to his father's control and overnight everything had changed.

He had changed.

Jayne's fingernails bit into her palms. She'd changed, back then, too. She'd gone from sensitive to wan and needy. And that had been before the discovery that—

"We were happy," he interrupted her thoughts. "For a while."

"Until I found out who you were, and everything changed." She took a long, hard look at him. He was still the most earth-shatteringly gorgeous male she'd ever met. His golden eyes glowed with intelligence. His high, slanting cheekbones, the arrogant blade of his nose above the chiselled lips, still had the power to make her heart race. But, clad in the *thobe*, the fearsomely muscled body hidden beneath the white folds, he looked foreign, dangerous and very, very powerful.

"Who I was should never have changed what we had."

"Oh, come on, Tariq. You can't honestly believe that? The pressure of being the successor to the Emir of Zayed, the hostility of your father—"

"Leave my father out of this!" His face darkened. "He never did anything to harm you. It was your behaviour, your treachery, that destroyed what we had."

Jayne shut her eyes blocking out the familiar invective. The Emir had hated her from the start, done everything he could to break up what they shared. And, in the end he'd succeeded. She'd been driven away, her spirit beaten, her heart broken.

Tariq had hated her.

"What does the past matter? You say it was my treachery that drove us apart. But in the end it was your lack of trust that killed what we had, Tariq. So what's the point of—"

"My lack of trust?" Fury turned the body beside her to steel. "You—"

"There's no point to all this, Tariq." She turned her head and stared at the water bubbling from the fountainhead. "It's over. I want a divorce…and once I leave I never want to see you or your father again."

"You may just get your wish." He drew a deep breath. "My father is dying."

Jayne heard his words from a distance; they didn't sound quite real. Six years ago she'd wished that the old Emir could…simply disappear out of her life…out of Tariq's life. Then, his death would have solved all her problems. Yet now she didn't care.

She felt numb. She told herself it was because she'd moved on. She had a life. And that life did not include Tariq. Not even if his father was dying.

"What does that have to do with me?" She kept her voice expressionless. "I don't care about your father. I don't care if he's dying." She swallowed her pain and flicked him a look. A flash of raw emotion glittered in his eyes. It was quickly suppressed. Her throat closed, feeling hot and tight. "I have no desire to see your father. Not ever again. When you told me to leave five and a half years ago, I told you that."

"You said you never wanted to see me, either." His mouth kinked into a mocking line. "Yet here you sit, in front of me. So, *nuur il-en,* never is a long time. Death has a finality that comes to us all. My father feels it is time for me to settle— he wants that reassurance before he dies."

He paused. The silence swelled darkly around them, coloured by the undercurrents between them.

"So?"

"Who better for me to settle with than my lawfully wedded wife?"

Jayne gave an uncontrollable laugh. It was hard and grating. Alien. As alien as the notion that the Emir would ever accept her as the consort for his son. "That's the last thing your father wants. He'd prefer to see me in hell." She gave him a twisted smile. "What about Leila? Why not settle down with her? Your father would approve that match like a shot."

"Unfortunately, Leila is now married. I do not approve of bigamy."

Unexpectedly, Jayne's heart lifted at the information. Then she quashed her exultation. It had nothing to do with her, who he married. "So divorce me and find another bride."

"There is no time. My father needs to be assured that I am married, happily reconciled with you. Now. And you are going to help me achieve that. As soon as he is dead you can leave. With this divorce you want so badly."

There was something savagely ironic at the idea that Tariq wanted her aid to deceive his father into thinking he was settled. But she had no intention of staying. She shook her head. "I want you to sign the consent to our divorce, then I want to leave."

"You never used to be this hard of heart—"

"Me? Hard-hearted?"

"You used to be gentle, loving." Tariq continued.

"Until you and your father got hold of me."

Tariq's gaze turned dark with bitterness. "Don't blame—"

"Oh, what is the use?" She wasn't going to get through to him. She gave a dismissive shrug. "I don't care anymore what you think of me. I've grown up. I don't need your approval anymore."

Tariq's lips thinned into a hard line. "But you do want a

divorce. And I'm not signing anything unless you stay. So unless you convince my father all is well between us before he dies, I will not consent to a divorce. Ever."

"I'll sue for divorce from New Zealand."

"And I'll oppose you. Even though our marriage was recorded at the New Zealand High Commission in London at the time, we were married according to the laws of Zayed and I am a citizen of that country. You need my consent. I have a lot of money to fight you with. And you know that I will succeed. Otherwise you would have applied for divorce in New Zealand. Not come all the way here to persuade me to give you this divorce."

He had her there. "Tariq, what you're asking is impossible."

Tariq glanced at his wife and suppressed the tenderness that threatened to spill out. She looked bewildered, off balance for the first time since her arrival. Not even when she'd been faced by those young thugs had she looked as shattered. She'd remained calm, unflustered, sitting beside him with her long lashes lowered against the porcelain skin he'd always relished, while he'd simmered with rage that any one dared touch his woman.

He'd wanted to arrest the youth, have him expelled from Zayed for touching Jayne. He'd fought the red, red rage for calm.

And in that instant he'd known that he was going to make this divorce as difficult as he could. But none of the seething emotion was revealed when he said, "I am not asking the impossible. It is my wish, dearest beloved—"

"Don't call me that. I am no longer your dearest beloved."

"That is true. You are no longer *my* dearest beloved." He knew she'd recognised his point by the way her body tensed against his. But he was not yet ready to open the wounds of the past. "Stay until my father dies. That is the last thing I ask of you, my wife—" he paused, waiting for her to respond to the subtle mockery, but her lashes again swept her cheeks "—before I grant you the divorce you seek so urgently."

He watched as she examined her nails. They were short, bare of polish. "How long?"

At her question his head came up. He narrowed his gaze, searching her averted face for guile. "What do you mean, 'How long'?"

"How long…must I stay?"

"Until my father dies."

"Yes…I know…but how long will that be?"

Something constricted in his chest as she flouted the conventions that frowned on such directness. Tariq felt a burning sense of…frustration…that she so clearly wanted out of their marriage, that she was prepared to ask him to quantify how many days remained for his father in this realm. He shrugged. "How long is a piece of thread?"

"That's no answer." At last she looked at him. "I want a time limit."

"I don't know." He stared at her, brooding. Hoped she didn't see all the way to his soul to the dark, black well of sorrow and confusion that lay there. "The thread of his life is close to snapping. He is very weak and in much pain. The doctors say it could be a week or two weeks. They don't give him longer than a month."

"A month!" She hesitated, her eyelashes lowered again. Her teeth closed on her bottom lip.

He waited, giving her time. She was impatient. Tariq narrowed his gaze on her teeth, the endearing gap between them, and wondered what it was about this Neil that had her so enthralled that she'd come back to the country she'd sworn never to return to, to get her divorce. The pictures of the man, procured from the detective agency he'd hired immediately after her call to his father's aide, showed an ordinary-looking man with a thatch of blond hair and an innocuous smile. Nothing pointed to Jayne having a sexual relationship with this man, this Neil.

Yet.

Right now that was the only thing keeping Tariq sane.

He had banished her. But he had not yet divorced her. He, Sheikh Tariq bin Rashid al Zayed, *owned* her. And what he owned he kept. Until he decided to rid himself of the troubling possession. As he would.

After his father died.

At last she looked up at him, her eyes darkened by shadows of turmoil. Her features pinched and drawn, a woman driven beyond her limits.

"Okay, I'll stay. But not for more than a month. I want your word on that. If your father hasn't…" Her voice trailed away.

"Died?" he supplied.

"Yes." She paused and shifted, looking dreadfully uncomfortable with the direction the conversation had taken. Then it came out with a rush. "Even if he hasn't…well…died, I want to go home in a month. I want you to swear you will give me a divorce."

It was time to cut her a little slack. It was extremely doubtful that his father would survive that long. "You have my word. Stay for the month and you will get the divorce you desire." Tariq allowed his voice to soften. "You will find my father…changed. He's very ill. He has moments when the medication takes effect and he is not himself." It pained Tariq that his strong father was so frail, so weak, in his body and his mind. It devastated him that disease had crept up undetected on the seemingly invulnerable Emir. "For that month you must promise me that you will strive to convince my father in his lucid moments that we are reconciled."

She drew a deep breath, then whispered, "I promise."

Three

The following morning Jayne crept silently into the Emir's quarters. A couple of men huddled in the antechamber murmuring prayers and didn't notice her sneaking past. The male nurse in the bedchamber nodded to Jayne as she entered.

Jayne was shocked at the change in the tyrant who had made her life such a misery. Sheikh Rashid lay in the high bed, his face gaunt, the bones showing through skin as pale as parchment, his lips drained of all colour. He turned his head when she paused beside him. Jayne had a glimpse of rheumy eyes, great black sunken rings around them, and then his eyelids closed again.

"He is not well today," the nurse said. "He has been drifting in and out of consciousness, confused about what is real and what is not. The painkillers are not helping."

"What exactly is wrong with him?" Jayne asked delicately.

"He has cancer of the bowel. It has been eating him, sapping his vitality."

So it was true. The old Emir really was dying. But Jayne felt no satisfaction…or even regret. Instead, a searing sadness followed by a vast well of emptiness filled her.

"I'm so sorry."

Sheikh Rashid's eyes opened. For a moment there was a flare of recognition. Jayne recoiled. The Emir muttered something indistinct.

"He is talking to you," the nurse said. "Bend closer."

Wary, as if he could bite, Jayne moved closer. She leaned forward.

"Lina," she thought he whispered.

Jayne frowned. "He's saying something." She waited a moment, then reached out awkwardly and touched the pile of bedclothes. "I am here."

"Lina," he whispered more insistently.

Her eyes troubled, Jayne said to the nurse, "I think he is confusing me with someone else." She patted the bedclothes, feeling the bony shoulder through the coverings.

His eyelids fluttered down and his breathing became regular.

"He's sleeping. Your presence is soothing him."

There must be some mistake. If he knew about her presence, the Emir would be rabid with rage. Withdrawing her hand, Jayne backed away to the door.

When Jayne went searching for Tariq a little while later, the disturbing sense of unease aroused by her visit to the Emir still had not left her. She found Tariq in the mews where the royal raptors were housed. Squinting through the dim light to the back of the building, Jayne made out Tariq's form clad in his distinctive white *thobe*.

She picked her way past a row of hooded birds perched on railings. There had been times in the past when she'd thought the birds were accorded more respect and affection than she had been.

The falcon perched regally on Tariq's glove glowered at her with suspicious eyes that reminded her instantly of Tariq—even though these were dark and his were pure gold. It was a larger bird than she'd expected to see. But the bird had the same long, pointed wings and dark eyes.

"That's not Khan," Jayne said, referring to Tariq's prized bird. The bird gaped at her, its beak open, a show of aggression to an unfamiliar intruder.

"This is Noor, a young bird that I'm training. Like Khan, she's a shaheen—a peregrine—but she doesn't know you."

"She's bigger." Jayne eyed the bird's open mouth with caution. The feathers on the falcon's head and neck were black, and a dark stripe extended down from the eye to the throat. Noor's throat and cheeks were white with narrow banded stripes on her breast and flecks across her back.

"She's a female, they're up to a third larger than the males. Here." Tariq passed Jayne a small piece of meat. "Place it in her open beak. It will stop her threatening you."

Jayne fed the bird gingerly, wary of the sharp beak. When the titbit was gone, Noor tilted her head expectantly. "No more for now," Jayne told the bird. To Tariq she said, "Where's Khan?"

"Khan died. A long time ago." The shadows in his eyes told her he was thinking of more than his beloved falcon.

Jayne could prevaricate no longer. "Your father is much worse than I expected."

"I told you that he is dying."

"I didn't—" She broke off. *I didn't believe you.* "I didn't realise how bad it was. The nurse said that he has cancer."

Tariq nodded. "He fought it with everything he had. He has lost the most important battle of his life."

"I'm sorry."

The words sounded so inadequate.

Tariq must have thought so, too, because he raised a mocking brow. "I doubt it. You always hated him."

Jayne stared at him mutely. Now was hardly the time to correct him, to tell him that Sheikh Rashid had hated *her* with a ferocious intensity that had sometimes scared her witless. The Emir had seen her as an interloper, and had taken every opportunity to make her feel like an outsider, until he'd poisoned even Tariq against her.

The falcon shifted restlessly on the glove, bringing Jayne's attention back to the bird. She studied the leather jesses bound to her legs. Noor was as captive as she had once been. "Noor wants your attention."

"She's hungry. She wants food." Tariq moved his other hand into the bucket containing strips of meat. The falcon tensed, her head coming forward, anticipation in every line of her body. Tariq placed the piece of meat on the glove and the falcon lowered her head and took it.

"Here, give her another piece."

Jayne fed it to the bird. This time Noor gave a squawk. Jayne gave the bird a wary look.

"She won't eat you." There was a hint of derision in his tone. "It's easy to come to an understanding with a falcon. The falcon simply has to stay hungrier."

Noor gaped at her again. "I don't think she likes me."

Tariq made an impatient sound. "She's a bird. Noor doesn't recognise like or love. She's interested in having her wants satisfied. She feels no emotion." He shot her a hooded glance. "A typical woman."

Jayne ignored the dig. "She's so graceful yet so strong." She moved to stroke the bird, Noor flapped her wings in warning.

"Careful. She's a wild animal, a predator. An opportunist. Not a house pet."

"Is she hungry? Will you take her out to hunt? Or will she fly away?"

"She's eaten sufficient. But even if I took her out she would not fly away. My relationship with Noor is straightforward, based on trust—unlike most male-female interactions. Noor trusts me to feed her. I trust her to return."

Jayne felt the jab of the barb. She started to protest. Then gave up. She wasn't going to allow herself to be drawn. Instead she said, "Your father spoke to me."

Tariq's gaze sharpened. "What did he say?"

"I couldn't make out what he was saying. I think he was confused, he thought I was someone else. He called me 'Lina.'"

His head went back, and his eyes flared to black. "That's impossible. You must've misheard."

Jayne considered him. What was that stark emotion in his eyes? Shock? Disbelief. And why? "What does it mean?"

"That was his name for my mother." Tariq's eyes were as empty as the stony desert she'd passed in the taxi yesterday.

"Perhaps he wants to see her?"

"No." He made a sudden, definite movement. The falcon reacted by flapping her wings and hopping up and down on the glove. "My mother is not welcome in Zayed."

Jayne waited. When Tariq failed to add more, she said, "I never met your mother. You never talk about her."

"As far as my father and I are concerned, that woman does not exist."

"Yet you see your maternal cousins, don't you?"

"That is different. Not only are we bound by blood, we are bound by business interests, too. My cousin Zac owns supertankers, I run refineries. There's a reason for us to get together. My cousins know that my mother is not welcome in my presence."

"Well, I don't think that's how your father feels any longer. He's dying. Perhaps he wants to make peace with your mother."

"My mother abandoned us—him—for another man. She has her own family—another daughter."

There was a flatness to Tariq's tone that had Jayne shooting him a questioning look. There must be pain about his mother's desertion. Somewhere. Deep inside him. They'd been married, yet she'd never been aware of this suffering within him.

"There is no space in her life for me or my father," he said, feeding Noor another sliver of meat. "Nor would my father want her back."

"Perhaps it's not a case of wanting her back. Perhaps it's more about wanting to tie off the loose ends in his life before he dies."

"You misheard. My father would never want my mother back in Zayed." The finality in Tariq's tone warned Jayne that the subject of his mother was better left alone.

Absently Jayne watched the bird preen, her beak stroking through her feathers, setting them right. "I'm sorry I mentioned it. I just thought you might know who your father confused me with."

"It doesn't surprise me that he confused you." A hand touched her hair. Jayne's gaze jerked upward. Emotion flared in his eyes. "You both have long, dark hair and pale ivory skin."

"I've never seen a photo of your mother." Jayne was sure his mother would be beautiful. Nothing like her. Ordinary. Plain Jayne.

"There are no pictures in the palace of my mother. As there are none of you. Both of you treacherous, two-timing—"

Jayne shifted abruptly. "I'm not listening to this. I was prepared to discuss this in the past. You wouldn't listen then and I'm not getting caught up in it all over again." He'd stonewalled her then, breaking her heart. "It's water under the bridge."

Water under the bridge.

The painful memories exploded inside her. She swung away from Tariq and made blindly for the exit to the mews, to where shafts of silver sunlight broke into the gloomy interior, lighting her escape. No footsteps followed. And she was glad.

She didn't want to talk about the baby that she'd carried in her body. The baby she'd lost. It hurt too much. It was something she could never forget, something that stayed with her every day of her life.

But what choice had she had?

The day dragged past. Jayne had bought some magazines at the airport in Auckland to read on the plane and she flicked through them listlessly. She itched for a book to read, but Tariq's library was a place she dared not go. It held too many unpleasant reminders of his distrust.

So she lay down on the bed and dozed, until every last wisp of jetlag had lifted. When the knock sounded on the door late in the afternoon, heralding Latifa's entrance, Jayne was ready for a distraction.

"There are many people in the palace this evening. His Excellency has been kept busy all day." Latifa's young eyes were kind and wise beyond their years. "I am sure Sheikh Tariq is looking forward to seeing the sheikhah tonight. There has been much talking today."

This was what had driven her mad the first time round. The long days with no sign of Tariq. The absence of anything to do, while the men closed themselves behind high carved wooden doors, wearing sombre expressions. And few of the women she'd met had spoken English, even though some had seemed nice enough. But apart from one or two invitations none had made any overtures of friendship to her.

In the past Tariq had told her to be patient. That she would make friends in time, that her loneliness would ease.

If only it had been so simple.

"Look, this came for you today." Latifa produced the box with the air of a magician performing a wondrous trick that deserved squeals of delight. Jayne didn't have the heart not to smile.

"What is it?"

"It is most beautiful." Latifa opened the lid to reveal a caftan and sheer *hijab* in shades of emerald shot through with bronze thread. "There are shoes to match and pants." She pulled out the high-heeled pumps like a rabbit from a hat. "And more clothes will arrive in the morning."

"I don't want clothes," Jayne protested.

But once dressed, Jayne had to admit that the colour suited her. The green accentuated the raven highlights in her hair, and her skin was paler than ever. Mascara, and a hint of *kajal* around her eyes to emphasise the shape, and she was ready to go. Draping the *hijab* across her shoulders and leaving her hair uncovered, she made her way downstairs, through the labyrinth of palace corridors.

The long table in the stateroom was laid with cutlery that gleamed in the light of the heavy chandeliers overhead. Men from the large delegation that Latifa had alluded to were already arriving; some in dark suits with only the traditional headgear, while others wore traditional dress. A few women were scattered around. A quick glance revealed that Tariq was nowhere to be seen.

An aide appeared and directed Jayne to where two vacant seats remained down the length of the table. Jayne kept her head down, aware of the speculative glances she was attracting. She was grateful for the welcoming smile from the woman seated to the left of her and they started to chat.

The woman introduced herself as Farrah Jirah in fluent English. It turned out that she was a doctor who practised in the maternity unit of the local hospital. Jayne found her charming, and she stopped worrying about where Tariq was.

When Tariq finally strode in, flanked by Ali and Mahood, Jayne could tell from the taut way he held himself that the latest round of meetings had not gone well.

Tariq's gaze flashed to the top of the table, took in the empty place at the head. His brow drew into a frown as he scanned the surrounding seats. The tension in his shoulders relaxed slightly when he saw her.

Jayne turned back to talk to her friendly neighbour. A moment later she sensed someone beside her.

"Are you okay?"

It was Tariq. He looked tired, the lines around his mouth

more deeply scored than they had been this morning, and his eyes held concern.

"I'm fine. You look tired."

A ghost of a smile flitted over his harsh features. "It's been a hard day."

"I won't even ask how whatever meetings you had went." Ali and Mahood were trouble. Vipers. She'd known that since the first time she'd met them. And Ali's daughter, Leila, was pure poison. Tariq was welcome to her.

Tariq sighed and said softly, "Ali is a powerful force in Zayed."

Jayne nodded. Ali controlled a lot of the northern territory, making him an important player.

"He can't be ignored," Tariq continued. "But he is disruptive. And this latest skirmish Ali and Mahood have gotten into over grazing rights with Sheikh Karim al Bashir is going to cause headaches."

"Are they fighting?"

"It hasn't turned violent yet. But Ali claims that Sheikh Karim is threatening war." Impatience showed in Tariq's eyes. "The sooner I intervene, the better."

Jayne felt a flutter of pity for him, for the predicament that Ali and his brother had put Tariq in. "But what about your father? You can't leave him now."

"My father wouldn't want this disagreement to flare out of control. We can't afford to be at war with Bashir. He will understand."

"Why can't Ali and Mahood understand that you're needed here?"

He looked at her. "No one understands that. Only you. To every one else my duty to Zayed must come before all else—

even my father. And now you must excuse me, *nuur il-en,* I must claim my seat at the head of the table before Ali usurps it."

Ali was sitting in the vacant chair at the top of the table, his head close to the man on his right, conspiring no doubt. Jayne shifted her attention to Tariq, watched him rise from beside her, his traditional robes swirling around him, the white *ghutra* over his head secured by the doubled black cord that made him look more formidable than ever. She pitied Ali and Mahood if they unleashed his full ire.

She picked at her food until she sensed someone seating themselves in the place Tariq had vacated, and turned her head. The welcoming smile she'd prepared shrivelled as she met the frigid gaze of Sheikh Ali.

The dinner dragged on and Tariq found it difficult to concentrate on the conversation swirling around him. His attention was riveted on his wife. He watched as she said something to Ali. But the response caused her to sag. What had Ali said to make her skin grow so pale?

As the meal progressed his attention kept straying back. Most of the time Jayne spent chatting to the woman on her left, Dr. Farrah Jirah was a nice enough woman and he'd hoped she might befriend Jayne. He relaxed as he saw Jayne smile. But then stiffened again when he noted that the few times she attempted to talk to Ali her attempts were rebuffed. Ali was flouting the social norms of Zayedi politeness at a meal table. As host, Tariq was within his rights to request Ali to leave. Tariq's frown grew more and more thunderous, until his dinner partners started to regard him with increasing wariness.

Ali said something to Jayne. She glanced down, and Tariq

saw the wash of colour high on her ivory cheeks. He started to rise. But Jayne beat him to it. Pushing back her chair, she was on her feet before he could move. By the time he reached the elaborate carved doors flanked by two palace guards, she was already gone.

He charged into the corridor, saw her disappearing into the study he'd had an aide show her to earlier in the day. With long raking strides he set off after her.

Jayne collapsed into the leather chair behind Tariq's desk. Her first reaction was to hop onto the Internet, to see if Helen was still awake. She felt lonely and isolated and incredibly homesick. She wanted her family, she wanted to go home, to leave this inhospitable country that had never brought her anything but pain.

The soft sound of the door closing brought the first hint that she was no longer alone.

"What did Ali say to make you leave?" An implacable anger glowed in Tariq's eyes.

"It doesn't matter." Ali had been his usual obnoxious self. He'd taunted her by saying that had his daughter married Tariq, she would have done her duty, borne him fine sons and done him proud as a hostess. She'd been stupid to let Ali get to her. Jayne shook her head, suddenly overwhelmingly aware of the heat of Tariq's body behind her, the soft hiss of his breath beside her ear as he leaned forward. Instantly, nerves started to churn in her belly. She lifted her hand from the mouse and spun the leather office chair around. Only to find herself face-to-face with Tariq. This close his eyes had the appearance of molten gold. Ensnaring her. Trapping her in the rich heat.

"It matters. You are my wife."

She held his knee-weakening gaze. "Not for long."

"For at least a month. And for that month I expect my countrymen to treat you with the respect that you deserve."

"The respect I deserve because I am your woman? Or the respect that I deserve in my own right?"

"Is there a difference?" He lifted his hand to touch her cheek. "I touch this skin. It belongs to my wife and it belongs to Jayne, too. They are one and the same."

"Jayne Jones is not your possession."

He didn't answer. His finger trailed down, across her lips, sensitising the soft skin.

"I should go," she whispered against his finger.

"I don't think so."

She stared at him, her breathing quickening, tingles of apprehension mingled with excitement shivered down her spine. Trouble.

"You're aware of me. Your body recognizes me."

"That doesn't mean you own me."

"My body responds to you, too. Even though I resist it. You own me every bit as much as I own you." Taking her hands, he pulled her out of the chair, against the hard, muscled length of his body. Instantly, she felt the hardness of his arousal against her stomach.

"I am leaving."

"Too late." His head swooped down, his mouth slanting across hers.

Heat and light and emotion scorched Jayne as his mouth met hers. All rational thought left Jayne as she parted her lips and started to kiss her husband back.

Four

All thoughts of her family, her sister, her nieces, flew away as Tariq's mouth plundered hers. His kiss was uncompromising and the flare of heat that started deep in her stomach took her by surprise.

It had been a long time.

Too long, since she'd last felt this intensity of emotion.

As his hand threaded through her hair at the back of her neck, his fingers brushed the sensitive skin of her nape and a frisson of delight ran through her. Tariq knew exactly where to touch…to arouse her, to turn her. The fingertips now moving in little circles sent shivers through her and his lips demanded a response.

Jayne gave a little gasp, taken aback by the pent up passion that Tariq had unleashed. Instantly he pressed closer, his tongue stroking into her mouth, tasting her, slower now, languidly, as if he could never get enough.

With a groan she reached up, locking her arms around his neck, conscious of her breasts growing taut and tender as her body melted against him. She felt like a flower blooming, unfurling, under the heat of the sun. Tariq's hands shifted against the back of her head, cradling her, bringing her closer still. She was sharply, disconcertingly aware of the tips of her breasts hardening under the loose fabric of the caftan, of the brush of his chest against the taut mounds.

Then, as suddenly as it had begun, the kiss was over.

The chill that followed the wave of heat shocked her. Jayne shivered with regret. Until those drive-me-crazy hands moved again, tilting her head, and his lips landed on the soft, exposed skin of her neck. A guttural sound exploded from her. She closed her eyes and let her head fall back, giving herself up to his touch, to the sheer indescribable delight. The fingers spearing through her hair released a fresh wave of shivers. And her body felt soft and pliable, boneless with want.

His teeth scraped her skin, his tongue followed, and Jayne gasped again. His mouth closed on the sensitive area beneath her ear…a trail of hot kisses, then a long stroke of his tongue set her on edge. Jayne waited…every nerve ending quivering…eager for what would come next.

In some distant space of her mind, she was half-aware of his hands leaving her hair, sliding over her shoulders, down her back, and she arched like a cat about to be stroked.

But when she felt his fingers stop, linger, and her bra strap give under the fabric of the caftan, she tensed, jolted by reality. *What was she doing?*

She should not be allowing Tariq to kiss her like this. Ali's words echoed hollowly in her head. Tariq needed a wife who would do her duty…and that woman was not her. So what on earth was she doing responding to her soon-to-be-ex like this? She couldn't jeopardise her newly planned life simply because Tariq still turned her on.

She'd almost left it too late. Jenna heard the rasp of a zipper, felt the caftan give.

"No!"

Tariq's hands stilled. "What do you mean 'No'? You are my wife!"

"No!" She shuddered. She couldn't survive the half world, the dry wasteland that had been her marriage. "I'll never be your wife again, Tariq. Our marriage is over." She wanted a divorce, to put Tariq and her marriage behind her and move on.

She tore out of his arms, ducked under his arm, and put half the length of the room between them. "I don't want this."

"Liar." His voice was flat, his face expressionless. The light in the golden eyes had been extinguished. "You responded to me."

He was right. She'd been far too…engaged. But she couldn't afford to let him know that. So she looked away. "Maybe I'd have responded to any attractive man."

"Any man?" It was a soft snarl, dangerous. "Not only me? So where does that leave the blond man who waits for you back home in Auckland, my faithless, lying wife?"

She stared at him blankly.

"Neil Woodruffe," he said silkily. "Or had you forgotten all about the poor bastard you are holding on a string?"

"How do you know about Neil?" Neil had asked her out several times over the past months. Lately he'd taken to visiting her apartment on flimsy excuses. She'd humoured him, inviting him in. But how did Tariq know about Neil? A sick tightness gripped Jayne. One glance at Tariq's face confirmed her suspicious. "You're having me watched."

He didn't deny it.

"That's disgusting." The words burst from her. She *hated* the thought that he was spying on her. "Does it make you feel powerful to follow the details of my life? That's sick!"

"I employed a detective when you initiated contact. You should remember that I have always believed information is key to any negotiation." He gave her a tight smile.

Jayne's heart thumped in her chest, so loudly that she feared he might hear. "Your lack of trust is the reason why I don't want to be married to you anymore."

"Do you blame me?" His mouth tightened. "No, don't answer that, there's no point in rehashing the past. Our marriage is over. In a month you will have your divorce, maybe sooner."

The next day Tariq stormed down the corridor to his father's apartments, his white *thobe* billowing behind him, still seething about how Jayne had managed to put him on the back foot the night before. Why was he thinking about her, when he had this whole disaster with Mahood and Ali to worry about…and he'd just been summoned to his father's side. Had the end come?

With his father dead, Jayne would get her divorce sooner than she'd hoped.

There would be no reason to keep her in Zayed.

The palace guard leapt to attention as he swept past. "His Excellency is awake?" he asked the male nurse who was filling out a clipboard in the antechamber.

"Not only am I awake—I'm refusing to take the drugs,

which is why they have called you." The voice was thin and thready, but the eyes that met Tariq's as he rushed into the bed-chamber, with the nurse at his heels, held a hint of the old fire.

"Leave us," Tariq commanded the nurse. Retreating with a respectful bow, the nurse closed the door.

"Father." Tariq sank to one knee beside the bed. "You must take the morphine, it will help the pain."

"I am feeling much better. The confusion and dizzy head is less now that I abandon the medicine." His father's hand rested on top of Tariq's head. Gone was the solid weight that had stroked his hair as a child. No longer the hand of a ruler feared and revered by his subjects, but the wavering touch of a dying man. Tariq swallowed the hot thickness in his throat.

"Hadi al Ebrahim has been to see me." Tariq's head rose as his father spoke. "He tells me the sheikhah has returned."

Hadi was one of his father's most trusted aides. Tariq nodded. "She came to see you but you were—" *drugged* "—sleeping." He watched his father carefully, unsure of what to say next. A couple of months ago, soon after the terrible diagnosis, Tariq had heard rumours that his father had sent Hadi on a mission to Sheikh Karim—a mission that he was not prepared to confront his father about now that he was dying. Instead he'd obliquely mentioned to his father that in terms of his marriage contract with Jayne he could take only one wife at a time. His father had looked fit to burst, calling Tariq a foolish monkey. Tariq certainly hadn't expected his father to be overjoyed by Jayne's return. But, for his father to die in peace, he needed to convince his father that marriage to Jayne was what he, Tariq, wanted more than anything on earth....

"Good. It is time that your wife resumes her position at your side."

Tariq's mouth fell open. While he was aware that his father wanted him contently married before he died, he'd anticipated a little more resistance. Especially as his father had evidently had other plans.

"Hadi is worried," the Emir said. "He says that Ali and Mahood can make a lot of trouble for Karim—and for you."

Tariq shrugged. "I'm sorry to say this, Father, but their trouble causing is not new." And if Hadi had been acting as a go-between to broker a marriage between Tariq and Sheikh Karim's half sister, then Hadi would have even more cause for concern.

"But this time they have angered Karim, you need to placate him, we cannot afford to have an angry neighbouring ruler—especially not one as powerful as the sheikh of Bashir. What will happen to our oil interests in Bashir if we are in conflict with each other?"

"I know. I have been in touch." Sheikh Karim had laid the blame squarely at Ali and Mahood's feet, saying they illicitly grazed herds of livestock over the border and had appropriated animals that did not belong to them. Karim had confiscated the whole herd the next time the animals had returned and impounded them.

Tariq gave a sharp sigh. "I will go—" He broke off and closed his eyes. What if his father died while he was gone? What if he missed these precious last days because of the stupidity and stubbornness of Ali and Mahood?

"When? You cannot wait."

Tormented, Tariq opened his eyes and looked into the dark orbs close to his own. Eyes that in the past had been filled with love…anger…disappointment…and now held only a stoic acceptance.

No, he wanted to yell. *Fight it.* Don't die.

Don't leave me.

Alone.

"You can't wait, my son. You must go. Now."

Silently Tariq shook his head. His father's hands were thin, the purple veins showing through the wrinkled skin. The skin that hung over his face showed a waxen cast…like a death mask, the eyes deeply sunken in the sockets.

"I order you." It was a command, gasped out by a man used to being obeyed.

Tariq stiffened. He knew that his father would read his refusal in his eyes. He would not go. He could not leave his father. Not so near the end.

"Please."

This time it was a plea. Tariq stared at the man who had never begged for anything in his life. The man that no one disobeyed.

"What if…" Tariq swallowed the words, unable to finish the thought.

But his father knew. "What if I die? *Inshallah.* It will not happen yet, I am feeling a lot better. But you cannot hover around waiting for that hour like a vulture in the noonday sky. You have a destiny…and Zayed needs you."

Tariq started to answer back.

"Do not argue with your father. I am an old, sick man." The bloodless lips curved into a ghost of a smile. "And by Allah, this will be the last task I ask of you, I promise that. Make peace with Karim and I will ask no more."

"He will expect an apology."

His father nodded.

"I will have to put something in it for him…land or oil leases."

His father nodded again.

"I will go tomorrow."

"Take your wife with you."

"What?" On his way to the door, Tariq stopped and stared at his father in disbelief. He'd already planned to take Jayne with him, in order to make it doubly clear to Karim that he was not in the market for a wife. Not even for Karim's ever-so-suitable half sister. But he'd never expected his father to suggest the same. He'd thought his father wanted the…merger…with Karim. It would've been convenient for all concerned. And for the two oil-rich desert countries.

"He needs to accept your wife…as I have. To know there will be no marriage between you and his sister."

There, it was out in the open.

So the rumours were true. His father had tried to broker a new marriage for him. But hearing that Tariq could only take one wife—a wife he had not chosen to divorce—must have dissuaded him from meddling further.

A gnarled hand reached out from the bed. "My son, do not repeat my mistakes with your own wife."

Crossing the room in one stride, Tariq closed his hands around the thin bones. "What do you mean, Father?"

For a while the Emir did not answer. Finally he said. "I am tired. Never forget, I am proud of you, my son. Now I need the morphine."

Tariq's hand went to the bell. The nurse arrived in a rush. The drug was administered, and his father's eyes closed.

Tariq lingered a few minutes, a deep sense of loss swarming through him. What had his father been about to reveal? Finally he leant over to kiss the wrinkled brow. In his heart he feared this was the last time he might see his father alive.

The notion shook him to his soul.

* * *

Jayne was sitting at the stone table in the walled arbour beside the fountain, catching a little morning sun and writing out postcards to Samantha and Amy when the sound of Tariq's footsteps clattered on the stone stairs.

"I have been to see my father," Tariq announced, his eyes unreadable.

He dominated the comforting enclosed space of the arbour. His height, his presence, the scent of the citrusy cologne that clung to his skin all overwhelmed Jayne. She set her pen down. "You talked about your mother?"

"No!" His answer was uncompromising. "You may have heard that there is trouble brewing between Ali and Mahood and Sheikh Karim al Bashir?"

She nodded. It would've been difficult not to have heard the rumours that flew around the palace, or the speculation about how Tariq would react. The Emir was dying. Would he placate his father's oldest friends? Or would he make amends to the furious Karim?

"Zayed must avoid a war with Sheikh Karim at all costs."

Her brow creased, trying to remember what she'd heard. "He's the ruler of a neighbouring sheikhdom, right?"

"Yes. We have many alliances—particularly over oil. We can't afford to antagonise him."

"Ali and Mahood are more trouble than they are worth," she said daringly.

"Mahood and Ali are my father's closest friends. Like brothers to him. I have to respect that bond."

Jayne said nothing. His reply left no room for argument. He would put up with Mahood and Ali and all their guile for his love of his father.

"The trip to the desert town of Aziz should take no longer than three days. I plan to travel swiftly."

He must fear that his father would die in his absence. Her heart squeezed at the sight of the pain etched into his features as he towered over her.

"What about—" *His father.* She broke off, her heart going out to Tariq. What if his father did die while he was gone? What if he left to sort out Ali and Mahood's skirmishes and never saw his father again? As much as she loathed Sheik Rashid, Tariq loved his father.

"What about you? Or what about the divorce that you desire so highly?" His mouth curled into an unpleasant smile. "Your first thought is about yourself."

It was so unfair! But her heart sank at the derision in his eyes, and for the first time she felt relief that she would be staying in the palace. Being surrounded by hostile aides was better than accompanying Tariq in this mood. "I have to think about me," she fired back. "No one else does. You've brought me all the way across the world to cool my heels and await your return and twiddle my thumbs. To waste my time. I have things I want to do." Like start her new course…and have a date with Neil…and start a new life, out from under Tariq's shadow. "What if there are delays and this all takes more than three days? Does that mean you will expect me to stay longer?"

The bubbling of the water in the fountain was the only sound that broke the silence. But the soothing sound did nothing to comfort her as she waited for his reply.

At last he spoke and his eyes were hard. "I won't leave my father for as long as a week. Not when he is so near the end. Nor will I be leaving you to cool your heels, *habiibtii.* You will be coming with me. Be ready to leave by daybreak."

* * *

The courtyard behind the palace was already bustling when Jayne got there the following morning.

Tariq was waiting beside a lone white SUV, clad in a *thobe* with a *ghutra* tied with two rounds of black cord around his head. The SUV had already been packed high with provisions. In the back, beside their bags, Jayne spotted a *kafas,* a cage with holes to allow circulation, holding Noor along with large storage bottles of water—a sobering reminder of exactly how remote their destination was.

Jayne slowed to a halt in front of Tariq. "Is this it?"

He raised an eyebrow. "You were expecting camels?"

Not camels. Anyway, the white SUV was the modern equivalent of the white stallion for a desert traveller. But she'd expected some sort of entourage. Tariq never went anywhere alone. Bodyguards. Aides. A veritable army accompanied him. "When we travelled before—"

"Last time I organised camels because that's what you wanted."

She gave up. They were talking at cross purposes. He was referring to the trip they'd made in the first few months after their return to Zayed not long after their marriage in London. He'd taken her into the desert—by camel. They'd camped out under velvet skies studded with stars as bright as diamonds.

"You expected the fantasy," he was saying, his eyes intent. "A desert romance. That excursion was supposed to be romantic—to make up for the honeymoon I'd never given you."

She clambered into the vehicle and muttered dismissively, "Another mirage."

"What do you mean?" He leaned in through the doorway, his brows fierce.

She shrugged, reluctant to get into a skirmish, and stared through the windshield determined not to look at him. "Don't worry about it. It's nothing."

"When a woman says 'It's nothing' only a fool believes her."

Jayne remained mute, pressing her lips firmly together.

She sensed him watching her. After a long moment he sighed and shut the door before walking around the front of the vehicle to hop in beside her. A flick of his wrist and the vehicle roared to life. Jayne put her head back on the headrest and closed her eyes.

Their desert romance had been nothing more than a mirage. Even that belated honeymoon had been cut short. After only two days a helicopter had landed where they were camped. Tariq had been summoned back to the palace. During the flight back he'd apologised. Promised that there'd be other times.

And Jayne had been left wondering if it had been another instance of the long hand of the Emir acting to destroy their marriage.

When she'd been taken ill with a violent stomach bug the next day, she hated everything in the desert…and Zayed.

But that was in the past.

In the end, the Emir had won.

Their entire marriage had been a mirage.

Now she'd finally made herself a new life. A real life. And she was ready to move on. Find an ordinary man with whom to create a real marriage with real children.

Turning her head, Jayne focused on the passing landscape. The morning was lovely. A smattering of clouds meant that the heat had lost the edge common even in the winter months.

"It's hot," she said a while later, more to break the throbbing silence than because the heat worried her.

"Tonight will be cool in the desert." His hand flicked a dial, and a blast of cold air swirled around her. "Better?"

She stared at the lean hands on the steering wheel, and a bolt of emotion shot through her. No, it wasn't better. The cold air did nothing to alleviate her inner tension. She swallowed. "Yes," she said finally. "It's cooler."

A sideways glance revealed a hard, hawkish profile. The white *ghutra* should have softened his jagged profile; instead it added to the mystique and ruthlessness of the man. Her gaze lingered on the black *agal*—the cords that wound twice around his headdress and hung down his back. Beside his mouth, the deep, scored lines showed the strain he was under. Tariq must be terribly worried about his father…and then there was this situation that Ali and Mahood had created. She had to remember that if she felt tense, he was under infinitely more stress. Finally she turned her head away and tipped her head back again, closing her eyes, and tried to doze.

Jayne woke suddenly to find that several hours had passed and she was chilled. The desert sun had vanished and a white blanket of cloud stretched across the sky. The air-conditioning was chilly enough to have Jayne reaching into her bag for a lightweight merino cardigan.

"Cold?" Tariq fiddled with the air-conditioning controls, and the rush of cool air slowed.

"A little. Despite the heat that is probably out there." She gestured to the desert that stretched out, bleak and inhospitable, in every direction.

"The cloud cover makes today cooler than normal." Tariq dipped his head and glanced up through the windshield. "I don't like the look of them, they've been gathering over the last hour." He slowed and examined a gadget that had to be a GPS.

Four-wheel-drive. GPS. What was she worried about? This was the twenty-first century. The desert was not as alien and threatening as she imagined. She was overreacting, allowing her dislike and resentment of Zayed to get to her. Jayne laughed. "Rain? Little chance of that out here."

"The desert does get storms, not often but they happen. They can be devastating because the desert does not absorb the water. So it gathers on the surface until there is sufficient for floods."

"Floods?" Jayne stared at the barren landscape and her apprehension crept back. Just enough to make prickles rise at her the base of her neck. "Hard to imagine."

"Believe it. As much as water brings life, rain can wreak havoc."

"Will we be able to reach Aziz before the rain comes?"

"Maybe. If it comes at all. The clouds may dissipate—not uncommon."

"That would be a relief." The prospect of a desert storm did not thrill Jayne. She stared out of the window at the clouds, then at the expanse of stony ground that stretched without end to the horizon. It gave the desert a foreboding feeling, even greater than it already possessed, and Jayne shivered.

Another hour passed. They'd stopped briefly to eat pita rounds filled with shredded lamb and lettuce and tomato and drink bottles of mineral water, before setting off again. Since the meal, Tariq had been silent, but Jayne thought that they'd picked up speed. The banks of cloud had been rolling, piling high into stacks that made Jayne's insides twist.

"I hate this place." Jayne's tension spilled over. "I really do."

"I know." Tariq's voice held a bleak quality that made Jayne give him a quick glance.

"You shouldn't have made me come back to Zayed."

"I needed you."

Her heart missed a beat. In the past she would have killed for an admission like that. But Tariq had been more focused on his father, on the good of Zayed than on her. She'd been lonely, her heart bruised by his lack of care.

"To convince your father that you will be settled after his death?"

"In my country it is believed if a man has given all his children in marriage through the course of his lifetime, then he has successfully fulfilled the duty of his life. Our marriage is not what my father considers a real marriage, so he considers that he has failed to fulfill the duty of his life. He wants me to be happily married. He believes it is time for me to have a family, children." Tariq sighed. "He's even tried to use a go-between to offer a bride price…he's been plotting to find me a second wife."

Second wife. She should've expected this. But still her heart plummeted at the news. Tariq with a family. With children. Once upon a time that had been her dream. "He can't do that," she said. "Our marriage contract—"

"Forbids that. I know. And I have advised my father that we added a clause that I may not marry another woman while married to you."

Jayne had insisted on it. Even young and desperately in love, she hadn't been able to overcome her greatest fear: that one day her gorgeous Zayedi husband would find a more beautiful, more accomplished wife and wish to marry a second time. Not even the status of being the senior wife would have made up for that. She'd wanted to be his only love. Forever.

Sadly, she'd never considered requesting a clause that allowed her to divorce her husband without his consent. If she had, she'd never have needed to return to Zayed. Back then, lighthearted with love, she'd thought that her marriage would last longer than the sands of the desert.

"Your father couldn't have been pleased." Jayne guessed that was an understatement. The Emir would've been enraged. Why hadn't he demanded that Tariq divorce her?

Immediately.

"No, he wasn't." Tariq's reply held a certain wryness. "But at least it appeared to put a stop to his quest to find me a second wife although certain…complications…were caused by his enthusiastic matchmaking."

"Serves him right! He never approved of our marriage. So don't expect me to be a hypocrite and stay for the funeral after he—" she swallowed "—dies."

"Why would I want you to stay for my father's funeral?" Tariq looked away from the road ahead. The eyes that met hers were full of turmoil. "You're not—"

The ring of a cell phone rent the air, interrupting what he'd been about to say. He hit the button where the phone rested in its housing on the dashboard. "Yes?" Tariq demanded tersely.

Jayne was relieved. There had been something in his eyes…

She suspected she wasn't ready to hear what he'd wanted to say. Not here stuck out in the middle of this inhospitable terrain with nowhere to run.

When he ended the call, he said, "There is concern about the weather. We will stop at a Bedu camp not far from here to take shelter from the cloudburst that the meteorologists are predicting."

Five

As they approached the Bedouin camp, Jayne stared with interest at the tents that nestled at the base of a rocky rise.

"These are Bedu tribal lands," Tariq told her as he headed the SUV for a huddle of tents. "You can't see it clearly from here, but on the other side of the ridge there is a village with a school and a clinic, and in the surrounding area efforts are being made at de-desertification."

"What do you mean?" Jayne turned to look at him and couldn't help noticing how he speeded up his speech, how his eyes sparkled as he spoke. He loved the desert and its people as much as she hated it.

"There are olive groves planted in the desert."

"But who looks after them?" She stared at their surroundings. "Aren't the Bedu nomads, always on the move?"

"In the past, yes, but things change…although some still follow the old ways, others are setting down roots."

Jayne gestured to the array of tents. "Some of those tents are huge. But are you saying there are brick-and-mortar dwellings?"

"Yes, over the rise."

"I think I prefer the idea of tents. I always wanted to stay in a Bedouin camp," she said a little dreamily.

"I remember." He gave a laugh.

"But we didn't find a Bedouin tent that time…although I did get to ride into the desert on a camel and camp in the tent you put up." Jayne thought back to that disastrous trip.

Seconds later Tariq pulled up to where a group of men sat outside in the thin shade of a tamarisk tree playing cards. They looked up. All play stopped.

One of the men jumped to his feet and came to shake Tariq's hand. "Excellency, we did not know you were visiting. We welcome you."

Tariq flung an arm to the overcast sky. "The weather has forced us on you, and we would be grateful for your hospitality for a night."

"Only a pleasure, Excellency. You are welcome for more than one miserable night. My residence is not far from here. It is new and you will not lack for luxury."

A smile played around Tariq's mouth. "I thank you for your offer. But the sheikhah has a fancy to stay in a tent—if that is not too much for us to ask."

The headman, whom Tariq introduced as Ghayth, looked at Jayne as if she were touched by the moon, then glanced at the sky. "But, Excellency, if the rain comes, the area outside the tent will be a mudbath."

Tariq raised an eyebrow at Jayne. "The tents themselves won't leak, they're constructed to withstand the elements, sun, wind, sandstorms. But are you sure you wouldn't rather stay under a solid roof?"

"As long as it's not going to cause problems for our hosts or uncomfortable flooding for you if the rains come, I'd rather stay in a Bedouin tent. It sounds like an experience of a lifetime." She was touched that he was trying to accommodate her quirky dreams, rather than practicalities. She gave him a small smile. "Thank you, Tariq."

The tent to which they were led was far larger than she had expected—and far more luxurious than the shelters on the outskirts of the encampment. Inside it was divided with drapes into two separate areas.

"This is the meeting area," Tariq said, waving to the large space around them furnished with several squat square stools covered with woven fabric and a long divan covered with similar material. In the corner stood a round table with four chairs set around it, and the walls and floors were covered with beautifully woven rugs. "Traditionally the curtained-off area is where the women prepare food in the day and where the family sleeps at night. But this tent is more ornate, probably kept for visiting dignitaries, that's why there are no cooking arrangements. The de-desertification program has been attracting a lot of interest—even from the UN."

"Oh." Jayne took in the rugs, the drapes that hung from the roof. "It's certainly not quite as modest as I expected."

Tariq pulled back the drapes to reveal a couple of broad low divans draped with rugs. The sleeping quarters. Instantly a subtle tension invaded the room.

"I think I need a wash," Jayne said, suddenly eager to get out of the tent she'd been so keen to experience. She had a feeling that she was going to be very pleased that the tent was a lot more spacious than she'd anticipated. Perhaps it would've been wiser to have accepted the offer of a stay in Ghayth's house…at least she would've had her own bedroom.

"You can bathe later," Tariq said, "after dinner. For now, use the water in the pitcher on the table to freshen up. Our hosts will be here shortly with our bags. Then we need to see that Noor has been fed and bedded down."

An hour later the clouds, while still ominous, seemed to have lifted a little. They no longer sagged with moisture overhead. Ghayth, the headman, met Jayne and Tariq as they headed back from feeding Noor, with an offer to show Jayne the nearby village.

Within minutes they'd piled into their host's very battered four-wheel drive, with the two salukis in the back, and roared down the dirt road that cut across the stony terrain. Tariq sat up front beside Ghayth, and Jayne sat beside his senior wife, Matra, whose name meant "pot that catches the rain," Jayne discovered as they drove past the olive groves surrounded by desert sand that Tariq had told her about.

From the pointing and the rapid questions he fired at their host, Jayne realised that Tariq was a lot more involved in the program than she'd suspected.

A little way on they turned down a track and the village came into view. A group of children were huddled around a bicycle that leaned against a scrawny tree and they all turned to stare curiously at the approaching vehicle.

Once they had stopped, Jayne descended from the vehicle and followed the men. Carpets in shades of ruby, garnet and topaz were spread out in the patchy sunlight, and a dozen or more women sat around weaving. Jayne caught her breath at vivid designs and colours. "They are beautiful."

One of the women gave her a gentle smile.

"How long does it take you to make such a rug?" Jayne asked, bending down to touch the design.

The woman looked at the men, a frown pleating her forehead.

"She does not speak any English," Tariq said, and rattled off in Arabic. The woman nodded and said something. "She says it depends on how many women are working on the design," Tariq translated.

"They must do well out of such rugs. The craftsmanship is wonderful."

"Not yet. The project has only been going for a couple of years. It's supposed to be self-driven by the village women, so it has taken some time for the women to get it off the ground."

"That's heartbreaking. The rugs are so amazing. I can think of people in Auckland who would pay a fortune for such finery." She thought of Neil, of his home in Remuera with the collection of fine furniture and antique books.

"There is no question of their talent, or their entrepreneurial skills. But some of the women are reticent. They are used to the men running things. But they are insistent that this is their project. They've had a lot to learn. Accounts. Running a business. Distribution."

"And a lot of us can't read or write, which makes it much harder," Matra said softly from behind Jayne's shoulder.

Jayne knew she shouldn't be surprised. But somehow she was. "I thought Zayed was progressive country, that a lot of the wealth from the oil fields is poured into education and development."

"It is," Tariq said levelly, and Jayne realised he'd taken her words as criticism. "But there are a lot of nomadic tribes in Zayed, too."

"And some of us are too old to learn," Matra said, her expression showing that it took a lot of bravery to converse with Tariq. Jayne considered her. "No one is ever too old to learn."

The daylight waned quickly as they returned to the camp. Night fell like a cloak over the desert, and Jayne found herself shivering as the temperature plummeted. Dark clouds swarmed overhead, but the rain that had threatened did not come, much to the glee of their hosts.

The Bedu had prepared an outdoor feast to celebrate their arrival. A fire had been lit and everyone sat around the flames.

An hour later Jayne sat back replete, and weariness seeped through her. She watched as the men seated around the fire clamoured for Tariq's attention. He listened, nodded, spoke a few words, then turned to the next person.

Matra came toward her carrying a copper pot with a long spout and murmured something Jayne did not understand. So she smiled and spread her hands helplessly.

"What is that?"

Before Matra could reply, Tariq was at her side. "Matra is offering you coffee."

Jayne nodded enthusiastically. "Coffee would be lovely."

Matra put the coffeepot down and disappeared.

"It's Bedu coffee," Tariq warned. "Strong and bitter. The coffee beans are roasted on a long shovel and then ground with a mortar before being brewed for several hours."

The other woman returned with a tray of tiny handleless cups and filled them from the coffeepot and handed one to

Jayne who eyed the greenish-brown liquid with suspicion. "It's not as dark as normal coffee."

"That's the cardamom. You drink the whole cup down in one sip."

"O-kay." Jayne took a deep breath and gulped, then almost choked as the bitterness hit her throat. "At least these cups only hold a sip or two," she murmured. "Otherwise I might have to develop a coffee allergy."

Tariq threw his head back and laughed. Jayne stared. How long had it been since he had laughed like that? When she'd first known him, his infectious laughter, his joie de vivre, had been one of the first things to attract her. Tariq had loved life—and lived it joyously.

She hadn't realised how much she had missed his good humour. Until now.

Matra was back offering the tray again. Tariq took another cup and smiled at the woman, who lowered her eyes. Sucking in a deep breath, Jayne reached for another cup.

"How am I going to drink this?"

"Slowly," Tariq responded, but his eyes danced.

She took a tiny sip and pulled a surreptitious face.

"Here, give it to me."

"It's okay, I don't want to be rude."

His hand closed around hers. He brought the cup up to his mouth. Under the pressure of his hand, she tipped the cup. He sipped. This close the gold eyes gleamed like burnished bronze. Caught in the snare of his gaze, she stared at him, suddenly breathless.

His lips lifted off the rim of the minute cup. "There is one last sip. For you."

His hands still cupping hers, she placed her lips against the opposite rim from where he had drunk. The cup tilted. She drank.

"How does it taste now?" His voice was husky. "Still bitter?"

She licked her lips clean of the last smears of coffee. As her tongue tip skimmed across her bottom lip, his eyes flared to the colour of midnight. The shock of the change from gold to dark sent a bolt of sensation through her.

She hurriedly retracted her tongue, swallowed and realised that the bitter taste had gone. All that remained was the distinctive flavour of cardamom. "No, not bitter."

How had this happened?

How had she become so aware of him standing so close to her, to his hand still grasping hers?

Jayne pulled away…and found Matra at her elbow. Jayne looked at the cups of coffee, glanced at Tariq and knew he, too, was supremely conscious of the heat that sizzled between them.

"Accepting a third cup means that you consider yourself one of the family. If you deliberately refuse this cup…it will be considered rude," he murmured softly.

Quickly she nodded to Marta. And so did Tariq. Following his lead, she tossed it back, trying very hard not to grimace and set the empty cup on the tray.

"Now you can refuse the next cup. Because after three cups it is considered rude to take another."

"Thank goodness," she murmured.

"You did fine. Come, it is time to say good-night."

A fine quivering sensation started deep in her stomach as they walked across the shadowed camp to their tent, the indigo night sky arching overhead. Jayne was aware of the darkness that stretched into the desert beyond their tent. The vast emptiness that surrounded them, broken only by the soft conversation of the Bedouin still gathered around the fire.

Their tent glowed inside, the soft light of candles diffusing against the drapes in a warm pattern.

"In the sleeping area there is a bath ready for you," Tariq said. "Matra arranged it."

"Oh." Jayne felt suddenly breathless. "I had thought there might be a washroom nearby."

"There is—with communal baths. No doubt Matra thought you would prefer to bathe in private."

Private?

With Tariq here?

Dragging her feet, Jayne made her way to where Tariq had pointed. A steaming bath waited, with a high back and a curved lip to rest her head on. After the drive and the long day, it looked too welcoming to refuse. Quickly she shucked off her clothes and stepped in, sinking down into the hot water. Shivers broke across her skin as ripples of heat enfolded her.

She tried to relax. But couldn't. Not with Tariq standing on the other side of that filmy drape.

Tariq lay sprawled across the divan in the outer compartment and listened to the soft lap of the water every time Jayne moved.

This was Jayne. The wife he'd banished. He shut his eyes, trying to block out the tantalising sounds. But then he'd hear it again. Slap, slap. He could visualise her. Naked. In the tub less than ten metres away. Her long hair secured on top of her head with a rubber band, her cheeks flushed from the steam.

No. He couldn't think about this. The kiss the other night at the state dinner had been an aberration. A mistake caused by the protectiveness aroused by the attack on Jayne in the city—and his reaction to the pain in her eyes at whatever cruel taunts Ali had made. The kiss was not to be repeated. It had been inspired by soft-hearted pity, his protective instincts. Nothing more.

He certainly couldn't *want* his wife. Not anymore. Not after—

Slap, slap.

She must be moving, causing the water to ripple. He couldn't bear it! "Do you need something?"

"No, no. I'm fine."

At last there was silence.

He told himself that it was relief that pooled in his stomach, that he wasn't thinking about the way her dark eyes had laughed up into his when he'd sipped from her coffee cup. He wasn't imagining her pale, soft skin slick with water; or the sweet curve of her breast, the dark cherry nipples that he'd loved to taste.

But as his body started to harden, he knew he lied.

The discovery was devastating.

"Tariq?"

At her call he was instantly on his feet.

"Don't come in," she said hastily.

He dared not. "I won't." It came out thick and muffled, like something was strangling him. He cleared his throat and tried again. "What do you want?"

What do you want? He shut his eyes and clenched his hands into fists as his words echoed in the intimacy of the tent.

"Some soap, please."

"How am I supposed to give you soap if I can't come in?"

"I don't know." Her voice was so soft he had to strain his ears to hear. "I suppose I could do without it."

"You'll feel better if you're properly washed."

"I suppose."

Tariq spied the soap. On the table in the corner, on top of a thick white towel. A shower cap lay beside it—and a bottle of shampoo.

"Would you like shampoo, too?"

"Yes, please, if it isn't too much trouble."

"No trouble." And wished that were true. He gathered up the bar of soap, the shampoo and the towel. Raising his voice, he said, "So how am I supposed to get this to you without stepping behind the curtain?"

"Close your eyes. Approach one step at a time. I'll tell you when you can drop them."

He strode to the curtain, shut his eyes, hauled in a deep breath that shuddered to the bottom of his chest and pushed the drape aside.

"I'm here."

A careful step in the direction of her voice. And another. She moved. He heard the lap of the water and prickles of arousal gathered in his groin. He thanked Allah for the towel that hid that evidence of his desire for her.

Only a small distance away, Jayne was naked.

Don't think about it.

Don't look.

How could he not? It had been too long since he'd seen those full breasts with the crimson tips and the tight stomach, below which lay the lush dark curls that…

Desire shafted through him, making him rock hard.

He fought the temptation to look.

And won.

Quickly he took another step. The scent of jasmine bath oil surrounded him, pungent, sensual.

"Stop!"

He obeyed, unbearably aroused by the hot steamy scent of the perfumed water, the thought that she lay naked less than an arm's length from him and the fact that he was performing personal, intimate chores at her command.

"Hold the soap and the shampoo out."

Like an automaton, he found his arms extending. The towel slithered down, landing at his feet. He heard the water swirl, knew she must be sitting up, that her breasts would be moving, glistening with moisture. He bit back a groan, and squeezed his eyes more tightly shut, leashing the urge to look.

"You can let them go."

Only then did he realise that he was clutching the toiletries so tightly that the shampoo bottle had buckled under the force. Jayne's hands, hot and wet from the water, reached for his. His eyes still closed, he bit back a groan, as her fingers slid wetly against his.

"I've got the bottle, let go!"

Hastily he released the toiletries. The shampoo bottle slid into her grip while the soap splashed into the bath. A moment later he heard the sensual lap of water against her skin.

Unable to resist, he opened his eyes.

The shampoo bottle sat on the lip of the bath. Jayne was leaning forward, both hands searching the water for the soap. From this angle, the beautiful breasts he remembered were hidden, and her back was pale and smooth and sleek under the lamplight. Her hair was piled on top of her head in a shining mass, and her nape was exposed.

Even conscious that she'd hate to know that he'd looked at her, that what he was doing was forbidden and wrong, Tariq couldn't stop staring at the wife who wanted nothing more than to be rid of him. Contrarily he itched to lean forward and place his lips against her nape, to stroke her wet back, dip his hands forward into the water and cup her breasts in his hands.

By Zayed, what was he doing? He would never take her back. What she'd done was too terrible to ever forgive…or forget.

He swung away. Grabbing a towel and a bar of soap off the table in the outer area, Tariq charged out the tent. Away from temptation. From ruination. By the time he returned after a long, ice-cold shower in the communal washrooms, Jayne was asleep.

She lay on her side, her hands pressed together under her cheek, looking barely a day older than when he'd first run into her in the Tate Gallery.

Picking up a woven angora rug, Tariq placed the extra layer over her, to protect her from the desert night chill. Then he sank down onto the wide divan beside her. He stroked the long strands of hair away from her face and stared at the alabaster skin, the red lips that had called for his kisses from the first moment he'd laid eyes on her, when she'd looked up at him, her mouth a startled *O*.

He fought the urge to kiss that terribly tempting mouth. His hands trembled a little as he gave her hair a last stroke. It shattered him that he still wanted his wife.

Despite what she had done.

Jayne awoke early the next morning. The tent was in darkness and there was no sign of Tariq. She rose, found the matches on the table in the outer area and lit a tall candle. Then she washed her face quickly using the bowl and cold water in the pitcher on the table in the outer compartment of the tent. And wondered where Tariq had gone.

Holding the candle high, Jayne returned to the sleep section and paused as she noticed the imprint of a bigger, heavier body on the divan beside where she had lain. Tariq must've slept beside her all night long. Heat uncurled in her stomach at the thought of him lying close beside her. And she hadn't even known.

Probably better so. She would've had to send him away.

Setting the candle down, she hunted through her bag for a pair of lightweight dark trousers with narrow-cut legs and a shift dress in a leopard print to wear over the top. By now the first rays of the morning sun crept through the open tent flap. Tying a chiffon scarf over her hair, Jayne picked up her sunglasses and ventured outside.

The early-morning winter air was crisp and chilly. The lack of mud on the hard sun-baked ground revealed the absence of rain during the night.

Yesterday Tariq has said that the clouds could dissipate into the ether, and he had been right, overhead the sky was a clear blue and the air smelt of dry desert dust. She scanned her surroundings, searching for Tariq. He wasn't in the immediate surrounds of the encampment. She walked around the tent, to where he'd parked the vehicle. It was gone.

Her heart jolted. Then she saw it parked a short way out in the shimmer of the desert. Nearby Jayne made out the form of a man and above his head hovered a falcon.

Tariq.

And Noor.

The distance over the desert was deceptive. It took her fifteen minutes of brisk walking to reach them. By the time she got there, Noor had returned to her master and sat perched on his glove.

Tariq turned his head. "Good morning. Did you sleep well?" Aside from the polite inquiry, Jayne could read little in the high-boned face, his dark gaze narrowed against the brightening light, but she sensed that he had withdrawn.

Why?

What had changed since last night when they drank coffee with the Bedouin, when she'd felt at ease with him? There'd been no coolness between them in the tent afterwards, before she'd bathed. To the contrary, there had been a flare of heat that she'd quickly doused. So why the feeling that they were now separated by a continent as cold and as vast as the Antarctic?

"Yes, I slept fine." Hadn't he? She examined his face. There were dark shadows beneath his eyes. Maybe not. Perhaps it was worry about his father that had kept him awake?

"Have you heard from the palace?"

He got her meaning. "I spoke to my father, he is sounding better. The nurse says he seems to have rallied and made an unexpected recovery." His gaze remained shadowed. "Not that it will change the ultimate outcome. But he does seem more comfortable."

His father would still die. "And at least he will be there when you return."

"*Inshallah.*"

If it is Allah's will. She sighed and examined the falcon. "I don't remember Khan wearing that," Jayne observed, changing the subject to one less bleak.

"That's a transmitter." Tariq's expression was hard to read. "I used to hunt the purist way, with no modern gadgets. But

I don't want to lose Noor, so I decided to make use of the technology at my disposal."

"What happened to Khan?"

"I lost him." His voice cooled even more. "Not long after you left."

Jayne decided against asking how. But her heart ached at the distance that yawned between them. And for a moment she longed for a replay of that moment when they'd laughed together while they'd shared that awful bitter coffee last night.

"But you still keep falcons," she said.

"Yes. It's a part of who I am, who I will always be."

Jayne suspected the statement held a warning. When he'd first brought her to Zayed she'd found the notion of hunting with falcons barbaric, a far cry from the romantic vision she'd carried in her head of nomadic Bedouin mounted on an Arab stallion while a falcon plummeted out of the sky to ride on the falconer's arm.

"You're a sheikh. And a falconer." There was a finality in her words. He was a world apart from her. They had nothing in common.

"And a man."

She stiffened at the flat, emotionless statement. Yet it reminded her of exactly what they did have in common. *He was a man.* His hot golden eyes reminded her of the fact. An ache stirred deep within her as their gazes entwined. *She was a woman.* They were bound together by threads of desire.

By sex.

And nothing else.

She broke the connection and looked away, reluctant to consider the unruly attraction that had existed between them. That was in the past. But was it? The kiss he'd pressed on her lips the other night flitted through her mind. Jayne shifted uncomfortably as she recalled her ardent response. The attraction was far from over. Noor shifted restlessly on his arm, drawing her gaze. Sucking a deep breath into her starved lungs, she said desperately, "Tell me why you became a falconer."

"I was five years old when I went with my father into the desert and experienced my first falcon hunt." His voice was low. "The Emirs are descended from the Bedu, it is customary for the ruling Emir to teach his son the tenets of falconry. I had not yet started school. I will never forget it. It was a memorable time of my life—less than a month later my mother left us."

Jayne recoiled. "I didn't know you remembered your mother. But you would've seen her from time to time afterwards?" Tariq's blatant refusal to discuss his mother had roused her curiosity. She hadn't noticed it in the past. She'd been young…in love…wrapped up in Tariq and later in her own misery.

"Every autumn houbara bustards fly south from the northern hemisphere to Africa and stop off in Zayed," Tariq continued, ignoring her question. "Peregrine and saker falcons migrate a little earlier. The canny Bedu falconers saw a way to supplement a sparse diet of milk, dates and bread. They would have only a couple of weeks before the houbara arrived. So they would trap a falcon and have to train it in a few weeks. The bird became a coveted ally to hunt houbara, which are good eating—considered by the bedu to be a gift from God through the winter months."

Jayne stared out over the timeless stretch of the desert. It was bleak and forsaken. He wasn't going to talk about his mother. Not to her. But at least that awful taciturn silence had been broken. And she couldn't help wondering if his mother had felt as out of place in the desert as she Jayne. She shivered. Beside her, Noor cocked her head and spread her wings before lifting gracefully into the air. "Is she hungry?"

"Probably. Noor missed a flock of pigeons earlier—they'd had a head start. I called her back."

"Will she find prey?"

Tariq shrugged. "If she doesn't I have a lure with meat in the truck." He tipped his head to the SUV. "But after the time spent in the *kafas* yesterday I wanted to give her a chance to fly for at least an hour before I cage her for the rest of the drive. There's a lot of space in the desert for her to stretch her wings. And plenty of birds for her to prey on."

"Plenty of birds? Here?" Jayne gave the surrounding wasteland a pointed stare.

He moved closer. "Yes, there are—more than a decade ago when the falcon and houbara populations became seriously endangered, I had to implement breeding programs throughout Zayed for both the falcons and the houbara. Now captive birds are released annually."

"So that falconers can hunt?" she challenged, tilting her head back to stare into his face.

"Without the hunters, there would be no falcons and no houbara—except for a few wild birds in zoos and the last of the numbers of the extinct birds stuffed for display in museums." He loomed over her. "Is that what you want?"

"No," she admitted, her attention fixed on his exquisitely moulded mouth.

"And there would be less people learning the ways of the desert and passionate about conserving the habitat that these creatures live in."

Passionate. Her breath caught. Finally she murmured, "I suppose."

Words spilled from Tariq. "I fiercely believe the ancient tenets that have come from our forefathers. A falconer should have love and respect for both the falcon and the quarry and have a deep concern for the hunting territory and environment."

Love and respect. That's what she'd craved from him. But bringing her to Zayed had killed his love. And she'd learned he'd never had any respect for her…for her love. As if it were yesterday she could remember him storming into the library where she sat with Roger talking about books they'd both read while he mended a first-edition copy of *The Letters of Pliny to the Consul* with reverent fingers.

Tariq had taken one look at their heads bent over the ancient book and demanded that she come with him at once. He'd been so furious that his eyes had blazed with a tigerish light and the generous mouth she'd loved so much had been set in a thin, implacable line.

Even now the memory caused her stomach to cramp into a cold, tight ball.

Jayne breathed slowly. In. Out. In again. She fought to relax and tried to concentrate on what he was saying.

"My forefathers released their falcons into the wild at the end of the hunting season—but now with more wealth after the discovery of oil in Zayed, falconers are keeping the better birds. So I have put a program in place where at the end of each season some sakers and peregrine falcons bred in captivity, who are trained in September and hunt through the winter, are released."

The falcons were far luckier than she had been. He hadn't released her. He had banished her, despite her tears…her pleas. He had been ruthless.

"Each season I personally train one bird that I will release—to join the wild population and strengthen the bloodline. That bird will be equipped with a transmitter and tracked by satellite to add to research on bird migration."

"I must admit, I didn't think of the hunter as carer," Jayne said. "If I thought of it at all, I thought of the lone nomad on his horse with his falcon strapped to his wrist."

Tariq gave a short, unamused laugh. "That age is gone. The world has changed. Falconry has changed. In the past, falconers followed on horseback or on camel—now we use four-wheel-drives. And GPSs and transmitters."

She gave him a once-over, taking in the *thobe* he wore, his dark tanned face. He looked like an ancient desert warrior. Timeless. Fierce. Unforgiving. Yet he was as comfortable negotiating state affairs abroad in a western business suit as he was here in the desert. "Do you miss the old Zayed?"

"It doesn't matter whether I miss it. Everything changes. *Inshallah.*" Something about the finality in the way he said the last made her suspect that he was thinking about his father. Once he died, Tariq's whole world would change again. His father would be gone, he could become the Emir of Zayed, a man powerful beyond belief…and he would grant her the divorce she wanted.

Nothing stayed the same.

Not even the desert. The dunes shifted under the fingers of the wind just like the evil whispers of the Emir had forever changed Tariq's love for her to hate.

A lump rose in the back of her throat. "Where is Noor?" she asked a trifle huskily. "Hasn't she had enough time up there? I need some breakfast."

"We must wait. A popular saying in falconry is: 'Who is training whom?'" He flashed her a grim smile. "The falconer must learn great patience...and trust."

Her heart turned over.

He smiled far too little these days. Even that sorry attempt had to be worth something. And he'd never trusted much at all. "You mean that you trust that Noor will come back?"

"Yes." His certainty was unequivocal. "And if you're hungry, there are some cereal bars in the truck."

Jayne walked away to forage around and emerged with the foil-wrapped bars. She gave one to Tariq. He tore the wrapper off and his teeth tore into the bar.

Those same teeth had once closed gently on her flesh... teasing...evoking delight and pleasure.

Looking away up into the empty sky, Jayne asked huskily, "How do you know Noor is still here? That she hasn't flown away?"

"Watch this." Tariq aimed the antenna at the empty sky and the signal boomed. "See? She's there. Right above us. Watching every move we make."

"Amazing." Jayne squinted upward, the light so bright, that even with sunglasses she needed to screw up her eyes.

A few minutes later Tariq breathed out. "Ah, now things are about to get interesting."

Jayne took in the change in him. The cool remote air had gone. His admiration for the falcon shone from his eyes. He'd transformed into a man of action, in his element. A falconer.

"See that?" Tariq was pointing at a bird about the size of a heron, flying swiftly towards them. "That's a houbara bustard, Noor's favourite prey." He placed an arm around her shoulders. "Come."

Under the weight of his touch, Jayne froze, her breath catching in her throat.

Breathe.

In. Out. In again.

"What are you waiting for? Hurry."

His grip tightened and a wave of emotion shook her. She sought desperately for something to say. "But it's so big. I mean, that's not a pigeon or something."

Far above them something flashed. Noor.

Jayne started to move.

"She's hunting." Tariq opened the passenger door of the SUV for her and slammed it behind her. An instant later he slid in beside her. "Noor will need all her skill to track down a bird of that size and speed. A falcon needs to hit a houbara hard to take it out and knock it to the ground. Noor is less skilled on the ground than in the air, and faced with a larger prey on the desert floor she may suffer injury if it can still fight."

"I hope she doesn't get hurt." Concern for the graceful falcon swept through Jayne.

Tariq turned his head to look at her. His gaze skimmed her face. Jayne's breath caught at the sudden spark of warmth in his eyes. For an instant time slowed, then he blinked. And the moment was past.

"Noor is a survivor." The SUV surged forward. "Let's go find her."

Six

Two kilometres on, Tariq and Jayne were still chasing behind the bustard with Noor hunting a long way above.

"She'll be exhausted," Jayne said in disbelief.

"Noor can fly for about an hour making repeated strikes. At the moment she's taking advantage of stealth," Tariq explained. "See how she flies above the houbara, with the sun at her back?" Jayne nodded. "The houbara won't see her coming."

"Good grief."

Just then the falcon tucked her wings and went into a dive, closing in on the bustard. Tariq pulled to a stop, and they both leaped out the vehicle. Even from the ground Jayne could hear the wind whistling through the peregrine's wings.

Tariq moved, hooking his arm around her shoulders.

When Noor struck, Jayne looked away. Tariq pulled her

into the crook of his arm. Her face buried in the heavy cotton of his *thobe,* she breathed in the rich, masculine scent of him.

When she raised her face from his shoulder the houbara was on the ground and Noor stood over her prey, her head bowed, ready to feast.

"She's waiting for my signal." Tariq gave a short sharp whistle and the bird started to eat. His hand rubbed up and down Jayne's arm, steadying her, offering rough comfort.

But the shivers that followed in the wake of his touch, had little do with comfort. Jayne bit her lip, determined not to let the melting sensation that pooled in her stomach undermine her good sense.

"Noor will not eat the prey without my consent," Tariq explained, the light rubbing of his fingertips torturing her. "If I were a nomad falconer, the bustard would feed more than only the falcon, and Noor would fly to hunt again."

It was savage. Jayne stared blindly at the bird. The desert was unforgiving. And the man beside her holding her was every bit as ruthless…yet once she had loved him with all her young heart. And he'd loved her with tenderness and reverence. Before his father had interfered and driven them apart.

When the falcon had finished, she fluttered over to them, half hopping, half skipping. She gave a cackle, breaking the silence.

"You're pleased with yourself, aren't you?" The falcon tilted her head at the gentle note in Tariq's voice and allowed him to squirt water from a spray bottle over her head and back. Noor closed her eyes, and Jayne could see her enjoyment.

"She's hot and tired." Jayne wished that Tariq spoke to her in that proud, soothing voice.

"See how full her crop is? Now she's ready to go back to her perch."

"Like a well-trained, tame female," Jayne said with a bite.

He looked at her through slitted, unreadable eyes. "Noor may be trained…but she will never be tame. Nor would I want her to be."

Glancing away, Jayne found herself staring into the dark bottomless gaze of a wild falcon. In that instant she felt a bond with the peregrine and something moved deep within her chest. Jayne was shaken by a strange sense that she balanced on the cusp of a revelation.

About the nature of the desert.

About Tariq.

And about herself.

Jayne glanced at Tariq. Why had she never noticed the untamed quality that clung to him? How had she ever mistaken him for another ordinary student in London on a backpacking holiday? Even when she'd learned he was studying finance, working in a London bank, the warning signs still hadn't gone off. She'd—mistakenly—imagined he worked as a clerk. And when she'd finally found out that he was a sheikh, the son of the Emir of Zayed, why had she ever imagined that she could domesticate such a man?

He was still so wrong for her…for what she wanted out of life. A man who loved her, a family, an ordinary existence. Yet she couldn't break the disquieting sense that after today nothing would ever be the same.

An hour later they had said their farewells to Ghayth and Matra and the rest of the tribe and were back on the road to Aziz. Tariq was exquisitely aware of the subtle scent that pervaded the vehicle. It came from Jayne's hair, from the shampoo he'd handed her in the bath last night. The memory of the want…the need…that had ripped through him while he stood beside his bathing wife was unwelcome. As was the inexplicable affinity he'd felt with her while Noor hunted.

Jayne hated the desert…hated falcons…considered him barbaric. How could he have felt such an unspoken bond with her, in the place she hated most? And he couldn't afford to feel any sort of affinity or desire for her.

It was not acceptable.

He lapsed back into brooding silence.

He would've preferred the foreboding from yesterday, the threat of the thunderstorm, to the fragile tension that stretched across the wasteland between them.

"Where do those tracks lead?" Jayne's voice broke the rising tension.

Tariq followed her arm to where she pointed at a sandy desert byway—little more than goat track—that branched off from the main road. "Most lead to grazing camps. They're access roads so that provisions and fodder for livestock can be delivered."

"Livestock?" Jayne sounded disbelieving. "It's hard to believe that anything survives in this hostile terrain."

Resentment surged within him, rising to sit hot and tight in his throat. "It's only hostile to you because you hate it so much. Many consider the desert beautiful."

"Maybe hate is too strong a word." She hesitated. He had the feeling she was groping for words. "After I fell ill on our camel trip, I wasn't in a hurry to repeat the excursion. Perhaps I just don't understand this world."

"It's my world."

Jayne didn't respond. She simply turned her head and stared out the window. And that gave Tariq no satisfaction at all. It certainly did nothing to quell the heat in his groin.

Don't think about it…and it might subside.

Sure.

To get his attention off the predicament that filled his thoughts—and tightened his briefs beneath the *thobe*—he tried to imagine the desert through her eyes. Bleak. Endless. Foreign. This far north the desert was much more sandy—less stony—and there were tufts of greenery that stretched as far as the eye could see.

"The desert changes as we travel north," he said, relenting a little. It wasn't her fault he wanted her. By Zayed, she'd made it clear that she couldn't wait to be rid of him. She didn't want him; his wife already had a new man lined up.

Neil.

Blond. Pale eyes. A man who'd grown up a stone's throw from where she had, according to the investigator's report. Who'd attended the same schools and churches as she had. A man who shared her upbringing…her world…and was everything he wasn't.

"There's actually some greenery here. Kind of like seagrass on a beach," she agreed and pointed out the window.

Tariq suppressed his infuriating thoughts and bent his head to follow her arm. "Those scrubby bushes provide cover for the wintering populations of houbara. Desert warbler and wheatear also inhabit this area. In spring they will return to the central Asian steppes to breed."

"Oh."

"Not so inhospitable. The desert teems with life. There are lizards and beetles and at night the gerbils come out. This area is a conservation habitat. No hunting is allowed."

"Not even for Noor?"

"Not even with falcons. Beyond this conservation area lies

the border with Bashir, and Sheikh Karim has declared an even larger corridor of desert a protected reserve, all the way down to the gulf. So when we get to Aziz, Noor will have to be fed from a lure, as hunting is completely banned."

"I want a falcon."

Tariq shot her a disbelieving glance. From her expression, the words had surprised Jayne as much as they had Tariq. His mouth twisted and he couldn't stop the cynicism that escaped. "Soon you'll be back in New Zealand…in the city. Where will you keep a falcon? Fly it?"

"I'll find somewhere. There must be clubs."

"And what will Neil say about your new…passion?" He drew out the "sh" sound in the final word to a sibilant hiss and she recoiled, pressing against the door. But she didn't reply. Fixing his attention back on the road, he gave a harsh bark of laughter. But he found no humour in the situation. Finally he said, "You've never appreciated anything from Zayed, why would you want a falcon?"

"What do you want me to say? Because I might grow to understand the power and secret of the desert?" Even as his head snapped around to stare at her, she was saying dismissively, "No, nothing as deep as that. Noor is so graceful. And I'd like the challenge of training a falcon like her."

For a moment, there, she'd had him going. But she'd been mocking him. If he'd thought that she would want to learn the ways of Zayed…he shook away the thought. *No.* It would make absolutely no difference. He didn't want her back, dared not take her back. "You'll need a lot of patience. Some birds are far more headstrong than Noor."

"I have a lot of patience."

He looked across at her. "So much patience that only a few

months after our marriage you fell into bed with another man and betrayed me?"

Jayne went very still. A sideways glance revealed her hands fisted in her lap, the knuckles white. Then she turned her head, and he caught a glimpse of eyes stretched wide with shock before he returned his attention to the road.

There'd been more than shock in her eyes. There'd been bewilderment…a gut-wrenching devastation that he'd torn open the subject that was tacitly understood to be taboo.

But this time she didn't shrink away. "Doesn't it strike you as strange that I demanded a marriage contract where you could have only one wife, and then I committed adultery?"

She hurled the words at him. For a very brief timespan he felt confusion, then he shrugged. "Since when has a marriage contract been a guarantee that one of the parties will not stray? That clause only meant you didn't want to risk your position. There was no guarantee if I married again, you'd be senior wife."

"You don't think that maybe I wanted our marriage to be a monogamous, once-in-a-lifetime love?"

"If that were the case, you wouldn't now want a divorce." Unable to look at her, he glared at the road ahead. "If that were the case, there would be no Neil waiting back for you in Auckland."

"Oh, what the hell is the point? First it was poor Roger and now it's Neil. You're never going to trust me. And I no longer want to be married to someone who doesn't trust me. It's as simple as that."

"Do not speak his name." He swerved off the road, yanked up the hand brake and swung to glare at her, baring all the rage and anguish he'd suppressed for years. "It's not simple at all. Not only did you betray me, you fell pregnant with the infidel's child."

She gave a gasp. The long, level look she gave him was filled with hurt and sorrow. The reproach kicked at his gut like a mule. But he refused to be swayed, to soften. "Less than fifty years ago, you would've been stoned to death in my country for such a blatant betrayal of your husband, do you know that?"

She stared back at him, her face cold and set like marble.

"Do you know that?" He wanted to shake her. Instead he clenched his hands around the steering wheel, terrified he might put his hands around her throat and choke her. "Have you any idea of what you did?" Her betrayal had emasculated him.

"Instead of a stoning, you accused me and banished me. You wouldn't listen—"

"To what? There was enough evidence. And you refused to take a DNA test—"

"An insult!"

"If you were innocent, you would never have hesitated to take the DNA test."

Jayne gave a groan of frustration. "Do you think I wanted a husband who needed a DNA test to prove that the child I carried was his?" Her face was tight and pale. "I wanted you to listen to my side—"

"I was so enthralled by you, I wasn't letting you whisper seductive, traitorous lies to me."

"Is that what your father said? That I would sway you with sex and lies?" Her velvet brown eyes were colder and harder than he'd ever seen them. "That's why you wouldn't listen to me? Because of your father's warped opinions?"

"That's what you always do. Bring my father into to it. You know that's a sure way to rile me."

"Didn't I have the right to defend myself?" Her voice rose. Then she went silent. Finally she said, "We can't have this discussion…or any discussion about the breakdown of our marriage…without bringing your father into it."

"I don't want to hear your poisonous lack of respect for my father. You sinned. You committed *zina*. I should've thrown you into prison. Instead I let you off lightly, I told you never to set foot in Zayed again."

He'd been enraged. And she'd left. He'd found her passport on their marital bed together with her wedding ring and known she would never return. The plain gold band she'd insisted on choosing, little knowing that the man who she was marrying could buy her anything in the exclusive jeweller's shop. That had been one of the things he'd loved about her.

The grief that had stormed through him after her departure had been fierce. He'd loved her with his whole heart. Then hated her with his entire existence. All that was left was to forget her, to drown himself in the Zayedi affairs of state… travelling abroad…keeping busy from daybreak to long after sundown. Until even his father had looked troubled.

In the years since, he'd tried never to speak of his wife. Unless pressed. Then she'd called demanding a divorce, and suddenly her name was everywhere.

"It's fortunate that you miscarried the child." He remembered the brief, bleak little letter she had sent him, several months after she had left:

I lost the baby.
Jayne

A couple of stark typed lines on a white sheet of paper. He'd torn it from side to side and hurled it in the bin. He'd been glad in a bitter kind of way. With the loss of the baby, the life she and the infidel had created had been lost forever. He remembered the humiliating moment of hesitation…the damning instant when he'd considered finding her, bringing her back to Zayed. He'd prayed for his soul that night.

And he'd resisted, humiliated by her evil act, which he knew would lead the way to others in the future. The shame of desiring a woman who took other lovers while married to him had been too much.

"Fortunate?" It was a low grunt of pain.

"The child might have grown up blond like his infidel father announcing your adultery to the world." Tariq didn't know what devil rode him.

"I don't want to talk about this." Her voice was ragged, and her dark lashes fell against her bleached cheeks.

After a long moment of silence, Tariq said, "Have it your way." Viciously he swung the vehicle back onto the road and stepped on the gas.

But last night, in that Bedu tent, Tariq knew he had come face-to-face with his demons. In spite of her ignominious betrayal, he still desired his wife. And he feared he would never be free of the silken threads of wanting her.

Not even after the divorce.

"What is that?"

As the angle of the hill slowed the SUV, Jayne roused herself from the silence she'd buried herself in for the last section of the drive and stared up at the dark stone building that rose in front of them.

"Mahood's, er, château."

"His what?"

"It's an old fort. Very historical," Tariq replied grimly, accelerating a little up the hill to the fort.

"It looks like the prison you said I was lucky to avoid." Jayne drew a deep, shuddering breath. Could it get any worse? She could've kicked herself as tension filled the car. "Like the kind of place that has dungeons and racks and implements specially designed for torture. Or, if I wanted to be fanciful, I could say it reminded me of Dracula's castle." She caught her bottom lip between her teeth. "If I go in, will I ever come out?" She was only half-joking.

"Don't worry. The walls are there to keep the inhabitants safe."

Jayne wasn't so sure about that.

"Relax, I guarantee that you'll be safe."

She gave a snort. "Thanks, your guarantees truly reassure me."

"Sarcasm doesn't become you, wife," he growled. "Now let us go and greet our hosts."

Another even less pleasant surprise awaited Jayne inside the fort. Leila—the woman the Emir had been desperate for Tariq to marry all those years ago, stood beside Ali, her father. Jayne shuddered inside. Could it get any worse? She should have expected with his wife dead, that Ali would need a hostess.

Leila inspected Jayne from head to toe through dark sullen eyes. When she'd finished, a dismissive smile twisted her henna-painted lips. Tariq moved closer to Jayne and put an arm around her shoulder. Jayne stiffened in surprise.

"Would you show us to our room? My wife is tired."

Leila's head jerked back at the reproof. "This way."

For the first time in several hours, Jayne started to feel a little more cheerful. Tariq kept his arm around her waist, and she was grateful for the support he offered.

Leila led them down a long gloomy corridor. Several twists and turns later, Jayne decided the fort could well be a place of torture. A short flight of stairs took them past a landing where slits in the walls for archers indicated the building's past purpose.

"Here, this is your room." Leila opened the door and they stepped into a large chamber with an immense canopied bed. On the far side of the room, latticed shutters had been flung open to reveal a view over the desert. But Jayne couldn't get her eyes off that bed.

One bed.

How had she thought things had gotten as bad as they could?

Clearly she and Tariq were expected to share that sensually draped bed. Images jumbled through her head like a relentless slide show. Tariq touching her, making love to her. Tariq telling her to go and never come back. Tariq kissing her the other night in his study. Her inability to resist. Tariq's hurtful conviction that she'd betrayed him with another man.

The dent on the divan where another body had lain beside her last night…

Jayne swung around. "I'm not staying here." Before she had finished speaking, she was heading for the door.

Leila's gaze glittered. "Our humble abode does not please the sheikhah?"

Tariq stepped forward. "Jayne—"

But his wife clearly wasn't in the frame of mind to be placated. "There's nothing wrong with the abode," Jayne said, her eyes flashing fire, her colour high. "But I have a problem with the accommodation."

"Exactly what is the sheikhah's problem?"

"Leila—" Tariq tried to intervene.

"I am not sleeping in that." Jayne pointed emphatically to the massive bed. "I want my own room."

Leila's gaze flickered between them, alight with avid curiosity.

Tariq felt fury and the familiar humiliation rush through his bloodstream. Before long everyone in Aziz would know that his errant wife refused to sleep with him. Leila would take great pleasure in spreading the gossip. By tomorrow it would reach Jazirah. He shut his eyes.

But would Leila guess what his wife really wanted? A divorce…

That rumour better not reach his father's ears. Not after he'd worked so hard to reassure the man he revered.

Leila stood in the doorway and smirked. "Of course, I will find the sheikhah a room of her own."

Jayne smiled sweetly at the other woman. "That would be lovely."

Leila had never been eager to lift a finger to assist Jayne. His wife had certainly never smiled at Leila with such glowing enthusiasm. Tariq decided he was ready to throttle them both.

Seven

That evening, accompanied by an elderly chaperone who had come to fetch her, Jayne left the pokey little room where Leila had installed her, daring her to object, and made her way to the reception rooms.

She stalked in, her head held high, ready to take on whoever gave her trouble.

Leila.

Ali.

Tariq.

She didn't care.

No one was getting the better of her tonight. For too long she'd allowed Tariq…his father…his political allies to walk all over her. No more.

But the sight of a young woman staring with dewy, adoring eyes up at Tariq was enough to stop Jayne in her tracks.

The nymph—she was barely old enough to be called a woman—wasn't touching Tariq…or even sharing extended eye contact, which could be dangerous, but she fluttered her lashes and every line of her body revealed her yearning. Suddenly Jayne felt quite ill.

She was thrust into the unwelcome mists of the past…of watching Leila making a play for Tariq. Of the poison the Emir had dripped into her ear about how Tariq should've married Leila. Not her. About the arrangement that had existed between Ali and the Emir that one day their children would marry and consolidate the northern and southern regions of the sheikhdom.

She swallowed. This young girl didn't carry the Emir's approval.

But she loved Tariq.

It was as clear as day to Jayne. Because once she, too, had yearned for him. Once upon a time *she* had gazed at him with soft velvety eyes, full of trust and love.

She looked away, not wanting to intrude on the girl's naked infatuation. And caught sight of Leila staring at the pair with unveiled hatred in her eyes.

Jayne's stomach cramped. The hairs on the back of her neck prickled. There was trouble coming. She could smell it.

To avoid the nastiness, she made her way to a table laden with *mezze* at the back of the room and helped herself to *kibbe,* the small, tasty, round balls of minced meat.

"You must be English."

She looked up at the man who had spoken in a transatlantic drawl. "No, I'm from New Zealand. Where are you from?"

"Texas," he said with a grin that deepened the laugh lines around hazel eyes. "Oil country."

Her spirits lifted at the wide uncomplicated pleasure in his face and she smiled back. "I should've known."

"Dexter." He stuck out a hand.

She took it and followed his lead, relieved that the anonymity of first names did away with the need for explanation. "Jayne."

"Now that you know what I do, it's your turn to tell me."

"I'm a teacher. But in the last couple of years I've become increasingly interested in literacy—so I'm studying further."

"So that's why you're here. To do research?"

She didn't correct him. Didn't want the questioning stares, the pointed silence when he discovered she was the sheikh's estranged wife.

Instead she started to talk about what she'd seen so far, about the education levels in Zayed and the Bedouin women in the desert, and he nodded, looking far more fascinated than the subject warranted. To head him off from getting any ideas about furthering their acquaintance, she said, "I must go find my husband."

"You're married?"

Not for much longer. But for once the thought no longer brought the delight it had only days ago. Unsmilingly, she nodded.

"He's a fool to leave you unattended."

What could she say to that? He always had. Tariq was too important to spend time chasing after her. "I had better go."

Tariq glanced around impatiently. Where was Jayne? He hadn't seen his wife since she'd stormed out of his bedchamber earlier. And he'd been too furious to find her later.

At his side stood Karim's stepmother, and her daughter, Yasmin. Yasmin asked him something, her voice soft and breathy. Irritatingly so, because he had to lean forward to make out what she was saying. From across the room he could feel the weight of Karim's gaze. Had Karim already heard the gossip? That Jayne had fled her husband's bed-chamber?

He frowned. Where the hell was Jayne? What was taking her so long? He needed her. He certainly didn't need Karim gaining the wrong impression about his intentions to Yasmin. Especially not after he'd taken such pains to twart his father's matchmaking attempts.

Just then he caught sight of the older woman who had been sent to collect Jayne from her room and escort her down. He touched her arm, lightly, getting her attention. "Was the sheikhah not ready to come down?"

The woman gave him a puzzled stare. "The sheikhah is here."

Here? *Where?* Tariq's head whipped around.

He barely heard Yasmin droning on about her favourite horse. Instead he froze as he caught sight of his wife.

She was laughing.

Yes, laughing—when she barely smiled with him—up at a strange man. A westerner with blondish hair and tanned features. Just like—

Tariq raked a hand through his hair. No, he was not think-ing about that. Not now. So he looked down at Yasmin. Her eyes were dark and glowing. Biddable. Waiting for him to say yes to whatever it was that she had asked.

Tariq muttered a reply, barely conscious of the words he was stringing together. Then, unable to help himself, he searched for Jayne again. She was still with the American who worked for Ali. Unable to bear looking at them any longer, he glanced away and caught a glimpse of Leila, hidden in a group of women. She was staring straight at him. Although he couldn't decipher her expression, a shadow passed over him. Jayne had always referred to the sensation as a goose walking over a grave. He'd hated the expression.

But it captured the malevolence Leila radiated.

How could this be? Why was it that the only woman he wanted was the woman he had driven away? The woman talking to another man…the woman who wanted nothing from him—except a divorce. And why could he not get her out of his mind? The memory of her dewy skin in the bath, the sweet taste of her mouth beneath his.

He was weak. He couldn't resist the sensual memories. And he'd thought he'd been so smart. When Jayne had contacted him about a divorce, he'd seen a way to let his father die in peace, satisfied his son was happily married. The last thing he had expected when his wife returned was to discover that he still desired his wife.

A wife who he could not keep faithful…a wife who hated Zayed.

What the hell was he to do?

Yasmin was speaking again, about the Arabian stud in Bashir where some of the world's finest horses had been bred. He listened with one ear, but his attention kept straying to Jayne, resenting the easy way she was talking to the geologist, her hands waving as she expressed herself. She looked relaxed and at ease, a far cry from the wary, tense woman who had pressed herself up against the door and watched him with cautious eyes when he'd pulled over at the side of the road only a few hours ago.

Why couldn't she relax like that with him? He gazed at her with a growing hunger. Why was she strung so tight when they were alone together? Was it their cultures that separated them, that made her unable to relax? Or was it him?

The thought made his heart burn with pain.

He wanted her to smile at him. He wanted her to talk to him with the same eagerness she spoke to the complete stranger in front of her.

So he glared across the room at her.

"The sheikhah's preferences for blond westerners are well-known." The soft murmur came from Yasmin. "It looks like this man fits her requirements."

Rage exploded within Tariq. He turned on the young woman. "You should not listen to scandalous gossip. You know nothing about what man fits my wife's requirements. If you did you'd know I was that man."

"But she refuses you, a sheikh!"

So even Yasmin had heard that Jayne wouldn't share his bedchamber and was willing to take advantage of the opportunity to gain his attention. No doubt Yasmin knew that he had banished his wife because she had bedded another man. Humiliation scorched him.

"And you will be Emir when—" She must have read something in his face because she broke off, her hand covering her mouth.

"When my father dies."

"I am sorry, I was impertinent."

Tariq bowed his head. "No. It is I who must apologise."

Yasmin might be young but she wasn't stupid. She instantly understood why he was apologising. And her eyes filled with tears. "So you will not marry me? Not ever?" Yasmin's lower lip trembled. "But Karim says—"

"I know what your brother thinks. He's been trying to

broker a marriage between you and me for months. It is not going to happen. And the Emir should have conveyed that. There will be someone else for you. One day."

More tears welled in the eyes in front of him. "It will be too late."

Tariq cursed in English. At the shock in her eyes, he apologised. "You were not meant to understand that."

A silver tear spilled onto her cheek. "Is it me? Is there something wrong with me? Am I not a good enough woman for you?"

Frustration surged inside him. And fury at Jayne. His wife should have been beside him to prevent this, not standing talking—no, laughing—with another damned man. "There is nothing wrong with you. It is with me—I am not a good enough man."

"You, come with me!"

Jayne stiffened at the high-handed command. It reminded her of that day in the palace library with Roger when Tariq had swept in and uttered the same words. All hell had broken loose afterward. She was not in the mood for a repeat performance. She was tempted to refuse. Then she shrugged. What could he do?

"How dare you shame me, make me the laughingstock of Zayed!"

Tariq's hand was hard under her elbow. Unused to the length of the kaftan swirling around her legs, she had to take small running steps to keep up with him.

"I will not share a bedchamber with you."

In a quiet corner of the room, he stopped and swung her round to face him. He moved closer. "Did I do anything to you last night? Did I touch you? Seduce you?"

Mutely she shook her head. Had she imagined that simmering tension between them earlier in the desert this morning? Or had the flare of desire all been one-sided? On her side only? Colour flooded her. She felt the blush rising up her throat, over her cheeks. She'd made a complete fool of herself. Clearly Tariq had no desire to touch her….

"What on earth possessed you to say such a thing to Leila of all people?"

"What do you mean 'Leila of all people'? You almost married the woman."

"Never." His eyes bored into hers. "I would never have married her."

"She still wants you. *Her* father thinks she would have made you a better wife. And *your* father wanted you to marry her."

"Please, let's not go down that road again. You're prejudiced against my father and I've grown weary of it." With his free hand Tariq brushed his hair back. "Leila is married to another, it's all academic now."

Jayne swung on her heel. "And I'm weary of all this." She swept a hand around indicating the throng. "I'm going to my room."

He jerked her back. "Oh, no, you're not."

"Where are you taking me?"

"I want you to stay beside me," he spoke through tight lips. "Where I can see you."

Jayne's spine grew ramrod straight. So this was about her conversation with the tall Texan.

"Why? So that no one else can talk to me?" Nothing had changed. Tariq still suspected her every move. Boy, she would be pleased to get out of here.

"I brought you with me to keep Yasmin at bay. I don't need trouble with Karim."

Yasmin?

The young besotted-looking woman.

And then the penny dropped....

"You brought me all this way as protection, didn't you?" He didn't answer. But he didn't need to. The flush of blood high on his cheekbones told all. "Body armour for you to wear to ward off other women." She turned away, infuriated.

"See it from my perspective. I don't want to alienate Karim. And he's been angling—"

"For you, the oh-so-desirable sheikh, the future Emir of Zayed, to marry his half sister—and create a dynasty linking two countries." To think she'd pitied Yasmin. Such a political match would undoubtedly have the Emir's approval. "Except there's one problem from Yasmin's point of view— you're still married to me."

"Soon you will leave Zayed, you will get the divorce you want so badly and once you're gone I have no intention of putting my head back into the bridal noose."

"What about your father's wishes for you to settle?"

Something shifted in his eyes. Then he shrugged. "My father will be dead. He won't know. And if he can see me from the paradise of the afterlife then it won't be the first time I have disappointed him."

He was referring to their misguided marriage.

Jayne couldn't resist the wicked self-flagellistic impulse to say, "You could do worse than Yasmin, you know. She's in love with you."

Tariq's jaw hardened. "She only thinks she is—mostly because her brother encouraged the fantasy."

"Without any help from you?" She raised an eyebrow. "How did he get that idea?"

"A long story." He sighed and rubbed a hand over his face. The lines were deeply etched. He looked tired and dispirited. Instantly her heart softened.

"So what have you told her?"

"Nothing. But Karim knows I am married to you and I'm not allowed another wife in terms of our marriage agreement." There was a bitter edge to his voice. Jayne wasn't sure she wanted to know more.

"I'm glad you remember that." But the topic had set her thoughts straying down a forbidden path. Her husband was a very virile man. They had been apart for years. "Not that a little thing like a marriage contract would stop you taking what you want."

He stiffened. The gold eyes were alight with anger. "What are you implying? I am a man of honour. Unlike my wife, I do not commit *zina*—no adultery, no extramarital sex."

Eight

Jayne had a sudden urge to smack Tariq.

He sounded so damned pious. She could imagine the uproar that such an act would cause, if the recalcitrant wife struck the sheikh. It was almost worth doing, simply to measure the reaction. She subdued the mad urge. "So, will you marry her after we divorce?" A funny little pain lodged under her heart. She didn't want to think of Tariq married to another woman. Not even the young and nubile Yasmin.

It shocked her.

Since when was her mission to gain a divorce no longer the most pressing desire in the world? Why did she suddenly want to spend time with Tariq…to delay the day of departure? She *must* be mad.

"No." He shook his head. "She's too young."

"She's utterly beautiful," Jayne said wistfully. "Those dark liquid eyes, her cheekbones, that slender figure."

"Beauty is nothing," he said disparagingly. "Dress up a stick and you get a doll."

"Easy for you to say," she muttered. He didn't know what it was like to be plain, never to attract a second look. Except from him. "Why did you ask me to have coffee with you that day in the Tate Gallery?"

"You had a beautiful smile."

"So you married me because you liked my smile?" she said facetiously. She'd been too bowled over by him, by the hot hunger in his eyes. Too busy falling in love with a man who was way out of her reach. If only she'd known who he really was.

"Not only your smile." This time there was a flash of that old hunger. "But you were gentle, too. Easygoing. And for the first time in my life I was with someone who made no demands of me. You've changed…you're not so—"

"Malleable?" She pursed her lips. "I was a doormat before." At least he didn't lie that it was her beauty that had blown him away. It was her lack of backbone more than her lack of beauty that he'd been drawn to, her very ordinariness. "Yasmin is young enough to be moulded. You could marry her and take another less beautiful wife, too. If that's what you want."

"One woman at a time is enough for me." Tariq's mouth twisted into a wry curve. "I think I want a woman who can stand up to me. A woman who has soft skin and silken hair… who responds like fire to my touch."

Jayne's breath caught. There was something in his voice… something that made her belly tighten and her breathing quicken.

Something primal.

Intimate.

Madness.

She stared at him her heart locked tight in her throat.

His chest lifted and fell. The silence stretched between them like a thread pulled tight. And then the silence snapped.

"Tariq."

Yasmin stood beside him. For an instant resentment surged through Jayne. *Why now?* Could the damn woman not have stayed away another moment or two?

Yasmin was making sheep eyes at him again. No, that was wrong. The young woman was too beautiful to be associated with a sheep. Her eyes were as wide and soft as a gazelle's, her mouth soft and trembling.

Jayne wanted to scream at Yasmin not to look at her husband like that. It was akin to an act of *zina*. The pang of poisonous emotion that pierced Jayne shocked her.

Jealousy. No! She couldn't feel possessive of Tariq. He was not hers. Could never be hers. Their worlds were simply too far apart.

And she had walked out of his world years ago.

Then the weight of his hand pressed against her side, propelling her forward. "Yasmin, I don't think you have met my wife, Jayne. You would've been a child when she first came to Zayed."

Hurt sparkled in the young woman's eyes at his implication that she was too young for him. The glint of silver tears, then she blinked. "No…I haven't." Her chin went up. "I thought you had left him years ago."

A declaration of war.

The unuttered "What are you doing back?" hung in the air.

How on earth was she to respond? Jayne glanced helplessly up at Tariq beseeching him for assistance.

He pulled her closer. Through her kaftan she could feel the

warmth of his body. "She's back now." Then one finger lifted her chin and he stared down into her eyes with a heat that melted the ruthless features. "Aren't you, *nuur il-en?*"

Jayne's heart skipped a beat as a pang of emotion stabbed her.

Steady on. This pretence was all for the benefit of the young woman watching. Tariq was simply using her to let Yasmin down. Gently.

So she nodded. And tried to smile, like a good, obedient wife would. Instead her gaze locked with his. At once the surroundings melted away. No one else existed. Except for her and Tariq. She thought she heard a stifled sob. And then Yasmin said, "You should never have left him. We all thought—"

"That the sheikh was a free man." Karim's voice broke in. "I would've welcomed him into the family—we grew up together."

Jayne wished Karim would shut up. Could he not see what he was doing to his sister? That he was making it so much worse?

"Even Leila has been praying for her husband to die of a heart attack, leave her a wealthy widow. There have been whispers of assassination. Leila would love to be Zayed's sheikhah."

"Stop." No hint of amusement lightened Tariq's expression. "You go too far, friend."

"Then I apologise." Karim bowed his head. "I apologise, too, for the trouble with Ali…and Mahood. It will not happen again."

"Hush, here comes Leila."

Through the black humour of the situation, Jayne felt a flash of pity for Tariq. The hunter had become the hunted…infinitely desirable prey to the women who fluttered around him.

What must it be like to be so in demand? To be so gor-

geous, so powerful and wealthy that every woman in Zayed...
and a few beyond its borders...wanted to ensnare him?

She stifled a laugh. But it really wasn't funny. All her life
she'd wanted a man who was ordinary. Who worked a nine-to-
five job at a bank and came home each night and helped her
raise two children. A man like Neil. Instead she'd fallen for
Tariq.

Gorgeous as sin.

A rich, powerful sheikh...who had turned her whole world
upside down and brought her nothing but misery.

Yasmin and Leila and all the other beautiful vultures who
fluttered around were welcome to him. He'd cost her too
much. She'd already lost her heart...her baby...and her
sanity.

Then his hand stroked up...over her hip, and heat shafted
through her. For all her defiance she still wanted the damn man.

And the wanting did not ease the following day. Tariq had
arranged to take Jayne on a tour of Aziz in the morning. He
hoped to have the discussions with Mahood, Ali and Karim
wrapped up the following morning and their departure the
next day was already planned. While she appreciated his
thoughtfulness, she could have done without the proximity to
the one man in the world from whom she most wanted to
escape.

The morning air was cool from the desert night. A blanket
of wispy cloud was forming in the north, blocking out the
pale-yellow sunlight.

Jayne wanted to see the *souqs,* the colourful exotic markets
packed with everything to be found in Zayed. The outdoor
camel *souq* smelt of the warm earthy creatures, and traders

haggled in loud, booming voices. Jayne touched the soft nose of a gentle camel who poked her head out to be stroked. The animal's long feminine eyelashes reminded her of Yasmin.

"Come, let us move on," Tariq said, with a quick glance at the sky. Jayne looked, too. While she'd been absorbed with the camels, the clouds had closed in overhead, giving the day a dark, brooding closeness.

At the indoor carpet *souq,* Jayne admired a glorious array of rugs. Then they visited *souqs* for fresh products…bric-a-brac…copper and rugs.

And gold.

Jayne's eyes widened. Here at the gold *souq,* the loud market cacophony was absent. It was subdued, refined, clearly a place where large amounts of money changed hands. There were necklaces, intricately worked and set with stones in all colours. Fine gold chains with bells. The merchant inside straightened and preened at the sight of Tariq.

"Gold for the sheikhah, Excellency?"

"What would you like?" Tariq's face was expressionless. "You can have anything your heart desires. They even have ingots if you'd like one of those."

Her insides twisted into a heavy ball. Tariq thought the price of her heart's desire could be bought with an ingot of gold?

If only…

"You're joking?"

"Not at all." He indicated a safe in the wall. "In there. But I'm certain you'd prefer something a little prettier than a gold bar. Come." He walked toward her, his arm outstretched. "Have a look."

She folded her arms across her breasts and shrank away from him. "I don't want you to buy me gold."

His vivid eyes flared more brightly than any precious metal. And then emptied of all emotion as his arm dropped to his side. He turned to the merchant and started to talk rapidly in Arabic. Neither man paid her the least bit of attention as the merchant silently took trays out and offered them for Tariq's inspection.

Unable to help herself, Jayne peered into the trays. Pieces lay against dark velvet set with pearls and coral and turquoise. Necklaces. Rings. Bracelets. "They're beautiful."

"Turquoise is believed to ward off the evil eye," Tariq said.

Jayne bit her lip and refrained from asking whether it would protect her from his father. The Emir had caused her so much unhappiness. "These are pretty." She pointed to an ankle chain with gold bells.

"The noise from the bells will chase away evil spirits." Tariq nodded his head at the merchant who removed them from the tray.

"I don't want anything."

A young woman appeared from behind the heavy drape at the back of the *souq,* hips swaying from side to side.

"My daughter," the merchant pronounced with paternal pride.

She sashayed past Jayne with barely a glance before halting beside her father. She gave a little bob in Tariq's direction, her eyes veiled.

Jayne suppressed the urge to roll her eyes. But she shrank a little inside and retreated to the doorway, determined not to watch yet another women making a play for Tariq.

Through the entrance she could see the storm clouds rolling across the sky. No trace of sunlight remained. She could hear the low hum of Tariq's voice behind her, and a quick glance showed him handing payment to the young woman.

Leaning toward him, she handed Tariq a heavily embroidered satin bag.

Jayne cast the bag a disparaging look. Too small to hold an ingot, no doubt it held the gold she'd told Tariq she didn't want.

Now the woman was smiling, almost brushing up against Tariq. Indecent. If she leaned forward any further her *hijab* would fall off, Jayne thought acidly. Tariq thanked her. Disgusted with the byplay, Jayne turned to the door.

As they walked out to the waiting limousine, a gust of wind hit her like a blast.

"Steady." Tariq grabbed her elbow. Her mouth pursed, Jayne wrenched herself free. "Why are you sulking? Do you think that I'm going to seek that woman out and commit adultery? Is that what you believe me capable of? Yes, she made it clear that she was available."

"So why don't you marry her then?" Jayne burst out.

"She's not suitable. And she's probably already married. And in my experience it is the woman who starts down the road to adultery, not the man."

Jayne clambered into the backseat. Wherever they went there would always be fawning women. And given his mother's betrayal—the betrayal he would not even discuss— and her subsequent desertion of both Tariq and his father, it wasn't surprising he had so little respect for women. But she'd had enough.

Once seated, she said tightly, "You might want to consider what it has always been like for me. Wherever we go, women give me one disbelieving look, then they dismiss me and fall all over you."

"I've never encouraged them." He looked defensive. "So don't accuse—"

"I'm not accusing you of anything." The irony did not escape her. Of the two of them, she had far more grounds for suspicion. It would've been easy for Tariq to be unfaithful.

The limousine rolled forward. "It's my wealth."

Jayne stared at him and shook her head slowly. "It's much more than your wealth…or even your good looks."

He coloured, bright flags high on his slanting cheekbones, but held her gaze. "Oh, please."

"You're gorgeous, Tariq. And I'm plain old Jayne. I never thought I'd hold you—"

"That's why you put that clause in our marriage contract. You thought I would find another woman—betray you—make you the second wife!"

Now, with his acute gaze narrowed on her, she wished she hadn't started this, that she'd simply withdrawn into the background and let it pass. Why had she felt the need to reveal her annoyance? It simply hurt too much.

It was too late.

Finally she said with a sigh, "Maybe."

"So you didn't trust me—"

"I didn't trust my own appeal. I would've been a fool not to have insisted on that clause. What I'm trying to say is that you have charisma. You draw people—especially women—like bees to a honeypot. Even if you had not a cent to your name, no sheikhdom to rule, you'd still be inundated with women. And every waking hour I had to live with the fact that you were surrounded by adoring women who came on to you, regardless of my presence."

"I never wanted them."

Her breath caught at the ring of truth in his voice.

"All I ever wanted was you."

That had never been enough. "But your father didn't. I was never going to be good enough."

"My father wanted me to marry a woman of equal status— like he did. My mother was the youngest daughter of Socrates Kyriakos, the Greek shipping tycoon, she came with a dowry of millions and valuable access to supertankers. Their marriage was dynastic. It was about oil and its distribution all over the world. The Emir of Zayed marries for power and the consolidation of wealth. For strategic reasons." He must have seen the horror in her eyes because his voice gentled. "Jayne, you must understand, it's the way things have always been done in Zayed."

"So why did you marry me?"

He looked away. "I was young. Idealistic. A student living in London. I didn't want to follow the soulless example of my parents' marriage. My mother never loved my father—and she hated Zayed. She went on a holiday to see her family, fell pregnant. When my father found out, he told her to go."

"Didn't he give her a chance to defend herself? To tell him that the baby was his?"

"It wasn't his."

"How can you know that?"

"I overheard their fight. She told my father that she hated him, that she had someone else, someone who made her happy. She told him that she wanted to have her lover's child. She wanted a life. And that their marriage had been a mistake from the start—because they had married for oil and money." He looked up at her. His eyes held a vulnerability she'd never seen. "I didn't want that. By marrying you I broke the rules."

She shook her head. "So the Emir drove me away because my family was not rich and powerful enough. Even though I loved you more than anything in the world."

The softness…vulnerability…whatever it had been, vanished. "*I* drove you away. Not my father."

"Because of what you'd overheard two adults yelling at each other as a small child?"

"No!" It was a harsh, grating sound. "I drove you away for good reason, because you were unfaithful to me."

Jayne rolled her eyes skyward. "So we're back where we started, you still believe I betrayed you. In that case, there is nothing more to say."

"Wait." He caught her hand. "We're not back where we started. I never realised how insecure you were, after we came to Zayed, how little you trusted my love for you. It must have been terrible for you when I travelled abroad without you."

"Yes," she whispered. She looked down at her hands, not wanting him to see the misery in her eyes. She'd hated it when he'd gone north or gone abroad. A finger under her chin raised her face to his narrow-eyed inspection.

"You thought I was unfaithful." He paused. "Is that why you did it?"

The car had come to a standstill. They were back at the fort. With a last look at Tariq, Jayne reached for the door handle. As the door clicked open, she shook her head sadly. "I am not going to deny it again. I'm through with that. You must believe of me what you want."

"I am trying to understand," he said. "Help me."

"I can't," she said quietly. "This is something you're going to have to figure out for yourself."

Nine

Without waiting for the doorman, Jayne pushed open the door of the limousine and jumped out. The first heavy splats of rain hit her as she crossed the forecourt. Clutching her purse, she ran for cover. But the heavens opened and the rain came down in torrents.

In seconds she was drenched.

She reached the overhang of the portico at the front of the porch, out of breath and very, very wet. She leaped up a step, out of the path of the water that was already streaming around the base of the solid stone walls.

"Are you okay?" Tariq stood beside her. His white shirt clung to his torso, plastered to his skin. She could make out the taut muscles of his upper arms, the tight wall of his chest through the saturated silk.

Quickly she averted her gaze.

"I'm fine." She pushed back the hair that hung like rat's tails over her face. "I can't believe how quickly that came out of nowhere."

"Aziz is a desert town, this is a desert thunderstorm."

Already the forecourt was under water, Jayne stared at the sheer volume of water that rushed down the steep slope of the road in disbelief. She could barely make out the shape of the limousine through the thick, grey veil of the rain.

"How long will this last?"

Tariq shrugged. "Not long enough."

"Not long enough?" Jayne stared with disbelief at angry torrent of water rushing below the step where she was standing. "You want *more* of this?"

"Look past the destruction." He gestured beyond the rain. "There lies the desert where water is life. A cloudburst is cause for celebration, even though it will bring grief, too. That's the desert way."

"It's hard."

"*Inshallah.*"

"How can you simply accept it? Just like that?"

"Breathe deeply."

"What?" She started at him blankly.

"Close your eyes and breathe deeply," he ordered.

"*Why?*"

"Do it and it will become clear."

Jayne closed her eyes and inhaled. "Like that?"

"What can you smell?"

She concentrated. "Wet. The fresh, steaming scent of rain."

"What else? What is missing?"

She opened her eyes. "Dust. The arid desert dust."

"Yes." He grinned down at her. "The rain is wonderful. It

washes away the dust and brings green and life. And, for a few days, there will be a fresh scent to the whole world before the dust and dryness returns for the rest of the year."

Jayne stared at the sheets of rain hammering down and gushing down the hill. "Where will all that go?"

"The city is ancient, and rain water was not a priority for the creators. The water will sit in large flat puddles on the surface until it evaporates. There is little vegetation in the desert to absorb the rain, so dry wadis will become rivers."

Jayne shook her head, and droplets scattered. She gave a little shiver as a wind gusted up the hill to where they stood under the overhang. The limousine had long since been driven away to the garages. The world felt utterly deserted except for the two of them. Ahead the sheets of rain obscured the view down the hill to the town on the one side and the stretching desert to the other.

"You are very wet. You need to change." Tariq's gaze lingered on the front of her dress, making her very aware of the way the sodden fabric clung to her breasts and how the cold wind had caused the tight nubs to jut out. She folded her arms and shivered.

"You need to change, too."

Thirty minutes later Tariq strode swiftly down the corridor, frowning a little as he took in the dingy darkness in the wing where he'd been told his sheikhah's room was located. No doubt this must be a quieter wing of the fort. He rounded a corner and stopped at the third door on the left. Raising his hand, he rapped three times. It opened a crack, and Jayne peered around the door at him.

"Yes?"

She didn't sound at all welcoming. He took in her damp

hair, the loose diaphanous caftan that covered her from head to toe, only the open neckline revealing that her skin was still damp from her bath.

"You were wet and cold, I wanted to see that you were okay."

That was his first excuse for being here.

Her expression told him she wasn't buying it. "I'm fine, a little water won't harm me. What do you want, Tariq?"

He tried the next excuse. "We will not be able to leave tomorrow. Floods have washed away the desert road! I have summoned the royal helicopter. But every helicopter in the country is busy with emergency missions in the wake of the cloudburst. I did not feel it right to divert them—not while there are people in need."

Now she looked a little less suspicious. "But what about your father…?"

"He is feeling much better. I spoke to him, too." Tariq moved a little closer. His father had told him to take time to get to know his wife, to become friends…lovers. Not to hurry back. "He knows we are stranded here for a few days. He told me to take my time, to do what needs to be done."

"How close are you to a resolution with Sheikh Karim?"

"It should not take much longer."

But he had not sought her out to speak about politics. He couldn't forget the look on her face when he'd challenged her that she'd believed he'd broken his wedding vows while they were together. Why had he never sensed how alienated she must have felt? He searched her eyes trying to read what lay behind the wariness with which she regarded him. "Let me in, we need to talk."

But still she did not open the door. Instead bit her lip and said, "What's there to talk about?"

He fixed his gaze on the spot where her white teeth played with her lip, the endearing little gap between her front teeth. He had a sudden wild urge to put his mouth, his tongue, exactly *there*. He glanced away before the impulse overtook him. "About the fact that you believed that I was incapable of remaining true to you—only you."

She gave an exasperated sigh and started to close the door on him. "Tariq, it's *years* too late for this discussion."

"Maybe not." He pushed it back, leaning forward against the solid wood. "I've only today learned of your irrational concerns about other women."

"Irrational?" Jayne stepped back, and the door flew open.

He brushed past her, and stopped dead. "*What the hell is this?* Is this where you have been sleeping?"

"Yes."

"In this hole?"

She nodded wordlessly.

He reached for her hand. "Come, we are leaving."

"I thought you said we couldn't leave yet."

He gave an impatient mutter. "We can't leave the town, but we can find accommodation elsewhere in the town." He pulled her toward him. "Ali has insulted me."

Oh, no. She could see the hard work of the negotiation all going up in smoke. "Tariq, wait. I doubt he even knows. This is Leila's doing, not Ali's, I'm sure of it. Ignore it. Don't let Leila cause more trouble than already exists."

"You are my wife." There was a white ring around his mouth. "There is respect due to you."

"How can you expect others to respect me when you don't?"

He looked at her, stark shock showing in his eyes, and then he got it under control, shuttering his reaction from her scrutiny. "What you ask is too much. The evidence against you was too heavy. *There was a child.*"

Jayne sagged. "It would never have worked anyway."

He caught her hand. The bones stood out beneath his skin, stretching it taut. "Do you know what the worst of it is?" His voice was low, tormented. "I still want you. Despite everything."

She knew what the admission must have cost him.

But it wasn't enough.

"I thought I could control this insanity. But when I saw you outside, your clothes clinging to your body—" he lifted his hand and cupped her breast "—every curve revealed, I wanted you. I'm surrendering. I can no longer resist."

"Tariq!"

But it was too late. His head was already lowering. His mouth closed over hers. For a moment she wanted to object. She should not be allowing this....

His tongue stroked across the seam of her lips…gently… tenderly. Emotion gushed through her. With a soft sigh, she relented and her lips parted.

One kiss.

Just one kiss.

But one turned to two. Then three. Then his mouth trailed a row of heated kisses along her neck.

"Tariq." This time it was a sigh of concession.

He pulled her closer, crushing her against him, and kissed her deeply, driving her wild. His lean length pressed against her, until a fierce tension vibrated through her. She threaded her hands through his hair, loving the soft silkiness between her fingers.

He moaned, a harsh, guttural sound. Then he raised his head. "I am not making love to you in this rat hole. Come with me."

Jayne went, dragged along by this devastating force that raged between them. Unseen, they hurried along the labyrinth of twists and turns until they reached his bedchamber.

Jayne caught a glimpse of the dark turbulent skies through the open latticed shutters, then Tariq kicked the door shut and yanked her back into his arms.

"I want you," he muttered.

Shivers chased down her spine at the raw need in his voice.

"Tell me you want me, Jayne."

For a moment she resisted. Boy, he could have any woman he crooked his little finger at. Why did he need her reassurance?

He hauled her closer. *"Tell me."*

His hardness pressed against her, leaving her in no doubt about the extent of his need.

In a low tone she admitted, "I want you, too."

"Good," he purred. "I want there to be no doubt about that later. No regrets."

No regrets? For a second she froze, almost pulled back. But then he swept her up, carried her to the bed and laid her down on the covers. She opened her mouth, glanced up at him…and all her thoughts flew out her head at the look in his eyes.

Hot.

Tender.

Almost…loving…? No, not loving, it was too intense, too carnal.

But it shook her to her soul. For a moment she felt an ache at the closeness she'd missed in the years they had spent apart. Then she excised it ruthlessly. Need—even love—was worth nothing without trust.

And he hadn't—still didn't—trust her.

So what the hell was she doing in his bed?

Seeking pleasure…seeking the completion only Tariq had ever given her. She moaned at the realisation. And Tariq took it for a moan of passion and reared back.

"You feel it, too?" His eyes blazed with joy.

How could she kill that?

Instead she nodded, biting her lip. The shutter at the window banged, caught by a gust of wind. She jumped.

"Hush," he murmured. "Everything will be right."

Not everything.

Not ever.

She shut her eyes against the sudden intrusion. His lips brushed her eyelids. Soft, butterfly kisses. Then his hands were sliding down her body, parting the front of the lacy silk of the caftan, pushing it off her shoulders, down her arms. A brief fumble with the clasp, then her bra was gone, leaving only high-cut briefs.

She waited, eyes still shut.

But the touch she expected did not come. Instead she heard the rustle of fabric. Her eyes flickered open. The white *thobe* he'd worn lay on the floor. All that remained were a pair of snug boxer briefs that hugged every bulge.

She blinked. "Goodness."

"It will be good," he growled, unsmilingly. And his eyes caught fire as he reached for her.

Her heart went into overdrive. His fingers closed on her shoulders, bringing her close. Her skin felt hot under his cool touch. The shutter slammed again, and a blast of wind blew into the bedchamber.

"Wait, I will be back in a moment."

Tariq got off the bed and crossed the room to fasten the shutters. Then he turned. For an instant he stood, proud, powerful.

Jayne could see the arrogance from generations of Emirs instilled in him. In the tilt of his head. In the sureness of his stance.

He bent down, pushing the briefs along his legs, then he was moving toward her, tall and straight.

And utterly naked.

For a moment she forgot to breathe.

He was beautiful.

The covers gave as he landed on the bed beside her. He touched her and she quivered. Waiting…

He kissed her. Until she was breathless. Before she could recover, his fingers slipped under the elastic of her briefs and slid them away. Tariq moved over her, his skin like silk against hers. Propping his elbows on either side of her arms, he gazed down at her. The golden eyes were hot and fierce.

"It has been far too long. I am not sure if I can hold."

Her eyes stretched wide. "Tariq?"

"We will take it slowly. Very slowly."

It sounded like a promise.

His fingers slid between them, he cupped her breast, then bent his head and tongued the pebbled tip. Her body responded, arching eagerly beneath him. His tongue touched her again.

Jayne gasped and closed her eyes.

Under her fingertips the slick silk of the bedcover felt unbearably sensual. Tariq shifted. His fingertips trailed down her body…over her belly…exploring the changes.

For a moment Jayne stiffened. A stab of loss shook her as his palm smoothed over her flat stomach. Was he thinking of the life that had once lain there? She sighed. No, he was probably doing everything in his power to forget it.

"Don't sound so sad, *habiibtii*. It will be good."

His words gave her pause. "Even if it is good. We should not be doing this." It was a whisper, but even against the whistling wind he heard it.

He raised his head and met her gaze squarely. But she read defiance in his eyes.

"Why not?" he demanded.

"Because we are getting divorced!"

Something flashed in his eyes. Then it was gone. "There is nothing wrong with making love. We are married, you are my wife. There is no sin in this."

"But there is no love, either," Jayne retorted, her ardour cooling a little.

"What is love?" Tariq's rough voice echoed in the bed-chamber. "We had love in the past and it was not enough."

Oh, what was the use?

He thought it hadn't worked because she'd found someone else. It hadn't worked for her because she'd needed his complete trust. Between them had stood the Emir, who held the alleged evidence of her adultery, the father who Tariq trusted with his life.

She got nowhere arguing with Tariq. And falling into bed with her husband was an even worse idea.

"Let me up." She tried to sit up, wanting to dress…cover herself. His hand stroked her stomach, moving lower. She shuddered as desire ignited in places she'd thought the embers long cold. "Let me up."

"Are you sure you want to get up, walk out that door? Never experience this fierce pleasure again?"

She hesitated.

"What do you say, *nuur il-en?* Light of my eyes?"

Light of his eyes. She stared into the gold flame of his gaze and all will to fight dissipated. Tariq read her surrender and growled, a hoarse, hungry sound.

"Is this what you want?" His mouth was all over her. Her body shuddered. She couldn't speak, she could only feel… and feel…and feel.

"Tell me," he demanded. "Do you want more? Or do you want me to stop?" His mouth ravaged the soft flesh of her belly, moving lower. She groaned again.

"What did you say?"

"Yes!" she burst out.

His lean, powerful body froze against hers. "You want me to stop."

"No, damn you." She was almost sobbing now. She reached for him, her hands knotting in his hair. "I want you to…" Her voice trailed away.

He held her off. "To what?"

"I want you to—" rage flashed through her, heated by desire "—I want you to make love to me. Now!"

"Good." He smiled, a hard ruthless curve of his lips. "I'm glad we've got that clear."

This time he touched her with purpose. No more teasing now. He was in control. She felt it in the stroke of his hand. Total mastery. Nothing less.

His fingers caressed her most secret places, causing her to gasp out loud. He touched again. This time she almost came apart.

"I can't." She bit her lip…fighting…fighting the waves of pleasure that threatened to crash over her and sweep her away. "What about you?"

"Don't worry about me." He gave her a wild, reckless grin. "I won't take long, *habiibtii*. Not tonight."

Then his hips fitted into the cradle of hers. He plunged forward. Jayne gasped as he slid all the way forward, sheathing himself deep within her.

Involuntarily her hips lifted. This time Tariq lost his breath in a husky moan. He started to move. Jayne reached for him, her fingers pressing into his spine.

"*Habiibtii*, if you do that it's going to be over before we've started," he whispered hotly in her ear. "So don't touch me— or it will be past."

She dropped her hands, clutched the silk cover.

Tariq pulled back, slid in. Then repeated the motion. The friction was slow and sensual and utterly delicious. Jayne felt the half-forgotten tension spiraling within her, tighter and tighter, as he continued to move. Until finally something gave, deep in the core of her, and the ripples started.

Tariq moaned. "Hold me."

Her arms came around him, pulling him close. And then his breathing became ragged and his body jerked in her arms.

"Do you know why I find you beautiful?"

It was past midnight. Outside the wind had died. The golden glow of light from the bedside table cast a warm hue on the walls and on Tariq's skin where he lay, head propped on his arm as he watched her.

A lump filled Jayne's throat. She shook her head.

"From that first time I saw you in the Tate Gallery, I

couldn't take my eyes off you. You glowed with serenity. You still do. Your skin has the radiance of the most prized Gulf pearls, your hair has the gloss of the sun on a raven's wing. When I touch your skin, your hair, it feels like silk."

"I'm not—"

"Beautiful? Don't tell me that! Whose standards do you judge yourself against? The magazines? Hollywood?" He shook his head. "They are of no import to me. There are many kinds of beauty…and to me you are beautiful."

The romanticism of his words swept her breath away.

She thought of Neil's advice that she cut her hair short. It suited her new studies, he said, her new career path as a departmental head of literacy studies. Short hair would look far more professional than her fly-away locks.

But she didn't want to feel professional. She wanted to feel feminine…desired…beautiful.

And that's what Tariq had achieved.

He made her feel alive. She stretched a hand out toward him.

"Wait, I have something for you." He leapt from the bed and rummaged through his clothes. A moment later he was back holding the satin bag from the gold *souq*.

"Tariq—"

"Don't refuse." He drew out the ankle chain she had admired. The little bells tinkled. Lifting her leg, he stroked it and fastened the chain around her ankle.

She started to object.

"Hush." He bent forward and placed a kiss against the soft skin beside her ankle bone.

Just as her pulse started to quicken, he straightened and his hand disappeared back into the bag. This time it emerged with a necklace. A circlet of gold threaded with large beads made of amber and turquoise.

"I can't accept that." The amber was the same colour as his eyes. Her heart ached. She didn't want gifts of gold. Yet he would never give her what she most wanted. His trust. "It's too valuable."

"Look on it as protection from any evil." His lips twisted. "To keep you safe. All the days of your life."

"Oh, Tariq." Her heart turned over. This was no ingot intended to buy his way into her heart. This was a farewell gift. Something to remember him by when it was all over. But she knew that she would never forget him, how could she? When part of him remained with her, every day of her life?

"May there always be a road for you, *nuur il-en,* and may it always be blessed. Now lean forward so that I can fasten this."

She obeyed.

He lifted her hair, and his fingers fumbled for a moment as he did up the clasp. His lips brushed her neck, then he was kissing her neck and shivers of desire swept her. Jayne turned in his arms and lifted her face. When the kiss came, it burned with suppressed passion.

She groaned and reached for him, closing her arms around him.

Tariq was late getting to his meeting with Karim the following morning. He drifted into the formal meeting room in a daze, still reeling under the passion of the long night.

"Sabah al-hayri," Karim greeted him.

Tariq pulled himself together. It would not do to look like a love-struck youth to his powerful neighbour. "Good morning," he returned.

But his mind kept straying from the negotiations. To visions of Jayne draped across his chest, her smile warm and sensual. To the memory of the silkiness of her skin under his fingertips.

"Tariq?"

He gave a start. Karim was staring at him, wearing a bemused expression.

"What do you think?"

What did he think? He blinked. He could hardly confess that he thought he should be in bed with his wife.

Karim was trying to be reasonable. For the first time in days Tariq had lost all interest in the settlement. He longed for his wife's arms...to forget the mess that his father's comrades had landed him in. More than anything he wanted to put an end to this internecine bickering and return to Jayne.

"What about I include that spur of land on the sea that lies on the Zayedi side of the border to apologise for the shame my kinsmen have caused you, Karim?"

Karim was frowning. "Let's not bring land into it. The last time land was promised to me by your family the deal was dishonoured."

"By whom?" Tariq shook his head to clear it and leaned forward, his elbows on the table.

"Your father."

A hot rush of anger followed Karim's accusation. All languor left him. "Don't lie. The Emir would never dishonour a deal."

Karim rose to his feet. "If you are going to call me a liar, then our business is done." He picked up his jacket.

"Wait." Karim was not the kind of man to cast stones at a dying man. Tariq bit back his rage and tried hard for a conciliatory tone. "You must understand, my father is a man of honour and he is—" Tariq broke off and swallowed "—very ill. Your statement hit a nerve."

Karim paused at the door.

Tariq took a deep breath and tried again. "Give me more details. Please. I need to investigate this." This must be a misunderstanding. His father would never break his word. Would never do anything underhand. Tariq would track down where the misunderstanding lay. And then he would deal with it.

"His Highest Excellency promised me a tract of land to extend the wetlands that we are building in Bashir." Karim's lips curved into a hard smile. "Ironically, they are not far from the spur of land you now offer me."

"I have heard talk of the gift." Karim's commitment to creating wetlands was well-known. It would have been the kind of thing his father might have done to better relations. Give a piece of marshland with not much value and receive a wealth of gratitude and goodwill in return.

"The gift was never made." Karim's jade eyes glittered. "Ali discovered oil there and persuaded your father to lease the lands to him."

"I know nothing of the discovery of any oil in that part of the country." Bewildered, Tariq stared at the other sheikh. "This cannot be true."

"Then there is nothing more to be said." Karim's hand reached for the door handle.

"Don't go." Tariq felt a burning behind his eyes. He didn't want to lose Karim's friendship. They'd played together as children in the Bedu camps and become firm friends as men. But it was important not to back down. This was a matter of honour. His family's honour. Yet Karim clearly believed what he said to be true. So to placate him Tariq said, "By Allah, if I find there has been dishonour, you will be gifted those lands, too."

He made the vow, comfortable that he wouldn't find anything like that. But he couldn't afford to alienate Karim. Too much depended on it.

There was something curiously like sadness in Karim's eyes. Pity? No, it couldn't be pity. Tariq shook his head to free himself of the notion.

"Tariq?" Karim's voice was low and very grave. "Arranging a marriage between you and Yasmin was an attempt to demolish the wall that was rising between Bashir and Zayed. Don't be too hard on your father when you get to the bottom of it. He is dying…don't spoil this last time by chastising him. He is only a man. Let him go to the afterlife at peace."

"My father is much more than an ordinary man, he is the Emir of Zayed." Karim didn't know what he was talking about. Even Jayne had come to realise that he would hear no criticism of his father. Soon he would have to step into his father's mighty shoes and he would be the Emir of Zayed.

But first he needed to convince himself that his father was at peace. That he would die fulfilled.

Shortly afterwards, Tariq shook hands with Karim and, after the other man's departure, he reached for his cell phone and dialled a number that he had never had cause to call.

Ten

The next couple of days passed in a haze.

Tariq spent most of his days in meetings with Mahood and Ali and Karim, but he'd told Jayne that a resolution was imminent. She lived from day to day, trying not to think about the future…or the past.

In the evenings Ali and his brother hosted elaborate state dinners with all kinds of entertainment provided. Singers. Dancers. But it was for the nights that Jayne lived. Nights spent clandestinely making love with her husband.

Jayne insisted on returning to her poky little room in the early hours of each morning and mussing the bed. Soon she and Tariq would be divorced. She needed to keep some sort of separation in her own mind. So she worked hard to maintain the fiction that they occupied separate rooms. It was difficult to think beyond the nights when they scorched the sheets before parting in the morning.

Their marriage was over, killed long ago by his distrust. But there was no reason why she couldn't make love with her husband. What damage could be done? And who would ever know?

That evening, the reception rooms downstairs were packed with people who had come to see the sheikh. Jayne watched as he was accosted and asked for advice.

"Sheikh Tariq is a master falconer. The kind of man who takes what he has learned in the desert and applies it to his leadership. He is wise, patient. He will be a worthy Emir."

Jayne started at the sound of Sheikh Karim's low voice. Every word only highlighted the difference between her and Tariq. Looking up at him she said, "If I'd known who he was when I met him, I would never have married him."

Karim raised an eyebrow. "Perhaps that is why he never told you."

"What do you mean?"

"He is a man capable of great passion. If only he could take the emotion he shares with his falcons and apply them to the people around him. He is more relaxed when you are around. When you are out of his sight he is restless, like a man who is incomplete."

"He doesn't need me."

"He needs you more than you might think. Why else has he never remarried? There has been enough opportunity."

Jayne felt her hackles rise. "He needs to divorce me first."

"Have you ever asked yourself why he has never done so?" Karim's smile was rueful when Jayne slowly shook her head. "Perhaps you should."

Jayne was still thinking about Karim's words when she crossed the cavernous entrance hall and made her way to the powder room. Why had Tariq never divorced her and remarried? Frowning, she pushed the door open and came to a halt.

Leila stood in front of the mirror, applying *kajal* around her dark eyes. Jayne hesitated, tempted to turn and run. Then she straightened her spine and stepped forward.

Without looking at the other woman, Jayne poured herself a glass of water from the tall ceramic jar that stood on the table and drank it down. Then she opened her bag, searching for a tissue.

A sound made her turn. Leila stood beside her, her lips curled back in a snarl. "You don't have what it takes to keep a man like Sheikh Tariq."

How was she supposed to respond to that?

Jayne decided to ignore her. She zipped up her bag and started toward the door.

"You are running away. Soon you will leave here and I will get Tariq."

Jayne paused at the door. "You are delusional. Tariq would never touch another man's wife."

Leila's face turned ugly. "I am divorcing my husband. And my father will make it part of these settlement negotiations that Tariq marry me—otherwise there will be war between Zayed and Bashir."

"That's not going to happen." Jayne had heard enough. Leila was a spoiled little witch who deserved to be taken down a peg. She turned the handle. "In terms of our marriage contract, Tariq has promised not to marry another woman while he is married to me. And I will *never* divorce him."

Why on earth had she said that? Jayne was still reeling from the surprise of hearing her own words when Leila gave a growl of fury and rushed at her, hands clawing at the air, eyes glittering with malice.

Jayne ducked. Too late. A painful stinging sensation slashed down her cheek. Jayne cried out and pushed the door, nearly falling into the corridor outside.

"Jayne." Tariq's hands caught her shoulders, steadying her.

She heard his breath catch. "You are bleeding. These are scratch marks. Who did this to you?" The sheer anger in his voice was overwhelming.

"Tariq—"

The door behind her opened and Leila stepped out. Tariq's fingers tightened on Jayne's skin and he pulled her close. His body was warm against hers, but she could feel the tightly coiled tension in his muscles.

"You have hurt the sheikhah."

Leila's eyes widened at the cold rage in the accusation. "I didn't—"

"Do not lie to me." Fury vibrated through each word. "You will be punished for this transgression."

"Please, no." Leila fell to her knees at his feet, bowing her head and grabbing at the hem of his *thobe*. "Don't you understand? I did it for you. *For us.*"

Tariq stared down at her. "Get up."

Jayne shivered at the icy tone.

"I have left my husband, we are getting divorced, so that I can marry you."

"What are you talking about?" Stunned amazement replaced his anger.

Leila raised her head. "I was always meant to be your wife. Not her. It will be made right. My father intends to speak to you."

"For the sake of Allah, can you not understand?" Jayne

shuddered at the impatience in Tariq's voice and buried her face in the soft fabric that covered his chest. "I already have a wife—I do not want another. I saw you watching me earlier, Leila. You are to visit the doctor, you need help. You will do so tomorrow. Agreed?" Tariq's voice had gentled but a core of steel remained. Jayne raised her head in time to see Leila nod and stumble to her feet.

Tariq held Jayne tightly to him. "Now I am taking my wife to tend to her hurts, and you will not threaten her again, ever."

A sense of wonder filled Jayne at his heated defence of her. A protective Tariq was almost impossible to resist.

That night Tariq's lovemaking was exquisitely gentle.

At first he touched her with fingers that were almost reverent, as if she were fragile and something infinitely precious. But slowly as the heat mounted, his hands ignited a wild response. Where he touched, fire followed.

The soft, devout kisses became hot sweeps of his tongue. Jayne twisted on the bed, her body stretched out, at the mercy of his loving.

It was wild. It was unfettered. It held a sweetness that had been lacking previously.

"Mine," he declared as his body thrust into hers, claiming her. *Mine.*

It echoed through Jayne's head as she started to move with him, under him, eager for the shivers of desire to engulf them both. When the moment came, Jayne cried out.

Tariq hugged her close to him, holding her tight, his body shaking with the force of their lovemaking.

And for the first time, Jayne wondered whether she could walk away from the man who had claimed her heart.

* * *

"So much for a three-day absence from the palace," Jayne said the next morning as they dressed hurriedly. They had both overslept. Jayne had wakened to find her limbs entangled with Tariq's and the sun already well up.

Tariq touched her face and stared at her with hot eyes. "The contretemps with Leila aside, would you have missed one minute of what we have shared?"

Slowly Jayne shook her head. "But I can't help worrying about your father. I don't want you one day to regret this time, because it cost you time with your father."

"I have spoken to him several times every day. He is in better spirits than he has been for a long time. But we should be able to leave tomorrow. The helicopter has dealt with the worst of the disasters caused by the rains."

Unexpectedly Jayne's heart sank at the thought of leaving here.

"If you'll excuse me, there's a call I need to make," Tariq said.

A little hurt at his brusque tone, Jayne flounced to the door. "I'd better start to pack." She left Tariq fingering his phone, checking on his father.

They left the following morning. As the helicopter rose, Noor gave a sharp squawk of protest from her *kafas,* and a sudden pang of sorrow shook Jayne. This time in Aziz had been so precious. Careful not to let Tariq see her face, she leaned forward to look out the window. Far below, the sun glinted off the silver pools where the town still lay under water. They flew over the desert and she peered down through the windows with disbelief. It had only been a couple of days since they'd travelled across the dry desert but already the desertscape had changed. Down below Jayne could see a sprinkling of green across the desert.

"It's the rain," Tariq said, pointing below. "The wildflowers will be blossoming, too. As soon as it rains everything comes to life."

The rains might bring life to the desert…but there was nothing that could bring their marriage to life. It had been doomed before it had ever started. Jayne swallowed. And, when it had ended, she'd had to make a choice that Tariq would never forgive.

If he ever found out…she shivered. She did not want to think about what might happen.

By noon they were back at the palace.

Tariq disappeared to visit his father and, left alone, Jayne made her way slowly back to her boudoir. Why had she expected anything to have changed with their renewed… closeness? Tariq was still a sheikh, a traditional male, and she would always take second place to his family…his political business.

And it wasn't as if she were back permanently, as his real wife. *They were getting divorced.* She had to stop thinking like a wife. But it was hard. Making love to him had bared emotions she'd never expected to feel again.

Not expecting to see him for the rest of the day, she retreated to the library, to the valuable collection of books housed there. Latifa found her there. She brought a cup of jasmine tea and some sweets, and Jayne heard how overjoyed the Emir had been by the return of his son.

There was relief in the younger woman's eyes. Jayne realised that she had not been alone in her fear that the Emir might pass from this world while Tariq was away settling Ali and Mahood's disputes.

By midafternoon Tariq was still not back, so Jayne settled down in Tariq's study and booted up his computer. She owed Samantha some information on Zayed, for her school project. She would ask Tariq for some photos to e-mail tonight.

There were e-mails from Helen waiting for her. Concerned e-mails. Her sister had seen the news about the floods in Zayed on television and the rescue efforts. She had tried to ring Jayne on her cell phone but hadn't gotten through. There was a photo, too, of Amy's first day at school. Amy looked so grown-up. So confident.

Jayne's throat tightened.

How she missed them all.

In the end, Jayne picked up the phone and dialled Auckland. It was good to talk to her sister and the girls. Curiously calming. By the time she said her farewells, she no longer felt as lonely as she had with Tariq busy with the affairs of state.

While Tariq divided his time between his father's sick bed and listening to the petitions of the citizens of Zayed who came from near and far each day, Jayne found herself spending more and more time in the raptor mews with the young saker falcon called Haytham that Tariq intended to release into the wild at the end of the season.

She was feeding the bird titbits when she received a visitor one morning.

"*Sabah al-hayri*," her visitor greeted.

"Good morning, Dr. Jirah." Brushing off her hands, Jayne

took off the glove and walked toward the woman with whom she'd chatted at the banquet what seemed an aeon ago.

"Kef Halak?"

Jayne paused. *"Ma atakallam arabi."* She stumbled over the words. "I'm sorry, but I don't speak Arabic."

"The correct response to my question, which meant 'How are you', is *zein al-Hamdulillah,* 'Fine thanks,'" said the doctor. "I am aware that you don't speak our language, but don't you think that if you are interested in falconry, in the Bedu roots from where the Emirs of Zayed originate, then, my dear, the time has come to learn to speak your husband's language?"

How on earth should she respond to the doctor's unusual frankness? Obviously, she couldn't confess that she and Tariq would be divorced in the near future—although the date of that event was becoming less and less important to Jayne.

Better to take refuge in half truths buried far in the past. "I tried to learn when I was here previously, but it was a struggle. And I never expected that we would stay in Zayed for long." She'd been so clueless. It had taken a while for it to dawn that Tariq was expected to succeed his father as Emir. There would be no life as a young married couple in London, raising children in a village a commutable distance from the city. And then there had been the difficulty in securing someone to teach her Arabic. No one had appeared to want to risk the Emir's displeasure by consorting with the daughter-in-law he despised.

Jayne had been an outcast.

And Tariq had been too busy to see it.

She'd had no friends, no social support network, and her husband had never been home.

He'd been sent on mission after mission, to neighbouring

Gulf states, to Europe, on political deputations. She'd been left in Zayed, alone and isolated and increasingly unhappy.

The only person who had talked to her had been Roger, the English book restorer charged with tending the Emir's library. And in the end that miserly friendship had cost Jayne her marriage.

How to explain that to the woman facing her?

"I heard you tried to learn a little and then you gave up at the first obstacle."

"I didn't speak well. I embarrassed the Emir with my pidgin Arabic."

Farrah waved her hands. "Who cares about the Emir—it is your husband you should be concerned with. It doesn't matter how you speak, at least be able to talk and understand a little—even if it is pidgin Arabic. It shows goodwill and soon you will make female friends who will help you learn—like I can."

"You would do that?"

"Of course. That's why I am here." The doctor gave her a smile. "And I have another agenda. But we will discuss that later."

"I couldn't speak. So when Tariq wasn't here, I started to refuse any invitations to go out and they tapered off."

"Not because your company wasn't wanted. But once you'd refused, no one wanted to put you in the embarrassing position of having to refuse again. To refuse two invitations is rude, and no one wanted to put you in that awkward place."

"Oh." That put a whole different complexion on it. She'd thought that everyone despised her. Boy, she'd been so young. So naive.

"It helps to have a hobby, too, one that keeps you busy

while the men talk and expect you to spend the evening with the other wives."

"What do you do?" Jayne asked with interest.

"I knit booties for the babies I deliver. There are lots of those." She smiled. "Sometimes the company can be very boring. That is why I hoped you and I could be friends."

"Where were you when I was here last?" Jayne complained. If only she had met this forthright woman then.

"Working in a hospital in London, completing my training."

"I'll think of something that would be better than twiddling my thumbs. I've always wanted to learn to do cross-stitch." Jayne could not tell her new friend that she would not be here to see the friendship through.

"Good," Farrah said briskly. "Now to the other reason I am here. I hear that you are interested in literacy."

"How did you hear that?"

Farrah smiled sphinxlike. "From a patient."

Dexter, the tall Texan. It had to be. Jayne tipped her head sideways and studied the doctor. "Do I detect a romance?"

"Perhaps. But it will take time and work to see if it will last."

Jayne envied Farrah her composure, her levelheaded approach. "I wish you luck."

"Thank you. Now back to my request about literacy."

When Farrah left, Jayne shook her hand and said a heartfelt, *"Shukran."* Thank you.

That evening Jayne and Tariq had settled down to search for photos to send to Samantha for her school project when a knock sounded on the door. Hadi al Ebrahim, the Emir's trusted aide, stood there looking very grave. "Excellency," he addressed Tariq. "There is a problem."

"My father!" Tariq was on his feet in one swift move.

"No." Hadi cast a glance at Jayne. "It is about the divorce, Excellency."

Apprehension tied Jayne's stomach up into knots. "What about the divorce?" she demanded.

Hadi gave Tariq a hunted look. "Can we discuss this privately?"

"This concerns me. The divorce is the reason I am here in Zayed." She voiced her worst fears, "Is something wrong?"

"There are rumours, Excellency," Hadi said delicately.

"What kind of rumours?" Tariq's brows drew low over his eyes.

"That you and the sheikhah shared accommodation."

Jayne shot Tariq a furtive glance. She flushed slightly as she remembered those steamy illicit nights they'd spent together in the fort at Aziz. Had someone seen her returning to her room in the early hours of the morning? Was that what this was about?

"We had separate rooms in Aziz," Jayne told Hadi. "But why is this important?" She shut out the thought that while they might have had separate rooms, they'd spent the nights in each other's arms.

"Not at Aziz," Wadi replied. "In the Bedu camp. It is said you shared a tent."

"So?" Jayne started to get annoyed. Tariq might be a sheikh but why did she have to face this invasion of her private life. "We're married. I've committed no sin. Even if we did share the tent, what does it matter?"

"Jayne—"

"What?" she turned on Tariq. "Why does this matter—"

"It matters." Tariq's face was expressionless.

Jayne stilled. She glanced rapidly from one man to the other. "What's going on? Why is this so important?"

"Jayne, listen to me—"

"No, I want to hear it from Hadi." She swung around. "Hadi, what's going on?"

The older man looked extremely uncomfortable.

"Tell me."

At last he said, "Sheikhah, under the laws of Zayed, a husband and wife need to live apart for five years to be granted a divorce."

"But we have lived apart for five years."

"Sheikhah, the night in the desert nullifies those years."

"What?" Jayne stared at him in horror. "How can it?"

"What Hadi is trying to say is that under our laws the couple need to stay apart for five years before they can be granted a divorce. If they spend the night under the same roof there is a presumption that they've had sexual relations, which would need to be disproved."

"But we didn't sleep together in the desert."

Hadi gave a cough of discomfort. "Then the sheikh and sheikhah have no problems. They simply apply to court and state on oath they have not shared—" he swallowed audibly "—sexual relations for the past five years."

Horror filled Jayne. How could she swear such an oath? It would be a lie. She glanced at Tariq. His face was blank, utterly expressionless.

"Hadi, thank you, you may go now." It was a dismissal.

"Thank you, Excellency." He bowed and walked backward to the great double doors. "The Emir will be saddened that the divorce is going ahead. He had such high hopes for this desert trip."

"You are not to say a word to him about the divorce," Tariq warned, his eyes hard.

When the door shut, Jayne turned on him. "You knew about this five-year provision?" Tariq nodded. Her brain started to click over. She remembered the night in his bedchamber. He'd just spoken to his father. He'd told her the Emir was feeling better. Had he been prepared to go to these lengths for his father's sake, to ensure his father died a happy man?

Was that why he'd made love to her?

"Jayne—"

"Don't talk to me. I'm thinking."

"Jayne, don't jump to conclusions—"

"You planned this," Jayne hissed. "You wanted to keep me trapped in Zayed."

Angry colour flooded his cheeks. "Why would I plan this?"

"Because this is what your father wanted—and you have always done what your father wants. You are a puppet on a string, Tariq."

His eyes flashed. "Watch what you say, wife. Why would I want you to stay? You hate this place—"

"I started to like—"

Tariq talked straight over her attempt to tell him that she'd changed her mind about the desert. "Why would I *want* a wife I can never trust near another man?"

Jayne gave a snort of disgust. "The old double standard. You are surrounded by temptation every day, yet you assure me you have never strayed. I believe you. Why can't you believe me?"

"*Because I have my father's word.* He saw you kissing Roger with his own eyes, caught you naked in the library."

"That's utter rubbish. I told you before."

Tariq's looked utterly tormented. "How can I not believe my father? He's a man of honour, the Emir of Zayed!"

"And I am your wife!"

"That would mean…"

She could see him thinking it through. She nodded. "Yes, the child I carried was yours, Tariq."

"No, that is not true." He shook his head. "My father would never lie. He told me it was Roger's child."

"So I'm the liar?"

Tariq raised his head and stared at her oppressively. "But what does it matter? The child is gone, there is nothing more to discuss."

"Except the end of our marriage." Tariq didn't answer her. She huffed out a heavy sigh. "And now I'm trapped for another five years in a marriage I no longer want. But you can't stop me leaving. Even if I can't have my divorce, I will not stay."

"Not until my father dies."

"Or the month is up. Whichever comes first. And then I want your promise that you will not come near me for five years."

"And what if I can't give you that, *habiibtii?*" Tariq's eyes were dark with some emotion that looked curiously like pain.

Jayne stared at him, at a total loss for words.

Eleven

Jayne was still angry and confused when she went down to the mews to visit Haytham, the young saker falcon the next morning. How could she have been stupid enough to have slept with Tariq in Aziz? She'd come to Zayed to get a divorce so that she could get on with her life and cut the ties with the past—and Tariq.

She kicked a stone off the path in front of the mews. Now it would be another five years before she could get a divorce. A memory of Tariq kissing her…of his hands lingering on her body…flashed through her mind. Images shifted like a kaleidoscope. Tariq drinking coffee and laughing. Tariq making love to her, his eyes burning.

Did she really want a divorce?

But how could she stay married to a man who didn't trust her? She'd planned a whole new life in Auckland, how could she throw it all away and come back to Zayed? And would Tariq even want her back?

Her head spinning, she entered the raptor mews and came to an abrupt stop at the sight of Tariq.

He stood beside Noor's empty perch, tall and commanding even in a pair of light coloured casual pants and a white T-shirt. Noor rode on the *mangalah* strapped to his arm to stop her claws damaging skin. With a hood over her head and a leash securing the jesses to the glove, it was clear that Tariq was taking her out to fly.

The falcon's feathers were pulled tight in anticipation and her head turned to the doorway where Jayne stood.

"You say you want to learn to fly a falcon. I'm going to exercise Noor with the lure. Do you want to come?"

Jayne nodded. But she knew that once she returned to Auckland she would give up that idea. It simply wouldn't work. It was another mirage.

They walked out to a flat piece of parkland behind the mews, surrounded by hedges and planted with tall date palms.

Tariq removed the hood to reveal Noor's dark eyes, her spirit on fire. The falcon shivered and gave a series of quick, excited chirps before stretching her wings, ready to head for the sky and hunt.

Jayne could feel the beat of her wings against the air as she rose. Noor was swift and agile and her enjoyment was evident.

"Her eyesight is about eight times as sharp as yours or mine," Tariq said, as she hovered overhead when he moved the lure. The falcon's shadow passed over them and she climbed into the distance.

"She's gone."

"She's waiting." Tariq sounded very sure. "If I flush those pigeons out of that date palm, she'll appear."

He strode forward, waving his arms. The flock rose.

"Look."

Rocketing groundward, her wings folded back, Noor swooped down on an unsuspecting bird. No hesitation. Strike. And feathers exploded.

Tariq signalled and she tore into her meal. When the falcon had finished he waved the lure but Noor turned her back on him.

"See? A falconer needs endless patience. Noor is not yet ready to come home."

His generous mouth was curved into a smile. Jayne's heart skipped a beat as the memory of Tariq's patience as a lover swept her. She felt herself flush. She had to stop thinking about his lovemaking.

Noor rose into the air again, beating her wings. She climbed higher, a flash of the sun on her wings, and she disappeared into the blue.

Tariq pointed the antenna upward. The signal sounded. "She's over on the other side of that hedge. She must have taken another pigeon without us seeing. I'll give her a few more minutes and then we'll go collect her."

A few minutes later Noor hadn't moved.

"She's feasting," Tariq surmised.

But when they reached the other side of the hedge, there was no sign of Noor. A search revealed the transistor lying on the ground and a couple of floating feathers indicating a scuffle.

There was a white line around Tariq's mouth. "Noor is gone."

Foreboding filled Tariq as he and Jayne made their way back to the palace. He was aware that she kept sending him little concerned glances. But he didn't want her to see his eyes, in case she worked out what he was thinking.

The last time she had left Zayed, Khan had gone missing and had never returned.

Now it was Noor who was gone.

Tariq couldn't stop the gnawing fear that it was an omen that Jayne was about to leave. And when she did, he would never see her again.

They spent an hour driving around, searching for the falcon, to no avail. When they returned to the palace, an older woman stood in the hallway. A western woman. Tariq slowed at the sight of her. Her eyes were the colour of jade and her dark hair was drawn off her pale face and secured into a chic knot.

Her gaze locked with his. She stepped forward, then halted. She started to say something, but then she simply shook her head.

Beside him, Jayne gasped.

"You are my mother?" His words sounded rusty.

She nodded. Her eyes glistened with tears. She appeared to be incapable of speech.

"Welcome to Zayed," he said formally.

Jayne rushed into the sudden silence. "I'm Jayne, Tariq's wife."

"I am so pleased to meet you. You may call me Athina." As his mother hugged Jayne, Tariq could see that her hands were shaking.

Then Athina drew a deep breath and turned to him. "Thank you for calling me. Can you ever forgive me, my son? I wanted to take you with me, when you were a little boy, but I couldn't. You were your father's first-born child, his only child. His heir."

Tariq inclined his head stiffly. "I know you could not take me. In terms of the laws of Zayed, all children stay with the father when the woman leaves."

Jayne went white. Tariq realised that she must be thinking of her own child. If the child had been his, she would never have been allowed to leave Zayed until the child had been born.

Was it possible that she'd been carrying his child when she had left? Was it his child that she had lost?

Had his father lied? A bitter, sinking sensation roiled in the pit of his stomach. On top of everything else that was happening…his father's illness…his mother's arrival…Noor's disappearance…it was all too much to take in.

"I never loved your father," his mother was saying. "Then I met someone else." His mother must have seen something in his face, because she quickly added, "It was wrong what I did. When I fell pregnant I had to make a terrible choice."

"So you went." His voice was flat, empty of the hurt that her desertion had caused when he had been a child.

"I couldn't stay. If anyone had found out, I would've been sent to jail, my daughter taken away. I'm very grateful that you have invited me to Zayed to say goodbye to Rashid…and perhaps start over with you?"

"We can talk later," Tariq said. "I called you because my wife believes that my father needs to see you. Your gratitude should be to her." Jayne's hand slipped into his, and Tariq gripped it tightly.

Since their return from the desert, Jayne had avoided the Emir's bedchamber and Tariq had visited his father alone. But with the arrival of his mother, Tariq made it clear that he wanted her to come along, and Jayne had no choice but to accompany Tariq and Athina to see the Emir.

What would she have done if she'd been faced with the dilemma that Tariq's mother had?

A cold fist clutched Jayne's heart. Perhaps it was better that Tariq had never believed that the child she carried was his. She would never have been able to leave her child behind. Where would that have left her? Trapped in an existence where she stayed in Jazirah simply to be near the child she'd lost?

A shiver snaked down her spine. That would've been unbearable.

When they arrived at the Emir's chambers, the male nurse sprang to his feet. "His Excellency has been tired today."

"I know," Tariq said. "He said so earlier."

Jayne lurked in the background, letting Athina and Tariq go ahead. The Emir shifted against the pillows. "Lina?" He murmured. "I have been praying that you would come. I need your help."

Athina took the thin, bony hand. "What is it, Rashid?"

"It is our son."

"What is it, father?" Tariq moved to his father's bedside. "You need to relax, take it easy."

"Where is your wife? Where is Jayne?" The Emir lifted his head off the pillow, but the effort was too much and his head fell back. "I need to talk to her."

Jayne sensed that the Emir wanted—needed—to talk, a burning desire she did not share. It was far too late for talking. Years too late.

"Jayne, can you come closer?" he said.

She stood her ground. Did he regret what he had done? Did he want her forgiveness before he faced death? He'd taken her dreams and trampled on them, destroyed the love in her heart. She didn't know that she had space for forgiveness in the withered remains of what had once been a heart.

Jayne turned to face him. "I came back to Zayed to get a divorce."

"Jayne!" Tariq grabbed her arm.

She yanked it free. "No, I will not lie."

The Emir's face fell, his eyes grew distant and bleak. "I had hoped…" His voice grew weak.

For a terrible moment Jayne felt…ashamed. Then she told herself she had nothing to feel ashamed about. She had never done a thing to harm the Emir. But he had plotted to destroy her marriage to Tariq. He had caused her to run…to collapse…and he had caused her to—

God! She couldn't bear to think about the loss. The loss that she carried with her every day of her life.

She owed him nothing.

Nothing!

She hardened her gaze—and what was left of her heart.

Let him go to hell.

Let him know what it felt like.

She hoped he suffered. He deserved everything that was coming to him.

"Lina, this is why I need your help." The Emir's voice was thready. "I have done our son's wife an enormous wrong."

"What are you saying, Father?" Tariq asked urgently. "Tell me."

"What have you done, Rashid?"

Only Jayne said nothing, her eyes fixed on the frail old man in the high cot. A chill had seeped into her. She felt as if she would never be warm again.

"I told Tariq that she had committed adultery and slept with another man."

"It was untrue?" Tariq's cheekbones stood out under his skin. He looked suddenly haggard.

"What do you think, my son?"

Tariq looked wildly around at Jayne. "She told me she'd never been unfaithful. But I wouldn't believe her. Instead I believe you, my father." There was terrible pain in his voice. And Jayne saw the anguish in his eyes as full impact hit him. Tariq reached for her icy hand. "My child! Jayne, I'm sorry you were alone when you miscarried our child."

He believed the child belonged to him. But Jayne didn't feel relief or jubilation. She simply felt numb, and she stared at the Emir and waited.

"Tariq, Jayne didn't miscarry the child." The Emir broke off.

"What do you mean?" Emotion flared in Tariq's eyes. "My child is alive? Where?"

"I have a grandchild?" Lina sounded overjoyed.

The Emir shook his head slowly from side to side on the pillow. He was deathly pale. "It is my fault. When Jayne left, I gave her money to abort the baby. I didn't want your first-born son belonging to a woman I had not chosen for you."

"Father!" Tariq looked shattered. He turned to Jayne. "You told me all this, that my father drove you away, and I thought you were paranoid."

Athina's hands cupped her mouth. "Rashid, these are terrible things that you have done."

"I know." The sheikh stared at his hard-faced son. "I ask your forgiveness. Your mother asked many times to see you while you were growing up and I refused to grant her access. She tried to get visitation rights through the courts, I blocked her at every turn. I want to make things right before I die."

Nausea rose in Jayne's throat. She turned and slipped out of the room. Down the passage she entered a bedroom and made for the en suite bath. She clutched her stomach and waited for the nausea to pass.

"Are you all right?"

Tariq came up behind her and swung her around into his arms.

"Yes," Jayne said, standing stiffly in his hold. But she knew she wasn't. This could never be made right.

"You aborted our child?" Pain glowed in Tariq's eyes giving the gold the sheen of fire.

Jayne recoiled. "I—"

He tilted her chin up and stared down into her eyes. "You wrote me a miserable little missive advising me you had lost our baby. Lost, what does that mean?" The lack of expression in his voice made the demand more lethal. "Did you *miscarry* my child?"

Slowly Jayne shook her head.

"Allah, help me!" He threw his head back and the skin stretched taut across his facial bones. His fingers dug into her arms where he held her. "You aborted my son."

Jayne pulled out of his arms and crossed to lean against the marble slab of the basin. "The unborn baby that you wouldn't believe yours was a girl. A tiny, perfect little girl." Pain splintered inside her. Jayne was beyond tears. "I held her in my arms, I named her. And then I lost her."

"Lost? She was born alive? She died?"

Crossing her arms over her chest, Jayne hugged herself tightly. The cold refused to recede. "She is alive. I gave her up for adoption." It was the hardest thing she had ever said.

Tariq came toward her. "You took my daughter away from Zayed…away from me…and gave her to someone else?"

"Yes." The look Jayne gave him stopped him in his tracks. "I gave her to my sister. Helen can't have children. Samantha is adopted, and now she has Amy, as well." Her voice grew fierce. "And you cannot take Amy away from her mother. I won't allow it."

Tariq looked shaken by her ferocity. "But you are her *mother.*"

"No, I am not her mother. And you are not her father."

"Tariq! Jayne…come quickly."

At Athina's frantic calls they both hurried out of the bedroom.

"What is it?" Tariq demanded.

Athina's hand was over her mouth. "Rashid is…not well. You need to hurry."

Tariq started to run.

By the time Jayne got to the sick room, the Emir's breaths were coming in loud rasps.

"Slowly, Father," Tariq was saying. "The doctor will be here in a minute."

Jayne came up to the Emir's bedside. "I want you to know that my baby is alive. Her name is Amy. She is beautiful."

The old sheikh opened his eyes. They held a faraway glaze. "Thank you for that, Jayne, daughter. Now I have a chance of looking forward to paradise. Look after Amy. And look after my son—he needs you."

Unexpectedly a lump formed in her throat. Jayne knew that the divorce she had come to Zayed to finalise would never happen. How could she ever leave Tariq? "I will."

"Tariq?"

Tariq came up beside Jayne. "Yes, Father?"

"There is a parcel of land I want you to gift to Karim." He

gasped and coughed, a hacking sound. "It has leases made over to Ali—"

"I will take care of it, Father."

"And look after your—" he struggled for breath "—your mother."

"Yes," Tariq vowed. And tears pricked at the back of Jayne's throat when she saw the look he gave Athina. There was a long road for them to travel to get to know each other, but clearly Tariq was prepared to make a start.

"And keep your wife happy. Learn from my mistakes."

"Yes." But this time Tariq sounded less certain.

"Lina…?" The Emir's voice was panicky.

"I am here." Athina moved to the other side of the bed and took his hand. "I won't go."

"Thank you." There was a long pause, then he whispered, "I loved you. But I never told you how much. You thought it was all about the oil."

Athina shook her head. From across the bed, Jayne could feel the woman's shock. Jayne's gaze lifted to meet Tariq's and her breath caught at the naked emotion she read there.

Twelve

The funeral took place two days later.

Jayne couldn't believe the number of famous faces that attended. Statesmen and businessmen from all over Europe and the Gulf region were present. Karim al Bashir was there. Farrah Jirah had come to pay her respects and so had Ali and Mahood, along with a very subdued-looking Leila.

Tariq's Kyriakos cousins had flown in from Greece. Athina introduced Jayne to her nephews, Zac and Angelo and their wives Pandora and Gemma. Afterwards, back in the palace gardens where coffee and refreshments were served, Jayne found herself chatting to Pandora, Zac's wife, and his sister, Katy. There was a sense of sadness about Katy, and Jayne made a mental note to ask Tariq about it later.

Angelo's wife, Gemma, was beautiful, with clouds of dark-red hair. She glanced from Jayne to Tariq, and Jayne sensed her curiosity about their off-again, on-again marriage.

A sudden familiar chirp caused Jayne to turn her head. There, on a pole sat a familiar shape.

Noor!

She looked around for Tariq and saw that he'd already seen the falcon and was moving stealthily to the base of the pole. She could see his relief at her return from the intensity of his expression.

Tariq loved his falcons. But he expected no love back from the wild birds. His love was unconditional. He'd loved his father. But expected no love back—only pride.

Her husband had grown up in a hard world surrounded by men…no women to soften him. No women to love him.

Except her.

And she did love him.

Yet he had no idea how to respond to her love. Should she really be surprised?

It's easy to come to an understanding with a falcon. The falcon simply has to stay hungrier.

His words echoed in her head.

Loving Tariq was never going to be easy.

"Jayne."

She turned and scanned Tariq's features. He was holding up well under the strain, but she knew that the suddenness of his father's death had taken him by surprise—even though the doctor had said it was not unusual for cancer patients to have a short upswing, at times to feel a little better, before the end came.

"It's great that Noor is back."

"I'm taking her back to the mews. I've hardly seen you

over the last two days. When I come back, we need to make some time to talk."

Jayne looked at him in surprise. In the past Tariq had never worried about her, about making time to spend time together, much less talk. But he was right. They did need to talk.

"I want to see…her."

They sat in Tariq's study in front of his computer. On the screen was a photo of Amy on her first day at school. Jayne had no need to ask who Tariq was referring to. He couldn't take his eyes off the computer screen.

"Why?" she asked baldly. "What will it help to meet Amy? It will only unsettle you. Amy can never know who you are."

He rocked forward on the chair. "I want my daughter back. What you did—kidnapping her—was illegal. She should never have been taken from me, or out of Zayed."

Jayne shook her head and apprehension blossomed inside her as she stared at him. "It's too late, Tariq. You cannot take her away from the only family she has ever known."

"The adoption is illegal. She should never have left Zayed."

Dread turned Jayne's blood to ice. "How can you say that? You banished me. I tried to tell you that Amy was your baby, that I had never betrayed you. You wouldn't listen. You wanted me to prove my fidelity with a DNA test."

"I was a fool!"

"You're being a fool now, too. You can't have Amy back."

"I have to see her."

Now a very real fear fluttered in her stomach. "Promise me, Tariq, that you will not take her away from my sister."

He turned his gaze away from the screen. His eyes were dark-gold pools of anguish. *"I can't."*

Jayne raised her chin. "If you use your power and wealth to take her away from my sister, I will never forgive you."

The flight to Auckland was long but passed without incident. After they'd booked into a five-star hotel on the Princess Wharf, Jayne called Helen. After she set the phone down, she turned to Tariq, "We've been invited to tea tomorrow afternoon."

"Tea?" Tariq looked hunted. "How am I supposed to drink tea at a time like this?"

"You have no choice," she replied with a touch of sadness and wished, for a brief moment, that everything had been different.

The following day they climbed into the hire car and Tariq drove them to Remuera where Helen lived. They pulled up outside the neat, modern town house and opened the gate to the fenced yard where a swing hung from the branch of a giant oak in the corner of the property.

Tariq looked around with interest, wanting to assess if his daughter had been looked after…or neglected. But there was no evidence of neglect here.

The house shone with love and care. A row of pots filled with colour stood along the deck leading to the front door, and the windows were clean and shiny. The house looked happy—like it was smiling.

He shook off the fanciful thought and strode to the front door. Lifting the polished brass knocker, he rapped three times.

The front door opened. And his heart turned over. His daughter looked up at him. And Tariq fell in love. Completely and utterly.

Amy was the most beautiful human he had ever seen. She had pale skin with the lustre of a pearl—like Jayne's, with Jayne's sleek dark hair. But her eyes were gold and wild. His eyes.

"You are—" He broke off. How could he tell this beautiful child she was his daughter?

The daughter his father had paid her mother to abort.

God!

"Hello," he said instead.

"Who are you?" she asked, her gaze steady, not returning his greeting.

His throat tightened, he answered, "I am your—" *father* "—your Auntie Jayne's husband."

"Then it's okay to talk to you. My mummy doesn't allow me to talk to strangers."

Stranger.

His flesh and blood. His child. It hurt. Unbearably. Her mummy was not Jayne, her mummy was Jayne's sister. He pressed the heels of his palms against his eyes.

God!

"Is your head sore?" There was concern in the golden eyes. Definitely his eyes. "When my head gets sore I sometimes drink some water and it helps the dehyd—" She broke off and frowned.

He wanted to kiss the frown lines away.

"Dehydration," he supplied.

"Yes, that's what it helps."

Tariq knew that water wouldn't help his pain. His heart was breaking. If he claimed this beautiful child, flesh-of-his-flesh, he would lose Jayne. He had no doubt of that.

He'd spent too many years without his wife. He wanted her back.

But he looked at Amy. They should have been a family. He, Jayne and Amy. But his distrust had killed that.

What in hell had he done?

Jayne watched her husband sipping tea from her sister's favourite bone china and marvelled at his ability to hide his thoughts behind those hawklike eyes. Looking at him, no one would have realised what this occasion meant—except for the hypersensitivity he displayed to Amy's needs. It was after he'd indulged her for the third time by passing her the plate of Tim Tams that Helen murmured, "He knows she's his daughter."

Jayne simply nodded.

"Oh, Lord, please help us." Helen sprang up and hurried from the room.

Instantly concern lit Nigel's eyes, but before he could rise, Jayne gestured for him to stay and went searching for Helen.

She found Helen leaning against the fridge, her eyes stark with misery. "He's going to take her from us, isn't he?"

"Helen—"

"How can we fight him? He has wealth beyond everything we know." Helen sounded wild with grief.

"Helen—"

"I cannot take the child from her mother."

Both of them turned. Tariq stood in the doorway, Nigel's anxious face appeared behind him.

Tariq moved forward. "I have lost my daughter through my own actions, my own stupidity. You will not lose your daughter because of my shortsightedness."

"You don't want Amy?" Helen breathed.

"Of course I want Amy! But in the past hour, I have discovered she is no longer mine. She speaks of her sister

Samantha, her mother and father, her school friends. She has a life in which the most I can hope to be is a favourite uncle." He sighed. "I lost all claim to Amy years ago. My stupidity lost Jayne her daughter, too. I have to live with that every day of my life. But I am fortunate enough that I have not lost the wife I love more than anything in the world."

Jayne's breath caught at the anguish in his eyes. "You love me?"

"Of course, I do, *nuur il-en*. I nearly lost you, too."

She moved up beside him. "There will be other children."

"But never a first-born with your hair and my eyes. She is lost to us forever." The pain in his voice made her choke.

"Tariq…" Helen's hand closed on his shoulder. "You and Jayne are welcome to visit anytime you want. Perhaps when she's older she can go and stay with you during the holidays—if she wants."

"You are prepared to let her visit us? Halfway across the world?"

"Helen is saying more. She's going to tell Amy who her parents are. That's what you mean, isn't it?" Jayne raised an eyebrow at her sister.

Helen glanced at Nigel. He nodded.

"Yes," said Helen. "We will tell her."

Tariq put his arm around Jayne and pulled her close. "If Amy—or Samantha—ever need anything, you tell me, and they will get it. I am a blessed man."

Back in their hotel room overlooking the harbour, Jayne said, "Are you going to say it again?"

"Say what?" Tariq dropped down onto the enormous bed and lay back against the pillows.

"Are you going to tell me you love me again?"

Tariq's face grew grave. "I am going to pay attention to my father's advice. My mother didn't know he loved her, so she found someone else. I am going to treat you far better than I did the first time around. I will not neglect you, and I will make sure you know I love you. I am not risking losing you again. And that is a promise."

"I love you, too," she said. She fingered the amber and turquoise necklace she wore. "I don't need you to buy me ingots…or gold. All I wanted was your trust."

"You have it, Jayne." He frowned. "Are you going to be able to leave Auckland…and Amy?"

She drew a deep breath, "When we were in the desert, Matra said to me that in the desert one Bedouin will inquire another about grazing by asking, *Fih hayah*."

"It means 'Is there life?'" Tariq said, looking a little puzzled.

"I want you to know that you are my water. Without you my life is a desert and there is no life."

"My wife!" His eyes flared and the heat started to burn.

"I can live in Zayed, I have grown to have a better understanding of the desert. Farrah is keen for a literacy program to be set up for the rural women. I'd like to do it." She moved to sit next to him on the bed. "And I can register for the studies I want to do through London. And that's the easy stuff. The hard part is that I will miss Amy—I have always seen her regularly. That will be hard. It's going to feel like a piece is ripped out of me, not to have her nearby."

"I am sorry."

And he was. Jayne could read the torment in his eyes. "Don't be. She is beautiful. And she has made Helen and Nigel very happy. She has completed their family."

"You are too generous, *nuur il-en.*"

"I can afford to be," Jayne said, as she leaned forward to kiss the husband who looked so fierce but melted under her touch. "I've got you, my heart's desire."

* * * * *

A sneaky peek at next month...

By Request

RELIVE THE ROMANCE WITH THE BEST OF THE BEST

My wish list for next month's titles...

In stores from 16th December 2011:

3 stories in each book - only £5.99!

☐ The Rinuccis: Carlo, Ruggiero & Francesco – Lucy Gordon

☐ Just What She Always Wanted – Amy Andrews, Alison Roberts & Lucy Clark

In stores from 6th January 2012:

☐ Millionaire: Needed for One Month – Maureen Child, Christie Ridgway & Susan Crosby

Available at WHSmith, Tesco, Asda, Eason, Amazon and Apple

Just can't wait?

1211/05

Mills & Boon® Online

Discover more romance at
www.millsandboon.co.uk

 FREE online reads

 Books up to one
month before shops

 Browse our books
before you buy

...and much more!

For exclusive competitions and instant updates:

Like us on **facebook.com/romancehq**

Follow us on **twitter.com/millsandboonuk**

Join us on **community.millsandboon.co.uk**

Visit us Online Sign up for our FREE eNewsletter at
www.millsandboon.co.uk

WEB/M&B/RTL4

Have Your Say

You've just finished your book.
So what did you think?

We'd love to hear your thoughts on our
'Have your say' online panel
www.millsandboon.co.uk/haveyoursay

- 🌹 Easy to use
- 🌹 Short questionnaire
- 🌹 Chance to win Mills & Boon®
  goodies

*Visit us
Online*

Tell us what you thought of this book now at
www.millsandboon.co.uk/haveyoursay

YOUR_SAY